LAST CALL

A Camden Ranch Novel

JILLIAN NEAL

Cover Design by
THE KILLION GROUP

Written by Jillian Neal

Cover Design by The Killion Group, Inc.

Copyright © 2016 Jillian Neal

Published by Realm Press

ISBN: 978-1-940174-41-9

Library of Congress Control Number: 2017954453

First Edition

First Printing – April 2016

To Everyone Who Fights – To remember, to forget, to recover, to be strong, to survive, to thrive, to move on.

And to My Brother – Who never failed to show supreme bravery on every battlefield including the one in his mind. Thanks for always being there for me no matter what battle I've taken on.

CHAPTER ONE

"Aaron Weber is watching you try to get that hay out of your bra, sis. In fact, he's been watching you all night long."

Natalie Camden leveled a cool glare on her sister, Holly. "Well, if you hadn't dragged me off of my horse and made me come out with you all, I wouldn't still have hay poking my boob...and he is not." Natalie was lying, and all of the Camden women seated around her knew it.

The hottest bartender at Saddleback's Honkytonk, who just so happened to be her sweet friend, *had* been staring at her, silently inviting her to come over and tell him what it was she wanted.

She'd called him the night before in a moment of weakness and told him she wanted to ask for a favor. But the impulse that had made her pick up the phone had been undone by his kindness.

He'd immediately sworn to do anything in the world for her, because he was Aaron and when he said things like that he meant them. But they were just friends. She'd blown all chances of him being more than that straight to hell a year ago. The favor she longed to ask was nothing more than an exercise in taking advantage of what a great guy he was. He'd pressed her to ask him. She'd called herself several less than kind names and changed the subject.

Wriggling again, she debated just sticking her hand down her own shirt and removing the offending hay. Why weren't there easy solutions for cowgirl problems? Currently she was surrounded by four dozen cattle ranchers, more than half of them skating on drunkenness. Flashing her cleavage probably wasn't the best idea.

The thought sent an all too familiar wave of panic throughout her. She dug her fingernails into the palms of her hands and tried to forget. God, why was it always right there just under her skin? Just out of reach so she couldn't take it in her hands and crush it violently. Why couldn't she just damn it all to hell the way she did most everything else she hated?

"Bet Aaron would be more than happy to help you with your hay issue, Nat," Summer, Natalie's sister-in-law, suggested with a sly grin. Her voice floated up above the low hisses of the beer taps and the drawl of the jukebox.

"Why aren't you even talking to him?" Holly asked. "I thought you were friends."

"Holl, I am not going to go ask him to get the hay out of my bra. We aren't *that* good of friends. How much have you had to drink anyway?"

"You don't have to do that." Holly rolled her eyes. "Just go say hi. It's weird you aren't up there. Besides, we all know he likes you."

"He likes me as a friend. We just established this."

"He likes you as way more than a friend, babe," Her brother Luke's wife, Indie, goaded. "Trust me, guys who are just friends don't stare at you like their hands are the only things they don't want to take off of you tonight."

"He's working. I'll talk to him later."

"Well, when you do talk to him, tell him you want to earn a few buckles in his bedroom rodeo." Indie laughed.

"No, no, no, Aaron's not a cowboy. She has to tell him she wants to become his peen queen," Holly announced rather loudly.

It was a testament to the amount of alcohol they'd consumed that everyone except Natalie erupted in hysterical giggles.

If she stayed at that table any longer, they were only going to get louder and more obnoxious. Rolling her eyes, Natalie stood with enough force to send her chair careening into the ancient jukebox. The inevitable collision switched the song from Hank Williams to Alan Jackson.

Aaron's chuckle shook through his upper body. His black T-shirt pulled across his pecs concealing a few of his tattoos while struggling to contain his tight Army-earned muscles. The jostle of his impressive body shook through her, the way it always did. What would it feel like to lay her head on that chest, to be enveloped in the sanctuary of him, and not run away this time?

"I hate that song anyway," he hollered across the sea of cattle ranchers.

When he winked at her, her feet carried her toward him of their own free will.

Stop. Stop walking. What the hell? What are you even going to say to him? You cannot ask him to pop your cherry and teach you all the finer points of love-making. If you go up there you're going to ask him. He's way too easy to talk to.

Half a dozen steps and two cowboys away from him, her better judgement finally shattered whatever spell his gaze had set on her. Heart double-timing to the tune of *"Where I Come From"* she skidded to a stop, changed course, and ducked into the restroom.

Slamming herself inside a stall, she jerked the hay out of her bra and tossed it in the toilet. The cool metal of the stall door against her back tempered the flare of shame. God, why did everything have to be so fucking difficult? Why had those few weeks all those years ago impacted all of the other perfectly normal moments? Why couldn't she just prance up to the bar, order one of those stupid pink drinks like other country girls did, flirt, and go home with Aaron or with anyone she chose? Maybe she could. Maybe it was high time she cowgirled up.

———

Disappointment crashed through Aaron as he watched Natalie disappear into the women's restroom. Dammit. What was going on with her? He'd been sure she'd make her way up to see him eventually. Slammed with a local rodeo crowd, he'd been pouring beer and mixing shooters for the last three hours straight.

Last night on the phone he thought they were finally getting some-where in the general vicinity of where they'd been a year ago when she'd run away in a fear he didn't understand. Addicted to the sweet sound of her laughter, he'd pulled out all of his best material just to hear her giggle. She'd said something about a favor. Now, she was avoiding him like an Amway salesman with a quota to meet.

The haunting fear that lingered in those beautiful hazel eyes of hers simultaneously made him want to hunt down and end anything that had ever frightened her while holding her tightly in his arms and swearing to her that he'd never allow anyone or anything to hurt her again.

"Hey, good-lookin', my cups lookin' empty…a little…empty…a little." The drunk blonde with tits the size of her head leaned forward on the bar just as Natalie made her exit from the restroom.

Her pensive stare whipped from his face to the ostentatious display of flesh on the bar. If Natalie Camden had rolled her eyes any harder, they would have lodged themselves in her skull. Shit.

Ignoring the blonde, Aaron scooted out from behind the bar and grabbed Natalie's hand. "Hey, I'm sorry we're so slammed. You want to hang out after last call?"

Jerking her hand out of his grasp, irritation clouded her eyes. "It looks like you already have your hands full."

"Come on, Nat. What's up with you tonight?" Just then the blonde decided to shove her shot glass into Aaron's shoulder. "I said I needed another drink," she screeched. "Make me another!"

"Yeah, you're done. If you don't have a ride, get one." Much to his relief, the pack of cowgirls she'd come in with took her hands and guided her out to the parking lot. "Come talk to me. She got dumped and was looking to get smashed. At least that's what her friends told me. You said you wanted to talk about something."

"I changed my mind." The impressive armor she kept firmly in place seemed to be strengthening the longer they stood there staring at each other.

"Changed your mind about what? Come over here." Praying she'd follow him back to the bar, he scrambled for what to say to get her to relax again. "Want a whiskey sour?"

"No. What was that chick drinking?" she asked.

"Pink lemonade shooters." Aaron rolled his eyes.

To his relief, she wrinkled her adorable nose. "Do those taste as ridiculous as they sound?" A glimmer of the Natalie he knew so well made a reappearance.

"Pretty much. Quick way to lose any inhibitions you ever hoped to have though."

"Maybe I should try one then." Visible regret chased the words she'd just spoken.

"I'm not making you a lemonade shooter. Where did that even come from? I've never made you anything but whiskey. I've always liked that about you."

"Why?" She seemed genuinely intrigued.

Aaron shrugged. "The world has more than enough vapid, pink lemonade, bubblegum, sorority queens. Needs a lot more cowgirls. How's Sundance?"

And there was the smile that summoned the golden flecks in her eyes and lit her entire face like a whiskey bonfire. He'd been to hell and back more times than he cared to recall but his one and only prayer lately had been that someday, somehow he'd get to call that smile his own.

"She's great. After we worked cattle this morning, I rode her all afternoon."

"Oh yeah? Bet she loved that."

"Not as much as I did. It was a tough summer. I was in the trucks more than I was on her. I hated it. Riding today was amazing."

How about riding me sometime, sweetheart? I'll make it so damn good for you. Just give me a chance. The words he would never voice staged a revolt on the tip of his tongue. The all too familiar longing took another swipe at his resolve. She was wary of men in general. And he was one hundred percent, red-blooded, all American male. He had to give her time to work through whatever had happened to her. If only he could pour up glasses full of patience the way he could fix glasses of liquid encouragement.

"Okay, how about telling me what you wanted to ask me, while I start cleaning up."

"I said I changed my mind."

"Yeah, I know, but what did you change your mind on? Did I fuck something up?"

"No," she sighed. "I just...I don't know. It was stupid."

"Last night, I told you about the time when I was a teenager and took a dare to jump out of the hay loft in the barn onto the trampoline at my foster parents' farm. I broke, like, seven bones. Whatever you wanted to ask me can't possibly be that dumb."

"Yeah, but kids do dumb shit like that all the time."

"Okay, how about this one. The first week I was living in the barracks, I locked myself out of my room wearing nothing but banana boxers and one boot. Had to wait outside all night dressed like that until my C.O showed up the next morning with the key. For years everyone in my platoon called me banana hammock."

That earned him a genuine laugh. He watched intently as the tense set of her jaw eased. "Why exactly did you leave with only one boot on?"

"I may not have been completely sober."

"Ah, that makes slightly more sense."

"Come on, Nat. I know you don't wanna go back over there and chat with your sister and all of your brothers' wives." He placed another whiskey sour in front of her. "Save me from everyone in here living high on booze and stupidity. Talk to me."

"Aren't bartenders supposed to want people to be living high on booze? Isn't that how you make the best tips?"

"Yeah, well, there's a reason I see this as a job not a career."

"Do you want to go back in the Army?" That was not an option, even if he had wanted to, which he didn't. A distinctive sadness darkened her eyes and filled him with another round of hope. Did she not want him to leave? God, that hope was going to be the death of him.

"Hell no. Just not entirely sure I always want to be a bartender." Just then a screech sounded from the kitchen right before the clatter of pots and pans echoed through the bar.

Natalie cringed. "Sounds like Ed and Eliza are at it again."

"Make that a bartender that moonlights as a marriage counselor. Be right back."

CHAPTER TWO

"What the hell did you say to her this time?" Aaron demanded of Ed Olsen, the owner of Saddleback's Bar and Grill. Both men ducked behind the industrial sinks as a soup pot flew end over end headed their direction.

"I just told her we made more tips when she stayed in the kitchen and out of the dining room. She needs to let the purdy young things wait the tables."

"One day, she's gonna kill you, and mark my words, I will tell the police you deserved it. Go apologize."

"I ain't going back there. She ain't worked through the iron skillets yet."

"Eliza." Aaron channeled his best drill instructor tone. "Stand down." Crouching, he edged closer to the supply room.

"You tell that moron I'm married to he can just go out and find himself a pretty young thang that'll make him tips and she can just have his sorry shriveled up butt all for her own."

"Beating my head against this brick wall would be more productive than trying to reason with you two," Aaron growled through his teeth. Grasping Eliza's hand before it landed on a nearby skillet, he willed patience and fought the inevitable anxiety that always resided just between his shoulder blades, another wound he couldn't reach to heal. "Now, Ed knows he's a dumbass that needs to learn to engage his brain before he opens his mouth, don't you, Ed?"

"Yeah, whatever. She's loonier than a cross-eyed cow that got in the still."

"What was that, Ed Olsen?" Eliza shrieked.

"Ed, so help me." Aaron shot him a warning glare. "I will hand her the skillet myself."

"You're purdy enough I s'pose."

Shaking his head, Aaron released Eliza's hand. This time an iron skillet sailed through the air landing hard on Ed's boot.

"Dag-blast-it, woman!"

"You know you deserved worse than that. Now, keep your mouth shut and go wash those dishes for her," Aaron ordered before he returned to the bar. "I swear there were days in the sandpit where I saw less action." Aaron sighed as he sidled back up to Natalie. The uneasiness of his boss's constant bickering continued to twist up his spine.

"What'd he say to her this time?" Natalie offered him another one of those rare full-faced smiles. For a moment, she looked happy he'd returned. His heart jerked to a stop before it flew.

"Something about the waitresses making more tips than she did. I swear he's a glutton for punishment. She took an umbrella to him a couple of nights ago."

Leaning closer to Natalie, letting the bar press into his abs, he attempted to memorize the exact melody of her giggle. That sweet sound could get a man through dozens of miserable nights. "What did he say to get beaten with an umbrella?"

Aaron shook his head. "She asked him what was on television. He said dust."

Her mouth dropped open and Aaron ordered every cell in his body to stop imagining his cock sliding between her lush pink lips. God, he'd wanted her since he'd first set eyes on her. For a moment, he'd thought she was some kind of dream. It had just been so fucking long and she was so perfect. "I would've beat his ass, too. Why doesn't he get up and dust if he wants it cleaned?"

"I never said he didn't deserve every bit of what he gets. I'd kick his ass myself for the way he talks to her if he didn't sign my paychecks." Hoping she'd meet him in the middle, he leaned closer still. Hay, saddle oil, and a distinct tang of her sweat filled his nostrils. Refusing to feel any shame he reveled in the aroma of Natalie. How fucking good would it feel, how sweet and spicy would she smell, if he worked her up until she was good and sweaty in his bed? What must the perfume of Natalie aroused be like? Heaven. He was certain. Patrons singing along to Miranda drowned out the low rumbled groan that escaped his throat from the thought alone.

"You smell really good," made its way into his ear. Her teeth sunk into her lower lip, trying to prevent more confessions it appeared.

"I was just thinking that same thing, Nat."

"You think you smell good, too?" Her teasing smirk taunted his determination to let her come to him this time.

"I smell good because I spilled garlic sauce on my jeans and I have Jack on my shirt. You smell good just because you're you."

Heat took up residence in her cheeks. Instead of staring up at him any longer, her gaze transferred to the wood grain of the long bar top. "I've been riding all day. I probably smell like sweat and horse."

"I don't smell the horse." Could she hear the hunger in his tone? Half of him prayed she could. The other was terrified she was going to bolt again if he didn't leash his lust.

The blink of her long eyelashes timed the moments between them. Two deep breaths in, realization furrowed her brow.

His breath stalled.

"You know that thing I said I wanted to ask you?"

"No, because you won't tell me." Powerless to stop himself, he reached her face and traced the tense angles with his fingertips, desperate to ease their strain. He needed her to look him in the eye. He'd spent the last year learning the kaleidoscope of colors and the meanings of her gazes.

"You can say no, if you don't want to do this." Fear and challenge competed for dominance in her tone.

"I want to do most anything with you. You know that. Just ask me." There was no way she was about to say what he'd been praying for a year to hear her say. If only he could convince his cock of that. Currently, it was going to bear the impression of metal teeth from the zipper of his jeans if he didn't get his erection to cut him some slack. Thankful for the bar concealing his need for her, he managed to keep a scant amount of blood flowing to his brain. Enough to keep prompting her. "Come on, Nat. Don't keep stuff from me. We're friends."

A harsh swallow contracted the long feminine column of her neck. "I know. That only makes this harder."

Harder. Oh, she had no fucking clue how much harder he was feeling at the moment. "You look like you're about to confess murder. Do I need to go find a shovel?"

"Pretty sure murder would be easier to confess." Defeat robbed her words of any volume.

"You have a ton of land. We could bury whoever it is that pissed you off out there. No one would ever find them."

"You'd actually help me hide bodies? I'm not sure if that's really sweet or very disturbed."

"Pretty sure it's both, but the point was I'd do anything for you so talk."

"I think... I'm kind of sure, actually."

"Sure of what?"

"I don't know how to do this." Her voice faltered.

"Can't be worse than murder, remember? Just keep going."

"What would you say if I said I wanted to sleep with you?"

Alarm bells blared in Natalie's head. No, wait. Aaron was ringing a bell. Panic swept through her. Fever shot through her veins and then burned in her cheeks. Oh my God. What had she just said?

"Last call," his low bellow ripped through the partying crowd. The cowbell above the bar blared on as he rang it with far more determination than was necessary. Her heart pounded out a frantic SOS in her throat. It took entirely too long for her brain to get the message to her feet that she needed to run. Her boots were twisted around the bar stool. Untangling them served only to slow her down.

Aaron's hand landed on her wrist, pressing it to the bar. Somehow, his grip never reminded her of what had happened before. Protectiveness radiated from his firm grasp. Possession resided in his fingertips, but it didn't frighten her. She didn't jerk away. If any of her brain actually worked, she would have hightailed it out of there, but for some unfathomable reason, she wanted to stay.

"Sorry, but you don't get to say that to me and then run away. We're gonna talk. Stay put." The order reverberated through her bones. Her stomach dropped somewhere in the vicinity of her ankles. "You've had more than enough, Gus. Get on home. I'm not making you another drink," Aaron made another command.

"What's the point of last call if you ain't gonna make me another?" Gus Peterson, a rancher from Ogallala, argued.

"The point is to get you the hell out of my bar. I've got things that need my attention. Go home."

"Just what do you think you're doing, son? It's barely 11:30. Why're you sending everyone home?" Ed Olsen's eyes bugged out of his head. Natalie was certain he was seeing dollar signs, not people, walking out of Saddleback's early.

"Don't you fuss at him Edward Olsen or I'll take my best frying skillet to your head. Now, Aaron probably has plans tonight, don't you, darlin'?" Eliza came to his rescue. "Oh, Natalie, how are ya sweet girl? I ran into your mama at the Feed and Seed this morning, said you all had been working calves this week."

"Uh..." The entire Sahara desert could not possibly have been more dry than her throat at that moment. The last words she'd spoken still haunted her. "Yes, ma'am."

"Yeah, they've been working calves all day and then she was out riding. She's worn out. You mind if I take her on home, Eliza?"

Well, wasn't Aaron taking all kinds of advantage that evening? Natalie hated the spark of excitement that lit low in her belly. She hadn't necessarily meant that night. She'd just meant maybe at some point in the future she might like to sleep with him if he wouldn't hate it. Another round of panic quickly vanquished the thrill. She wasn't mentally prepared for this to happen tonight.

"I wouldn't mind at all. Ed and his big fat mouth can clean up tonight, can't you Ed?"

"You ready to go, Nat?" Holly appeared at her side.

"I'll bring her home. Tell Dec I said hi." Once again Aaron directed everyone's evening plans.

A broad grin climbed across her sister's face. "I'll tell him. You two have fun. Don't do anything I wouldn't do."

"Which is what?" Thankful her voice had made a recovery, Natalie couldn't resist the taunt. She clung to the normalcy of teasing her sister. Nothing else made any sense.

Aaron's discreet chuckle gave her another shot of courage. "You definitely do not want her to enumerate that list. Come on. For once in my life, I'm getting out of here early."

"Aaron." The panic was still too easy to access. "I'm not sure I meant tonight. I'm not sure what I meant at all." There. She'd said it.

"Yeah, that's what we're going to discuss." He wrapped his arm over her shoulders and guided her outside. Weak against his steady strength she allowed her lungs to inhale the masculinity surrounding her. His heat permeated her side and in that exhilarating, terrifying moment she allowed herself to picture being in bed with him. His naked body pressed to hers. That hunger that consumed his eyes when he thought she wasn't looking, apparent in his every move.

Her mind was restless and unsure, but her body was beyond certain what it wanted.

CHAPTER THREE

A cold slap of Nebraskan wind whipped Natalie's long hair in front of her face and rushed the panic back to her mind. Wishing she'd worn her favorite cowgirl hat, she stumbled on the loose gravel parking lot. Aaron kept her upright, while she shoved the hair out of her eyes.

"Deep breaths for me, okay? I'd never do anything you didn't want me to do." The words somehow sounded rehearsed, like he'd been preparing to say them for weeks.

"I know." That was one of the many reasons she'd asked him to do this for her. The way his T-shirts would occasionally swing to the side while he worked the beer taps and show off the chiseled pillows of his abs, his substantial shoulders that could easily have carried the weight of the world, and the low rasp of his voice all made the list as well. Guiding her to his old Chevy truck parked behind the bar, he opened the passenger side door.

"Hop on in. We're just gonna talk. Then I'll take you home."

"And?" She had to know what to prepare herself for. A knot of tension continued to expand in her stomach. It grew until she swore it reached her throat and robbed her lungs of air.

"Talk first." He dominated all the spare room in the cab of the truck. The nearest city lights were two hours east but the moon offered enough light that evening for her to see. "Look at me, Nat."

She lifted her eyes to his.

"Talk to me. You said you were sure. Does that mean you've been thinking about this for a while?"

"Yes...but if you don't want to..."

"I want to. I want to more than you know. Trust me."

"I do trust you. That's why I asked you to help me."

"You didn't ask me to help you, sweetheart. You asked me to fuck you."

"That's the thing. Doing what you just said would be helping me, and I swear I won't be one of those girls who gets all clingy and stupid. I won't let anything ruin our friendship. It's just I need to do this because..."

"Because why?"

"Because I've never." She refused the words. Every muscle in her body tightened, bracing for impact she knew wasn't coming.

"Damn." His Adam's apple contracted enticingly. How was it possible his neck was one of the sexiest things she'd ever seen? "You've never...? You're a...? I mean, no one else has ever...?"

"I hate that word. Once you say it, people lose the ability to complete sentences, like I should be wearing one of those ridiculous prom queen sashes, Natalie the Virgin." She made no effort to erase the accusation in her tone.

"Okay, sorry. I'm still processing all of this. It's nothing to be ashamed of. I'm honored you asked me, but can you tell me why you've never slept with anyone else?"

The adamant shake of her head brought on a full body shiver.

"Hey, it's okay." Aaron dug behind the bench seat and produced a Kansas City Chiefs sweatshirt. "I'd turn the truck on but the heater is shit, and I don't want Ed to know we're still here. He'd find something for me to do." Before she could protest, he eased the sweatshirt over her head. Static clung to her hair drawing it out in long points from her head like antennas. The scent of pine trees and Aaron surrounded her. Every breath brought another round of him to her nostrils. Her shoulders dropped in relief and her jaw eased its fierce clench.

Chuckling, he ran his fingers through her hair and tucked it behind her shoulders. That motion alone flooded her entire body with heat. She wanted to beg him to continue. Maybe if he would just play with her hair long enough, she could relax and then he could do other things with his hands. She'd be so content it wouldn't bring back any memories she wished she could sever from her life with a blade.

"I know something happened to you, Nat. If you scoot any further away from me right now just talking about having sex, you'll be sitting out in the parking lot. I need to know if there are things you don't want me to do. I will not let what happened to us last year happen again. I refuse. I have to make sure I never do anything that scares you again."

"Nothing happened to me, and I'm not scared of you. I just almost always fuck everything up." Self-hatred filled her. How could she lie to him? She couldn't look him in the eye.

If she'd backhanded him, it would have hurt less than her lying to him. "Jesus, Nat, just tell me you don't want to talk about it. Don't lie to me."

Low-level rage ate at the ease he was trying desperately to portray. Wherever the bastard was that had done this to her, that had scared her like this, that had taken something she wasn't willing to give, needed to be on high alert. If Aaron found him, his fist would be the last thing the motherfucker ever felt.

Confessing her virginity and asking him to be her first already had him on a knife's edge of arousal. Whatever had happened to her, he had to know so he didn't fuck this up epically. He'd already done that once. He had to take this slowly, but his overly anxious cock was still hung on the fact that she was a virgin and he was her choice.

Shaking off that information, he reminded Aaron Jr. of the way she'd looked at him that night a year ago, so frightened she'd gotten in her truck and had flown back to the ranch. She'd refused to leave for almost a month. If they were going to do this, they had to take this slowly, painfully slowly. His eager eyes watched her shake the horseshoe charm on the delicate necklace she almost always wore back and forth, a sure sign of her nerves. Her bottom lip slipped through her teeth as he reached a negotiation with his body. He would take this slowly just as fast as he possibly could.

"Fine, I don't want to talk to about it."

"So, something did happen to you?"

"Kind of."

"Kind of is a yes and nothing is going to happen between us until you tell me more. I'm not going to risk frightening you again. Believe me, I've seen a lot of shit in this world. I've survived a lot of shit. I can take it. You ever think telling someone about it might help?"

"You sound like Dec and Holly."

"Well, they are psychologists. I've been seeing Dec for a long time. They know what they're talking about."

"I spent years seeing a therapist, too. I went when I was younger. I'm so sick of Holly and Dec and everyone trying to fix me. I don't want that anymore. I just want to sleep with you."

"Yeah, you keep saying that."

"You said you wanted to." Desperation perforated her tone.

"Do you seriously think since I'm not throwing you in the bed of my truck and being done with it all tonight means I don't want to?"

"I don't know." She erupted. "I don't know anything. I don't know why we're here talking. I don't know what you're thinking. I don't know why I even asked you. I don't know what happens next. I don't know why I acted the way I acted last year. I hate myself for that. The only thing I know is that I do not want to talk about *that*. I need it not to have any part of whatever is or isn't going to happen between us."

"Never hate yourself for anything, especially not for being afraid. I pushed too hard last year. It was my fault."

"None of it was your fault. I freaked out and refused to talk to you. I was once again a tremendous bitch because of..." Her jaw clamped shut once again.

"You were not a bitch. Never say that again. I of all people get the shitstorm that comes when your past decides to override your future."

"I know you do. That's part of why I thought maybe we could try again."

"I need to know more than you're a virgin and you want me to sleep with you, Nat. I need some information between those two things. Have you ever kissed anyone besides me?"

"Yes, but not since I kissed you, and not all that often before you either. It makes me nervous."

He called himself a rat bastard for the possession that coursed through him. She was his, and he was finally going to get the chance to prove that to her. That fact made him ache.

"That's what I need to know. When do you get nervous?"

"Do we have to do this?"

"Yeah, we do. Just hang with me a little while longer then we can talk about anything else you want." Racking his brain, he tried to remember exactly what they'd been doing when she'd leapt up off of his sofa and made up an excuse to go home. "You know what the bases represent?"

"I have three older brothers." She managed her customary eye roll.

"Yeah, I figured you did. Let's go with that." Bile crawled up his throat from the thought of some asshole having his hands on her, but he had to know. "Any man ever gotten to second base?" His gaze zeroed in on her slight cleavage. His palms itched to explore the tender swells of her breasts, to feel her nipples pebble and press against his exploring hands. That was what had been on his mind the night she'd fled.

"Define man," she sighed.

Holy fuck. "Do I get to ask what that means?"

"Barrett Peters and I went out for a few months when we were nineteen. Not sure he'll ever qualify as a man, though. He still lives with his parents and last time I saw him he was getting money from his mama for a slushy at the rodeo."

Is he who I need to maim? Aaron longed to ask but he wouldn't push her. Pushing made her disappear and he wasn't certain he could live with himself if he caused that again. "If you don't think he's anything more than a mama's boy, why'd you date him?"

"He was safe." Her lips folded under the pressure of her teeth as soon as those three words made their escape.

"Safe because you weren't actually attracted to him or safe because he's weak?" Was she protecting her heart or her body? He had to know.

"Barrett has nothing to do with what I'm asking you to do." The girl had always dodged like a pro. No more. He'd lean harder on the skills he'd acquired for getting information out of people.

"So, both then?"

Leveling a moonlit glare on him, she sighed. "He was like dating instant mashed potatoes."

"Tasteless, boring, and no one would notice if they got up and walked off your supper plate."

"Basically."

"How old were you when whatever happened, happened? If you won't tell me what it is at least tell me when."

Pain broadcast from every beautiful curve of her body. Her eyes hollowed. The flecks of gold he could make sparkle with a joke or a flirty smile disappeared entirely. "It stopped happening a week before my twelfth birthday."

"My God, Nat. Twelve? Is this guy still breathing? Because I'm gonna burn for all the shit I've already done. I've got no issue adding another name to the list."

"Yet another reason we are not having this conversation, and you are not."

Unmitigated fury shot through Aaron's musculature. What kind of sick bastard would...? No, he couldn't go there. Not right now. Later. When he'd gotten her through this portion of life she'd completely missed out on. And he would. He was going to be the one to make certain she was worshipped head to toe and back again. He'd show her how fucking desirable she was, what she did to him. He'd do his damnedest to erase every terrorizing memory. He'd make certain she felt no shame.

Two things were painfully obvious, even if she was still concealing most everything he needed to know. She was attracted to him and she sure as hell didn't think he was weak. His ego stirred right along with his cock.

He'd wondered for years why he was even still here. There were days and weeks when he had no desire to take up space or to continue drawing breath. He'd seen no point. Somehow, he'd managed to come through that hell. Maybe being a man for Natalie Camden, being the one who bridged the gap between the harrowing land of fear where she existed to the sanctuary of his arms and the carnal knowledge, he could give her was his purpose. Maybe this was his chance to prove he wasn't a weak bastard that couldn't deal with what he'd been through.

All he knew was no one would ever be allowed to hurt her ever again.

An idea sprang to his mind. "Hey, okay, how about this? Where in the baseball diamond do you get the most afraid? Is it second base?"

"Not exactly there. I don't know. I don't have much experience, like I said. I guess somewhere between second and third scares me most."

Not better. Not better at all.

"So, do you think we could have sex without that? Maybe that would work." Hope lilted in her voice and shattered the remnants of his heart.

"If we're going to have sex, Nat, we're going through all the bases, including shortstop, until you're not afraid anymore, which is precisely why we won't be doing this any time soon. I know you hate the word or whatever, but you are a virgin, so those steps are extremely important. I will not hurt you."

"Had a feeling you were gonna say that."

"Look at me." She lifted her eyes to his once again. "I can make this so good for you. I can show you what it's like to come undone, to let everything go. I want to help you work though what happened, but not until you tell me what that was. And this is not going to be a one-time deal. I'm not bedding you and walking away. We're together. We're going to actually date this time. Couple-shit like movies, and rodeos, and the county fair, hanging out at King's Creek. That sound okay to you?"

"You really want to date me again? I was a disaster last time."

"Nothing wrong with a do-over, babe. I've wanted you since I first laid eyes on you. If I get the chance to date you again, I'm sure as hell going for it."

"I liked dating you, if that's what we were doing. I didn't know what I was doing. I just...felt safe with you, until..."

"Until I fucked everything up."

"You didn't. You never did anything you shouldn't have done."

"I did, and I'm going to do right by you this time."

"You never made a single mistake when you were with me. I got scared. It had nothing to do with you."

"If I'm the guy lucky enough to get to take you to bed, it has everything to do with me. I will not mess this up again. You're sure you want to do this with me?"

"I think so."

"I need you to be sure. We both know I'm sure as hell not a saint."

"If I get scared, will you stop whatever we're doing?"

"Of course." He tried not to be offended but truthfully he was. "I would never force anything on you."

"If I tell you not to stop even though I'm scared, will you keep going? I'm pretty sure I'm just going to need you to keep going."

"Babe, I can't do that. Nothing is going to happen until I know you're not scared of me."

"I'm not scared of you, but what if I don't know how to not be scared of this? When I was a little girl, nothing scared me. I could outride all of my brothers. I could go faster, jump higher, do it all. The more dangerous it was the more I wanted to try it. But after all that stuff I was scared of everything. I don't want to be scared anymore. I want to feel brave again."

Gutted. He was absolutely gutted. He'd held kids in his arms trying to save them from road side bombs. He'd buried men who were like brothers to him. Thinking about Natalie being afraid tore him apart. "Sweetheart, you're about the bravest woman I've ever met. Doing this with me is pretty fucking brave. We're going to figure everything out." *And then I'm going to hunt down the bastard that hurt you and end him.*

"Since I've already completely made a fool of myself and I'd like to get all of the talking about this over with, can I ask one more favor?"

"You can ask me anything you want anytime. In fact, as soon as I know you're ready, I intend to have you begging for things from me every single time I take you to bed. Get used to it."

Another eye roll. Aaron fought the smirk taunting his own lips.

"I will not be begging for anything ever," she informed him.

Not only did the smirk escape but it was followed by a chuckle. "So much to teach you. You'll beg for me, babe, I'll make sure of it. But what did you want to ask?"

"I don't just want to have the regular sex kind of sex. Maybe. Kind of. I don't know, but I think I don't only want that."

God, she was so damn sweet and innocent. He had no clue how he'd managed to be lucky enough to get this opportunity, but life had fucked him over on the regular for the last several years. She needed him and he desperately needed her.

"What exactly is irregular sex, Nat? Be specific."

"No."

"So, I just get to guess then? What happens if my definition is significantly dirtier than yours?"

"I'm sure yours is dirtier than mine, since I have no clue what I'm doing. I just want you to show me...I don't know what exactly."

Frustration tensed his jaw. *Take it slow, Weber. Man the fuck up. This is part of the deal.* Reviewing every ounce of knowledge Natalie had provided him throughout their friendship, he took a well-educated guess. "Does it go something like you want to know what it might be like to experience all of the stuff your sister and sisters-in-laws run their mouths about every time they come into the bar?"

"Yes."

His mind scrambled. What if this was somehow one of those damned dreams that would haunt him for the rest of his life? Natalie asking him to kink it up with her after popping her cherry couldn't possibly be a reality. He just wasn't that lucky. Life didn't like him that much.

Three deep breaths. He counted backward from twenty.

"Aaron?" Natalie's hesitant touch on his knuckles finally grounded him. His cock throbbed out a desperate pulse. My God, this was real. "Do you not want to do that stuff with me?"

"Jesus, Nat, I want to do every single thing you want me to do and probably a dozen more you're too sweet to even know about. I just can't go there right now. We have to take this slow, sweetheart. I have to do things in order. If I get carried away, I'll scare you again."

Her bottom lip slipped through her teeth and another harsh swallow drew his gaze to the tender skin on her neck. A flood of saliva filled his mouth. He was so thirsty for her. Fear and hope fought for placement in her eyes. Turning his palm up, he took her hand. "Whatever it is you're thinking, say it."

"Sometimes when I'm alone and I can push the stupid memories away, I like to think about what it would be like if we got carried away."

A low, rumbled groan thundered from his chest without his explicit permission. Her eyes widened and those perfect heart-shaped lips opened a half-inch. He searched her expression for any sign of fear and came up empty. Intrigue and desire paraded through her eyes. Her chest lifted and fell with her rapid breaths. Fucking hell. She was going to kill him.

"You think about me when you're alone? Think about what it would be like to be with me? Tell me," he demanded.

A single nod and then her arms crossed over her chest. Cool air swept in and erased the warmth her hand had brought to his as soon as she jerked away. In his former life, he was a highly-skilled intelligence officer. He could read body language with more ease than most people read stop signs. He was treading on thin ice and he knew it. The warning flags were all there. She was going to run. His jaw clamped in a futile attempt to dam back the words, "When you're thinking about me when you're alone, baby, are you touching yourself?"

"Just take me home." If she'd carved the word yes in the hood of his truck the answer couldn't have been any clearer. Another hungry throb of his cock made him long to show her just what she did to him.

"I swear I will in just a sec. Look at me again."

"No." She turned her entire body toward the door.

"Fine, but know this, every single time I've jacked off in the last year, it's always you I'm thinking about fucking, you who's underneath me staring up at me while I take you over and over again, and you who's begging me for more."

CHAPTER FOUR

Agitation continued to tick through Aaron's blood, running hot and fast, while he paced outside Pleasant Glen's own mental health clinic the next morning. Dammit, where was Dec? The clinic was supposed to open in fifteen minutes. His frantic pulse kept the time.

Saddleback's opened at eleven, and he was working the early shift. He had shit to do before he had to clock in. Namely, taking the information he was determined to get out of Dec and figuring out exactly what to do next.

His fingers twitched. His bottom lip longed for the comforting weight of a wad of tobacco. He'd given it up and started back a half-dozen times. Natalie frequently commented on how much she hated the practice. It was time to quit for good.

Opening his mouth wide, trying to pop the tension out of his jaw, Aaron continued stirring the gravel between his truck and the front door with his work boots. He checked his watch again and decided to go on with the next item on his list.

Bringing his cell phone to his ear, he kept watch on the empty parking lot and the passing car on the single road that ran through Pleasant Glen.

"Triple A. 'Bout damn time I heard from you. To what do I owe the honor, Sarg?"

A broad grin spread across Aaron's features against his will. "I'm not your sergeant anymore, and sorry, I should've come out there last week. Just been busy lately."

"How goes the mixing of drinks in that half-a-map-dot town?"

"Lay off the Glen, T. You can't judge the whole place on the one crazy-ass cowgirl you picked up last time you were out here."

"Dude, she was coo-coo for Cocoa Puffs. Still texts me every few weeks wanting to know the status of our non-relationship."

"I told you not to take her home. You didn't listen."

"Yeah, well, I'm listening now, and you sound determined to either fix something or fuck it up. How can I help?"

Aaron knew he would never deserve the kind of brotherhood he had with T-Byrd or Voodoo or any of the remaining members of his team. Something about walking slowly straight through hell together cemented the men who'd survived it. "How's business? You still doing your thing?"

"I'm offended."

"Why? There cannot possibly be that many people in Lincoln who hire four dim-witted, ex-army show-offs to figure out if their wife is cheating on them."

"The agency does more than track down cheating spouses, and you know it. Last four jobs we've taken were security details. Two of 'em for gorgeous women who needed to be kept safe."

"Oh, I bet you did a whole helluva lot more than keep them safe."

There was far too much pride in T-Byrd's laughter. "Can't discuss cases outside the agency. However, my job offer still stands."

"No thanks. I have no interest in any job that requires me to wear my name on a chain or constantly be looking over my shoulder for a living ever again, but I do need to know where someone is."

"You got a name?"

"Not yet."

"Male, female?"

"Male."

"Description?"

"I doubt I get more than a name, but I'll have it soon."

"Even I'm not that good, Triple A, and I'm the best."

"I'll have you a name this afternoon. What else do you need?"

"When I find this guy what are you going to do to him?"

"Depends on what I find out about him."

"Interesting."

"How long will this take?"

"To make sure we have the right person, I'm going to need more than a name. You have a last known whereabouts?" T quizzed.

"Where the hell did you learn to talk like a cop?"

"Here, moron."

"I'll get you all the information I can, but it may take me a little time if my first source isn't willing."

"You never had trouble getting people to talk. You always knew how to apply just the right amount of pressure, if memory serves. That's yet another reason I want to hire you."

"Yeah, well this is different."

"Different how?"

The roar of Dec's Harley announced his arrival. "Gotta go."

"That kind of different then."

"Bye, T."

"Later."

"'Bout damn time," Aaron spat under his breath as Dec slung his leg over the bike.

"Holly will be terribly pleased you're here early this morning." Dec chuckled as he unlocked the front door.

"Oh yeah? Why's that?"

"Because I'm assuming you're here to discuss Natalie, which will delight my wife."

"Yeah, her and a few other things."

"Am I allowed a mere moment to put my things up and pull your file or are we going to have this session in the waiting room?" The smirk on the doc's face fed the ire in Aaron's blood.

Narrowing his eyes, he saw no reason not to be more than forthright. He always had been before. "Last night, when I dropped her off, she worked up the courage to kiss me on the cheek. That was it. I nearly came in my shorts."

"You know, I married the woman who has that effect on me."

"You and I both know no one in their right mind wants to be married to me, but trust me when I say, I'm more than anxious to talk to you. We can do it wherever you want, but we're talking now."

"Understood." After stowing a few files, Dec opened his office door and gestured Aaron inside.

Too antsy to sit, Aaron avoided his normal spot on the couch and continued to pace. "Tell me exactly what happened to her when she was a little girl. I know you know." Not generally the best way to gain actionable intelligence, but he had a plan. Keeping his eyes trained on Dec he watched every twitch the doctor made. Three to five that was all it took. He'd have to come up with his next move on the fly, but what he found out in the next three to five seconds would tell him exactly which way to go.

"Have a seat, Aaron."

A non-answer always held far more information than the informant intended. Switching to peripheral questions was the safest move. He'd get back to his goal when he had Dec more distracted.

"Fuck. So, it's that bad then?" Every muscle in both his arms and chest tensed in anticipation. He took his seat. If that was the prerequisite for figuring out who'd hurt Natalie, he'd deal.

"I didn't say that and I cannot tell you what happened to Natalie."

"Yeah, I get that. I just can't stand to think that someone who hurt her is out there possibly hurting other people." He leaned in driving home his point. Concern he hadn't had to force perforated his tone. Guilt was always the easiest emotion to manipulate in an informant.

"Aaron, if you'll sit back and look at the degrees hanging behind my desk you might remember that I am a psychologist. Now, I doubt I have even half the training you do in reading people and gaining information, but I do know what you're after. If you want to know what happened to Natalie, she's going to have to be the one who tells you, just like I would never tell *her* the things you and I have discussed."

Undeterred, Aaron shifted in his seat, relaxed his shoulders, and casually crossed his legs. He needed Dec to be more comfortable with him. "So, Natalie has talked to you as a patient?"

"I'm going to ask that you stop making assumptions now."

"I'm not assuming anything. Seems to me we're both on the same team of keeping Natalie safe. You'd go crazy if someone had hurt Holly when she was barely more than a baby." Feed them a lie and let them correct you. Almost always worked, psych degrees or not.

"She was a few years older than a baby," Dec slipped. "And yes, I suppose I would. I get where you're coming from."

Standing in her pajama pants, her favorite torn T-shirt that informed everyone to Buck Off, and an old pair of Luke's rubber boots, Natalie dumped another bucket of water from the lake into the stock tank. Sundance whinnied her approval. "There you go, girl." Natalie ran her hand down her horse's neck.

"Nice of you to dress for work, Nat," her brother Austin chuckled when he entered the paddock.

"Shut up, Austin. I'm tired."

"Yeah, I'll bet since Aaron Weber's truck didn't drive through the gates 'til midnight," Luke tried for a friendly tenor but missed the mark.

"Why is it all of you feel the need to keep tabs on where I am and who I'm with all the time?" Focusing on Sundance, she refused to watch the hesitant glance her brothers always shared when she asked something like that. She already knew the reason they were more protective of her than they'd ever been with Holly.

"Because you're our baby sister. It's our job to look after you," Grant huffed as he slung his saddle off of the shelf in the barn.

"I thought you liked Aaron," Natalie tried a different angle to get her brothers off her back. It had taken every ounce of courage she'd ever hoped to have to survive that conversation in Aaron's truck. The last thing she needed was her stupid brothers trying to scare him off now.

"I like him just fine as a bartender and as a friend, not so sure I like the idea of him as your boyfriend," Austin explained.

"He is not my boyfriend, and even if he was what business is it of yours?"

"You not hearing real well this mornin' or something, sis? It's our business 'cause we're your brothers," Grant came right back.

"You know I kinda thought by the time you all was married and making babies of your own that I wouldn't have to say this, but leave your sister alone and get. We got a hundred and fifty pairs to work." Natalie's father, Ev, came to her rescue. An automatic smile spread the width of her face.

"Thank you, Daddy." She couldn't resist sticking her tongue out at her brothers even if she was entirely too old to do such things.

"Brat," Austin taunted just before he had her in a headlock. His fist pressed to her scalp, giving her a noogie.

"Austin!" With a quick twist of her body she dug her shoulder blade into her brother's abs.

"Did I not tell you to leave her be?" Ev ordered again.

When Austin finally released her, Natalie stumbled forward and almost collided with their cousin, Brock. Panic shot through her veins. She felt the blood drain from her cheeks. When he reached his hands out to steady her, she leapt out of his reach. Thankful Brock didn't seem to notice, Natalie went through the taxing mental process she'd developed for just such an occasion.

"What are you all doing to her now?" Brock shook his head.

"We're just showing her our brotherly love," Grant teased.

"Poor kid." Brock laughed as he pulled on a pair of work gloves.

"Brock we're working your calves first so we're heading that way as soon as the horses are saddled and loaded. You all get on. I'll be right behind you." Ev gave the day's orders.

"Hope's making lunch for everyone. She'll bring it out wherever we're working," Brock added.

"Baby girl, you planning on working this mornin' or are you goin' back to bed?" Concern perforated her father's inquiry.

"Unbelievable," Austin shook his head. "You imagine what he'd say if any of us showed up down here in skivvies?"

"She worked two-hundred pairs yesterday, son, and I'd throw your sorry ass in the lake if you showed up down here in your drawers 'cause you'd clearly need to be sobered up."

Her brothers all rolled their eyes. "She didn't work 'em all by herself," Luke pointed out.

"Good Lord, I'm workin' today. When have I ever not worked? I just wanted to brush Sundance and give her some oats before we started, since I know you all didn't do it last night when you put her up."

"That horse is almost as spoiled as you are." Austin guided his horse out of the barn.

"Come on, baby girl, I'll walk you back home so you can change." Her father's offer struck the tone of an order.

"Fine," Natalie sighed.

They hadn't made it fifty paces outside the paddock before her father started in.

"You and Aaron Weber dating again?"

"It's been less than seven hours since we decided that. How the hell did you hear about it so fast?"

"A daddy knows. You didn't throw your brother on the ground when he had you in a headlock so I figured you were in a good mood about something, and I saw Aaron's truck drive by on the way to your house last night."

"Does anyone on this ranch ever sleep?"

"I don't sleep 'til I know all of my young-uns are safe and sound on my ranch."

"He said he'd like for us to go out a few places again, so I guess we are."

"Seems to me you either are or you're not. I don't much like the idea that you're only dating him because that's what he wants."

"I want that, too. And when have I ever done anything I didn't want to do?"

Ev's soothing chuckle eased the irritation and fear Brock's appearance in the barn had brought on. "Honey, no one, and most certainly not me, has ever doubted your ability to be stubborn when that's what you set your mind to do. I just don't know much about the bartender. You didn't date him too long last time."

"Well," Natalie filled her lungs with the fresh scent of hay, manure, and sunshine. A broad grin formed on her face. "That's why we're trying it again, maybe."

"What's he got all them tattoos for?"

"Daddy."

"You're my little girl. I got a right to ask that."

"No, you don't."

"He didn't get all them in prison did he?"

"Dad."

"I'll go ask him if you don't answer me, Natalie Camden."

Making no effort to hide her eye roll, she shook her head. "I'm fairly certain he's never been to prison."

"So, you ain't real sure?"

"I'm going to find Mama."

"No, now don't do that. You ain't gonna get any are ya?"

"And what if I did?"

"I don't know why you young-uns want to do that to yourselves."

"Probably because it bugs you all so much."

"Are you trying that reverse psychology on me? I'm pretty sure that's supposed to work the other way around."

"You stopped asking me about Aaron's tattoos, so I'd say it worked just fine. I'll be out as soon as I change." As soon as her house came into view, Natalie picked up the pace.

"You ain't gotta work out there if you don't want to." Her father made the customary offer he'd been making her for the past several years.

"I'm fine, Daddy. I am always fine."

CHAPTER FIVE

"I thought it'd be a good idea for you to give me some tips on how to handle this relationship, since she's a little afraid of being physical and this is my first real relationship since...everything." Aaron waved his right hand wishing for the thousandth time that he could simply brush off the hell he'd created. "I just need to know how to keep her safe." *And who to keep her safe from.*

Dec was a sex therapist by trade. Letting people ease into discussing things they knew a great deal about made them feel safe. Americans who felt safe often gave up information they hadn't intended to. Europeans in general were different, and Brits were no exception. It took a little more to get them to divulge personal information, but he was up to the task.

"Did Natalie ask you to keep her safe or did she ask you to introduce her to the finer points in lovemaking?"

"I care about Nat, more than I care about most anyone out here. We've been friends for a while. You know that. Whether we sleep together or not, it has nothing to do with the fact that I will always make sure she is safe physically, mentally, and emotionally. Didn't you teach me that trying to be something I'm not is an exercise in futility? I'm being me."

"I know. And I can help you handle a sexual relationship with a victim of assault if you'd like to discuss that instead of something I simply cannot and will not tell you."

"Fine, but before we discuss any of that, I do need to know if she is in any danger. You don't have to tell me from who, or from what, but I will not let anyone hurt her." The word assault shot bile from his gut to his throat. He welcomed the burn. It drove him. Telling the informant all they didn't have to share occasionally helped get the information you needed them to tell you.

"Natalie is not in any imminent danger that I am aware of. The likelihood that what happened to her would ever be repeated is infinitesimal by my estimations. The person who hurt her will never be allowed back on the ranch. Do remember that she has an extremely protective family all of whom would lay down their lives to save hers. Perhaps even more importantly, you need to remember that Natalie is a force unto herself. She never gives away anything she isn't willing to share. If she asked you to be romantically involved in her life, that says a great deal about how much she trusts you."

Aaron sure as hell knew that Natalie was fierce. It was one of the many things he adored about her, but infinitesimal wasn't small enough, not by a long shot. And he had just been handed actionable intel he could make use of. *Back on the ranch.* Wasn't that interesting? *Sick bastard, I'm coming for you.*

His goal remained in the forefront of his mind, but he needed Dec to believe that he was moving on now that he'd been assured Natalie was safe. "I want off the meds, both of them."

Dec tried to hide his grin and pull on his standard concerned expression anytime Aaron brought this up. "I take it the side effects aren't something you're willing to gamble on with Natalie?"

"Damn straight. I hate them anyway." That was God's honest truth.

"You've already worked yourself down to your current doses every other day. The next step is yours to take, but I do need to warn you the nightmares and panic attacks could become more frequent off of the meds. If you're determined to come off of them, you might need to find other ways to handle those."

Aaron hated the weakness he associated with needing the pills. He loathed that he'd ever required them in the first place. The way they muted the world around him wasn't worth it. He'd deal. He had to be all in when he was with Natalie.

He wanted to experience every shiver of her sweet little body, feel her breath on his skin, taste the hunger on her lips. He was determined to see the trust in her eyes that he'd somehow build. He needed to see the streaks of warmth he could summon with a touch, the wet heat he would draw from her, and her pussy swollen and greedy for his cock. He'd gladly take his table in hell to memorize the tight slick space between her thighs that he was going to make all his own. Choking back a ravenous groan from the thought alone, he knew Satan had nothing on what men could do to each other anyway. "I'll work out more. That helps."

"That's good. You might find that sex solves myriad problems, as well."

"Yeah, well, we're taking this slowly, so it'll be a while before I know just how much that's gonna help."

"Taking things slowly is an excellent idea. You could also come in more often if you find yourself needing a little additional help."

"We'll see. I'm worried about her. I'll deal with whatever happens to me."

"Soldier through and through."

"I know what it's like to have some tiny ridiculous thing send you reeling into a flashback. I won't put her through that. I just need to know if there's anything I shouldn't do with her?" He went on and called himself an asshole. He did want the answer to his question because he couldn't go on living with himself if he did anything that dropped her off the spiraling cliff of doom he'd climbed out of too fucking many times to count, but his motivation was twofold. What exactly did the person who'd been on Camden Ranch when Natalie was a little girl do to her?

"As you know flashbacks can be triggered from any number of places. A sight, a smell, a noise, a completely unrelated situation, a single word that prods the wound in your subconscious. Since you've been back on American soil, no one has done any of the things that happened to you while you were in the Middle East, however, you've had some pretty terrorizing memories surface. If Natalie flashes back to her attack, it is not in any way your fault, and you are probably the best person to help talk her off the ledge."

Dec always referred to PTSD as a wound. That's why Aaron continued to see him. Dec's degrees were worth quite a bit, he supposed. He knew the trauma was some kind of infection no one could reach to cut away. He knew that hell changes a man, changes who they were, who they are, and worst of all, changes everything they'd ever hoped to be.

"I will also point out that psychological traumas are not signs of weakness. They are signs of unfathomable strength. She gets up every morning, faces her fears, climbs on her horse and deals. Exactly the way you get up every morning and do the things you do to get through the day. You'll find that women with the highest, most reinforced walls often have the deepest amount to give this life. If you'll give her a little time and make certain you never break the trust she's extended you, if you can really make her feel safe in your presence, it could be life changing for both of you."

The words sank slowly through Aaron's mind. He tried to make sense of them. His shoulders eased of their own accord. The concept that Natalie wanted to share herself with him finally settled squarely in his chest, bringing warmth to the constant chill he'd carried for so damn long. The battered remains of his heart managed each beat with slightly more ease. "Okay, fine, tell me the best way to give her what she needs from me. Tell me how to make her feel safe."

"You and I both know consent is a very sexy thing, but for someone with Natalie's past it is absolutely crucial that you have her permission to be in any kind of physical contact with her."

"I'd figured that much out myself, Doc. Shocked the hell out of me when she kissed me last night. I thought I was going to have to sit on my hands to keep from touching her."

"You might find yourself in that position several times over the next few weeks."

"I figure it's not medically possible to die from a hard-on, so I'll deal. I'll never go into another mission I don't know I can handle. I've got this. Just thought you could give me a few specific directives."

"I'm going to take this opportunity to encourage you not to think of Natalie as a mission. You don't need a briefing on having a relationship."

"It's sure as hell not something I've ever done before. Hookups and hangouts I ultimately worked into hookups are the only things I've ever accomplished with women. This is different. Nat's different." This was going to be more.

"Good. Because hookups are highly overrated and you both deserve better."

"I told her that last night. Told her we weren't just going to sleep together, that we were going to figure out couple-shit to do, too."

"And she said?"

"That she'd liked dating me." Choking back the rest of her confession, he refused to admit to Dec that he'd scared her in the past.

"Then you're already ahead of the game, aren't you? Figuring out what she likes to do when you're together will ultimately help you build a relationship beyond the physical one both of you are seeking. Reaching deep and going after her heart will get you what you're wanting. If you don't want her to be afraid, teach her to trust you outside of your bedroom first."

"Yeah, that was already in my plan."

"Care to elaborate on this plan?"

"I was an intelligence officer, Doc, and I definitely consider that need to know information."

"I see. Might I ask if you intend to tell Natalie about Najaf?"

Ire streaked up Aaron's chest singeing his throat. "Why in God's name would I do that?"

"You want her to tell you about what happened to her."

"The last information exchange I involved myself in lost me seven members of my team."

"I see, so you really just want me to tell you things you likely already know. A bath after her first time will help the tenderness. To make certain she's with you and not back in dark memories either visibly or by her telling you she is whenever she's in bed with you. A great deal of foreplay and lube might make things easier. Those were the kinds of directives you were after, correct?"

"Something wrong with that?"

"Correct me if I'm wrong, but I believe you played Dom at a few sex clubs in Europe several years ago. I am not worried about your ability to make love with Natalie. I'm worried about the highly unsteady psychological and emotional ground both of you will be walking. Let me make this clear, I'm almost more worried about you than I am about her."

"I'm in this. We'll make it work."

"Before you go into this be aware that sexual fantasies often hold the very thing the mind needs to heal. Keep that in mind for both of you."

"Are you ever going to tell me what you and Aaron did last night or am I going to have to tickle it out of you?" Holly threatened Natalie while they mucked horse stalls that afternoon.

"There's nothing to tell. We didn't do anything."

"So, you just came home in his truck an hour after I left Saddleback's? You sat in silence and did nothing else?"

Natalie rolled her eyes. "We talked."

"About?"

"None of your business, Holl."

"Come on. I'm dying over here. I'm your baby sister. You have to tell me."

"No, I don't."

"Are you dating again?"

"You're not going to drop this are you?"

"Nope."

"Fine. Yes, we're dating again." That odd sizzle of heat shimmered under her skin again as she made the confession. Natalie desperately needed to know what about dating Aaron was causing that. Every time she'd thought about him, her body reacted oddly. Her heart beat too fast. Her skin took on a hunger for his touch. The wet heat she was somewhat accustomed to gathered in her panties. Her mind flew into overdrive. Her ears longed to hear him make that grunting groan he'd made in the truck the night before. Once they slept together, would all of that go away? She debated asking Holly but couldn't bring herself to say any of it out loud.

"You kept staring off into space today while we were working. You know if a cowgirl thinks about a guy while she's on the back of her horse he has to be important."

"He is important."

"How important?"

"I'm going home now."

"Because you're going to Saddlebacks? Want me to come? I can be your wing-woman."

"Officially on my nerves, Holly."

"I am one and a half semesters away from being a full-fledged sex therapist. Let me help you."

"I don't need anyone's help. Would you stop trying to fix me?" That last phrase escaped Natalie's mouth without her permission. Sinking her teeth into her bottom lip another round of self-hatred filled her. Why was she always such a bitch whenever she thought about any of this? "Sorry."

"It's okay." It wasn't okay. Defeat broadcast from her sister's features, darker duplicates of her own. "I don't think anything is wrong with you, Nat. I'm sorry I made you feel that way."

That was also a lie. She knew what had happened. The final occurrence it had been her scream for their daddy that had stopped things from going further. It had also stopped it from ever happening again. Her little sister had been her saving grace.

"It's fine. I know you're only trying to help. Uh..." Natalie searched for something she could share with Holly to suture the wound she'd inflicted. "I can't seem to stop thinking about him, actually."

"That's a good thing." The sparkle returned to Holly's eyes and a grin climbed across her face. "Anything specific?"

Remembering that she owed her sister for so many things, Natalie succumbed to her fate. "I really like his neck and his forearms and the way he does this thing with his lips that isn't actually a smile or a smirk. It's like a combo of the two but better. So, there is actually something wrong with me because that can't possibly be normal."

There were so many other things about Aaron that she found fascinating, but the way he listened to her, the way nothing ever seemed to frighten him, the low throaty notes of his voice that had taken on the consistency of gravel the night before when he'd told her that he thought about having sex with her, and the way his capable hands made her feel safe instead of terrified just weren't things she wanted to share even with her sister. They were her own. A private sanctuary he didn't even know he constructed for her every time they were together. A place she went in her head whenever the world was simply more than she had the willpower to deal with anymore.

Holly's giggle eased a little of the strain between them. "Sorry to tell you this, sis, but you're completely normal. A bad boy with good lips is hard to resist. Believe me, I would know."

"I really don't want to hear about your fascination with Dec's lips. Thanks though."

"His lips, the tattoo over his collarbone, and that place under his jaw where his beard is somehow a little scruffier."

"Are what?" Natalie immediately regretted asking. The next pause in conversation she needed to escape. She didn't even have anything to discuss with Holly yet. It had taken a dizzying amount of courage to brush a kiss on his stubbled cheek the night before. She hadn't come up with another way to communicate that she wasn't afraid of him before he'd dropped her off. She'd been aiming for his lips, and in her complete ineptitude had gotten his cheek. Stupid nerves.

"The first things I noticed about Dec that night in the bar."

For some reason, Natalie's brain failed to get the message to her mouth to stop talking. "Can I ask you something?"

"Yes." The excitement in her sister's tone shot another round of regret through Natalie's veins. "That's the whole reason we're still in the barn."

"Right. I just wondered if you slept with Dec on your first date or whatever? Did you go home with him from that bar?" *I know you did because you're not afraid. There's nothing wrong with you.* Why had she even asked?

"No."

"You didn't?"

Holly shook her head. "I offered, but he turned me down."

"You're such a liar. You two are like rabbits. I don't believe he ever turned you down for anything."

"Now we are, but he had a lot he had to deal with, Nat. Everyone has issues. We worked through them. We were actually on a one-week rule."

"What's a one-week rule?"

"No sex for the first week we dated."

"Oh." A cold wave of dread speared through her stomach as Natalie tried to determine if she'd be prepared to go through with this in one week's time. Is that what Aaron thought would happen? Was one-week a thing? Is that what everyone else did, everyone who wasn't afraid?

"It doesn't have to be a week. It can be as long as you and Aaron want it to be."

Natalie assumed it was a testament of their bond and the mastery of her classes that had Holly reading her mind

"Yeah, I know." Stowing the brushes on the tack shelves kept Natalie from having to look her sister in the eye.

"Do something for me."

"What?" She prayed whatever Holly wanted would be something she could provide.

"Don't push yourself to do anything that makes you uncomfortable. He'll be patient with you. I know Aaron's going to understand a lot more than you think he will."

CHAPTER SIX

"You came." Aaron looked far more thrilled than was really necessary when Natalie scooted from the front door to the bar at Saddleback's. That weird fizzy feeling in her stomach started up again as soon as she saw him.

"You texted me three times asking me to meet you here." Natalie held up her phone. The dinner crowd was comprised of mostly ranch families. No one appeared to have had too much to drink as of yet. Her muscles eased and she focused on the grin Aaron was still sporting. Holly was right. His lips were awfully sexy.

"I know I did. Just wasn't entirely sure you'd follow orders." Another one of those winks assured her he was only teasing. If only she could convince the heat in her cheeks to lay off every time he did that, things would be good.

"Well, I don't care for being ordered around, normally, but I wanted to see you."

"Really? Well, trust me that feeling is very mutual. I get off in an hour. Want to go do something?"

"Isn't that what dating is?"

"Yeah, I just didn't want to assume that I got to be your evening plans, babe. I'm trying to make you think I'm cool."

I think you're so much more than cool. "And what would you be doing if you weren't trying to make me think you're cool?"

"Probably something that would show you just how fucking anxious I am to let every single asshole in this bar ogling your ass in those jeans know that you're taken. I'm trying to quell my possessive side for the time being anyway."

Whipping around to face the dining room again, Natalie's mouth fell open. There was indeed a table of men in the back all staring at her. The ease she'd felt a moment before was ripped away from her. Chill bumps lifted every hair on her arms. She narrowed her eyes in a hateful scowl, lifted her chin and refused to show off the effect their lascivious gazes had on her. Crossing her arms over her chest, she tried to make herself as unappealing as she was able.

Suddenly, there was no longer a bar between her and Aaron. He was right beside her. "Hey, it's okay, sweetheart. I'm right here. Can I hug you?"

She managed a slight nod and then found herself wrapped safely in the strength of his arms. Burying her face in his chest gave her lungs a heady dose of his musky scent. A shot of courage bolstered through her. A tender kiss landed on the top of her head. Would that be enough to let the men know that she wasn't all alone? Was that enough to keep them away?

"I've got you. I'm sorry, I should've kept my mouth shut. I thought you saw them when you came in."

"I was distracted."

Another one of those hungry grunts sounded in her ear. *Do that again.* She wanted to beg. That sound, the low thrum of Aaron aroused, soothed her frayed nerves and fed the desire racing up her spine.

"You know you kill me when you say stuff like that, right? Hey, you say no if this makes you uncomfortable, but I could grab your sexy ass while they're staring and let them know you're mine."

Utter delight zinged through Natalie. "Do it." She tried not to giggle.

"Yes ma'am." His massive hand cupped her right asscheek. When he squeezed, a breathy moan escaped her mouth without her permission. God, why did that feel so good? She rocked against him, colliding with his burgeoning erection, all heat and steel hard. Reminding herself they were standing in Saddleback's, she bit her tongue to keep from asking if she could touch him.

"You feel what you do to me, sweetheart?"

She managed another nod.

"Tell me to stop, Nat, or I swear I'm never going to be able to." Another grip of his hand brought a rush of wet heat to the crotch of her panties.

"I don't think I want you to stop either, but you're going to get into trouble if Ed sees us." One singular brain cell had come up with that bit of logic. She clung to it fiercely, lest she beg him to just keep going. Throwing caution to the wind was far too appealing as of late.

Making one more quick check of the men in the far corner, to make certain they'd gotten the message that she was not available to be gawked at, flirted with, or to have drinks procured in her honor, Natalie lifted her head and watched the dark fire she loved dance in his eyes when he stared at her.

"I'm stopping, I swear." He patted her backside and then stepped back.

"What did you mean when you said I was killing you? And don't work too hard to keep that possessive side under wraps. I like it." She watched his head turn as he made a quick check of the bar and scan of the dining room. "Do you need me to let you work?"

"Nah. There's nothing more important than you in my world currently, but you were right. I just needed to make sure Ed isn't going to come out here and start busting my ass for not being behind the bar. He's working the late shift tonight, but he's not here yet. Look at me."

Natalie's gaze found his once again.

"I came up not having much to call my own. Sharing is a way of life in foster care. When I was in the army what was mine was also my team's, and that was fine by me. But there haven't ever been many things in this life that were all mine, and only for me. Whenever I get something that is just for me, I take care of it. My dogs, my truck, and my room. That's been pretty much it, until you told me last night that you want us to date again. Possessiveness when it comes to you is as natural as breathing for me. I don't need you to encourage it, because my God, I want to walk over there and knock heads together just because they looked at my girl, and thought about things that are going to belong only to me. Drives me crazy. But I also have no intention of scaring you again by showing off my caveman side. Just know this, I will always take care of what's mine."

"I keep trying to tell you I'm not scared of you. I don't need you to fight my battles for me, but it's kind of nice that you want to. I definitely don't mind being someone that belongs to you and that you take care of. I feel the same way about you. Can't we just take care of each other?" Measuring her words carefully, Natalie made certain she'd said all of that right.

"I don't need to be taken care of. I just need to do right by you."

She was just too sweet, too good, too innocent. He was an asshole for not turning her down the night before. He didn't deserve her. He didn't deserve anyone that wanted to take care of him. Just then, she nuzzled her face against his chest. That one tiny movement bolted his boots to the hardwood floor. He wasn't going anywhere, not as long as she was in his arms.

"You plan on making drinks tonight, Weber, or is this job gettin' in the way of your love life?" Ed stormed into the bar.

Shit. "I'm making drinks, Ed. Just took a quick break. Haven't done that since we opened."

"I'm not payin' you to take breaks, son. I'm payin' you to serve beer."

"Yes, sir." The words tasted like battery acid on his tongue. "Hang tight, babe. Let me do refills, and I'll be right back." Directing Natalie to a barstool, Aaron grabbed a pitcher of Bud Light and made the rounds.

When he neared the back table, he narrowed his eyes. "Keep your eyes to yourselves, gentlemen. I'm not in a forgiving mood. She's taken."

"Last time I checked the bartender gets no say in who I choose to look at. Pour me another, son." The monogram on his shirt sleeve said the cattle rancher had more money than good sense. He drummed his fingers on the table.

The idiot next to him rolled his eyes and then checked his Rolex. "If we're going to make Cheyenne by nightfall, we need to go, Dad." *Dad.* What the hell? Aaron's palms itched to beat the guy into oblivion, but Ed would make his life hell for fighting and Natalie would run. Not worth it.

"Nice example you're setting for your kid, dumbass. You'll make Cheyenne, because you're leaving now. Last time I checked, anyone who makes my girl uncomfortable ends up eating parking lot gravel. I'm the bouncer and bartender here. Don't let the door hit you in the ass, and pay your tab on the way out. The sheriff's sitting right there." Aaron pointed to Sheriff Wilheim reading the paper at a nearby table.

Removing their mugs from the table wasn't nearly as satisfying as removing their eyes from their skulls would have been, but Aaron made do. "Out." He pointed to the door.

When he returned to the bar, Natalie was wide-eyed with shock. "Did you make them leave because of me?"

"They've been on my nerves all afternoon. Been taking up a table for four hours and drinking way too slow. Hey, you want a drink while you're here?" He knew she didn't. He'd embarrassed her throwing the douchebags out. She wanted to leave. Stiffled motion seemed locked in her limbs.

For the moment, she was right where he'd left her, staring up at him. How the hell was this suddenly his life?

"Not really. What do you want to do when you get off?"

You, baby doll. Keeping that response locked behind his teeth, he shrugged. "Anything you want."

Her bottom lip slipped through her teeth. His eyes locked on her mouth. When her fingertips located the horseshoe charm around her neck he realized his mistake. He should have made plans. Some boyfriend he was turning out to be. Scrambling for most anything nearby, which wasn't much, he took a shot in the dark. "You wanna drive out to Ogallala and see a movie?"

"They're redoing the theater. It won't be open until Christmas. We could go get Lulu and Buster and take them over to Luke's and play with them."

While it was true that Aaron's dogs had a grand time playing with Luke's Beagles, Bailey and Bella, it couldn't be a good sign that she wanted her big brother around for their date.

Aaron had been so intent on getting intel out of Dec and getting her to the bar he'd forgotten to plan anything. What the hell was wrong with him? Thinking about what had happened to her had scrambled his good senses. When he added in what she wanted from him he was rendered effectively useless. He had to get it together.

Keeping a mask of consideration firmly affixed to his face so she wouldn't see how disappointed he was, he forced a nod. "We can do that if you want."

"Do you want to?" Hesitation perforated her tone.

"I told you I'm good with anything you want to do. Lulu and Buster will be so freaking glad to see you they'll lose their damn minds. They've missed you almost as much as I have. They've got to be sick of me by this point anyway."

"I've missed them, too. I love them more than I love Bailey and Bella, just never tell Luke that."

The things she said to him. The way she'd occasionally admit things without any pretense or plan. The way she loved his dogs. The remnants of his heart beat out its frantic approval. If she needed Luke around for the night, so be it. He'd make it work.

The lengthy list of things he'd rather do extended as he popped open the register drawer to clock out. Locating the jar he kept under the counter, he shoved his tip money into his pocket. Less than forty bucks. Working the lunch shift sucked.

He reminded himself that nothing was more important than simply being in Natalie's presence, even if he was going to have to put up with her big brother.

He'd much prefer to get her out of the bar and get his hands up that light pink tank top she was wearing that was nothing more than an invitation to sin if he'd ever seen one. Only adding fuel to the fire in his groin was the fact that she had no idea how drop-dead gorgeous she looked, so innocent and sweet. Curious. Eager even, but for what she didn't seem to know. The semi he was just going to have to get used to was quick to throb out its reminder that he could teach her anything she wanted to know.

Leaving bruising kisses on those lush lips, getting her drunk on him, showing her how good he could make it for her, marking her all for himself, exploring her body until he memorized the sounds she made at his touch, making her feel safe enough to explore, all tallied in his mind right behind showing her how beautiful she was. Ordering those thoughts away, he clung to the knowledge that pushing her too far, too fast would only end in disaster. He'd get her there, when the time was right.

Knowing the history behind your mission was one of the commandments of army intel. He had to keep everything in order and do nothing until she was ready.

Taking one more quick glance at the clock over the bar, he sighed. "Five more minutes. Then we can head to my house."

"It's fine." She fidgeted with her necklace again. Focusing on slowing his breath, Aaron's scrambled brain continued to try to come up with better plans for their evening. "Holly asked me about you before I came out here," leapt from her mouth.

Clearly all of the Camdens were going to play a pretty big part in this relationship. He quelled his sigh this time. "Oh yeah? I don't know Holly nearly as well as I know Dec. What'd she ask you?"

"You know how she is. She's my baby sister, and she firmly believes she can help everyone. She thinks I should tell her everything going on with me. It's annoying but that's always how it's been with us. She's like that with everyone, really."

"I have a few army buddies from my old team that get antsy if they don't hear from me on the regular, even if I have nothing exciting to tell them. They're my family. Is it kind of like that?"

Those golden flecks shimmered in her eyes as she studied him. Everything about her exploring gaze should have panicked him. Even after she'd run out of his house all those months ago, she always looked at him like she could see through him, like she already knew things he'd never tell her. It had been his job since he was barely eighteen years old to keep his personal shit to himself. What the hell was going on in that brain of hers when she stared him down?

"Family can have its perks, I guess. I got lucky. As much as they all drive me crazy, they love me, but it can be awful, too. It's like you're bound to these people your whole life. What if you end up with a terrible family? It's not like you get any choice in the matter."

"That's an interesting take, Nat. I always thought the Camdens were like the Waltons or something. They're the backbone of this entire town. Everyone knows them. Your parents have that classic entity thing going on, don't they? Your brothers are pretty cool. All of the Camdens seem like good people."

"Yeah...I guess they are, and Mom and Dad are definitely going down in the history books."

There had been a few dozen moments since he'd finally signed the medical separation papers terminating his career in the army where he wished he didn't know what he knew. He wished he'd never learned to decipher every single thing a person didn't say, wished he couldn't read the empty spaces between the lines, and desperately wished he could somehow turn off what now happened naturally.

The pause before she'd answered was far too long. The quick swallow and touch of her index finger to her lips spoke much louder than her verbal lie. Holy fuck. What had he just inadvertently discovered?

"You ready to go, sweetheart?" Everything in him was poised to protect her. His muscles were strung tighter than a racked hammer on a pistol. Suddenly, hanging out with Luke didn't seem like such a bad plan. There was more information he needed.

She slipped off the barstool and he settled his jacket on her shoulders, longing to cover her with his body instead.

"Thanks." She gave him that grin again.

He doubled down on his plans to find and decimate whoever had hurt her as he whisked her out of the bar with his arm around her.

Aaron released Natalie's hand to fish his phone out of his pocket when it rang on the way to his house. Glancing at the screen, he debated. This was clearly not his night. Ignoring T-Byrd's call would only earn him endless attempted calls for the next several hours. Talking to him in Natalie's presence wasn't a great idea either.

"Aren't you going to answer that?" Her brow furrowed.

There was no way out now. "Hey T, little busy at the moment."

"Thought you worked the early shift on Wednesdays. You never called me back after you got your intel. I'm bored. Throw a brother a bone. I'm in the mood to figure something out."

"Stay in that mood and be patient."

"What's that mean?"

"Means some things take time."

"I'm betting it means you couldn't get your contact to talk. What the hell, man? You're the best."

"Yeah, well I'm a little out of practice."

"Nah, that ain't it. You gonna introduce me to her?"

"To who?" Aaron had learned early on how to lie his way out of trouble. Necessary way of life for most any foster kid. Extremely handy skill for any intelligence officer. He'd lied his way out of capture twice, but lying to T-Byrd wasn't going to fly, and he knew it.

"Don't bullshit me. To the girl who's clearly fried your brain. I've never heard you so rattled."

"Not any time soon."

"Bring her out to the Hi-Way tomorrow night." Dammit, she really had fried his brain. He'd forgotten the Sevens standing diner night, first Thursday every month at the Hi-Way diner in Lincoln. No one was allowed to miss unless someone they knew had died. Those had been the rules they'd all made when they were discharged.

"She does not want to come with me to Lincoln tomorrow night."

Natalie's pointed to herself and mouthed the word, "Me?"

Aaron nodded his agreement.

"Why wouldn't I want to go?" she asked with more volume.

"Ah, she speaks, and she does want to come. We'll be good, Triple A. I swear on my old socks."

"The ones we used to use for kindling? I'm not subjecting her to you all."

"Afraid she'll trade you in on a better snake eater?" T-Byrd chuckled.

"Fuck off." Snake eater. God. How long had it been since he'd been called that? Aaron couldn't remember. The slang for Army Special Ops brought back too many unwelcome memories.

"Geez, she really does have you wound tight. Bring her out here. I have to meet the woman that can undo you. I didn't believe she existed. Besides, she clearly has something to do with the guy you're wanting me to find. Might help if I met her. Seems to me Team Seven did its best work when we were together."

There was enough truth in that to amp the gall coursing through Aaron. "I'll ask her, okay? But don't count on her being there."

"You have any other sources on finding this guy you want to kill on her behalf?"

"Yeah. I'm still working on it. Patience, remember?"

"Never my forte, remember? And I'll get a table for six."

Shaking his head, Aaron wondered what Natalie would make of his old team, and what would she want to know after she met them. "Bye, T." He ended the call.

"I take it we're going to Lincoln tomorrow night." Natalie laughed.

"You don't have to come. It's just this thing I do every few weeks with some old friends of mine."

"Old army friends? The ones you just told me were your family, which means you are not skipping out because of me."

"And my mouth gets me in trouble again." A strained chuckle accompanied the pained words as they left his lips.

"What does that mean?"

Aaron threw the truck into park when he pulled up to his home, a single room above Old Man Rasmussen's garage. "Not a thing."

It wasn't the first time his dogs had saved him, and he doubted it would be the last. Barking loudly as soon as they saw his truck, Lulu and Buster bounded out from where they were resting in the shade of a cottonwood. They greeted Natalie heartily as soon as her boots hit the dirt.

CHAPTER SEVEN

"Let me make you something to eat before we head over to Luke's," Aaron offered.

"I ate at Mama and Daddy's before I came to the bar. We could stop by there before we go to Luke's so you can eat. Mama always has leftovers."

"Nah, I'm good. I'll just grab a protein bar." His missions went to war in his mind. Adding her parents into their evening surely wouldn't help warm her up to his touch, get her comfortable with being alone with him again. For a moment, he prayed Indie would need Luke to help out with their twins or something so he could work their way to Natalie's house. If they had to go to the ranch, at least they could be alone. But being alone wasn't going to help him figure out who'd hurt her. His suspicion that he was somehow related to Natalie meant the answers would likely only come from another family member.

He'd been the best damn intel officer in the army before everything had gone to hell. No reason he couldn't handle both missions. Just had to take one before the other.

Retrieving a Builder bar from the stash near his hot plate, Aaron tore off the wrapper.

"Who's this?" Natalie pointed to that damned envelope he'd stupidly left on the kitchen counter. The picture of him and Josh from boot camp graduation stared back at him, mocking him for not throwing it in the boxes under his bed where he kept every other thing he never wanted to see again. "You look so young here." She beamed at him.

"Just a guy I used to know. Graduated with him." Trying to keep it together, he eased the photograph out of her hands, grabbed the envelope full of letters, and shoved it in his desk drawer. The muted clank of Josh's tags as they slipped down the envelope roiled in his gut.

"Will he be there tomorrow night? You know, at the thing in Lincoln?"

"Uh..." Aaron hated the quiver in his tone, "...no. He won't be there."

"Oh. Sorry."

"What are you apologizing for, Nat? You didn't do anything wrong." He didn't even recognize his own voice. It had taken on the effect of the tunnel she'd thrust him into, a nonstop, direct flight to his past. The envelope had arrived two weeks ago. It had been mailed two months before, but that was standard delivery for anything in Pleasant Glen. Damned mailman was useless. Why hadn't he put his foster mother's letter away?

"I shouldn't have asked about it. I was being nosy."

"It's fine. Let's get out of here while there's still some sunlight left." Blood rushed back to his brain and breath filled his lungs as soon as he got Natalie out of his house. There was no sand in the humid air. Trees surrounded them. *Let it go, Weber.* If only his Detachment Commander's voice wasn't so readily accessible in his psyche, he'd have been able to convince himself quicker that he was no longer in the desert.

Grabbing the half-gnawed Frisbees and leashes from the hook in the garage, he ordered himself to focus on his current missions, not the ones from his past.

Suddenly, Natalie laced her fingers through his once again. Her touch yanked him back from the cliff he was teetering over. It erased a portion of the memories he was so anxious to escape. The tender concern in her hazel eyes further freed him. "This is going to sound stupid, but I like holding your hand."

A genuine smile formed on his face. The motion felt foreign for a moment. "Oh yeah?"

"Yeah, and trust me, that's a big deal for me, even bigger than you grabbing my ass or whatever."

"I told you I was going to do right by you, sweetheart. Sounds like maybe I haven't fucked this up too bad."

"You haven't fucked anything up, Aaron. Why do you always think you have?"

Because that seems to be my M.O. "Just want to make sure I keep doing things you like. Holding hands is a big deal. People don't get that. It's a connection. Touch is important." Taking a chance, he lifted their joined hands and brushed a kiss along her knuckles.

The connection shot a jolt of lust from his lips to his chest like a live wire. Her smile climbed from her lips all the way up to her eyes. Jesus, if kissing her hand made him ache what would having her in his bed be like? Saliva filled his mouth at the thought. He was so damned hungry for her.

"I think so, too."

"Soon, I'm going to do that on your lips, Nat. I'm gonna take my time, learn my way around there again. Might spend hours with your lips on mine and my hands on your body. Deal?"

"Definitely a deal. Maybe we could do that tonight."

"That sounds like a plan."

Lulu helped herself to the front seat when Aaron opened the door for Natalie. "Not this time, girl. Natalie gets to ride shotgun."

"Aww, she can ride up front with us. I don't mind."

"She'd lick you to death before I got you to the ranch. Get in the back, Lu." He popped the tailgate. Formally trained as a therapy dog, Lulu immediately complied. Buster, a mutt Aaron had rescued from a shelter on Josh's birthday a few years ago, followed suit, though not without a few whines of contention.

Certain she should be officially named the world's worst person to date, Natalie dug her nails into her palm. Focusing on the slight pain kept her from talking and making things worse.

Clearly, he did not want to go over to Luke's. She should never have suggested hanging out with her big brother. Why had she even said that? He also didn't want her to go with him to Lincoln the next day. She'd only asked because she'd felt so bad about ruining their first date. Then to ice the cake of stupidity, she'd lost the leash on her curiosity and had asked about a picture that was none of her business.

She doubted she would ever possess the ability to erase the haunted pain in his eyes that her question had wrought. Whatever had happened to the boy in the photograph, it had deeply wounded Aaron. She of all people should've known not to ask about his past. The pain contained in the past couldn't be mended. It was finished yet somehow incomplete. A wound that bore a visible scar nothing could erase. It was untouchable, unchangeable, and there was no escape.

He'd probably be happier if it was Lulu up here instead of me. At least dogs never say anything that make him sad. Crushing defeat sank her lower in the seat.

"Hey, you know the one and only perk of having an ancient truck is that there's still a bench seat." With that crooked grin that was entirely too fascinating he gestured to the middle of the seat and stretched his right arm over the top of the bench, arranging himself so he would have his arm over her shoulders if she scooted closer to him. "Thought you kind of liked it when we were touching."

"I do." Complying immediately, Natalie scooted against him. His warmth and protection washed through her. Maybe she hadn't screwed up too badly. He had said he wanted to kiss her. Having his tongue in her mouth would keep her from saying anything else stupid, she supposed. Plus, spending time with their lips touching was about as close to heaven as she'd probably ever get.

Every single thing about that night a year ago was still locked firmly in her mind. His eagerness, the sounds he'd made, the hunger on his tongue. The scrape of his beard on her chin. The rough wool of his sofa against her calves. The dark fire in his eyes. The masculinity surrounding her. The safety of his arms, the sanctuary of muscle he'd enveloped her in. The tender ache of emptiness that had taken up residence between her thighs. The need for him to fill her.

One moment, she'd been certain she'd never want to exist

anywhere else. Her nerves over not knowing what to do with her hands or if she was being too eager taunted her constantly, but she'd kept going.

He'd traced his hands up her thighs, brushing the denim skirt out of his way. Her body had begged for more. Until the motion had taken up residence with the case of nerves and sent her reeling backward in time, a collision course she was powerless to stop.

The icy grip of fear had robbed her of the heat between them. Her lungs temporarily forgot how to take in breath. The ever expanding balloon of terror expanded outward from her chest until it choked her.

Escaping had been the only thing her body understood. She couldn't fight. She had to fly. Her legs had carried her out the front door before her mind understood what she was doing. Regret sank its teeth deeper into her.

Chancing another quick glance at his lips and pausing a moment more to admire his slight beard and mustache, she wished for the millionth time that she'd been able to reason her way through that fear.

If only she'd handled that night better, everything would be different. She might know who the guy in the photo with Aaron was. She'd know what had happened to him. She might even have told him what had happened to her, why she'd been so scared that night. She'd know how to help him not be so sad.

He kept wanting to take care of her. If she hadn't blown it, she'd already know how to take care of him. More than all of that, she wouldn't have had to ask for a redo. She would already know what it was like to be with him, to feel the rasp of his fingertips against her skin, to feel his weight against her.

The emptiness pervaded her soul.

"You're awfully quiet, Nat. You okay?"

"Kind of."

"What's wrong?"

"Me, I guess."

"There's nothing wrong with you. What made you say that?"

"I don't know. I was thinking about that night when we were dating before."

As soon as he made the turn onto the gravel road that would ultimately lead them to her family's ranch, he locked his eyes on hers.
"You didn't do a damn thing wrong that night. That was all me. I
pushed too hard. I fucked it up."

"But you didn't. I just don't know how to do any of this. I'm sorry I
suggested going to Luke's. I know it's not what you wanted to do.
Eventually dating someone who doesn't know how to date is going to
get old, don't you think?"

"Hey, stop it. I'm no good at dating either. If I was, I would have
made plans for us tonight. Let's just figure it out together. Stop
thinking you're doing something wrong."

"Only if you stop thinking you're fucking something up. Deal?"

"Yeah, I guess. But you don't have to come with me to Lincoln
tomorrow night. It's a hole-in-the-wall diner, not the kind of places I
wish I could take you, and a bunch of washed up army ops with
nothing better to do."

Natalie debated. She wasn't certain if he didn't want her to go or if
he somehow thought she wouldn't have fun. Her brain continued to
confuse itself. For some unfathomable reason, she wanted to go simply
because he would be there with her.

"You don't want to go. I knew it," he sighed.

"Actually, I do want to go. I'd like to meet your friends. You just
kind of showed up in the Glen a few years ago. I know you were in the
army, but I don't know much else. I just don't want to intrude or be a
third wheel or whatever."

"You're never intruding, sweetheart. I'd love for you to come
with me."

"Really?"

"Really. We can talk more about the Sevens on the way out there
tomorrow. You know there's a lot about your past I don't know either."

"Because I don't want my past to have anything to do with us."

"Yeah, you keep saying that, but you just called me on keeping mine
away from you."

"That's different."

"How so?"

Because yours is probably brave and heroic and mine...wasn't. "It just is."

"I was an intelligence operator in the army."

Panic erupted from Natalie's core. Was he really going to tell her about his past? Did that mean he expected her to share as well?

"Uh, I've never wanted to be anything but a cowgirl." There. That was something.

He quirked another grin. "I wasn't going for a sharing session, Nat. I don't do that. I was just pointing out that I know a fair amount about reading people and figuring out what they mean even when they don't *say* what they mean. *It just is* isn't much of an answer, but it is an answer in and of itself."

"Meaning what exactly?"

"Promise you won't freak out if I tell you this."

"Okay, I promise." Natalie wondered if she'd just lied to him. How was she supposed to promise not to freak out when she had no idea what he was about to say?

"*It just is* wasn't the answer your brain came up with. It wasn't your truth, and I know it wasn't by how long it took you to come up with that as your lame-ass answer, babe."

"So, you're like some kind of human lie-detector or something?" Flipping through the emotions residing in her body, she tried to locate fear, or irritation, or even outright anger but came up empty. All she could find was relief. None of her reactions made sense anymore. What was he doing to her?

"Not exactly. Lie detector *machines* can be wrong."

"Cocky much?"

"Only about a few things."

"And those are?"

"Knowing when somebody's lying to me, knowing when they're about to do something that could hurt themselves or someone else, and knowing how to make you come over and over again, making you so needy for me you beg for more. The rest of life I'm basically shit at."

Another round of heat burned in her cheeks. She knew he wasn't exaggerating. Forcibly pushing his sexual prowess out of her mind for a moment, she attempted to focus on the lie detector business. "I wasn't trying to lie to you, but I'm also not telling you the thing you seem so hung up on. Let it go."

"You're not the first person to tell me to do that. Never been very good at letting things go."

CHAPTER EIGHT

Luke was seated on his front porch with one of his twins in his lap. Aaron wished he could tell the girls apart. They looked just alike. Whichever one it was, she wiggled down out of her daddy's lap and took several hesitant steps toward the stairs when Natalie hopped out of the truck. She applauded her aunt's appearance and lifted her arms upwards.

Natalie scooped up the little girl while Aaron let the dogs out of the back of the truck.

"You giving Daddy a hard time, Savana Jane?" Natalie kissed her niece's cheeks. Savana cuddled into her, babbling excitedly.

"How do you know which is which?" Aaron hoped that wasn't a rude question.

Natalie's answering smile erased his concern. "Savana has a pudgier belly and is a little shorter than Dakota. And they had them on oxygen for a couple of weeks. The way they laid them with the tubes shaped their ears differently. Savana's go to the right." She traced the shell of Savana's ear. The little girl shivered before she began pulling on Natalie's right ear. "And Dakota's go to the left."

Luke ambled down the stairs. He shot Aaron a warning glare before crossing his arms over his chest. What the fuck? Studying Luke, Aaron racked his brain trying to determine who or what had put his dick in a knot. They'd always been good friends.

"Somebody piss in your Wheaties, man?"

Natalie glared at her big brother. "No. That's his attempt at an intimidating, don't mess with my little sister look. Ignore him. He's being stupid."

At that moment, Indie exited the front door carrying Dakota. Bailey and Bella, their Beagles, skirted by her and bounded down the steps to greet Lulu and Buster.

Indie's glance made a quick trip from Natalie to Luke to Aaron. "Oh, dear God, Luke Camden. Back the truck up, honey. Natalie doesn't need you to protect her anymore, and I have no patience for you being pissy tonight. I pulled an engine, replaced a transmission, put on two new belts, and changed oil on four cars today. I'm tired."

Anymore. So, at one point Nat did need Luke to keep her safe. Interesting. Aaron tempered his humor over Luke's sudden change in attitude toward him. Luke clearly had intel he needed.

"You want me to give you a free shot at my face or something? Let you play big brother or are we going to be okay? I'd never hurt her. Surely you know that."

"I am standing right here." Natalie sneered. "He isn't going to hurt me," she informed her brother. "I will be fine. I always am. Would both of you stop trying to protect me? I can take care of myself."

Taken aback, Aaron started to apologize but Luke huffed, "No, I will not stop trying to protect you. I'm your big brother. It's my job."

"No, it isn't. Get over yourself, Luke. Who I date is my choice."

Ignoring his sister, Luke turned back to Aaron and menaced, "You just make sure I never need to take you up on that offer."

Aaron debated pointing out how many ways he knew how to kill a man, or how often he worked out. "Guess if I had a little sister, I'd be just as overprotective."

"Well, you don't so you have no idea what it's like."

"Nope, I don't. She wanted to come out here and let the dogs play. I can always take her back to my place." The threat was implicit. If they were on the ranch, Luke got some say and had his eyes on them. They did not *have* to remain on the ranch that evening.

"It's fine. You're welcome here anytime. I just...it just... I don't want to think about it. Do not make her cry. Ever. You hear me?"

"I know you won't believe this, but even thinking about someone making her cry makes me want to beat a guy seven ways straight just for an appetizer, so I get it. I care about her. I have no intention of ever making her cry."

"Good."

Indie rolled her eyes. "Come on, Nat. Come help me change the girls' diapers before the boys break out the rulers."

"Can you both not be doing this..." Natalie gestured between Aaron and her brother, "...when I get back?"

"You got it," Aaron immediately agreed. Luke offered nothing but a noncommittal grunt. "Any particular reason you're acting like I'm the son of Satan all of a sudden?" He leapt as soon as the front door closed behind Natalie.

"Natalie isn't like other women."

"No shit."

Luke rolled his eyes. "I don't mean like that."

Now, they were getting somewhere. Aaron edged closer. Luke stepped back into the slight shadow cast by the porch. Interesting. There was clearly something Luke Camden knew he should keep hidden. He was struggling. "Then how did you mean it, man? I'm crazy about her. Have been since I drove into town. Seems to me you were all about us dating the first time around."

"Yeah, I was. I still am I guess. This is different. I can tell. She's acting different about you this time."

"Different how?"

"Damn near 'bout rode her horse into a fence post this morning."

Years of practice controlling his facial expressions all went to hell. He managed to keep from pumping his fist in the air but a broad grin formed on his face. Running his hand over his chin he hoped her brother didn't notice his delight. "Meaning what?"

"Like you don't know."

"Nat's the only cowgirl I've ever dated. Not sure what it means when they ride horses into posts or whatever. Guess I should ask if Sundance is okay?"

"Horse is fine. Natalie's mooning over you like a schoolgirl with her first crush. It's weird. She doesn't do shit like this."

"She's a grown woman, Luke. I'm sure as hell not her first crush and I won't be her last. Why are you up in arms over us? Why are you so protective of her? You didn't go after Dec when he and Holly got together."

"Holly's different."

"And we're back to different how? Just tell me why you're so angry." *Tell me why you blame yourself for what happened to her?* Guilt was laced in every word Luke Camden spoke, in every expression that tensed in his features, in every slight movement he made. Aaron could read him like a book.

"I don't want to see her get her heart broken."

"I have no intention of breaking her heart, but that isn't what you're really worried about."

Irritation flashed in Luke's eyes. "She know what you used to do in the army?"

"She has some idea."

"There might be things that she don't want you poking your nose in with all of your intelligence gathering know-how and whatnot."

Considering his words carefully, Aaron nodded. "I have no plans to do anything that might make her uncomfortable. There anything you want to tell me? You look like a man who needs to get something off his chest."

That wasn't actually true. He looked like a man who needed a good night's sleep, a shot of whiskey, or to get laid, maybe all three.

Lifting his cowboy hat, Luke ran his hands through his hair. He worked his jaw. The weight of consideration settled in the air around them. He stared into Aaron's eyes seeking permission perhaps, or more likely a confidant. He'd seen similar expressions on hundreds of men who needed to rid themselves of the burdens of knowledge they didn't want to possess. Luke needed someone to help him keep Natalie safe.

Aaron's pulse timed the seconds it took for him to speak. "I want to keep her safe just as much as you do." He forced his tone to a reassuring, measured tenor. Stepping back, he let Luke feel the relief of more space between them.

If he needed a partner, Aaron was his man. The confidence he'd thought long gone returned to his musculature. He barely recognized it. In Iraq, he'd blown everything to hell. He could never repair the damage he'd caused. Somehow keeping Natalie safe, nurturing her, worshipping her, it all felt like a balm to his internal wounds. This was all the do-over he would get. At that moment he wondered if it was the only one he'd needed for so long.

"Nat's never really dated anyone. She has no experience at all as far as I know. Men scare her. When she was a little girl..."

Natalie and Indie burst through the front door and Luke's mouth sealed shut. Dammit all to hell.

"There's a puddle under Lulu she's been standing there with the Frisbee drooling for so long. What were you two talking about?" Natalie asked.

"Your brother was just making a few more threats. It's all good. Sorry, girl." Aaron immediately took the Frisbee from Lulu and tossed it out into the nearby pasture. The dogs took off after it.

Knowing Luke, he probably was driving home his threats. Her brothers were all idiots.

When Holly and Dec drove up in her truck, she knew this was going to be a disaster. Why in God's name had she brought him back to the ranch? This was not how dating couples acted. If she'd ever actually dated someone significantly, she would have known that.

"Saw your truck headed this way. Hol insisted we come see the babies and the dogs," Dec explained to Aaron before he and Holly worked their way through the swarm of dogs that had come to greet them.

"Nice to see you," Aaron sighed.

Holly and Dec were followed by Natalie's parents. Jessie's Suburban pulled up to the side of Luke's house. A moment later her parents were upon them.

"Saw you two drive in. Thought we'd come out here and check on everything," Ev explained. Natalie cringed as her father overtly studied the stars inked on Aaron's arm. "You ain't one of them pain junkies are you, son?"

"Pain junkies, sir?" That smirk she wished didn't affect her quite so profoundly formed on Aaron's features. Her heart sped its approval.

"Daddy, stop it," she demanded.

"No, now, before you go off dating my little girl I got a right to ask. You don't get all them tattoos because you've taken a likin' to pain, makes you feel woozy and whatnot."

"Everett Camden where in God's name do you come up with this stuff?" Jessie huffed.

"I seen a documentary on people with lots of tattoos. Made me wonder."

"Dad!" Natalie tried again.

Holly sank her teeth into her upper lip but couldn't seem to stop the taunt. "You know, Dad, pain and pleasure come from very similar receptors in the human brain."

"Don't you start with all of your psychology. I don't want to think about it."

"Uh," Aaron cleared his throat. "I promise I don't have a thing for pain, sir. Just like ink."

"You ain't getting any more are ya? You have enough don't you think?"

"Daddy, please stop. I like his tattoos." Natalie's attempt at a rescue only served to enflame her cheeks.

"Maybe I should get Nat's name somewhere." Aaron winked at her.

"Ah geez. Jessie do you have my Rolaids?"

"I'm sorry I asked to come here." Natalie spoke through her teeth. "I didn't know my whole family would show up or that my dad would break out his tattoo lectures."

Aaron folded her into his embrace and spoke directly into her ear. "No worries. They just love you. Want to make sure I'm going to treat you right and apparently they want to be assured that I'm not a masochist."

"They're being nosy. You haven't done anything to me at all," she lamented.

He made that noise again, the hungry grunt he'd made the night before. "You sound a little disappointed by that, babe." His hands eased up and down her back. He pulled her closer. For one perfect moment the ranch, her brother and sister, her parents, the entire world disappeared. She existed in a sanctuary of steady strength. "I grabbed your ass, remember?"

"I remember." Her own giggle surprised her.

His ability to make her laugh no matter how badly she'd screwed something up made no sense. It had taken her a month to leave the ranch after the night she'd run away from him. She was terrified to see him and have to relive her embarrassment. As the universe would have it, as soon as she stepped foot on Main Street, he was standing there. Instead of making her feel more ashamed, he'd apologized and then immediately told her a story about Buster making off with Old Man Rasmussen's underwear and taking them to Mrs. Larson, the widow who lived across the street. She'd been in the middle of hosting Bible study in her living room for the Ladies' Aid Society. Aaron and Natalie had laughed until all of the tension and embarrassment she'd carried with her for weeks had disappeared. He'd smiled at her. The forgiveness she'd been offered was more than she could ever have asked for.

"Let the dogs play for a little while and Dec and Luke attempt to scare me off. Then we could go back to my place or down to your house."

What happens when we get to my house? Searching for courage somewhere in the recesses of her body she came up short. Stubbornness, however, she always had at her ready disposal. She forced a nod. She was going to do this, no matter how awkward and scary the first time was sure to be. Maybe he just wanted to kiss her. She was definitely interested in that.

Aaron nuzzled her hair and worked his mouth directly beside her ear. "We're not having sex tonight."

"How do you always know what I'm thinking?" The words leapt from her lips.

"You went stiff as a board but kept hugging me. Knowing what people are thinking used to be my job."

CHAPTER NINE

"I kind of think I might like your whole mind-reading ability thing." Words continued to spew from Natalie's mouth. She was tired of trying to stop them. Aaron's truck bounced over the cattle guard between Luke and Grant's portions of the ranch. They were heading to her house, and she was using all available brain power to keep from panicking.

"I can't read your mind, Nat. I can just tell when something I say or do bothers you. And I'm glad you kind of like it because I kind of can't turn it off. Sometimes I wish I could."

"If you know what I'm thinking, then even if part of me gets scared while we're...you know...we can still keep going because you'll know I'm not scared of *you*."

"Not how that's going to work. If you're scared, we stop until you're ready to keep going. Doesn't matter why you're scared or who you're scared of."

"I'm ready. I think. I don't know. I told you I was terrible at all of this."

"You're not terrible at anything."

"Oh, so you mean going over to Luke's was a good idea for a date?"

"Okay, we both suck at last minute plans. That wasn't your fault. I should've planned something. I'll do better."

Natalie rolled her eyes. "We'll both do better. I'm sorry he threatened you. He's always been like that. I'm also sorry my father has apparently traded the PBR channel for Kat Von D."

Aaron's genuine laughter sent a rush of fresh air back to her lungs. She could handle whatever was about to happen. He was one of her favorite people. She just had to get it together.

"Don't worry about your daddy. You're his little girl. I get that, but Luke hasn't always been this way."

"Yes, he has."

"We went out a half-dozen times over a year or so ago and he encouraged it. This time he's pissy about it. Says you're acting different this time around."

"Oh God, you didn't tell him I asked you to sleep with me did you?"

Natalie's body lurched forward when Aaron slammed on the brakes. Intensity was aflame in his cool blue eyes. It rolled off his body in waves. Instinctively, she slid back from the heat of his gaze.

"Nope." He caught her hand and pulled her back toward him. "Not running away this time. Listen to me. What we share, what we do, what you ask me for, what you're scared to ask for, the way I'm going to make you feel, the way I'm going to get to see you, the knowledge I will own, that's all for me and no one else. I would never share any part of our relationship with anyone, most certainly not your brother. Do you understand that?"

Natalie managed a haggard nod. She swallowed twice, trying to remedy the dryness in her throat.

"Good." He eased off the brake and they were on their way again.

Uncertain if the trip to her house had taken a week or a minute, Natalie stumbled out of the truck. Time seemed oddly variable all of a sudden. Aaron caught her hand and with another one of those cocky smirks, steadied her on her feet.

"Do I make you dizzy, babe?"

"No." *Yes, damn you.*

His chuckle said he knew she was lying once again.

No one ever locked their doors in Pleasant Glen. Thankful she didn't have to try to unlock anything, as she was beyond certain she did not currently possess the ability to slip a key in anything, she opened her front door and let the dogs inside. "I'll get them some water."

"I can do it, just tell me where bowls are," Aaron scoffed.

"There are some old mixing bowls in that cabinet. Do you want anything to drink?"

The twitch of his full lips shot another round of pure lust through her veins. She made herself a glass of water after he'd filled the bowls for Lulu and Buster. Mixing alcohol in with her current woozy condition couldn't possibly be a good idea.

"You want my honest answer or a polite one?" His tone lowered to that throaty rasp she loved.

"I always want your honesty. I guess. Maybe." *My God, Natalie, make a fucking decision. Who are you?*

"I *honestly* don't want anything to drink because I don't want any flavor in my mouth but yours." He licked his lips driving home his point.

"I thought you said we weren't..."

"We're not. That sure as hell doesn't mean I don't want to know the flavors of your mouth and your skin though, sweetheart. There's so much I want to know."

Spurred on by curiosity and stubbornness, Natalie forced her feet to move forward. No more looking back. She was doing this. Resolve strengthened in her spine. "What else do you want to know?"

Another dark chuckle. He leaned back against her countertop, casually. Why did she have to be the only one who was nervous? "Still want honest?"

She nodded. "Yes. I always want honest."

"You're sure now?"

"I'm sure."

"Good. Come here to me." His darkening eyes drew her to him with just as much force as his hand taking hers and pulling her closer. "I'm about to be all kinds of ungentlemanly. Don't tell your brother."

"I won't. I promise."

"I want to know which way you lean your head when I'm hungry for your lips. I want to know what they taste like. I want to know how pink and swollen I can make them. Throwing all sense of politeness out for the moment, I can't fucking wait to know the same things about your pussy lips as well. I want to know the kinds of sounds you're going to make when I make you forget how to speak. And I will, honey, I will make you forget everything but my name and I'll make you scream that.

"I want to know every square inch of your body. I want to know how tight and achy your nipples will get for me. I want to know the flavor of them as well. I want to know what your tits feel like swollen and full in my hands. I want to know precisely where I can touch you to keep you right on the edge of release. I want to know how long I can keep you there before you beg me to give you everything you need. I want to torture you in the most delectable ways. I swear you'll like it. You'll ask me for more. I want to know what your pussy looks like wrapped around my cock. I want to know how slick and milky I can make it. I want to see it covered in my cum. I want you to know how hard I get for you but how gentle I'll be until I know you're wanting more. And that's just the beginning of all the things I'm going to discover about you. You okay with all of that?"

"Oh my God, yes."

He'd given it his all. The long line of patience he'd been extending since the night before disintegrated into smoke with her greedy declaration that she wanted all of that as well. Forcing himself to enjoy this moment where she'd lost a little of her trepidation, he traced his thumbs over the hollows of her cheeks.

Her eyes fell to half-mast.

"I'm about to kiss you, baby. That okay?"

"Please."

He caught the single word with his lips, trapping the consent between them. She wanted this. She needed this. Maybe not quite as badly as he did, but my God they both deserved a relationship that could heal them.

The confection of her lips melted against his. He brushed his tongue against her mouth, constantly seeking more, needing her to open to him and for him.

Her lips parted. His moan rang with his own victory. But she stiffened and drew back, before his tongue could begin a thorough exploration. Dammit all to hell.

He lifted his head. Before he could apologize, Buster leapt on his hind legs landing his paws on Natalie's chest, attempting to thank her for the water she'd provided them.

"I love my dogs but they do not get to feel you up before I do. Get down, boy. Go sit." Aaron pointed them to the living room.

Natalie laughed. Okay, so maybe he hadn't screwed up too bad. "I'm sorry I got nervous. I just... I never..."

"Never what?"

Heat bloomed across her features adding to the arousal he'd brought to her cheeks.

"Just tell me, baby? Never be embarrassed with me."

"That's easier said than done."

"Come on."

Her gaze landed somewhere in the vicinity of the cabinet above his head. "I never know what to do with my hands." She wrung her hands as if trying to rid her body of them. "I'm the only grown woman on this planet that doesn't know how to kiss."

Trying to temper his humor over her confusion, he winked at her. That always seemed to make her smile. If that wasn't addictive as hell he didn't know what was. "Trust me, you kiss like a dream. Drove me wild. Did the last time we did that, too. Just relax for me. Want me to do something with your hands? Then you won't have to worry about them."

"I guess that depends on what you do."

"Let's give it a try, okay?"

This time he only got a nod, but he'd take it. Guiding her to a wall between her kitchen and living room, he turned caging her between a rock and his hard place. "This good?"

Another nod. Improvising happened to be one of his specialties. He'd make do with whatever she was comfortable with. "Look at me,

Nat. Be right here with me." That was key. He had to remember that. No flashbacks for either of them.

Her eyes met his and he gathered her wrists gently in his hands. Her breaths disintegrated into shallow gasps. "I would never hurt you or make you do something you don't want, baby. You know that."

"I know. I just don't know what you're about to do."

"I'm about to do this." With his right hand he pressed her wrist against the wall over her head. He repeated the action with her left.

"Oh God," she choked on a half-moan. Well, well, well, perhaps he'd just discovered a little something.

"Then I'm going to do this again." He layered his greedy lips to hers, letting her flavors soak through him. Her chin moved against his beard and she allowed him in without prodding this time. Soft, open-mouthed, needy kisses. The perfect antidote to most anything in the world.

Her tongue filled his mouth. His baby was so hungry for him and still afraid to ask for what she needed. Innocence was penned in the flavors of her saliva.

The knowledge racked like hot, leaden weight in his balls. He memorized the wet heat and the hunger, the inexperience and the desire. Desperation shot through his veins. His muscles ached with need. She was his. He would be the only man who ever knew what she felt like when she came. What she felt like when her body squeezed and flexed around his cock.

When their teeth bumped, he lifted away from her, leaned the other way, and helped himself to another heady dose of Natalie.

She arched into him this time. Her denim trapped pussy moved instinctively against his groin. A low growl wrenched up from his gut. Fuck. If she kept that up he was going to come. It had been too damn long. He'd dreamed about this too fucking many times. He'd wanted her since the moment he saw her.

She ground with more vigor, so damn needy.

His groans were constant now. He had no more hope of keeping them contained than he did of making her stop.

She bucked again, spreading her legs more this time. The heat of her made him throb against her. This time it was her giving him a needy whimper for more.

His entire body drew taught. He released her hands. They traveled down his chest, nearing his now painful package. "Shit. Baby, stop." He spoke the words while his own hands toyed with the end of her tank top. Skin. He just needed to feel her soft skin in his hands. Needed to know where she most wanted his touch.

His face moved from her mouth to her neck. He inhaled the scent of her.

Glancing down at his jeans he was shocked they weren't actually on fire. Unable to help himself, he traced his index finger along the low collar of her shirt. Her head fell back offering him more. "Tell me to stop, Nat. Jesus, just say it and I will. I swear." His hand encapsulated her right breast. His mind willed her bra and shirt away.

Her gasp held no note of fear, only of need.

Her body knew how to ask for what she wanted, even if she couldn't verbalize it. She thrust against him again, faster now.

Refusing to come in his jeans, something he hadn't done since he was seventeen, he stepped back.

Her eyes flew open. "Why did you stop? Did I do something wrong?"

"I sure as hell didn't want to stop, Nat, but I'm not doing this tonight. We're taking our time. If we keep this up it's all going to be over way too soon." He tensed his jaw and tried to discreetly adjust himself. A mischievous grin spread across her face.

"I did that?" She pointed to the bulge against his zipper line.

"You did that." He chuckled. "I'm strung so tight I may not be able to walk out to my truck."

She gnawed on her lip for a moment, furrowing her brow.

"What? Just say it."

"I really liked all of that. I'm sorry you can't walk though."

"My God, I'm an asshole."

"Why do you think that?" Genuine confusion lit the golden flecks in her eyes.

"I wasn't going to go that far. You're just so sweet and I'm a greedy bastard."

"I'm not sweet. I prefer to think of myself as a badass, thank you very much."

"Oh yeah? Well you're the most beautiful, innocent badass I've ever met."

"You're supposed to be helping me lose the innocent part."

"And you're one hundred percent sure you want me to do away with it all right now?" He knew the answer.

"Not one hundred percent, maybe."

Keeping his eyes on hers he leaned in for one more quick kiss. "That's what I thought. You sure you want to go with me tomorrow night?"

"I am sure about that. It'll be fun. I don't know much about your life before you got here. I'm excited to meet your family."

"I'm not really related to any of them."

"Blood isn't necessary for family."

Aaron knew in that moment if he wasn't extremely careful he could end up falling head over army boots in love with Natalie Camden.

"I'll pick you up around 4:00."

"I'll be ready."

CHAPTER TEN

Feeling rather proud of herself as she parked her truck back by her house after Aaron had taken her to retrieve it, Natalie debated the ice cream in her freezer.

If she concentrated, she could still taste him on her lips. She didn't want to lose his flavor. *That was definitely the girliest thing you've ever thought.* She wondered about this new side of herself. Being lovesick didn't sound too appealing, but being into a guy was a normal thing for a woman to feel.

Bliss danced under her skin. She even seemed to have some kind of small flying creatures in her stomach, not something she'd ever experienced before. Luke was right. It was different this time. It was different because she refused to let what had happened with her uncle ruin this for her.

Power surged through her. She could leave it in the past now. She *would* leave it in the past. She'd taken the bull by the horns and hadn't thought about those months when she was eleven for that entire kiss. Take that, Uncle Mick! Even thinking of his name shot bile to her throat. Nope. Not tonight. Nothing was going to ruin this night.

When her phone rang, she leapt across the sofa to answer it. Okay, so maybe she was just a little lovesick. She gave herself a pass. This was a guy she'd had a crush on since she'd first seen him in Saddlebacks. A man who knew all the things she needed to learn. And heaven help her if he wasn't the sexiest thing she'd ever laid eyes on.

"Hello." She remembered to actually answer the ringing phone in her hand.

"Hey, baby."

The deep gravel of his voice sent the butterfly-like things in her stomach into overdrive. "Hey." She inwardly mocked her own singsong voice.

"You okay?"

"Yeah. I'm really, really good."

"I'm glad *you* are. I may need to spend all night in a cold shower."

"Sorry about that."

"Stop apologizing. I'm just teasing you."

"I know. Can I tell you something?"

"You can tell me anything. I wish you'd tell me everything."

"I wish you'd stop asking me about everything, but in a way this kind of has to do with that."

"We'll talk all night long if you want."

Natalie knew he would. If she really wanted to rehash all of the confusion and shame, he'd listen and he wouldn't judge. He'd do everything he could to help her understand, but that was the very last thing she wanted. Nothing was going to overshadow what they'd just shared. Even if it wasn't mind-blowing sex, it would be someday. She just had one question about it all she wanted an answer to.

"I shouldn't have liked that." There. She'd said it.

"Shouldn't have liked me kissing you?" Disappointment was laced in his response.

"No, the kissing was great. I'm supposed to like that and I did. The hand thing is what I shouldn't have liked."

He bound her hands. Sick fucking bastard. Aaron doubled down on his resolve to brutally tear whoever this sorry excuse for a human being was limb from bloody limb just before he put a bullet through his skull.

She was safe in her house alone and had questions about what they'd just done. His vengeance would have to wait for a few minutes anyway.

"Sweetheart, there are absolutely no rules about what you should or shouldn't like. Never think there are. When it's just you and me the things you're curious about or the things that turn you on, they're perfect, just like you are."

"I'm not perfect."

"By my estimations you are and we're going to slowly explore all of the things that make my girl fly when she's in my arms. I know it's hard to do but try to leave all of those rules you've got in your head about what you should or shouldn't want outside the bedroom door, okay?"

"I don't know what I want exactly."

"I keep telling you we'll figure it out."

"I have another question." Her tone turned accusatory.

His mind immediately conjured up ways to get out of the inevitable question she was about to ask. "Shoot."

"Who taught *you* the things you like?" And there it was. A blur of European and Middle Eastern sex clubs flashed through his mind. Prostitutes. Nameless, faceless women he'd had no business drowning his sorrows in joined the parade. He'd never deserve someone like Natalie. How had he ever thought he would?

"I have a lot of experience I wish I didn't have. I'm sorry."

"It's okay." She sounded sincere.

"No, it's not."

"I figured you'd say something like that. I just wanted to know where you get all of your experience."

"All over the fucking world, but, Nat, I swear what we're doing, this means a lot to me. You mean a lot to me. I'll do right by you. I was a stupid kid back then. I didn't know what I was doing. I never knew how much I'd regret. You shouldn't have given me another chance, and you did. I won't do anything to fuck this up."

"I'm really not upset you slept with other people. Still a little irked you kissed my sister once."

"Thought we agreed never to talk about that again."

Natalie laughed. "When did we agree to that?"

"That time I begged you never to bring it back up. You know it was her idea."

"You told me you were loopy on some kind of depression meds and that you'd just gotten to town."

"I was but she caught me staring at you that night at the bar. She might've mentioned that you kind of liked me and that if I kissed her you'd likely take notice. That's why I agreed."

"Are you lying to me?"

"I swear, Nat. Ask Holly."

"I don't really care enough to do that. It's just one of the things I try not to think about. I'm oddly glad you know how to teach me everything I'm missing out on. Don't be so hard on yourself."

"That's not really an option. You sure you're good with everything. Want to ask me anything else?"

"Will you tell me about the guys we're having dinner with tomorrow night? I don't want to get off the phone yet." *How the hell is she even talking to me? How did I get this lucky?*

Never fucking deserve her. Ever. "I told you we'll talk all night if you want. Get in bed. I need to know you're warm and safe then I'll tell you about the Sevens."

"Do you think someday I could sleep with you? You know, after we have sex or whatever?"

"I'm not a great sleeper but you can stay here anytime you want, sweetheart. I'll hold you all night. We can do that before we have sex if you want. No rules, remember?"

"Why don't you sleep?"

"Sleep is complicated."

CHAPTER ELEVEN

The sun crept slowly over the fields, warming the grazing cattle and the cool Nebraskan dirt, as Natalie stomped through the wet grass to her sister's house early the next morning.

She'd already fed and watered the horses. She'd go check her cattle after she talked to Dec. Pounding on the door, she prayed her sister wasn't currently tied to the bed or anything. Dec and Holly were into some pretty kinky stuff.

Envisioning herself tied to a bed with Aaron over her swirled excitement through her limbs. Guilt over her own curiosity rushed the feeling away a moment later.

Dec flung the door open wearing nothing but flannel pajama pants and a frustrated scowl. He brought his mug of tea to his lips. "Holly's in the shower. You okay?"

Relieved she hadn't interrupted anything, Natalie nodded. "Sorry, I know it's early. I have a question I need you to answer."

"Come on in. I'm heading to the clinic in a few minutes."

"You're secretly praying Holly doesn't use up all the hot water, aren't you?"

"Everyone who lives on this ranch always has that prayer, don't we?"

"Yeah, but I used to live with her. I know what it's like never to get a hot shower."

Dec smirked. Natalie held up her hand. "Don't say what you're thinking. I don't want to hear about you two showering together."

"A man has to do what he has to do." Dec laughed. "Want some tea?"

"Do you have any coffee?"

"I'm shit at making the stuff. Holly won't let me touch the maker anymore."

"It's fine. I had some at home."

"How long have you been up?"

"I already brought in all of the horses and fed them."

"That's early even for a cowgirl."

"I was up anyway."

"Something wrong?"

"No. I was up because I'm excited." Dammit, how did Declan always manage to get her to confess things she didn't intend to? Had to be some kind of psychologist superpower or something.

"Excited about Aaron?"

"Yeah, and he's who I wanted to ask you about."

"Sit." Dec pointed to a chair at the kitchen table.

"Last night Aaron told me he has trouble sleeping. He wouldn't elaborate much. I know that you know why he can't sleep and I want you to tell me."

Setting down his mug, Dec's head fell into his hands. "Jesus H. Christ, I'm going to end up losing my license over you two."

"Why?"

With an audible sigh, he shook his head. "I cannot discuss anything that goes on in my practice or with one of my patients with anyone else. It's against the law."

"But I'm family."

"That doesn't mean there aren't laws."

"I'll ask Holly."

"She won't tell you either."

"Ha!" Her familiar stubbornness held the line. It was the one thing in her life she could always count on. Marching up the stairs in her sister's house she flung open the master bathroom door. "It's me."

Dec followed her into the steamy bathroom.

Holly poked her wet head around the shower curtain. "One of you hand me that hair conditioning mask I left on the counter."

Natalie grabbed the jar and handed it over.

"Is it not at all strange to you that your sister is in our bathroom?" Dec asked.

"Nah." Holly ducked back around the curtain. "This mask has to sit for ten minutes but then I'll be out to make coffee."

"I don't need coffee. I need to know why Aaron has trouble sleeping at night," Natalie shouted over the sound of rapidly falling water.

"He has PTSD."

"Holly!" Dec scolded.

"What?"

"Oh, I don't know, HIPPA."

"He's not technically my patient. I'm also not technically a doctor yet and she's my sister."

"Dear God."

"Told you." Natalie laughed in Dec's face. "What is PTSD?"

"I'm going back downstairs to pretend I do not hear any of this."

"Hang on. I'll get out and tell you then get back in and rinse this out. The things I do for you." The incessant fall of water halted abruptly. Holly stepped out with her hair up in a plastic cap. She wrapped a towel around her. "PTSD stands for Post Traumatic Stress Disorder. It's awful. A lot of patients have night terrors from it. They can also have flashbacks that are also usually worse at night. That's probably why he can't sleep."

"Holly, for the love of God," Dec bellowed from the bottom of the stairs.

"All right fine. There's probably tons of info on the internet. I don't know any of Aaron's specifics but I told you he'd understand some of the stuff you don't like to talk about."

So that was why Holly had given in so quickly. She wanted Natalie to talk to Aaron about what had happened to her. Too bad. Maybe whatever kept Aaron from sleeping had to do with the guy in the picture with him. She couldn't ask him. Not yet.

Maybe she could figure some of it out when she met his friends that night. "Would you mind checking on my calves? I need to do some research."

"Yeah, okay, but you owe me big time. Never ever tell Aaron I said anything. Dec really could get in trouble."

"I swear I won't."

Holly held up her wet pinky finger. Grinning at her little sister, Natalie linked their hands. "Pinky swear."

She raced back down the stairs. "I'll never say anything to Aaron. I pinky swore to it."

"Oh, good. That's sure to hold up in my state disciplinary medical board hearing," Dec huffed.

"You have to love me because you married my baby sister."

"Yes, well, she's been nothing but trouble since the very beginning."

"She's worth it."

"She's more than worth it, and you can quote me on that."

"I'll be sure to tell the disciplinary board." Natalie raced out of the house.

Aaron had told Natalie a few stories about crap the Sevens had gotten into back in the day, but he'd kept it to quick, insignificant tales. He didn't want to describe them to her. He didn't want to reduce them to their scars. He couldn't. They were so much more than remnants of the worst day of all of their lives.

"I used to go to the Hi-Way Diner when I would come out here to visit Holly while she was at UN. I love their fries."

"They do have killer fries. We like it because it's quiet and even when there are dozens of people in there you can hear yourself think."

"Not like Saddlebacks."

"Saddlebacks isn't as bad as some bars I've been in. Ever been to Europe?"

Natalie shook her head. She also wound her fingers around his right hand as he drove with his left. Perfection. "I've never been any further than Vegas. We used to go to Cheyenne every summer but you can't really vacation when you run a ranch. The animals are rather fond of eating."

"True. I was just thinking about how obnoxiously loud every fucking bar in Amsterdam was. Drove me nuts."

"Sounds like Vegas."

"Yeah, probably. Never been there. Have no desire to go."

"I hated it. I went to see Austin compete for the PBR title. Good thing he won or I would've been pissed I went to watch him lose." She laughed.

"People still come into the bar talking about his title. Must've been one hell of a ride."

"It was, but I was ready to come back home. I like quiet, too. It's soothing."

Aaron took his eyes off the expanse of road in front of them long enough to smile at her. He brought her hand to his mouth and brushed a kiss on her knuckles, wishing it was her mouth instead. "Can I ask you something, baby?"

"Sure." She shrugged.

"Why'd your brother like getting his ass thrown off of bulls? Sounds like he had a death wish. Your dad should be worried about him being a masochist not me."

"No joke. I never understood it and I used to help him practice. Well, after he was sixteen I kind of understood it, but before that we were all worried he had some kind of brain injury from birth or something."

"What happened when he was sixteen?"

"His best friend was killed in a car accident. Austin was driving."

"Damn." A sudden chill lifted every hair on Aaron's arms. He signaled and changed lanes just to have something to do. He knew all about losing your best friend. He knew about it being your fault. He sure as hell understood the desire to make sense of it or to kill yourself trying.

"It was awful. He went on for years refusing to believe it wasn't his fault."

"Yeah, I get that."

Natalie kept staring at him. Almost studying him. He wondered what she saw. Unlike his friends, his scars were almost always covered, as long as he was clothed. Without granting himself permission first, he pressed his tongue to the inside of his right cheek. The long gash was concealed by his beard.

Two hours later, Aaron pulled into the parking lot of the Hi-Way Diner. Griff's brand new, jet-black Silverado and was parked in the lot right beside Smith's Acadia Denali. He'd never regretted sending his army pension to his foster parents, but he wished he had a little money to spoil Natalie with. Opening her door for her, he wrapped his arm around her and guided her inside.

The crack in the sidewalk just outside the door and the low hum of the patrons in the Hi-Way were drenched with familiarity. Aaron pulled Natalie closer. The rhythmic click of her boots washed away as they stepped from the tile to the carpeted floor. He found himself missing the sound. For a guy who preferred silence, it was an odd sensation.

"All right, try not to drool or make her wish I'd never brought her here," Aaron commanded as they approached the table in the back corner, the Sevens customary spot. Despite his warning, Smith and T-Byrd let out low wolf-whistles when Natalie offered them a sweet grin.

She tucked back into Aaron and he glared at the men he'd walked through hell with. "Don't embarrass her either." He popped T-Byrd on the back of the head. "I can still beat the shit out of all you at the same time."

Griff at least looked amused.

"Natalie, this is T-Byrd, Griff, Voodoo, and Echo or Thomas, Griffin, Vincent, and Smith if you'd prefer. Idiots at large, this is Natalie Camden. For the love of God act like you have some kind of human DNA."

"He talk to you like he talks to us, sweet thang?" Voodoo tipped his cowboy hat to her. "I've got cuffs in my truck and I can shove a napkin in his mouth to keep him quiet if you want."

"He's a lot nicer to me." Natalie wrinkled her adorable nose.

"He better be." T-Byrd stood and offered his hand. Natalie pretended she didn't notice the jagged, thinned skin that ran the length of his hand and disappeared under his rolled up sleeves, but Aaron knew she'd seen them. "Triple A is all about getting people out of trouble, honey. But I can get you into all kinds of trouble if you'd like to trade in one snake eater for another."

"Snake eater?"

"It's a stupid name for Army Operatives. Ignore him." Aaron pulled out a chair for Natalie and shot another predatory glare to his friends.

"Operatives like Special Ops?" Great. Now she was curious.

"Yeah, want me to order you some fries?"

"Sure. And I take it you're Triple A?" She elbowed him.

"Something like that."

Natalie turned her questions to the Sevens. "Do I get to know how he got his nickname? I'm sure he won't tell me."

Aaron snorted. "Because you're so forthcoming with info, babe."

She stuck her tongue out at him and his friends erupted in laughter.

"Oh, I like you." Smith chuckled. "You should come with Triple A every month."

"Well, maybe I will if you tell me why you call him that."

"A negotiator. Now I know why he fell for you."

"Shut it," Aaron ordered.

"Geez, get him a beer. He got the nickname partly because he's Aaron Alexander Weber but mostly because he got us out of trouble more than a few times," T-Byrd supplied.

Natalie gave him one of those full force smiles that took his breath away. "That sounds like him. Why are you T-Byrd?" She wasn't going to let this go, and T looked far too thrilled for Aaron's liking.

"'Cause I'm in and out hard and fast, baby, as many times as you like."

Her brow furrowed. She didn't understand the joke. Jesus help him. "T," he growled.

"Sorry." A half-second glance Aaron shared with T told him everything he needed to know. She was that naive. She needed to be protected. Whatever had happened to her had affected the rest of her life. "Uh, my name is Thomas Thursten Byrd because clearly my parents hate me. Nickname went with my job as a HALO jumper. I can get in, find who or what we need, and get out."

"What's a HALO jumper?" She was loving this. Aaron wondered if he could make up some reason they needed to leave. He didn't want to go there. Not tonight. Never again.

"Stands for High Altitude Low Open jumps. T was the best at them," Aaron forced an explanation.

"Like parachute jumps? You jumped out of planes?" The entire restaurant had to have heard her.

"On occasion. Could we just order?" Aaron pointed to the waitress standing by their table.

"Sorry." Her teeth sank into her bottom lip and Aaron hated himself all the more.

Fuck, he was being an ass for no good reason. She was always curious. That was one of the things he adored about her. "We were a Special Ops team back in the day. Team Seven. That's why we call ourselves the Sevens. We were airborne, specialized in search and rescue and intelligence acquisitions but that was a long time ago."

"Wow, I had no idea. That's amazing. I can't believe you jumped out of planes."

"Used to love it." Aaron tried desperately to give her something other than the ragged remnants of his soul. The red and yellow glow of the neon diner lights leached from his sight. The grayness he fought constantly crept slowly across his skin.

"Tell us how you and Triple A met." Griff came to his rescue, he always did.

"I'm from Pleasant Glen, where he works. It's pretty rare that anyone new moves in. We started talking one night at the bar. We've been friends for a while. He's one of my favorite people, actually." She squeezed his thigh.

Breath expanded in Aaron's lungs. His pulse steadied. Life itself jolted through him. How the hell could that be true? He was nothing. He was broken beyond repair. But he swore any fragment he had left he'd give to her if he could just keep being one of her favorite people.

"Yeah, we're pretty fond of him, too, even when he is being an ass," Smith taunted.

"What's it like to jump out of a plane?" She asked T.

"Well, I could show you sometime if you want."

"You still do it?"

"No rush like air hitting you in the face at 120 miles per hour."

"I'm way too much of a coward to ever do that."

"No, you're not," Aaron's voice returned to him. "You're one of the bravest people I know and that includes all of these yahoos."

Natalie's scoff said she didn't believe him. He added that to his mission specs. Prove to her how strong and brave she was.

CHAPTER TWELVE

"So, we get down to this tiny bumblefuck town in Georgia the day before we start Airborne school." T launched into yet another tale.

"Don't tell that story," Aaron groaned. Truthfully, he didn't mind. Once he'd gotten over himself, he was actually enjoying watching Natalie absorb everything his army issued brothers discussed. Having her there somehow made every story better. He inhaled her fascination like a drug. It eased the pain of the times no one told stories about.

"Aww come on, this one's on me anyway. That was the first time you bailed my ass out of a sling," T-Byrd vowed.

"I want to hear it," Natalie urged.

"We go into this bar that's supposed to have cheap beer and ladies with a thing for men in uniform."

Aaron shook his head, laughing at what was to come. "I feel the need to tell you that I went back to the barracks alone. T did not."

"That's the truth," T confirmed. "Anyway, I got nice and cozy with this redhead in the bar and decided that no one would ever know if I snuck her back in with me for a little while."

"I take it that didn't go as well as you thought it would." Natalie giggled.

"That would be a very safe bet, sweetheart," Aaron assured her.

"I got her on base just fine. It's just that I'd had enough beers to drown a sailor so I passed out as soon as I blew my wad."

"T! You kiss your mama with that mouth?" Aaron admonished.

Natalie shook her head at them. "It's okay. Keep going. I have lots of brothers."

"We were supposed to be in formation at 0430 the next morning," Aaron picked up the story. "T's nowhere to be found. I know he's gonna get his ass chewed up and spit out and might even get sent back, idiot that he is."

"Yeah, so, Triple A tells the C.O. that I'm taking a—uh, that I was in the head. Would've worked too, except right about the time I made it to formation Red comes stumbling out of my room."

Natalie cringed.

"That's not the worst part," Aaron assured her. "Tell her about SF training."

"Yeah, so I find out many weeks later that her daddy is the head of weapon's instruction for all of Special Forces training. Someone from jump school gave him a call when they saw her coming out of my room that morning. He had a grudge to pick. As soon as my boots touched the ground, he was on my ass. Until Triple A figures out that the guy is a huge University of Alabama fan. A is a fucking brilliant bastard if you haven't figured that out yet. He tells Instructor Asshat all about how his daughter had too much to drink and that I was worried about her going home with some other guys she was hanging out with that night. Then he casually lets it slip that the guys she'd been hanging with went to Auburn. Triple A tells him that I'd actually stayed in *his* room that night. That I'd just bought her back to the base so I'd know she was safe while she slept off the booze."

"In the South football is like a religion. I knew it would work," Aaron explained.

"Like it isn't here?" Natalie reminded him.

"Right, so from then on I was a hero. A's saved my life too fucking many times to count but that will always be the one I appreciate the most, I think. All the others it would've been over much faster anyway."

"I couldn't listen to any more of your whining about what he was making you do. I had to do something."

"I bet that wasn't it." Natalie's lips landed on the scar under his beard. For a brief moment, the memory of it was erased as well. "I'll be right back." She grabbed her purse and headed to the bathroom.

"My God, she's gorgeous." T leapt as soon as she was out of earshot.

"I know."

"She's good for you." Griff's earnest vow was weighted with importance.

"I need to be good for her."

"Tell me what you know about this guy who hurt her?"

"Not much. Whoever he is he was on Camden ranch when she was eleven."

"Are you fucking saying she was eleven when whatever happened, happened?" Griff growled.

Aaron nodded. "Now you know why I want to kill this bastard with my bare hands." The Sevens all nodded. "Possibly a family member but I can't come up with who that would be. Could also have been some kind of ranch hand she thought of as family. It was definitely someone she trusted at some point. I had her brother softened up last night but we got interrupted before he gave me anything actionable. I'm betting he'll go cold now."

"If you know he was on her ranch when she was eleven all I need to know is how old she is now. Get me all the info you can on her and I'll find this fucker," Smith vowed.

Before their lives had been blown to hell, Smith had been one hell of a communications sergeant. He could make anything from an old school CB radio to the latest greatest satellite comm unit sing for him. Hell, Aaron would put good money on him being able to rig up some kind of communication device out of conch shells and rubber bands. There was a reason they called him Echo.

"Before she gets back, who owns this ranch?" T leapt into action. The remaining members of the Sevens all took out their phones.

"Been in the family for generations. The kids all own a portion of it. Everett and Jessie Camden are her parents. I'm betting the entire thing is really in their name and parceled out to the kids."

"What's her middle name?"

"Uh, it's Jessica, after her mom."

"Birthday?"

Aaron had taken Natalie out to the lake to hang out with her siblings and some of their friends last year for her birthday. "Shit, it's soon. September twenty-first maybe."

"Better memorize that real quick-like, A." Griff chuckled as he typed. "Do not want to fuck that up and it's in three weeks."

"Noted."

"Natalie Jessica Camden born September 20th right here at St. Elizabeth's. Father is Everett Lucas Camden. Mother is Jessica Suzanne Camden. Would that be her?" T-Byrd held up his phone displaying a copy of Natalie's birth certificate.

"That's her. How'd you find that so quick?"

"She's got nothing to hide. She isn't camped out under a rock in the Middle East. It's a lot easier to do what we're doing now than what we did before."

"We're taking this job pro-bono, T, hope you know that," Voodoo declared.

"I already told him we were," T huffed.

"You can't let her know I asked for your help," Aaron warned.

"Dude, we have been in and out of countries without my mama even knowing we were out of the driveway. We can be discreet."

"Whoever hurt her is going down," Griff vowed.

"Here she comes," Smith spoke through his teeth.

"You're so full of shit," Aaron laughed like they'd continued on with their reminiscing while she was gone. Just as they'd always done, the Sevens joined his laughter, playing right along. They'd never let him down.

"I get why they're your family, Aaron. They're great." The hours of fascinating conversation that evening spun round and round in Natalie's head as Aaron drove them back to Pleasant Glen. She had so many questions. Questions she knew she had no business asking him.

"They thought you were pretty awesome, too. Thanks for going with me. I liked having you there."

"You sound surprised," Natalie teased him.

"You know how you told me last night that you shouldn't have liked me holding your hands against the wall like I did?"

Natalie nodded.

"I shouldn't have liked you being there. Those stories get to me sometimes but tonight, they didn't bother me."

"Do you think that means maybe we're good for each other?"

Aaron squeezed her hand. "Yeah, maybe. Not sure how good I am for you, but I'm trying."

"I'm really glad I asked you to sleep with me." Natalie prayed the moon outside her window didn't reveal the streaks of heat in her cheeks.

"Trust me, sweetheart, I'm really glad you did, too."

Raking her teeth across her bottom lip for the fourth time, she tried to come up with something to ask that would explain exactly how he'd gotten PTSD. She'd read everything she could find on it for most of the day. She wanted to help him. She just had no idea how to do that.

"So, um, when did you all decide to get out of the Army?"

"Didn't exactly decide that." His voice was suddenly hollow. He pulled his hand away from hers and put it back on the steering wheel. It didn't appear that he'd even noticed he'd done it. *Definitely not a good question.*

There were seven identical military-looking stars tattooed from his left wrist to his elbow. "Are your star tattoos for the Sevens? That's such a cool way to memorialize everything you all must've accomplished together."

His long eyelashes made three quick blinks. A harsh swallow contracted the muscles in his neck. His Adam's apple bobbed like he was choking back an answer. "Kind of," escaped his lips before they sealed shut again.

"I won't ask anything else. I'm sorry." *Way to go, Nat. You really are an idiot.*

"No. Fuck. I'm the one that's sorry. It's just...you know that thing you refuse to tell me?"

"You aren't telling me because I won't tell you what happened to me?"

"God no, it's just we both have shit in our pasts we don't want to talk about. All those stories they told you tonight, those were the good times. Times weren't always good."

"I'm really sorry for whatever happened, Aaron."

"Yeah, me too, baby. For both of us."

"So, they all own a business together now or something? That's what it sounded like."

"Yeah, T got the brilliant idea to open a security firm. They're pretty much just glorified P.I.'s as far as I can tell. They love it though." He shrugged.

"Is it bad that I'm glad you work at Saddlebacks and not with them?"

"Not at all. I'm glad you like having me around, sweetness. And don't worry, I don't want to have anything to do with any kind of profession that requires me to carry a gun ever again. I love the Glen. It reminds me of one of my favorite places growing up. Our tiny town definitely does not need a P.I, so I'm good tending bar."

"Except for when Ed and Eliza start in on each other."

"They drive me crazy but it's worth it." He returned his hand to hers. Natalie grinned.

"Did you see how Voodoo kept trying to flirt with our waitress and she kept shooting him down?" She ventured back to safer ground.

A haunted smile returned to Aaron's features. The effort that must've taken physically affected Natalie. Her chest ached for all he'd been through. "I saw him. Did you see him slip his number in when he signed his check?"

"I didn't see him do that. What did she do?"

"Rolled her eyes. Voodoo has probably been a womanizer since preschool. Needs somebody to settle his ass down. We were on the same chopper when we got sent to Ramstein. I came to for a few minutes and Voodoo's strung out on painkillers but still trying to flirt with the doctor who's redoing the stitches he gave himself."

Natalie forced a slight chuckle. What was Ramstein? She needed to remember so she could search for it later. The words, *came to, painkillers,* and *stitches he gave himself* churned in her stomach. "I'm glad you're okay. Scares me to think about you not being okay."

Aaron's seeking gaze finally landed on hers. "I'm fine."

"I always say that, too." Her voice was devoid of any emotion or any volume. He didn't respond. Determined to find some way to help him, she refused to be deterred from the plan she'd come up with when she'd stumbled upon a medical website that outlined the sleeplessness and nightmares that were common with PTSD.

The darkened ranch was almost silent when Aaron drove them through the gates. The occasional bellow of a cow and screech of a hawk just weren't soothing that night. Unable to work out the best way to ask this, she decided to just let the words leap off her tongue. She was sure to mess it up anyway.

They neared her house. "Uh, I was thinking..."

"I'm hoping the next words out of your mouth are about kissing you again."

"Well, yes, but no."

"Gonna need a little help with that answer, Nat."

"I was thinking I'd really like you to stay with me tonight."

The rapid, rhythmic clicks of Aaron's parking brake echoed inside her skull. "You want me to stay here tonight?"

She knew enough about Aaron to know without a doubt he would never stay if he thought she was doing this for him, and he would never turn her down if he thought she needed him to stay. He would always come to her rescue. He would always keep her safe. Triple A through and through.

"It's just sometimes I have weird dreams. When I was a little girl, my therapist said it was my brain trying to heal or make sense of... everything. Sometimes I can sense when I'm going to have one before I even get into bed. Kind of feels like carrying around a ghost that you can't get rid of. It feels like it's bigger than my body. I can't contain it but it won't go away. When I'm with you, I feel safe." That was all true. She wondered if he carried around ghosts as well.

"Come here to me."

Before she understood what was happening, he'd scooped her into his lap. She nestled her head into his neck as he cradled her in the soothing warmth of his arms. Maybe staying with her wasn't all for him. Maybe she needed this as well.

"Baby, I'll stay with you as long as you need me to. I swear to you I will never let anything or anyone hurt or scare you ever again."

"I know."

CHAPTER THIRTEEN

Aaron Weber was standing in her bedroom staring at her bed. Nervous energy trilled through Natalie's stomach. Then it did a few unnecessary somersaults, which weren't in anyway helpful in this situation.

"We can sleep together the real way if you want." Her words were without conviction. She knew he wouldn't take her up on the offer.

"Not tonight."

The ocean blue of his eyes was heavy with concern. He stroked her cheekbone with his thumb. Her eyes fluttered closed. She reveled in his tender touch.

She had no idea how to go from fully clothed to her torn pajama pants with him there. She had no clue what he normally slept in, or what side of the bed he might want, or what would happen in the morning. All she knew in that moment was there was nowhere else she wanted to be.

"I probably have one of Luke or Grant's old T-shirts around here, if you want to change."

"I don't wear much to bed. That okay with you? I could just sleep in my clothes. I don't want you to be uncomfortable."

"I won't be." Holy crap, what did *much* mean exactly?

"You sure? I want you to sleep, baby, not worry about me. Spent more nights than not sleeping in the sand. I'm good."

"I'll be fine."

"And what does my beautiful cowgirl sleep in?"

"Nothing particularly sexy or anything. Usually a T-shirt that says *Buck Off*."

Aaron's half-smirk and the glimmer in his eyes made their return. Natalie rejoiced at their appearance. His rumbled chuckle shot sparks of heat straight to her core. "You have any fucking idea how sexy you'd be in nothing but one of my T-shirts?"

A shiver worked through her as his hands gripped her ass, bringing her to him.

"Kiss me." His commanding thrum made her weak. The emptiness she'd grown so accustomed to it had taken on a numbing effect as of late ached to be filled.

His hungry lips found hers and she swore the wet heat from his mouth was nothing compared to what was flowing between her legs. Her stomach hollowed as he coaxed her tongue into his mouth. A whirlwind of desperate need whipped through her.

His fingers worked under the tight knit shirt she was wearing. Delicious heat flowed from his palms to her back. He lifted the shirt slowly as if every inch was a question of consent.

Natalie prayed her moans of approval were answer enough. Her heartbeat flew faster than Sundance at full gallop. His potent erection pressed into the cradle of her hips. Uncertain what she was doing, she rubbed against him letting her body take what it wanted, what would feel so good. Her mind was hazy with lust.

"Fuck," he grunted. "Not tonight, baby. Soon. Jesus Christ, it's gonna be soon. I swear."

His hands landed on the strap of her bra. She shook as he expertly popped the clasp.

"I want a taste, Nat. I *need* a taste. Give me a taste, honey."

"Yes," flew from her tongue a split second before her shirt landed on the floor. He moved the ministrations of his tongue to the top swells of her breasts, easing the bra down her arms.

Her back arched in invitation. Her body rolled against his. A wave of nervous energy broke over her but desire to feel his hands and his mouth on her skin washed it away. The waffle-weave of his shirt abraded her tender skin. One tiny brain cell that was capable of any thought at all insisted this wasn't fair.

Tugging his shirt from the waistband of his jeans, she wanted to feel the ripple of his muscles under her touch. He gripped her hands. "Not yet, honey." His expression was loaded with undiluted need. His fingertips raced across her chest. "So fucking gorgeous."

Before she could process his declaration, his mouth encapsulated her left nipple drawing it to a hot stiff peak.

A knot of pressure pulsated behind her mound. How was he doing that with his mouth on her breasts? "Oh my God," she whimpered.

"That feel good? Tell me, baby."

"Yes." She had no capacity to answer with more than single word responses.

He returned to her left breast, kissing a trail of fire around her pulsating nipple.

"You need more don't you?"

"Please," came from her next.

He lifted his head. The victorious gleam in his eyes let her know what he was thinking before he spoke. "Told you I'd make you beg. Every single time we're together, I'll make you so needy you plead for more."

Narrowing her eyes she drove her fingers through his thick black hair and shoved his head back to her breasts.

He licked and suckled before chuckling. "And there's that cowgirl spite. Drives me wild."

Every nerve ending in her body sizzled. Her skin was raw. Pressure mounted constantly. She had no specific knowledge of what she desperately wanted, other than her favorite vibrator, which seemed woefully inept when she compared it to the man standing before her, solid muscle, heat, and might. She wanted more of whatever he had in mind.

His hands returned to her ass. With every grope he drove her body against his erection. She hummed out a needy approval. When his hands traveled around her waist and popped the snap on her jeans, she panicked.

"Aaron," her voice vibrated through her lips. "What happens next?" Shame burned through her. She should know this. She should know some way to make him feel as needy as she did. He wouldn't let her touch his skin. Desperation for contact joined the embarrassment swamping through her veins. She wanted to hide.

He lifted his head and cradled her face in his capable hands. The fire in his eyes had softened. A little of his earlier intensity had slipped away. "What do you want to happen next, sweetheart?"

"I want you to take your shirt off, too."

"I'm pretty intent on getting you out of those blue jeans. Can I do that first?"

As soon as he stripped his scars would be visible. This night wasn't about him. This was about her exploring with him. Bullet wounds would have no part of this experience. She'd finally admitted that she was scared. Come hell or high water he was going to prove himself to her. He would show her that he would always keep her safe. Her inevitable questions about what had happened to him wouldn't distract him from his mission.

She offered up a hesitant nod. Her teeth sank into her bottom lip. Her fists were in knots by her side. Her nipples were drawn in tightened buds, flushed the most perfect shade of a ripened peach. Aaron suspected that was from fear not arousal at this point. My God what had that bastard done to her?

Treading with more care than he'd take to walk through a minefield, he eased her back into his arms. "I've got you, baby. I'm right here." He had to teach her to trust him. Her standing before him in nothing but a pair of worn Wranglers and cowgirl boots had all but done him in, but he refused to rush her as badly as he wanted to.

Dipping his hands down the back of her open jeans and the innocent cotton panties she was wearing, he groaned out his hunger. Cupping her perfect asscheeks, he let his mind conjure what she would look like naked before him but he kept her covered, exposing nothing to his starving eyes.

He needed her drunk on him, needed her to forget everything that had come before this moment. "This okay?"

"God yes." She came back to the present. Elation rode on the tidal wave of blood surging straight to his cock.

"Can I see you, baby?"

A slight tremble led to a nod.

"Step out of your boots for me."

She did as she was told. Her gaze seeking as she toed out of the boots.

The head below his belt reminded him how fucking much he loved to be in control when he was with a woman. There were a dozen subs in sex clubs all over Europe that would attest to his skills. The head on his shoulders knew this was entirely different. It was more. It was better. Even if he didn't get to direct their lovemaking the first hundred times he fucked her, he'd eventually get her there. He'd show her the strength in giving yourself over to a lover. He'd teach her to let go. Teach her to ask for what she wanted with no shame. Teach her to wait to get it. He'd make her fly.

But not tonight, and not anytime soon.

Careful not to allow her panties to come down with the jeans, he slipped the denim three inches over her delectable ass. The sight of the light pink panties stretched across the firm globes of her backside made him throb. "So fucking sweet and beautiful you're going to kill me, but if I have to go this is sure as hell how I want it all to end."

Her body continued to tremble. Determination set in his jaw. *Slowly, Weber. Act like a man that deserves her even if you aren't.* "Want me to stop, sweetheart?"

"No."

Aaron weighed her response. She was both lying and not. Her eyes were locked on his. Her lips were full and hungry. Her arms were covering her breasts. Some part of her wanted him to keep going. Another part was terrified.

Shit. If he gave up on her now and insisted they go to bed fully clothed, she'd be furious the next morning. He knew her. She'd set her mind to something and once Natalie Camden did that there was no stopping her. She would be angry, not with him but with herself. He wouldn't allow either one.

"Come here then." He guided her back against him, providing her cover to what he so desperately wanted to see. Instead of dragging out what she clearly thought of as torture, he scooted the jeans down her legs.

He eased back and stripped out of the shirts he was wearing. Her eyes slowly traveled down his chest taking in each and every line of the black Eagle's wings that stretched across his chest. She licked her lips, but a half-second later her mouth fell open. Her eyes blinked rapidly. The circular, white puckered markings mixed in with the scalpel scars were just as vivid as the inked Special Forces logo around his navel. They followed the lines of his abs. His tattoo artist had refused to cover them. He'd tattooed around them offering Aaron slight conceal-ment from his past.

Concealment. He knew how important it was. She had no visible scars from her past. The invisible ones were far worse.

"Are those...?" She reached to touch his abs. He flexed automati-cally, tightening his fists and closing his eyes against her pity. "I'm sorry." Her fingers never made contact. His eyes blinked open. She'd withdrawn her questing hand.

"No questions tonight, okay? Please."

Another nod. "Okay."

Working quickly, he pulled the undershirt away from the long sleeved shirt he'd worn and eased it over her head. It slipped down her slight curves, covering her body. He simultaneously hated it and was thankful for it. He told himself the relief painted on her features made it worth it. It was a lie but he clung to it with everything he had.

"Like a walking wet dream, baby."

"What?" Her brow furrowed.

"That's precisely how fucking sexy you are in my T-shirt."

A harsh swallow contracted her throat. How perfect would she look with his mark on that delicate skin? God, he wanted to see it there, longed to brand her as his own. Need seared through his veins, burning away the shame of his scars.

If he didn't get some relief the heat of his body was likely to set her bed on fire when he crawled in beside her.

Her attempt at stepping toward him had her toppling forward. Her ankles were still trapped in the jeans. He caught her as she leaned toward him. Chuckling, he held her hands while she kicked them off.

"I'm not usually so klutzy." She sounded disgusted with herself.

"Does mighty things to my ego to think I make you just a little off balance, honey."

"You definitely do. Hopefully, I'll get over that once I'm more used to this."

"Oh, I hope not." With that, he scooped under her legs and cradled his sweet baby in his arms. Her body covered the reminders of every single thing he wished he could erase from existence.

Gently, he eased her under the unmade covers on her bed. Stepping back, he unbuckled his belt. She watched his every move. Her eyes were locked on his package. Damn if that didn't just make him harder.

Without thought, he gripped himself, desperate for relief. Her lips parted in intrigue. A flash fire of desire lit her darkening eyes. One stroke. She moaned. On the next, she sat up in the bed. He made one more pull before he unsnapped his jeans trying to give his cock room to breathe. "You still good with this?"

"Keep going," she urged.

"I'm counting that as begging, too, just so you know." He shed his jeans and kicked them away.

His anxious cock tented his boxers and there wasn't a damn thing he could do about it. When her hand shot out from the covers, reaching toward him he leapt back. "Nat, baby, if you put your hands on me right now it's gonna get messy."

Walking to the other side of the bed, he prayed she'd let the idea go. Her eyes narrowed in consideration. She wasn't letting this go. He should've known better.

"I don't mind messy. If I beg to touch you, will you let me?"

"You getting me off without me making you come isn't how we do this."

"I want to feel you. Please."

"Fucking hell." He wasn't a saint. The patience he'd been trying so hard to extend went up in the flames exuding from his body.

"Please." Her fingertips hesitantly traced through the slit in his boxers. His body and the bed shook from the force of his restraint being ripped away from him.

"Shit," he grunted. "Nat, stop."

"I don't want to stop."

Damned woman. "You sure you want this? Speak up now, honey. I'm about to wrap my hand around yours and show you how bad I need this."

"Do that. I'm sure I want you to." She pressed her hand through the slit and he lost all ability to reason with himself or with her.

Gripping her wrist, he pulled her hand away.

"I'm trying so hard to be brave, please don't make me stop."

"Baby, I don't want you to have to be brave but I'm beyond any ability to stop you." Slipping his boxers over his ass, he guided her hand back to his cock. "You're sure about this?"

Her hand wrapped around him. Fascination and trepidation fought for dominance in her eyes. That was all the consent he was going to get.

Capturing her small hand in the strength of his massive one, he pressed her fingers to his head. His cock was weeping for her, weak bastard that he was. "Use what's coming out of me to get me slick," he commanded.

Again, she did precisely as she was told. His cock throbbed out its dominance, his command over her. The way she obeyed. She was perfection. He would burn in hell for this. He knew. He just couldn't find it in himself to care.

She gave an experimental tug and ranchers three counties over probably heard his greedy growl.

"Looks like I could make you beg, too." Naughty little minx gave him one hell of a sex kitten grin. Her confidence made a comeback.

"You want me to beg, baby? Do it just like this." He jacked himself with both of their hands slowly, just the way he'd imagined it so many times. Up and down. All on her own she circled his crown with her thumb on the next upward glide. His entire body quaked. His mind scrambled.

Natalie, his Natalie had her hand on him. In that moment she wasn't afraid. She was fascinated with the power she held with every tug of her hand.

"I swear next time I won't blow like a teenage kid on his first ride. It's just been so fucking long," he choked.

Thrusting against their hands. God all he wanted in the world was to bury himself so deep inside her she forgot every single thing in the world but him. He wanted to be the only man who knew how she felt, knew how wet she got, knew how tightly she seized, saw the look of ecstasy on her face when she came. He was going to be the man who opened her, claimed her sweet little cherry all for himself, owned her so thoroughly she'd never want another.

That thought decimated him. White pops of light shattered in his eyes. The scent of Natalie aroused mixed with the perfume of her bed. His orgasm barreled through him. Spurts of hot cum shot over his abs and soaked their hands.

She gasped as he shook. A string of expletives flew from his mouth. "Damn, so fucking good. Such a good girl."

She jerked her hand back and scooted away from him.

"Nat? What?" Quickly reaching for tissues on the bedside table he attempted a quick clean up while gasping for breath. Tossing them on the side of the bed he reached for her but she scooted farther away. "I'm sorry for whatever just happened. I should never have let you do that. Dammit, I knew you weren't ready." All consuming self-hatred rushed the lust that had filled him a split second before.

"That wasn't it." Her whisper was barely audible. The light in her eyes was gone again. Her body caved in on itself. Her arms were wrapped around her legs pressed to her chest, like she didn't deserve to take up room. What had he done?

"Nat, honey, I'm sorry for whatever I did but I need to know so I never do it again. Please tell me."

A shiver shook through her. She scooted under the covers and he hated himself all the more. "Baby, please." He stood, determined to redress, certain she didn't want him in nothing but boxers in her bed.

"You don't have to get dressed."

"I have to do something. I will do anything to fix this."

"It wasn't what we did," she finally confessed. Her voice was tender, almost raw with the brutal scars from memories he wanted so desperately to erase from her mind.

Nodding, he seated himself on the end of the bed, as far away from her as he could possibly get and still be on the same piece of furniture.

"Can you tell me what it was?"

She wasn't running and she hadn't thrown him out yet. He tried to console himself with that fact.

"It was what you said." Tears pricked her eyes.

"Oh my God, baby, please, please don't cry. I won't touch you. I swear. I'll leave." Racking his brain, he tried to remember what insanity might've flown out of his mouth while cum flew out of his cock. She'd been into it until he'd lost it all.

Good girl. His mind finally landed on what had to have been it. God, he was such an idiot. "I'll never ever say that again. I swear. I wasn't thinking. It's hard to think right then but I'll never let it happen again. I'm so fucking sorry." When he found the scum of the earth that had done this to her the pathetic piece of garbage was going to burn. He'd set him on fire himself. A bullet was too quick, too easy. Didn't hurt enough. Aaron knew.

"Okay," she squeaked.

"I'll go."

"I don't want you to go. Just give me a minute."

"Take as long as you need. I'm really sorry."

"It's okay."

"No, it isn't. We shouldn't have done any of that, and I sure as hell shouldn't have said that."

"You didn't know. It's not your fault. It's mine."

"No." He longed to march to her and pull her into his arms. He stayed seated by the force of his own determination to fix what he'd done. "It is absolutely not your fault. Do you understand me? None of this was your fault. Nothing that happened when you were a little girl and nothing that happened tonight. None of it was because of you."

A hesitant light made a reappearance in the golden flecks of her hazel eyes. Tempted to fall on his knees and thank God for it, he searched the room instead. There was a small chair in the corner of her room covered in clothes.

Sliding the clothing to the floor, he seated himself. "If you want me to stay then I'm gonna sleep here. I'll be right here all night, unless you change your mind and want me to go."

"I don't want you to sleep over there," she fussed.

"Well, I'm going to."

"I want you to hold me in the bed."

He'd served with the finest Green Berets in the army, the toughest Navy SEALS, and fierce marines capable of decimating anything that stood in their way. He watched them all stare down bullets and traverse land littered with IED's like it was nothing. Yet she was without a doubt the bravest person he'd ever had the pleasure of sharing the earth with.

Refusing to get back in the bed mostly naked, he pulled his jeans back on. She didn't argue. Slowly, measuring every step, giving her the precious time he knew she needed, he made his way back to the bed.

"You're sure?"

"I'm sure." She turned off the lamp on her bedside table. Darkness concealed them.

"Still want to be held?"

She scooted closer. "I'm sure, Aaron."

"I don't deserve this." With precise care, he guided her head to his chest and wrapped his arms around her.

Her entire body relaxed against him. Clearly, the good Lord thought he deserved a few favors. Aaron made a mental note to drop all of the tips he made the next day in the collection plate Sunday. "Go to sleep, sweetheart. I've got you. I'll never say that again."

Her eyes fluttered closed. A half-hour later, her breaths finally steadied. Wishing for a wad of coffee to put between his lips and gums, the way he'd always done on fire watch to keep himself awake, he refused any kind of rest.

He wouldn't risk scaring her again with a nightmare of his own and he sure as hell would be alert and ready if she had one herself. He'd find some way to undo the damage he'd done.

CHAPTER FOURTEEN

Trying to ease his phone from the pocket in his jeans without waking Natalie proved tough. She whimpered when Aaron shifted to the side. Okay, screw it. He wanted her to sleep. He'd been planning to catch a few hours of shuteye before he had to go to work, but he could live without. His dogs needed to be fed and watered, too, but he assumed they'd forgive him this once.

The sun was barely up anyway. It couldn't be that late. He'd heard Natalie talk about how early she normally awoke and wondered if her family was out doing ranch chores. Would it piss somebody off if she wasn't there? Were they avoiding her house because his truck was out front? What would Luke and her old man make of that?

A hearty dose of rebellion brought a smirk to his face. He called himself a bastard for good measure.

The knock on the door answered his question anyway. Clearly, someone in her family wanted to know where she was. Aaron automatically hated whoever was awakening his sweet baby.

"Make them go away," she fussed and tightened her arms around him.

Chuckling, he kissed the top of her head. "My pleasure. Give me just a sec."

Working his way out of the quilts and sheets piled on her, he skipped the shirt when the persistent knocking got louder. His long strides made quick work of getting to the door. Debating the best way to respond, he took a deep breath before answering. Telling her brothers he planned on returning to bed with her for another hour or two before he left was one thing. Telling her father that was another.

To his shock, Dec was standing at the door. He chuckled. "Thanks for putting pants on before you answered."

"No problem. You need something?"

"I don't, but I honestly don't think I've ever seen Ev Camden so pissed and that includes the night Holly brought me here after I'd gotten her thrown out of school. I decided to come see if I could help get you off of this ranch before he locates one of his many shotguns."

Hearing Natalie moving around in her bedroom, Aaron tried to speed things along. He wanted a few more minutes to revel in her cuddling into him, to assure himself he was forgiven for his misstep the night before. "I'll take my chances."

"Had a feeling you'd say that. Everything go okay last night?" Ah, so the family thought exactly what he would've thought had someone else's truck been sitting outside her house all night long. Was Dec checking on him or on Natalie? Didn't matter. Neither was necessary. What went on between them wasn't anyone else's business, even if Dec was a sex therapist.

"Think I'll leave last night between me and Nat."

Before Dec could respond Natalie was at Aaron's side. His T-shirt still hung loosely off of her curves but she'd added a pair of tight black yoga pants, concealing what was only for Aaron from her brother-in-law.

"Is Dad pacing or shoveling manure?" She yawned.

"We're way past that," Dec rolled his eyes. "He's unable to form coherent sentences."

"Good grief. Okay, I'll be out in a minute."

"I'll handle your daddy, Nat. You go back to bed," Aaron huffed. Her hair stood in a wild mane around her face. Her cheeks were flushed pink and her eyes were the precise shade of the sugar maples outside Fort Carson in Colorado, caught somewhere between summer and fall, half green and half gold. The imprint of the collar of his shirt marred the alabaster skin on her shoulder. Her scent filled his nostrils as he put his arm around her, drawing her closer. He damned the world outside to hell. Why couldn't everything else just leave them be? Hadn't it taken enough from the two of them?

"Can't. Have to go gather cattle and move them to another pasture." Another deep yawn contorted her delicate features. When her mouth closed, she turned, threw her arms around his shoulders, and buried her face back in his chest.

"That's as good an answer to my question as any. I'll leave you to it. Good luck with Ev. My only tip in dealing with him when it comes to the Camden women, be very, very humble," Dec offered.

"He doesn't need to be humble because I'll go talk to Daddy. Bye, Dec." Natalie shut the door. "I don't want last night to be over with."

Well, you didn't fuck it up too badly. Overwhelming thankfulness had him squeezing her tighter. "Me either, baby. I'm working the early shift again. Let's go do something tonight when I get off. Nothing's over. That's the best part about dating. I swear I'll come up with real plans this time."

"Okay." He felt her grin against his bare chest.

"Nat, I'm really sorry about last night."

"Stop saying that. I'm erasing that one part from all of the really good memories. It's harder to do that if you keep bringing it up."

"Sorry. I won't say anything else about it. I just need you to know how sorry I am. I wasn't thinking. I let you down because I was an idiot."

Her index finger landed on his lips. Lifting his left eyebrow in challenge, he licked her fingertip and then began to suck it. Her nipples rose once again to stiff pearls against the cotton of his T-shirt. Damn, but he needed more.

She pulled her finger away and he replaced it with her lips. A needy moan and her tongue filled his mouth. Oh, hell yeah. He opened his eyes to change position and saw her father heading their way.

"Baby, your daddy's not too far from here. Let me get dressed and meet him outside."

"You sure you want to talk to him? He's ridiculously overprotective of me."

"Well, then we have some common ground. I can work with that. Trust me, I've talked my way out of worse situations."

Natalie followed him back to the bedroom. "I guess you want this back." She started to remove his T-shirt but there was regret laced in her words.

"I'd rather you keep wearing it. Maybe send me a pic of you in it when I'm at work. Give me something to look at until I can see you again." Aaron threw on the long sleeved shirt he'd worn the night before and stepped into his work boots.

"You really don't mind if I keep it?" Almost instinctively, she brought the soft cotton to her face and inhaled. He loved her lack of pretenses, loved that she never played games with him. She liked him and it might've taken her a long time but she'd finally spoken up. "I kind of like smelling like you."

A greedy grunt sounded from low in his gut. "I told you it turns me on to think about you in nothing but my T-shirt and trust me, I like you smelling like me, too. I'll come pick you up as soon as I clock out."

"Okay. If Daddy's awful to you promise you'll tell me."

"Promise." He'd bet a week's worth of tips that her definition of awful was quite different from his, making that an easy promise to keep.

Warmth from the rising sun heated the sizzle of nerves under his skin. He'd never had an encounter with an angry father. Pissed off drill instructors, angry officers, hell, even furious terrorist insurgents at the end of their rope he'd dealt with. This was all new to him. Truthfully, he'd never dated anyone seriously. No one's father even knew of his existence. He never used his real name in the clubs. Part of his job had been to make it appear for all intents and purposes that he didn't exist.

But Ev Camden did indeed look like someone had shoved a few dozen corncobs up his ass. "Mr. Camden, sir." Aaron waved to him while walking to his truck like nothing about that morning was unusual. Guy needed to get used to this. This sure as hell wouldn't be the last time he stayed over.

"Where is...Hol, no, Gr, no, Jess. Ugh. Where is my daughter?" he fumed.

Aaron ran his hand over his mouth to keep from laughing. "Uh, well, I have no idea where Holly is but Natalie is getting ready."

Rage flashed in Mr. Camden's eyes. "What did you, no, I don't want to know. Why isn't she...barn...horse?"

Okay, this was comical. "We slept in. She was tired, sir," he added for good measure. "She'll be out soon though."

Aaron watched the man's chest expand and his fists clench. He took a step back. He knew that stance.

"She is my little girl," he finally managed with a shaky voice. Pain broadcast from his eyes and the deep sun-drenched lines of his face.

"I know, sir. I would never hurt her. She asked me to stay last night."

"She isn't ready for this." Ev gestured to the house.

"I would never push her to do anything she didn't want to do."

Ev shook his head, lifted his cowboy hat, and ran his hands through his sweat-drenched hair. His eyes closed and he appeared to be counting. Aaron waited. He reminded himself that her father knew what had happened to her and most certainly would want to keep her safe.

"Sir, I..." He had nothing to offer this man to make him okay with this and he knew it. Hostile negotiations could only be calmed when both parties had something the other wanted. He offered the only thing he had in his possession. "I'll always make certain she is safe. I promise you that. I know you don't like this, but she means the world to me."

Ev's shoulders relaxed and Aaron knew he was getting through. "Is she okay?"

Whoa. Okay, that was a turn he wasn't expecting. Genuine empathy welled in Aaron. This poor guy, a hard-working cattle rancher who loved his kids more than life itself just wanted to make sure his little girl was okay.

Clearing his throat to buy himself a little time, Aaron considered the weight of his words. They clearly meant a great deal to Everett Camden, a man he respected, a man he would be proud to have the respect of. He sorted through the night before. There had definitely been far more good than bad. Who could really ask for more than that?

"She's the strongest woman I've ever met, sir. She's good. She's ready for a relationship. She deserves a good guy, someone who'll take care of her. I want to be that for her more than I've ever wanted anything. I will do right by her."

Her father gave him a nod but the agreement didn't reach his eyes. "When she was a baby... Jesus, I don't know why I'm telling you this."

Because people tell me things. They always have. Made being an Intelligence officer just a little easier and makes being a bartender effortless. "I think you're telling me this because you love her, sir. Because you're worried about her. Believe me, I get that."

"When she was a little girl she wasn't afraid of anything. She was five the first time she killed a prairie rattler. Stared it down, stuck her tongue out when it did, and drove a shovel that was three times her size through its neck. She never even flinched. When she was barely eight, she used to jump the fences like they weren't even there and that was when she wasn't sneaking calves into my house cause she wanted to take care of 'em. Scared her mama and me to death. Then, all of a sudden, she was afraid of everything. It was all my fault."

Seizing the opportunity, Aaron took a step closer. "What was your fault, sir?"

He shook his head. The grip of his jaw dammed back the words Aaron desperately needed him to say. "Get off my ranch. And so help me son if you hurt her I will make you sorry you ever stopped your truck in Pleasant Glen."

"You have my word. I will never hurt her."

"Good."

"Daddy, please stop." Natalie appeared at Aaron's side. She was in her standard long sleeved shirt and jeans. Her shit-kicking boots were firmly in place and her hair was pulled back in a ponytail. "I'm better than I've ever been."

"Your mama's got breakfast, little one." The quiver of his voice betrayed the tears he was trying his damnedest to blink away.

Aaron had spent the majority of his adult life watching the most abhorrent pain men could render on one another out of hate. This was the first time he'd seen the kind of pain love could wield, somehow it was both better and worse.

Natalie threw her arms around her father's neck, the same way she'd done Aaron that morning.

"I'm fine, Daddy."

"You've been saying that for years, baby girl."

"I know but this time I really mean it." She turned back to Aaron. "I'll see you tonight." She blew him a kiss. Twenty-four hours earlier, if he'd seen any man pretend to catch a thrown kiss and bring it to his heart he would've called him a pussy of the highest order. Things had changed. He caught the kiss and laid his hand on his chest not giving a damn what the rest of the world might have to say about it. The rest of the world had fucked both of them over. In that moment, watching her cling to her daddy's arms he knew he was staring at his saving grace.

"He ain't even a cowboy," Natalie's father huffed as soon as they seated themselves at the breakfast table.

"Ev, honey, put food in your mouth," her mother Jessie ordered.

Natalie giggled. "You're the only cowboy I need, Daddy."

That earned her one of her father's customary grunts. Her sister and sister-in-laws all offered her sympathetic glances.

Katy, Grant's wife, shook her head and winked at Natalie. "Hard for daddies to let go."

Her brothers were all staring at their breakfast plates like the scrambled eggs and bacon had personally offended them. She didn't care. If Aaron staying overnight caused them this much distress, they really needed more to do. Surely, her life wasn't that interesting.

A symphony of grunts ranging from irritated to furious sounded around the Camden table.

Rolling her eyes, Natalie shoved eggs onto her fork viciously. "I don't know what you're all up in arms over. Not like you all haven't had people stay over."

Holly nodded her agreement. "Oh, you know they can do whatever they want but God forbid *we* do anything that makes us happy."

"I'm going to assume I'm not being lumped into this," Dec quizzed.

"No, you're not. You are evolved."

That brought on another round of grunts.

When her mother's lips pursed and her eyes narrowed, Natalie knew they'd gone too far. "Luke Camden, you have two daughters who need to be fed before your wife goes to work and then you need to move your hay to the new field. Grant, I feel certain your wife needs her back rubbed before you go get on that horse of yours, seeing as how she's pregnant, again. Austin, son, you chased a belt buckle and skirts for so long your daddy and I were concerned you were going to be solely responsible for infusing the world with more cattle ranchers than cattle. All of you get over yourselves or get up from my table because you are being ridiculous. And Ev, honey, why don't you go find some fence to fix 'fore I find a frying skillet to take to your rear end. She is not a little girl anymore."

Natalie and Holly shared a conspiratorial grin.

When her brothers downed the last of the eggs, even though she'd wanted more, they filed out of the house solemnly.

Holly grabbed her forearm. "Let's do dishes!"

"You're awfully excited about dishes, Holl. What's up?"

"You. You're up. Don't I get a few details?"

"A few details on what?"

"Nat. An extremely good-looking guy spent the night at your house. What did you think I was talking about?"

"I don't know. It was kind of great, except for one stupid little part I'll forget about soon."

"Wait, what stupid little part?" Her sister's excited tone turned worried in a heartbeat.

"Nothing. It was almost perfect. I hope he stays tonight, too."

"Good. That's good. Does, uh, anything feel sore? It doesn't have to. That whole thing about your first time being extremely painful is a myth if the guy knows what he's doing."

"What? Why would...? Oh." Humiliation taunted the fringes of her consciousness. She should have had her first time last night. That's what everyone thought had happened. That's why her daddy and her brothers were acting insane.

Just lie. Just get this part over with. But it wasn't in her. She'd been asked to lie about something several times the weeks before she turned twelve. Lying wasn't something she would ever do again. "We didn't have sex."

"Oh." Extreme confusion formed on Holly's features before she was able to reshape them into faux understanding. "Well, that's totally fine. It's good even. Yeah, it's good. You should take your time."

"Yeah, that's what I think, too. Aaron's fine with it." He all but enforced it, Natalie reminded herself.

"Good. He's a great guy. You know, if you won't talk to me, you could at least talk to him. Maybe."

"We do talk."

"I mean about what happened."

"I don't ever want to talk about that again. Quit bringing it up."

"All right but if you have any questions or anything you know where to find me."

"I'm fine, Holl."

"You always—"

Natalie held up her hand. "This time I mean it."

CHAPTER FIFTEEN

Scrubbing his hands over his face, Aaron blinked away the exhaustion from his eyes. He told himself he could grab an hour of sleep, shower, then go to the drug store, then be at work on time.

The dogs had other plans. Buster was all over him when he walked into his apartment. Lulu was sulking. She circled him giving him reproachful looks with her huge chocolate-brown eyes. "Sorry, guys. It was for a good cause, I swear."

Glancing around the relatively empty room, he tried not to note the threadbare blanket on his bed. The warmth of Natalie's body as he'd held her all night long and the sunny ranch were absent here. The constant chill he'd brought home from Iraq always compounded here.

Aaron followed the dogs out into the yard to let them run and take care of a few things. Old Man Rasmussen stalked down from his front porch a hundred yards away looking angrier than usual.

Aaron racked his brain. Rent wasn't due until the first. His portion of the last water bill was on the low side. Dogs never really got into any trouble. He'd been eating at the bar so he wasn't using his hot plate too often.

Lulu bound back toward Aaron. She barked at his approaching

landlord, not something she did unless she sensed Aaron was in distress. Aaron patted her side. "It's okay, girl. I'm all right."

She turned to face Rasmussen and bared her teeth. She'd never liked the old man. Aaron assumed it was because he ran a steady temperature between grumpy and pissed-the-fuck-off. Aaron agreed with his dog's assessment. He loathed the guy. There just weren't any other rooms available to rent in Pleasant Glen.

"When I agreed to rent you my room I didn't know you'd be coming in at all hours and taking up with the likes of them Camdens."

Dear God, Aaron needed sleep before he even attempted to dismantle that level of insanity. "When you rented me my room you never said there was some kind of curfew. Where I am and what time I come back isn't really any of your business."

"Eliza Olsen was flapping her gums all over town about you dating one of them Camden girls."

Of course she was. "Clearly, should've added who I date not being any of your business either."

"Nothing but trouble the whole lot of 'em. Thinkin' they up and run this town."

"Way I hear it if Camden Ranch wasn't here none of the Glen would be. So, I guess they do run this town, don't they?"

Since his arrival in the Glen, Aaron had never heard so much as a cross word spoken about the Camdens. Everyone adored Ev and Jessie. They willingly helped anyone who needed it. Jessie Camden would cook for half the town if the power went out for too long. They were at church every Sunday. Since his landlord hated everyone, Aaron didn't think too much of it. Some men lived to complain. It was the air they breathed and the nourishment they sought. Nothing Aaron could do about it.

"Which one of them girls you taken up with? Spoiled brats the both of them."

Decking the old man crossed his mind. Knocking his remaining teeth down his throat would be extremely satisfying. He reminded himself of the lacking real estate market. "Mind your tongue, Rasmussen. Somebody needs to teach you some manners."

The old man spat far too close to Aaron's boots. *Beating up an old geezer would not make Natalie's dad like you more.* He clung to that, steadying his breaths, and digging his fingertips into his palms.

"One of 'em married that foreigner a while back. You dating the other one, then?"

"Well, I'm sure as hell not dating a married woman so that's a safe bet, don't you think?"

"Smart mouth army brat. Didn't they beat any of that disrespect outta you in boot camp? Back in my day..."

Aaron rolled his eyes. "Why do you care who I'm dating?" Unable to listen to stories of some Vet's glory days, he cut him off.

"That other one's the one who caused all the trouble."

The hair on the back of Aaron's neck stood. His jaw twitched. The vengeance he carried constantly in his gut twisted like a caged animal ready to strike. "When did she cause trouble, Rasmussen? What the hell are you talking about?"

"Low down thing to do to a good man."

Control was always key when you had an inadvertent informant. They could never know they were being turned into a source. Nonchalance was always the way to go. Easing his stance and his jaw. Aaron knelt down to pet Lulu. She was still snarling at Rasmussen.

From his vantage point, Aaron proceeded with caution. When a man was below you whether in height or because they'd lowered themselves for whatever reason, it usually put the taller male at ease. Perceived control was a heady sensation for someone like Rasmussen and an extremely dangerous drug to buy into.

"You telling me Natalie did something to someone she shouldn't have? I heard she could take on rattlers. I've never seen her do anything to anyone else though."

"Lying to get her daddy's attention if you ask me. 'Course they took her word. Women always screaming about men being men. They teach 'em to do that shit when they're girls. Low down thing to take a man's land if you ask me."

Holy fuck. "Whose land did they take?"

"I don't want you hanging out with the likes of a lying bitch like that. You just make certain I don't see her over here."

Aaron rose to his full height, towering over the old man. "You just make certain I never hear you calling her names ever again, you got that, old man?"

"You remember whose name is on the deed to this house, Weber?"

"You remember who knows you're running a still out on the back forty, Rasmussen? Seems to me I heard something about you claiming me as a dependent to the IRS. I'm sure the sheriff will be in Saddle-back's for lunch today. Maybe I should mention a few of those things to him."

"You keep your mouth shut."

"You do the same."

Flying back up the stairs, with the dogs hot on his heels, Aaron had his phone to his ear a split second after he slammed the door.

"T, wake the fuck up."

"Give me a minute. I'm off today."

"Want me to call Griff?"

"No. Just give me a sec. You sound like you got intel."

"Maybe."

"All right, I have coffee. Go."

"Natalie must've told her parents what happened to her. They took land away from someone as a direct result from what I can tell. Not sure if it was their land or some other land, but something went down. From what I know, Camden Ranch has never changed hands since it was purchased by her great-great-great granddaddy or something. They have acquired other ranches though. There was a big thing back when Austin won the PBR buckle. He used some of the money he won to buy more land. There has to be public record of all of this somewhere."

"There will be, and you know I'm your man."

Aaron heard T typing on a keyboard.

"All right, so we're looking for any kind of land grant changes in Lincoln County from the very late nineties to the early 2000's, right?"

"I'm not certain it's in Lincoln County. I heard her brothers talking a few months ago about some kind of wheatgrass property they have in Oklahoma for doing something with calves. Could be there."

"Bet it's backlotting."

"What's backlotting?"

"Basically fattening them up. That's interesting."

"What's interesting?"

"That they run a massive cow-calf operation and have enough money and land to run a backlot as well."

"In non-cowboy terms please."

"Get your girl to explain ranching to you, A. Bet she'd love it."

"You grew up on a ranch."

"Yeah, but right now I'm in the mood to dig into intel and not in the mood to shoot the bull about ranching. See what I did there?" T chuckled. "Somebody hurt my girl and I plan to help you mount their sac on your rearview as a warning to others."

"She's *my* girl," Aaron growled. His own fury shocked him.

Another chuckle sounded in his ear. "I know, just wanted to make sure you knew that. And I wanted to hear you say it. Now, let me work. I'll call you when I find something."

"You better."

Skipping the nap, Aaron showered, gave the dogs extra treats as an apology, and straightened up his humble abode. "Can't promise I'll be back until tomorrow morning. Trust me, when I tell you this is worth it. I'll be fine. You be good." Aaron assured Lulu who was still had her ears pinned back and barked whenever she neared the front door.

Ten minutes later, he pulled his truck into the parking lot of the CVS. For some reason the locals still referred to the drugstore as Wilton's. It had been a CVS for years. Some people just couldn't let go of the past, he supposed.

Making quick work of throwing shaving cream, toothpaste, deodorant, and some new Frisbees for the dogs, in his basket he glanced around and headed for what he'd come in to purchase. Buying condoms and lube in a small town reminded Aaron of training up new troops. Everyone watched your every move from the recruits to your superiors and no one let you forget a single misstep.

This was his first condom acquisition in the Glen, but it had been the same way in Gentry when he was seventeen. His foster parents had gotten no fewer than five phone calls about his purchase before he'd even made it back to the farm. The last thing he needed was some busybody calling Ev Camden to let him know that Aaron was purchasing lube for his daughter. That would go over about as well as a lead zeppelin.

Feigning interest in a copy of Farm and Ranch magazine, he noted the position of everyone in the store. Pharmacist was busy. Girl at the checkout was gossiping with a cattle rancher buying liniment. Teenage girl who couldn't have been old enough to drive was meticulously studying a nail polish display. Few other customers were scattered throughout but they all seemed interested in their own purchases.

He turned down the aisle he needed and grabbed two boxes of condoms without notice from anyone. Half of the mission was accomplished.

Stalking farther down the aisle, his eyes goggled. Determined to do anything in his power to make Natalie's first time a good one instead of a miserable experience, he reached for a bottle of KY, but instead encountered dozens of bottles of lube, all offering different sensations for the users. Warming, cooling, a mix of the two, massage cream, intense, some kind of moisturizing bead, something that said it offered changing sensations throughout the session, natural, organic. Passion, love, sensuality. Did these people actually think you could bottle that? What happened to plain old lube. "What the hell?" he huffed under his breath. Finally spotting a simple bottle with clear liquid, he leaned down to make the acquisition.

His ass collided with someone else's. Jerking upright he spun into none other than Austin Camden. *Shit.*

Both men glared at one another. Aaron noted a pregnancy test in Austin's hands. Austin was eyeing the condoms in the basket and the lube in Aaron's palm.

"Want to just pretend we never saw each other in here?" Aaron extended an olive branch.

"Don't hurt my little sister. You got that?"

"I got it."

"You break her heart I'll break your spine. Nat's different."

"So I've been told." Weary of constantly being threatened, Aaron popped the crick out of his neck. "You ever take time to remember that Nat and I have been friends for a long time. She could've gone after any guy she wanted. Could've been one that doesn't give a damn about her."

An audible huff of breath filled the air between them. "Yeah, all right, I know. This is just weird for us. For as long as I can remember, we've been the one to look out for her. Not easy to hand over the reins. I worry about her."

"Why don't you worry about Summer. Looks like she might need a little extra looking after." He pointed to the pregnancy test. "I've got Nat. I swear to you. I'll keep her safe."

Austin nodded. "Yeah, Summer's so sick she couldn't come to town to get this. I keep trying to tell her I know she's pregnant. I can always tell. She wants proof."

"Sometimes seeing it with your own two eyes means something."

"I s'pose. We lost one a few months back. She's scared."

Aaron knew Summer wasn't the only one who was scared, but Austin Camden would never admit his own trepidation. "I'm sorry, man. Really. That's rough."

"It was that. The whole damn town'll know as soon as I buy this thing, too."

"Yeah, I'm in the same boat." He did it without thinking. Commiserating with your opponent almost always softened them up. It was engrained in Aaron.

"Nat won't care. She never lets the town chatter get to her."

"I hope you're right."

"The first person who calls up to the house to give Summer unneeded pregnancy advice will piss her off good, though. And that'll happen 'fore I get back to the house."

Aaron chuckled. "My foster dad used to say if people in small farming towns would use their tractors as much as they use their telephones we could feed the world."

"Ain't that God's honest truth. I'm half tempted to drop a twenty on the counter, tuck this, and run. If this one don't work out and everyone knows..."

"There are cameras but I can tell you the one by the door isn't actually on. You want to slip out with that, I'll make it happen."

"Ain't that illegal? Me ending up down at the courthouse over a pregnancy test ain't gonna make my wife any happier."

"You're paying for it. You're just not waiting on a receipt, so to speak."

"You really think I could get out of here without anyone knowing?"

"Stick to the walls on this side of the store. Keep it down by your left side so the camera in the back doesn't catch it. Give me the cash. I'll leave it on the counter when I check out. If you go up there, you're made. Camdens are fairly recognizable in this town."

Austin grunted. "Don't I know that, too. Hey, how do you know which cameras are working?"

Red light isn't on. Camera isn't moving. Back wiring is disconnected. Aaron shook off the information his mind processed constantly. He couldn't turn it off. "Security cameras are something I have a little experience with. Extra set of eyes in the field kept me alive more than once."

"I forgot you were in the Army." Austin slapped the twenty in Aaron's palm. "Thanks for this. I'll still kill you if you hurt my little sister but I owe you."

"I'll take that."

Aaron's phone vibrated in his pocket. Out of habit he waited until Austin disappeared, rather discreetly for a famous bull rider, out the sliding doors.

The text from T-Byrd read: *There have been twelve land acquisitions by the Camdens in the last fifty years. I'm looking into each acquisition starting with the ones that occurred after Natalie's birth.*

Let me know if I can help. Aaron responded before heading toward the checkout.

Willing the color in her cheeks to fade from florescent red to something slightly less enflamed, Natalie stared at herself in the mirror. She turned side to side deciding how exactly to go about taking this selfie.

Aaron's T-shirt swayed back and forth against her thighs. She shivered.

Good girl. The voices of the two men who'd spoken those words blended in her mind. She gagged. Nope. Nope. Nope. That did not happen. She banished the memory once again. The night before had been far too close to perfect to let two stupid words ruin it.

The scars on his abs crossed her mind. She picked up her phone determined to send him a sexy picture but touched the phone app instead of the camera. The Sevens had made a big deal about putting all of their numbers in her phone. It had been funny and sweet. They'd all told her to call if Aaron ever got out of hand.

Touching T-Byrd's name she stared at his number trying to come up with a nonchalant way to ask about Aaron's scars. "You can't nonchalantly ask about him being shot," she scolded herself. She didn't know why it was so important that she understand exactly what had happened to him. She wanted to help him. She wanted to heal him. She just didn't know how to go about it.

T probably wouldn't tell her anyway and she shouldn't ask. She closed the phone app. There were certainly things she didn't want him to know. Maybe the gunshots were like what happened to her. They should just be left in the past. That was the worst part about scars both visible and invisible. They were always in your present and they would always be in your future.

Shaking off that truth, she attempted a sexy come-get-me grin and snapped a picture in the mirror. It looked more like a mugshot than a sext. Brushing her hair over her left shoulder, she turned to the side and tried again. It was a little better. Adding cherry Chapstick to her lips, she rubbed them together. Sliding the T-shirt down so it revealed more of her breasts, she tried once more. Bingo.

Ridiculously pleased with herself, her grin expanded ear to ear. She snapped another picture with a genuine smile. It was even better than the last. Maybe she could do this girlfriend thing. She wasn't completely inept. Last night she'd proven to herself that she wouldn't remain trapped in her past. She was going to move on. The distance the years provided hadn't worked but doing this with Aaron would. She was determined.

Deciding to send the picture without accompanying text, she gulped in a breath and hit the blue send arrow.

"Oh my God. Come back," she ordered the picture. The swoosh sound of it flying off into cyberspace made her whimper. What would he think? What would he say? Would he remember that he'd asked her to send him a picture or did he just say that? What if someone else saw it? Oh, my God.

She stared at her phone willing the picture to come back or some kind of response. Each second felt like an hour. Why hadn't he responded?

She dropped her phone to the tile floor when it buzzed. "Shit." Scooping it up she prayed it wasn't broken and there was a response.

You are so fucking beautiful, baby. My God, I don't deserve this. Thank you. <3

She stared at the heart emoji at the end of the text. Relief catapulted through her. She sank down to the cool tile floor and leaned up against the tub. The feel of the chilly tile seeped through her panties. The parts that burned with need when she was with him grew uncomfortable. She needed him.

You really liked it? She responded. Okay, so she needed a little more reassurance. She'd never sent a sexy photo to anyone.

He sent back a gif of a cartoon dog drooling copiously with his eyes bugged out. The sound of her laughter echoed off the tile. She wished he were there to laugh with her.

Another text came in. *Next time, warn a guy though. I almost dropped my phone in a pitcher of beer.*

Her body shook against the tub from her continued laugher. *Next time?*

If you won't send me more pics I'll have to come see the real thing. I can't go too long without a hit of my girl.

His girl. She liked that way more than she probably should, more than was probably safe. Right then, she didn't care about her heart getting broken. Being his girl was worth a little risk.

Come see me, baby. I miss you.

She sighed. This was far too good. She pinched her thigh to make certain it wasn't a dream.

I thought you were picking me up later?

Can't wait that long. I want you.

Pure bliss fizzed in her stomach and danced under her skin.

Hopping up off of the floor, she raced to her closet. *I'll be there as soon as I get dressed.*

You getting dressed is a damned shame. Shouldn't cover something that gorgeous.

She rolled her eyes. He was laying it on thick. Not that she minded. *Are you saying you want me to come to the bar without pants?*

I don't share, honey. I'll just have to get you out of your pants later.

CHAPTER SIXTEEN

Aaron spent every single moment of the short break Eliza offered him staring at the sexy picture Natalie had sent him. Damn, damn, damn but she was perfection. Showing off her yet unexplored naughty side set up longing in the marrow of his bones. He was going to be sporting a semi for the rest of the night. That brought him back to the hand job he'd received the evening before. He doubled down on his determination to peel back the layers of her sexuality slowly. So far, he was sure as hell enjoying every inch they gained.

He'd fantasized about her jacking him off dozens of times. Nothing he'd dreamed up would compare to her hesitant hand exploring every hard ridge of his cock. His mind offered up an image of her on her knees before him, her arms bound, her lips covered in his cum, her gorgeous ass as pink as her pussy from his hand. Her begging him for more.

Blinking rapidly he brought himself back to his current reality. *Not yet, Weber. Not fucking yet.*

When he returned to his station behind the bar, the blood drained not only from his cock but from his entire body. "What the hell are you doing here?" he demanded of T-Byrd and Griff seated at the bar. "Natalie is on her way down here."

"Well, I didn't know that. Just be cool. We'll tell her we came to see you," T reassured.

"Why are you really here?"

"Land grants came up empty. More questions than answers. The way the land is divvied up must be in the Camden wills. I'm gonna go make friends with the sweet old lady at the courthouse, see if I can't stumble into the wills and records room."

"How do you already know Mrs. Snyder works at the courthouse? How long have you two been here?"

"Long enough to get the lay of the land."

"It's one street, T," Griff goaded. "We had it down in ten minutes."

"Everyone in this town knows everything about everyone else. You two are gonna stick out like sore thumbs. She cannot know I asked you to find this ass-wipe."

"We know. We know. We've got this. Trust us," T ordered.

"I wouldn't have asked for your help if I didn't trust you morons. Just don't let anyone know what you're looking for. It'll get back to the Camdens instantaneously."

"Like I said, trust us."

"Does this mean you didn't find anything online?"

"Dude, you're a bartender. Shouldn't you take our order before you start your interrogation?" T laughed.

Rolling his eyes, Aaron made certain no one was near enough to hear them. "Fine. What can I pour you and make it quick? I want an update before she gets here."

T drummed his fingers on the bar top pretending to consider.

"So help me," Aaron huffed.

"Fine. Something dark that comes out of a tap."

"Sounds good," Griff agreed.

Aaron slammed the glasses down before them. "Talk."

"I couldn't find paperwork on all of the land they've purchased in the last fifty years. I'm sure there are titles and bills of sale in the courthouse. Stuff like that wasn't recorded online in little towns until about ten years ago. However, every purchase they made in the last ten years they actually paid more than the land was worth. Lots of the acreage they purchased was about to go to up on the auction block with foreclosure notices all over it. They bought their neighbors out of debt in most cases. You have any idea why they would do that? Why not wait and get it cheap?"

"I've been told no less than a hundred times since I moved here that Ev Camden is the salt of the earth. From everything I can tell and the times I've talked to him, I'd say it's the truth. He would've paid more for the land so the people losing it had something to live on."

"Didn't know there were men around like that anymore." Griff sounded genuinely impressed.

"I didn't know there were women like Natalie anywhere until I met her," Aaron confided.

Griff and T both laughed.

"Dude, you are aware that you're in love right?" T quizzed.

"You had a good ride but you're done for, my friend." Griff lifted his glass in a mock toast.

"Doesn't matter if I am. She deserves better than anything I've got to give for the long term."

Their laughter was erased from the air. They both stared up at him. The memories of all they'd lived through and the ones who hadn't survived reflected in their eyes.

"Don't say that," T argued.

"It's the truth. Why not say it?"

"Moving on," Griff demanded.

"Fine but don't fuck this up because you think you're damaged goods or whatever. You're not the only one in love. She's all about you. I could tell every time she looked at you last night," T vowed.

Hope was the most dangerous emotion humans were capable of experiencing. Offer a prisoner hope that one day you'd set him free, they'd last endlessly. The will to get something you wanted so badly you could taste it kept many men clinging to life itself. Aaron refused the hope that rode stupidly astride T's vow. When the rubber met the road he had but two things Natalie needed: his strength and his sexual prowess.

When he'd taught her everything she wanted to know about passion and satisfaction and made certain whoever had hurt her no longer polluted the air by breathing, she'd find someone who could give her everything else she wanted in this life, everything she deserved. "Thought we were moving on."

"Fine. I couldn't find anything about them taking any land from anyone. I want to see the plot map from the original purchase, which if I'm extremely lucky will be somewhere in the records office."

"Their family has owned that property for centuries."

"I know, but you'd be surprised. If I can't find the original I want the earliest possible one they have on record. From that I can figure out which land was theirs from the beginning. I can piece it together. Might lead me nowhere but you never know. Hey, do you remember Maddox Holder?"

"From the 101st?" Aaron hadn't thought about Mad-dog in years. Guy was wild. Never turned down a dare. They'd had some fun together back in the day. Hell of a Screaming Eagle, too.

"Yeah. He's back on his family's land in Oklahoma. He helps us out on occasion. He's looking into the land the Camdens have down there for me."

"Thank him for me. Just how big is this organization you all have going on?"

"We call in favors all over the country when we need to. I didn't put together a half-assed security firm, A." T sounded offended. "I know what I'm doing and the moment you decide to make a real living on top of what you send your foster parents you'll take my job offer."

"Gotta say I'm impressed, but I still don't want a job." He sensed her presence before he lifted his head to watch her walk through the doors. The way she affected him was unlike anything he'd ever experienced before. If he was in love, it was sure as hell rattling his cage. "Nat just walked in." He spoke through his clenched teeth.

"I've got you covered." Griff lifted a denim jacket he must've stowed on the barstool beside him to keep anyone from sitting too close.

"Is that hers?"

"Yep."

Aaron retraced their time at the Hi-Way. She had been carrying the jacket when they went in but he didn't remember it appearing again until that moment. "You took that from her didn't you? You lifted it when she went to the bathroom?"

"I kind of figured we might need to come out here to help you with your case and I know this town is all kinds of up in everybody else's business. Made a good cover," T explained. If it hadn't been such a brilliant plan Aaron would've had more to say about their stealing from his girl.

"Hey, I didn't know you two were coming out here." Natalie's broad grin snatched Aaron's breath from his lungs. Okay, so this had to be love. He hadn't even slept with her yet. How was he already falling for her? He knew the answer. He'd fallen for her the moment he'd laid eyes on her.

She'd been the hope. She'd been the very thing he'd wished for that had kept him going. A chance with her was what kept him from ending it all on the nights when he couldn't rescue his present from his past. Now, he was just feeding the ceaseless cravings.

"You left this at the Hi-Way last night. A told us he'd let us drink for free if we brought it to you," T thrust the jacket into her hands.

The neon lights of the bar twinkled in her gaze as she lifted her eyes to his. "That was so sweet of you but I'll buy your drinks. You didn't have to bring this all the way out here. I keep forgetting stuff for some reason lately. I think I'm losing my mind," she fretted.

T and Griff both smirked. "You know A's gonna take credit for making you forgetful. Don't give him ammo, girl." Griff winked at her.

She laughed. God, that laugh. His heart pounded out its approval. His cock leapt back to attention. He'd survived a lot of things in this fucked up life. He wasn't certain he was going to survive her, however.

"Are we all going out?" she forced a smile but gave him a disappointed glance.

Fuck him, she didn't want to go out with his friends. She just wanted him. Of all the things he'd screwed up, the brothers he'd gotten killed, for some unfathomable reason she only wanted him.

"No, baby, they're heading back to Lincoln in a little while. Just the two of us tonight. I promise." Her fake smile was immediately replaced with a genuine grin that reached her eyes and lit the tiny faded freckles across her cheeks.

Griff and T both hid their chuckles. Being discreet wasn't one of her talents. Aaron hoped that proved true in bed as well.

"Is there some kind of memorial service for a man's wild days when he gets himself tied down? If that's not a thing it should be because we need to plan one for you." Griff stuck the tip of his tongue between his teeth and laughed. Natalie turned the shade of sunburnt strawberries but Aaron caught the thrill that lit in her eyes.

"You know our man is kinky as fuck. Bet he's the one who'll be doing the tying down," T goaded.

"I swear, T. Shut the fuck up," Aaron huffed. "He's joking," he vowed to Natalie.

Relief swept a little of his fury away. Natalie didn't look horrified or frightened. He studied her eyes, they were the windows to her every thought. A dozen years of studying human expression and mannerisms told him she looked intrigued.

T went as far as to hum the opening cords of "Here Comes the Bride."

"Actually, we're not going back to Lincoln tonight. We're on a case," Griff volunteered to Natalie. Aaron appreciated his attempt to distract her and he had enough experience running ops with Team Seven not to panic. He steadied his pulse and his breathing like he was about to scope in on a kill. How far would Griff extend the truth until he would be forced to run into lies?

"Really?" Natalie settled on the barstool beside him. "Surely not in the Glen. Nothing ever happens here."

"Nah, not here," Griff scoffed. "Down in Cottonwood Springs."

"Oh." Natalie nodded. Aaron wiped down the bar to have something to do. He wanted to see what she was going to ask next. She was curious. He could tell. "Can you tell me what kind of case it is?"

"Nothing out of the ordinary. Trying to find someone who doesn't want to be found." T looked her in the eye, judging her reaction. Dammit, if he blew this, Aaron would strangle him.

"That sounds like it could be dangerous."

"Danger's my middle name, sweetheart."

Aaron and Griff both laughed at him outright. Natalie shook her head. "Pretty sure your middle name is Thursten which is decidedly not dangerous." She went as far as to pat him on the head and Aaron doubled over.

"Oh God, I love her," Griff howled. "You did good A. Hang on to this one."

"For as long as she'll let me," Aaron assured no one but Natalie, who was staring at him with enough soul for the both of them penned in her hazel eyes. He'd left his back in the desert sands. Maybe he could just experience hers for a short while. He winked at her. As if on command her grin expanded the width of her face, and that warmth he was already addicted to licked at his spine.

"I have to go do refills. I'll be right back." Aaron grabbed the pitchers and made his way toward the patrons gathered at tables.

Natalie stared unabashedly at Aaron's ass as he walked away. It was something she'd been doing since the first time she'd ever seen him. Now, she knew what he looked like mostly undressed but still hadn't really gotten to admire the tight firmness she wanted to dig her fingers into and squeeze.

The night before had gone by in a blur. She hadn't gotten to explore as much as she wanted and she had no idea how to ask him if he would lay very still and just let her touch him. She was fairly certain he'd let her if she asked. He'd probably give her the moon if she requested he climb up and hand it to her. Asking was only half of her fears. If he agreed, she'd have to follow through. That kept those thoughts locked up tightly in her head where they belonged.

She wondered just how kinky Aaron really was. If she wasn't so inexperienced he probably would've done more with her already. In concept being tied up and at his mercy sounded sexy as hell. In reality, having some kind of panic attack while tied to his bed would be horrifically embarrassing.

Griff's laughter brought her back to the bar before her. "We already know you like him, sweet thang. You don't have to stare after him while he's gone."

"I do like him," she admitted. "I like him a lot."

"I can assure you the feeling is mutual. A has a bad habit of never thinking he deserves what he needs. Don't let him pull that shit with you. He deserves good in this life even if he doesn't think he does."

"Why do you think he thinks that way?" Here was her chance. His friends had come all the way to the Glen to bring her a jacket she'd stupidly left behind. They must like her and they clearly loved Aaron like a brother. Maybe they could help her out with some knowledge as well.

T shook his head. "Only one thing you can say about life that's always true: it ain't fair."

The cryptic response told her nothing and she was fairly certain T-Byrd knew that.

"Can I ask you something else?" She had to know how to help Aaron. He was doing so much for her. She wanted to give him something in return. Peace was the best gift anyone could ever give. Her parents had given her some semblance of it when they'd banished her uncle from the entire Midwest. She'd clung to it fiercely for the last two decades.

"Uh, okay." Suddenly, T didn't sound so certain.

"Aaron has some really bad markings, scars I think. There are long white lines and then...others." She gestured to her own stomach. "They...well...they look like they're...they look like they came from a..." When she was nine, she'd been playing with the BB gun she'd gotten for her Christmas that year. It was all she'd wanted. Her brothers had them and she hated being left out. She'd accidentally dropped it and it had gone off. The BB had lodged in Austin's knee.

Eventually the scar had blended in with all of the others he'd earned getting himself thrown off of bulls. But she remembered how guilty she'd felt. She'd apologized to him every day for a year until he'd begged her to cut it out.

The puckered white marking resembled the ones on Aaron's abdomen. Only Aaron's were much, much worse.

She couldn't force the words bullet wounds from her lips, however. She couldn't bear to think about it. He couldn't have been shot that many times and survived.

T and Griff shared an uncomfortable glance. Griff shook his head discreetly. T offered her a kind smile. "If you're asking us, I'm betting you've already tried to ask him."

"He probably refused to tell her," Griff sighed.

"I can't tell you what happened, Nat. I wish I could but it's not my story to tell. Do me a favor, if he doesn't want to talk about it don't push him. He's a fucking hero, braver than any man I've ever met. I can't believe he did what he did. But he... he doesn't remember it the way it went down. Maybe someday he'll talk about it with you. But you'll never hear it from me."

Natalie nodded. "Okay. Sorry."

"Hey, loving A is nothing to apologize for."

Loving him? Natalie reached for the charm on her necklace. She shook it back and forth. Did she love him? If she did how was she supposed to know?

Aaron set the empty pitchers back under the spouts and grinned at her.

The rough scrape of T and Griff's barstools against the old wooden floor marked their standing up. "We have to get. Lots to do before sundown. You two go get wild and crazy. Life's short, right?" T winked at Natalie. Griff pulled a Texas Longhorns baseball cap low over his eyes and they both disappeared into the humid haze of the late afternoon.

"You okay, baby? You're looking at me like they just cancelled your favorite television show," Aaron asked as soon as they left.

"I'm fine."

"Hey, Nat, all that shit T was saying about tie-ups and all that. It was a lifetime ago, okay? I don't want you to be afraid of anything, baby. Certainly not me."

"I'm not afraid," she vowed. "Nervous maybe but not afraid. I'm not even opposed to being tied up." She glanced around to make certain no one heard her. "Just might have to psych myself up for it first."

"We're taking this very, very slowly, remember? No one's bringing tie-ups into this for a long time. I don't want you to have to psych yourself up for anything."

CHAPTER SEVENTEEN
T-Byrd

"I say we just wait until sundown and come back with my lock pick set. This place barely has a front door and the windows are all unlocked. There can't possibly be a security system." Griff sized up the smallest courthouse T had ever seen.

"Let's just go in and see what we're up against. I want to get a feel of the clerk. Then we'll come back tonight."

"All right, fine, but if we go in now and then come back later and they eventually figure out someone was in there who do you think they'll come looking for? I'm not doing anything that might get Triple A in trouble. We spent too much time in the bar with him and Natalie. People saw us."

"Yeah, maybe. My gut says we should go in now and see if we can't make friends with someone in there. Tonight feels a little iffy to me."

"Do I need to remind you how fucking many times A's bailed us out? He's got a good thing going on in this town, if that's what this is. I'm not fucking it up for him."

"Oh, my lands, T-Byrd, is that really you?" The screech T had spent the last six months trying to erase from his memory clawed through the air.

"Shit."

"Looks like you already have friends in town, T," Griff huffed. He made no effort to hide his irritation. "Who the hell is she?"

A half-breath later, Cheryl something-or-another was upon them. "Did you change your number? I call, and call, and call and never get through. I mean I know you got moved to Anchorage but I figure we can just keep in touch until you move back."

T forced a pained smile. Griff rolled his eyes.

"I won't be moving back. Anchorage is a permanent assignment. I'm just here to see an old friend." An idea sprang to T's mind. This is why he always went with his gut. He came up with his best ideas when his balls were to the wall.

As he recalled the claw marks Cheryl had left up and down his back he remembered why he'd ever put up with that voice of hers.

"Who?" Cheryl pouted. "I thought you didn't know anyone out here except me."

Bile swam in T's gut. "Natalie Camden. We go way back. Do you know her?"

Griff eyed him cautiously. He shook his head but T knew he wished he'd come up with the idea himself.

When a woman like Cheryl thought they were in some kind of competition with another woman they always came out swinging. And in the dressing down she was sure to offer, there would be information they could use.

"Oh, well, yeah everyone knows Natalie. If you ask me she should spend more time at the beauty parlor than on that horse of hers. With money like the Camdens have surely she could do something about her looks. Besides she's kind of a bitch. My mama had me invite her to a cosmetics and skin care party a few years ago. I told her she wasn't all that ugly and that makeup would do a lot for her. She told me she'd rather gouge her own eyes out with a stick and that I could...well that's not for polite company.

"Oh, and I heard she's taken up with that no good bartender at Saddleback's. If you ask me he has more tattoos than good sense. I mean, where did he even come from? My mama says he's not to be trusted and I agree. Leave it to the Camdens to go around befriending all of the wrong kinds of people. Have you ever met Austin's wife? Met her on the rodeo circuit, so he said. I went over there one time to ask Austin about something and you would've thought I set fire to their barn. She was all over me. Told me Austin was taken, like I didn't know that. I was there to congratulate him on all of his rodeo winnings. Some people."

Griff rubbed his temples. "Seriously, her?" he mouthed behind Cheryl's back.

So she went after Austin Camden, one of the brothers, T recalled from his digging, after he'd won the PBR buckle and all of the money that went with that, and Austin's wife had called her on it. T only knew what the Camden family looked like on paper, but from what he'd heard he'd say he liked them.

"Get rid of her," Griff demanded silently. He glanced toward the street where they were drawing a small but interested crowd.

"Listen Cheryl, we're heading out. We're leaving for Anchorage tonight. It'll be a long trip. It was nice to see you." One of the many things he'd learned in special ops training was how to lie. That had served him well.

"Well, at least give me your new number so we can keep in touch. You still own that business you were telling me about. It sounded so lucrative and exciting."

T never told anyone outside the agency what he actually did for a living. He searched his mind for exactly which story he'd told Cheryl.

"Company went bankrupt," Griff explained. "He lost everything. Can't get a job doing anything but working the pipelines in Alaska. Rough work. No money. He's got nothing to show for it but debt." He slapped T on the back consolingly. Okay, so T wasn't the only one who occasionally came up with brilliant ideas.

"Oh." Cheryl took two steps backward and T almost laughed out loud. "Well... uh... it was nice to see you." She ran away from them like they'd suggested she go back to Camden Ranch and take on Mrs. Austin Camden again.

"Okay, I owe you one," T sighed.

"Oh, dude, you owe me more than one. What the hell? Did you sleep with her?"

"I was hard up."

"You see the statue of the cowboy on the horse right there?" He pointed to the small concrete statue in front of the courthouse. "Even *he* is not hard up enough to go there. Now, since someone in this town besides Triple A knows your name, we're gonna go get lost until tonight when we can come back and do this right, fucker."

"Yeah, all right. Where the hell do you get lost in a town like this?"

"Let's take a drive and figure out what we can see of Camden ranch."

T's phone rang while they drove past the Camden's land. It extended on for miles. "Biggest cattle ranch I've seen in a while," he commented before taking the call. "Talk to me, Mad-Dog."

"Two hundred and fifty acre farm of sorts. Nothing on it but wheatgrass. They've got it leased to Orpington Cattle for the moment and a feedlot management company in town is managing it. Nothing out of the ordinary. Lease agreement says the Camdens have owned it for the past twenty-five years. There's been no changes in ownership or any sign that they sold any of it off or purchased more. Sorry, T. Looks like this is a dead end."

"Marking something off the list isn't a bad thing. Easier for me to figure this out if it's up here anyhow. Triple A says to thank you for your help. That goes for me, too."

"No problem. How's he doing?"

"He's got it bad for a cowgirl. If he doesn't fuck this up you might get a wedding invite sometime."

"Oh, yeah? Good for him. He deserves something good in this life. Tell him to give me a call sometime."

"Will do." He ended the call. "Got nothing to do with the land in Oklahoma."

"I figured," Griff sighed. "If land changed hands records of it have to be in that courthouse."

"What time do you figure everyone in this town goes to sleep?"

"Well, you gotta give Junior time to do his chores and his homework then there'll be some top ten rides or some other shit everyone'll watch on the PBR network assuming the satellite signals don't give out 'cause we're out here in Bumblefuck. God, I do not miss this," Griff spat with far more anger than was necessary.

T loved growing up on a ranch. The wide open prairies of Camden Ranch made him long to turn down the gravel road and baptize himself in the sanctuary of it all. Hell, he'd even shovel manure if they'd just let him stay for a day or two. Griff hadn't fared as well. He still held a grudge.

"Want to have a conversation with me that we'll swear we never had?" T hoped he'd agree. This had been eating at him ever since they'd seen Cheryl.

"Is it gonna be about how fucking gorgeous Natalie is and how jealous Cheryl is and why women do shit like that?"

"Yeah."

"We got nothing to burn but time. Why not?"

"She's pretty, right?"

"She ain't my type but she's all kinds of Triple A's. You see her ass? Damn. This town wants to build a sculpture and put it in front of the courthouse that's what they ought to show off."

"You know they get that way from riding."

"Guess the country does have something going for it."

"A's always liked 'em small with an ass men would donate a nut just to see."

"Well, he got it all then. She's gorgeous and more importantly she's smart and sweet and all kinds of into him. Cheryl's a gold digger with three functioning brain cells and they're all squealing give me mon-eee. I'm done with this conversation now. A's in love with her. That's all I need to know."

T chuckled. "Yeah, all right."

By ten o'clock, the honkytonk where Aaron worked was the only thing open. The rest of the main thoroughfare through town was dark and empty.

"Let's park at the bar, keep to the shadows, and see what we find," Griff commanded.

T parked behind the bar. "Wonder where A and Natalie are tonight?"

"His bed if he's got any sense left."

"Oh, come on Griff. How have you not figured this out yet?"

"Figured what out?"

"Whatever this guy did to her scared her badly enough to be afraid of men. That's part of why A wants this guy dead instead of just mangled but breathing. I'll bet you a Benjamin he hasn't gotten her in his bed yet. He'd never want to scare her more."

"Poor kid. Now I want him dead, too. At first I just wanted to beat the shit out of him because A didn't like him. I didn't know what he did was that bad. Sick bastard."

T-Byrd nodded. "So, let's go find this shitwhistle."

"Yes, sir."

CHAPTER EIGHTEEN

Aaron rang out his register drawer and emptied the tip cup. There were two fifties in it along with a handful of ones and a few fives. What the hell? T-Byrd and Griff. Shame slithered over his skin. He didn't need their charity.

"You made somebody's day." Natalie beamed at him.

"They shouldn't have done this."

"They wanted you to have it. That's what friends do for each other, right?"

"Maybe." Deciding to spend it on her, he grinned. "Okay, so it's lady's choice this evening." He took her hand and escorted her out to his truck.

"What does that mean?"

"I came up with three date ideas and you get your choice."

"Okay." Her brow furrowed but delight danced in the moonlight in her eyes.

"First option, you tell me your favorite place in this tiny-ass town and we go there and hang out. Second choice, we go out to the County Fair in North Platte."

"I love the fair. I haven't been in years. I didn't even know it was in town."

"Then let's go, baby."

"No, wait, what's my third choice?"

"We go to Ogallala and get Runza's and then go to the drive-in that they opened back up since the theater's being rebuilt."

"Wow, when you decide you're going to make plans you really go all out."

Aaron chuckled. "I am definitely not a man who does anything halfway, babe. Besides I figure whichever two we don't do we can do another time."

"I really don't care what we do. I just like hanging out with you."

"Well, I was planning on being with you on all three dates," he teased her.

"All right, smarty pants, take me to the fair."

"Yes, ma'am." He ran his right hand over her ass as she climbed up in his truck.

"Or we could go back to my house and do more of that," she offered hopefully.

He climbed in the driver's seat and turned the key. "You are going to be the death of me, woman. We'll get to all of that later. I might even cop a feel on the Ferris Wheel."

"Luke got caught with his hand down Indie's jeans at the fair when they were in high school. The North Platte Sheriff called Mama and Daddy and her parents. I thought Mama was going to kill him. Every time they went out for a year after that Grant and Austin would ask him if he wanted to take his gloves with him." She giggled.

"Poor guy. Rough getting caught by the sheriff."

"Don't feel too bad for him. He can talk his way out of anything. It was just that the sheriff didn't know who he was. It was high time he got caught doing something."

"What's your favorite ride at the fair?"

"I like anything where you feel like you're flying. The Skyflyer is my favorite. I love how the wind whips in your face and you're so far off the ground you can barely see the people below you."

"You ought to try jumping out of planes." The words fell out of his mouth without much thought. He used to love that feeling, too. Those moments when you floated between the clouds and the ground, where no one could reach you, when destiny stretched out in front of you, the rush and the free fall, the lift and rip of the chute, he'd lived for that a lifetime ago.

"I can't believe you used to do that."

"Came with the job."

"I know your job was probably awful but did you like that part?"

"It wasn't always awful. I lived for the jumps."

"Whenever I get to really fly on Sundance it's the greatest part about being a cowgirl. No one can touch you while you're flying. Everything blurs around you. Everything that's important matters and everything that doesn't just fades away. It's like in that moment life makes sense. No one can get to you, you know?"

"Yeah, baby, believe me, I know."

CHAPTER NINETEEN
T-Byrd

Glancing back over his shoulder once more, T watched Griff extract the lock pick set from his pocket. They were in the shadows of a huge cottonwood but not quite as covered as he would've preferred.

Griff had spotted a side entrance to the courthouse. It was a safer bet than walking in the front but it was a push-handle door. Picking it would be far more difficult.

Taking a chance, T pulled on a glove and pressed the latch handle. To his shock, it opened.

"What the hell? They don't even lock up the freaking courthouse?" Griff huffed quietly.

"Middle of Nebraska my friend, not the middle of Baghdad. Bet the front door's locked but not this one."

They slipped inside and Griff eased the door shut. "I'm locking this. I don't want any interruptions."

"Just remember to unlock it when we leave."

"We have to go out this way, genius."

"See, if we'd come in this afternoon we could've seen all of this in the daylight," T reminded him.

"We were too busy with *Cheryl*."

"How the hell was I supposed to know she'd show up?"

"It's a small town, T. Everyone shows up because showing up is all there is to do."

T clicked his Taclight on and kept it low. There was a front counter, a desk in the corner, eight by ten photographs of mayors from the last hundred years along one wall, and three rooms with shut doors behind the counter. One was conveniently labeled *Land and Family Records*.

"This is going to be like taking candy from a baby." He immediately took photographs of the room with his phone so they'd be able to restore the things they went through to make certain no one knew anyone had been in the courthouse after hours.

"I don't know. This computer looks like it crawled up from the Carter administration. We should've brought Echo with us," Griff huffed.

"We don't need Echo for this. Boot it and see if there's anything interesting but I'm betting everything we need is in there." He pointed to the door.

"I'm not sure it'll even boot without defib paddles, man. Hang tight, I'll see."

The threadbare carpeting in the front room appeared to be older than the computer, but T was thankful for it. It did a decent job of masking their footsteps.

Griff shook his head. The computer groaned to life only to display a picture of three kids with jelly smeared faces sitting in a tree. Had to be somebody's grandkids.

"Looks like this is mostly for show. This is probably the only court-house in America that didn't get metal detectors after nine eleven.

"Nah, I bet none of these ranching towns have 'em. It's a different world. You know that."

"Yeah, I know and I want to get back to the real one. Let's check the records room."

T tried the door. "Well, you are gonna get to use your lock pick kit after all."

"Good. I'm glad something's secure. This is way too fucking easy."

The lock took less than five minutes to pick and Griff was pissy again. T rolled his eyes. "Not everything has to be difficult."

Metal filing cabinets lined every wall of the room. Griff tugged on the drawer label with a handwritten C. "Spoke too soon, my friend. Every one of these drawers is locked too." This seemed to please Griff.

"Good thing I hired a guy who can break most any lock." This lock proved no more difficult than the door.

Griff extracted a handful of manila folders. "The Camdens." He laid them on a folding table in the center of the room.

T rubbed his hands together. "I love my job."

"You take the first half. I'll take the second."

T set a Rothco anglehead flashlight on the table and they dug in. "Okay, I love my job slightly less."

"I take it you just figured out there's no filing system here. They just stick stuff in the folders however feels good."

"Mm-hmm."

An hour later, he stumbled upon something very interesting. "Hand me those birth certificates." He pointed to a neat stack by Griff.

"Okay, so Ev and Jessie have five living children, right?"

"Uh yeah, I've got Lucas, Grant, Austin, Natalie, and Holly. Here are their records."

"Yeah, so who is Brock Camden?"

"Uh..." Griff dug through papers until he located another yellow sheet of paper. "Birthdate in 1982. No death certificate that I see. Mother's signature is here. Her name is Mary Mendell Camden. No father's signature."

"Apparently, half of Camden Ranch actually belongs to him. Looks like it's nothing more than a gentlemen's agreement. It's not even typed, just handwritten."

"But he isn't one of the kids."

"Right, so who the hell is he?" The familiar feeling of discovery and digging surged through T. He loved this part.

"Hang on. Okay, I've got a marriage certificate for Everett and Jessie and one for Henry and Camille from 1952. There's one for Austin and Summer, Lucas and Indieanna, Holly and Declan St. James, who I also have immigration paperwork on, one for Grant and Kaitlyn Sommerville, and one for Brock Camden and Hope Hendrix. They've been married a while and had to have gotten married here for the certificate to be here."

"Was he adopted?"

"I haven't come across any adoption paperwork and you and I both know if he had there'd be four more folders of just that." Griff sighed.

"And I'm back to who the hell is he."

"Answer has to be here somewhere. Dig."

"Holy fuck." T lifted another set of birth certificates from one of his folders. Certainty and accomplishment surged through him. This was why he loved his job.

"What?"

"Looks like Henry and Camille had two children, Everett and Michael."

"Who's Michael? Why haven't we seen more of his shit?"

"No idea, but I'm betting I know who Brock belongs to."

"Interesting. Did Cheryl ever mention any of the Camdens while she was trying to calculate your net worth, specifically whoever Michael is?"

"I wasn't interested in her telling me all about the residents of Pleasant Glen."

"Work from what we know. Find everything you can on Brock."

"On it." They continued reading every piece of paper and stacking them according to generation and then individual families in each generation.

"There's got to be more somewhere. We're missing something. I feel it. Do you feel that?"

"No, but after serving with you for twelve years I tend to trust your feelings," Griff allowed.

T stood, stretched out his right calf. The steel rod they'd put in, making him able to walk after the incident, always made him stiff if he sat too long.

Stalking to another set of filing cabinets, he tugged on yet another drawer labeled C-L. "Dammit, open this one, too."

"Don't get your g-string in a knot." Griff popped the lock and then returned to his methodical searching.

Flipping through folder after folder, nothing caught T-Byrd's eye until he reached the last folder in the drawer. "What do we have here?"

He extracted a file from a lawyer's office. He turned to Griff with a sly grin. "I just found the Camden wills."

"Well, bring them over here. We don't have all fucking night."

T flipped through all of the standard lawyer speak laid out in every last will and testament until he reached the special family allocations and instructions.

Ink written over the typed print on one of the final pages of Henry and Camille Camden's will immediately caught his eye. "Well, I found Michael."

"And?"

T shoved the will in front of Griff. "Looks like Michael Brock Camden was written out of the will September 27, 2000. Everything was given to Everett and it was done in red ink."

A low whistle slid between Griff's teeth. "Bet that made for some bad blood."

"Yeah, but hang on. Everett's will gives each of the six children, not his five, their agreed upon portion of Camden Ranch with the stipulation that it be given to their children equally upon their deaths."

"Wait, when did A say her birthday was?" Griff sorted through one of his piles until he found Natalie's birth certificate. "September 20, 1988."

"He said whatever happened, happened just before her..."

"Twelfth birthday?"

"Holy fuck."

"If my brother molested my kid I'd do a whole fucking lot more than throw him off my ranch," Griff snarled.

"You and me both."

"So, that's what happened. This is the land they took away. Is he who we're looking for?"

"Seems like it. Sketchy details on everything but the dates though. They didn't exactly take land from anyone. It already belonged to the Camdens."

"It makes sense though. Ev gave Brock back the land that was originally willed to his sperm donor a few years ago. Who knows if Michael is even still alive?"

"I can find that out from Lincoln."

"A's gonna want harder evidence than this. You know how he is about taking shaky intel."

"Yeah, but this is it. I can feel it."

"I'd feel better if we had something more substantial."

The sound of a siren outside had both men standing and making their way to the front windows. T's heart hammered out a frantic warning. A police car from the next town over flew past the courthouse, never even slowing down. He let himself breathe again. Before he returned to the paperwork, something caught his eyes. "We're both from small towns, right?"

"Don't remind me." Griff rolled his eyes.

"Someday, I want to know what the fuck happened to you that made you so surly. Right now, think back. If anything of any significance happened where you grew up, where's the first place people went to find out about it?"

Griff began methodically placing papers back into the files they'd come from. "The newspaper," he finally stated.

T pointed to a diminutive office beside the library across the street labeled The Pleasant Glen Gazette. "Don't you think the wealthiest family in town, the one with the most land and, hell, probably the most kids, being broken up would've made the papers?"

"I'd say it's a safe bet. Guess it's too much to hope there's an online archive."

"You're dreaming. Google News is not saving stories from the *Pleasant Glen Gazette*. Trust me. But I'll bet they're on film in that newspaper office and I know there will be a microfiche machine in the library."

"They don't have metal detectors in their courthouse but they have a microfiche."

"The ways of the small town, my friend. It's kind of nice."

"We clearly have different definitions of nice and you know my rule. I only break into two buildings in one night," Griff chuckled.

"But you'll bend that for Triple A."

"Yeah, all right let's clean this up and I'll figure out how to get into the library and the newspaper office."

Fifteen minutes later, T was keeping watch while Griff silently picked the lock on the library door. It was a safe bet there was an interior door between the library and the newspaper offices, but there was only one entrance into the Pleasant Glen Library and it was front and center on Main Street.

T gave two low deliberate whistles. Their sign for hurry it the fuck up. Griff huffed in response. When he coughed, T left his position, stuck to the shadows outside the streetlights, and met Griff on the porch.

Griff pointed to a sign beside the door as they eased inside. Pleasant Glen Library Hours 9:00–7:00 Wednesdays and Saturdays Head Librarian: Hope Camden.

"Brock's wife is the librarian? Maybe we should do a little more checking in here besides just making use of the microfiche."

"I love how you seem to think the sun isn't coming up in a few hours. I keep telling you we don't have all night." Griff stalked quickly to a door on the side wall between shelves lined with books.

"Hey, I was right about there being an interior door to the newspaper office," T reminded him. "So, in a way, you are only breaking into two buildings in one night."

"Want me to get you a Skittle?"

"Red's my favorite," T goaded.

"Dude, shut the fuck up and hand me my jack knife. Everyone knows purple's the best."

A half-second later, the door to the newspaper office gave a loud pop and opened. T and Griff both cringed and stood deathly still to make certain no one had heard the door. The seconds ticked by. Nothing happened.

Griff eased inside the office and gestured for T to follow.

T shook his head. "You pull the archives for the month of September 2000. I'm going to find the machine."

Twenty long minutes later, Griff returned. His hands were full of film. "I don't think there's anything on these. I tried looking at them with the light on my phone."

"You can't see anything that way. I put the microfiche in the bathroom. Only place where we can turn it on without lighting the whole place up."

"There aren't windows in the bathroom?" Griff tilted his head right and left, popping an imaginary crick out of his neck. Something T had seen him do dozens of times, always when he was nervous. T knew Griff had been taken once, before he was with Team Seven. He didn't know what had happened to him, but he knew Griff didn't care for being in tight places with no way out.

"There are windows against the ceilings. If we keep the microfiche on the floor the little bit of light will blend in with the moonlight."

"Let's just get this done. I don't like this place."

They made quick work of setting up and started going through film. The Camden name would pop up often, but nothing of any significance. Natalie had won a horseback riding competition. Austin was calf riding at a local rodeo. Brock and Luke were working on some kind of 4-H project.

They moved on to the week of Natalie's birthday. The Camden name was oddly missing from every paper published that week. The following week was the same.

"Something not being here isn't evidence," Griff sighed.

"Nope. It isn't. Weird though."

"Agreed. Hang on I want to grab a few more rolls. I want to know when the Camdens returned to the papers." Griff slipped the rolls they'd been through back into their canisters and headed toward the newspaper file room.

T slipped back into the library. Heading to what had to have been Hope Camden's desk, he picked up a picture of two toddlers in a silver frame. There was a wedding photo of Brock and Hope's wedding and another of Brock with one of their sons on his shoulders. Looked like a stand-up guy but pictures could be deceiving.

He slid open the desk drawer and extracted a few file folders. Book orders and paperwork on some kind of book donation drive. Nothing out of the ordinary for a library. But there under the folders was a letter.

"I knew there'd be something in here," T spoke to the ether. There was no return address but the postmark was from Wilmington, North Carolina.

The envelope had already been opened, the letter already read. Keeping his Taclight between this teeth, T opened the letter.

Boisterous laughter filled the silent night. "Fuck." T slipped the letter in his jacket and darted for the bathroom. The front door banged against its casing. "Fuck, fuck, fuck." Hoisting the microfiche into his arms, he bolted through the library and shoved it back on the low shelf where he'd found it.

Griff knew the protocol if they were ever interrupted. Quickest means of escape. Phone call an hour later.

Returning to the bathroom, T climbed up on a toilet and slid one of the ancient windows lining the low ceiling to the side. Using his massive upper body strength, he hoisted himself up to the ledge and wiggled back and forth trying to squeeze himself through the small opening.

The front door of the library burst open and another round of female laughter made its way to his ears. Whoever she was she had male accompaniment.

Fuck. The glass panel of the window popped. Glass shattered.

"What was that?" The male asked.

Double fuck.

It was already broken. Maneuvering his knee upward, T kicked it out giving himself ample room to escape. His boots hit the hard dry dirt a second later. The shock of his calf trying to absorb the impact brought him to his knees.

Pain seared up his leg all the way to his groin. Bile shot to his throat. *You're a fucking Green Beret. Get up.* Gripping the brick building, he tried to pull himself upright. His leg protested. Clenching his jaw, T took two deep breaths and tried again. This time his managed to stand. Steadying himself, he knew running wasn't going to be an option so he limped toward the tree line twenty yards away.

Sirens blared. Red and blue lights were far too close for comfort. Not running was no longer an option. Gasping through the pain, he raced farther into the woods praying Griff had gotten out.

CHAPTER TWENTY

"This was so much fun. Thank you for bringing me out here." Natalie knew she was gushing but it had been the most perfect date she could ever have fathomed. She'd dreamed so many times about being a normal woman who went on dates with Aaron Weber like it was no big deal. Tonight, she'd done just that.

He was having fun too. She could tell.

"You're so damned beautiful." Intensity was once again alive in his eyes as he stared at her in the lights of the Midway. His right hand gently cradled her face. His thumb traced along her cheekbone. She loved when he did that and couldn't quite catch her breath. Her stomach leapt to her throat and then bottomed out and tumbled toward her feet. His touch was better than every single roller coaster they'd ridden.

"I am not," she scoffed. "I don't even wear makeup, just Chapstick."

"You don't need makeup. And I know you're not ready for all of this but if you keep saying shit like that the first kinky thing we try out will be me paddling your ass," he whispered in her ear.

With all of her stubborn might, Natalie tried not to be intrigued.

Another rush of wet heat soaked the crotch of her panties. Her nipples puckered against the lace of her bra.

The lift of his right eyebrow said he'd noticed. Great. "Do people really do that?"

"Lot of people really like it." He wrapped his arm over her shoulder and pointed to the cotton candy booth. She'd said she wanted some.

"My sister likes it when Dec does it."

"That's more info than I needed, babe, but why'd you ask if people really do that if you know they do?"

"I thought maybe they did it because they're both sex therapists. I figured they do a lot of stuff other couples don't do. They're... adventurous."

"Nothing wrong with being adventurous as long as you're both in agreement on what's going to happen. Pain and pleasure run very close together. Enjoying a little of one and a lot of the other makes the whole experience better for most people."

"So, you are a masochist," she teased.

"I won't lie to you. There's definitely a high that comes when you get inked. That's not why I do it, but it's there."

"You do it because there are things you want to remember don't you?"

"I'd say it's more like there are things I refuse to forget."

Biting her tongue to keep from asking what it was he refused to forget, Natalie inhaled the sweet, sticky air surrounding them and memorized the feeling of this night. He wanted to remember. She wished she could forget. Maybe those two things were like pleasure and pain. They ran oddly close together.

Not wanting their pasts to interfere with this date, she debated.

"What are you thinking about, sweetness?"

"Reading my mind again?"

"Trying my damnedest."

"What happens if I end up liking being sp—?"

Before she could quite get that last word out his lips were on hers. She gasped as his tongue dove past her lips. A soft moan slipped out next as she allowed her body to melt into his. When he pulled back, he gave her that half-smirk. "Let's maybe not ask that surrounded by kids at a fair."

White hot embarrassment, singed through her. She covered her face. Sweat broke out across her forehead. How had she forgotten where they were? There was a family with four kids all under the age of ten in front of them and a line of preteens clutching dollar bills tight in their fists behind them. Aaron was chuckling.

"I'm an idiot."

"You are sexy as hell. Griff and T-Byrd keep telling me I'm falling hard."

"Are you?"

"Oh yeah, baby."

"Me too."

"You can ask me anything you want once we're back in the truck. Want to skip the cotton candy and get out of here?"

"Definitely."

Guiding Natalie away from the innocent ears of children, Aaron wrapped his arm over her shoulder and tucked her against his side. Her warmth spread through him, easing him, healing him.

"I can't believe I almost said that back there. I really should see a doctor. I left my jacket at the Hi-Way last night. I think you're making me crazy."

Aaron vowed to himself that someday soon he would tell her T had lifted her jacket. He hated lying to her. "I thought it was my job to drive you crazy."

She stared up at him with her lips pursed and the light in her eyes more alive than he'd felt in a decade. He tried to memorize their exact color and the glow, her full pink lips, the teasing look stamped on her features. Lifting his phone from his pocket, he snapped a picture instead.

"Why did you do that?" She laughed.

"I told you, you're beautiful."

Pops of gunfire crackled behind them. "Shit. Get down." Aaron wrapped his arms over Natalie and pulled them behind a ticket booth. Pushing her head down he kept her surrounded by his body as another round sizzled closer this time.

The orange flares of the machine guns lit in his mind.

"Aaron," she whimpered.

"Shh, I've got you."

I've got you. The words wrapped around his neck, strangling him and dragging him backward in time. *"I've got you, Josh. Just fucking stay with me. Don't you die on me. Not you, too! You stay with me. You hear me?"* He grabbed his own gut. Blood filled his hands.

"Aaron!" Another voice shattered through the sand-drenched wind. His body shook. Shit was he hit again? His stomach clenched. Reaching, his hands encountered soft flesh. The world morphed around him. His vision blurred.

"Aaron! It's me! Please!" she shouted. "You're okay."

She? His eyes blinked rapidly.

"Aaron?" Her voice wavered. Was she crying? He held her tighter. Who was she?

"Aaron, it's Natalie. It's okay. Open your eyes."

Her hand touched his cheek. His fist closed around her fingers, a lifeline.

"Aaron? It's me."

She came into focus. He gasped for breath.

"Nat?" Why was she there? She shouldn't be there. He had to keep her safe. He had to get her out of there.

"It's okay. We're okay. Stupid fireworks. I'm right here. We're okay."

He nodded though he didn't fully understand.

"We're getting out of here," she vowed. When she tried to stand, he moved with her. Keeping her safe was the only thing that made sense to him.

She grabbed his hand and started to run. Running was good. Running made sense. He caught up with her.

Another round of pops shattered the darkened sky. Something inside him shook. He couldn't make it stop.

"Faster," she shouted over the crackle in the sky overhead. "Fly with me." She took off. He'd follow her anywhere. His boots pounded against the ground until he'd overtaken her. Scooping her up into his arms, he flew with them both.

CHAPTER TWENTY-ONE

"Hey, you know I've had flashbacks before. I know how awful they are." The silence in the truck cab ate at Natalie. Why wouldn't he talk to her? He just kept sitting there staring at the pumps in the gas station parking lot.

"I know. I'm sorry. I'm..." He shook his head.

"Angry, sad, embarrassed?" She listed all of the things she knew were the results of a flashback. "Your muscles and your brain ache like you've gone ten rounds with a prize bull?"

"Yeah. All of that."

Bile singed the base of her throat but she forced herself to go back to the last flashback she could recall. It had been a few years ago. Brock had grasped her hand to keep her back from a snake she hadn't seen in the grass. His hands looked so much like his father's. She'd screamed. Everyone thought it was because of the snake. It was *a* snake she supposed just not the one in the prairie.

Luke had understood what was actually happening. He'd taken her back to her parents' house. Holly and her mother had talked her through it. She remembered what had finally helped her grasp reality.

"I mean it's just such a stupid fucking thing. Fireworks. Who thought that was a good idea? It's basically colored gunpowder. So stupid. Literally no one needs that in their lives." She gave him a place to start. She gave him an out. Something to hate, somewhere to place all of the anger he refused to forget. She threw a life preserver out in the freezing sea where he was sinking before she jumped in herself. She wouldn't let him drown. Being angry at something that should never have happened was a step toward accepting it. She knew.

He stared at her with pain and hope fighting for placement in the haze of confusion in his eyes. "Yeah, they are really stupid. People get hurt fucking around with them, too."

"I know. I read that kids get burned every summer. It's ridiculous."

"Houses and barns go up in flames with them, too."

"Oh, I know. You know the farm near the Kilroys? Their kids were messing with them and caught an entire field of corn on fire. Do you know how much money they probably lost?" Natalie let the adrenaline she'd felt drive her.

"Stupid fucking things."

He gripped her hand again, clinging to her. If he needed a lighthouse, or someone to hold on to in this life, she would be that for him. Leaning across the bench seat, she brushed a gentle kiss on his cheek. There was a gash there. She'd noticed it the night she'd missed his lips and gotten his cheek instead. Every wound he'd endured she would find a way to heal. Every scar he clung to she would find some way to help him accept.

"I even read about how fireworks cause flashbacks," she continued.

Suddenly, his brow furrowed. Okay, maybe she shouldn't have said that. He managed a nod but he'd keyed in on that point more than any of the others.

"I'm really sorry about all of that. Want me to take you home?"

"No." No, no, no. She would not let him take her home so he could crawl into some kind of internal hole with no light. Never. Searching for something, anything, for them to do an idea sprang to her mind.

"Let's go in the gas station and get scratch-offs."

"What?" At least he seemed to have let that last point on fireworks go.

"When I turned sixteen, Luke gave me this huge box of scratch off lottery tickets for my birthday. It was so much fun. It's probably my favorite birthday gift ever. It's like a reminder that there's always a chance. We might win some money. We might not but that's not the point. Come on." She popped open the door of the truck praying he'd follow.

When his fingers laced through hers, she let the breath she'd been holding escape her lungs. If it had been her, she would've wanted him to pretend nothing had happened until she was ready to talk about it, so that's precisely what she did.

Marching into the gas station she gave him a beaming grin. That wasn't difficult. He always made her smile. "Okay, for scratch-offs we need Dr. Pepper, and Red Vines, and Air Heads, and Flamin' Hot Cheetos." Picking up a basket by the door, she guided him to the snack section.

"You're gonna be sick, sweetheart."

"Nah, I'm kind of a junk food junkie. My stomach has learned that there are times I need Cheetos."

"I was aware, but this is extreme even for you."

"It's the rule for scratch-offs. Don't harsh my mood, Weber," she teased.

The light made its return to his eyes. He was there with her, fully now. She thanked the universe for that.

"Never, baby." Winking at her, he picked up four snack bags of her favorite Cheetos and placed them in the basket before locating bags of Red Vines. "You sure you're okay with... everything?" leapt from his lips.

"I'm here with you. I'm much better than okay. Come on."

They made their way to the register hand in hand. "We want ten Quick 7's, ten Ruby Red Roundups, and ten Seven Elevens."

Aaron pulled one of the fifties from his wallet and laid it on the counter. She started to protest but sealed her lips instead. He'd already proven what a weak asshole he was that night. The least he could do is pay for her lottery tickets.

She all but skipped back out to his truck. When he'd come to, he was pressing her into the ground like they were being shot at. How had he not freaked her the fuck out? Strongest, bravest woman on the planet. There was no doubt.

Ripping open the bag of Red Vines, she handed him one and took one for herself. She held hers up. "To getting rich off of scratch-offs."

"I'd rather Red Vine toast you." He touched the candy pieces together.

That infectious giggle of hers worked its way through his ears and settled squarely in his chest. "Scratch." She handed him a ticket. Fishing in his pocket for the change from their purchase he handed her a quarter and did as he was told.

Keeping the tip of his tongue between his teeth kept him from apologizing constantly and begging her to forget that this night ever happened.

"Nothing," she sighed, tossed her first ticket back in the plastic sack, and grabbed another one.

"Hey, look at that, this one's worth five bucks." He showed her his match. An odd sense of satisfaction chased away a little of his hopelessness.

"See, I told you it's fun."

"Give me another one."

His next was a dud but the one after that was worth a buck.

"Look you're rich," Natalie laughed.

"Oh yeah, this six bucks is gonna get me places."

"Keep going. You're on a roll." She pressed another ticket in his palm. He gripped it and her hand. Guiding her in, he stared into her eyes. Their breaths mingled. Electricity sizzled between them.

"Kiss me," she whispered.

The ticket was lost in the floorboard as he drew her in and layered his lips to hers. She tasted like cherry candy and her, confection and heat. That sweet little gasp she always made when he did this erased more of his shame. Her right hand worked down his chest. She stopped at the end of his rib cage, leapt over the scars on his abs, and palmed his cock.

His hum of approval vibrated against her lips but he wasn't doing this again. He refused to take more than he gave. Never again. The next time he came with her it would be deep inside her pussy after he'd made her weak with orgasm after orgasm.

Their conversation standing at the cotton candy stand rushed back into this consciousness. Things had been going so many good places before his past had ruined everything. Why couldn't he escape the damn thing for one night? Just one fucking night.

Her head fell back offering him an undeniable invitation. He spun his tongue and suckled with his greedy lips against her throat. She shivered and his cock pulsed out its hunger for her.

His hands traced the cups of her bra. Her breasts spilled over the top. Her nipples strained against the lace between them and the palms of his hands. His sweet, needy baby. "They hurt, sweetheart? Are they tender for me?"

"Oh God, yes." Her breaths quickened.

Before he lifted her shirt, the sound of a truck horn reminded him where they were. She jerked back. A truck driver parked at the diesel pumps gave him two thumbs up. Aaron cringed.

"Okay, maybe we shouldn't park here." Natalie squeezed her eyes shut.

"I can't get anything right tonight."

"Stop it. We're having a good time. Let's finish the tickets, go get our money, and then we could go up to King's Creek."

King's Creek had long been the make out spot of couples young and old in Pleasant Glen. "You ever been up there before?"

She shook her head. "Not with a guy."

He'd be her first. He'd make her come for him, in the fogged up windows of his old truck, grinding in his lap with her tits bouncing in his face, calling out his name. A wave of greedy arrogance washed through him. Instead of calling himself an asshole he rode it for all he was worth. That night, after everything that had happened, he needed the jolt of confidence.

"Give me the tickets. I want to get you out of here."

She licked her lips. "I want that, too."

They worked through the tickets. Aaron's last scratch was actually worth a hundred bucks. His mouth hung open in shock.

"See! You never know. There's always a chance. Things get better," she vowed earnestly.

"Nah. I think you're just good luck."

"I kind of think we're good together."

"I think so too, Nat. I'm really sorry about…"

Her index finger landed on his lips again. "You have nothing to be sorry about. Let's go get your cash."

"I'm spending it on you."

"You better not."

"I am. Hey, your birthday is coming up. What do you want?"

"To do something with you."

The girl sure as hell knew how to stroke his ego and his cock. "Okay, what do you want to do with me?"

A decidedly naughty grin formed on her kiss-swollen lips.

"You think I'm gonna be able to wait that long? You're giving me way too much credit, babe."

"Never said anything about it being the first time." She batted her eyelashes at him as he threw open the door to the gas station for her.

CHAPTER TWENTY-TWO

Excitement bubbled in Natalie's stomach. She willed Aaron's truck to move faster. She wanted his arms around her again, his lips against her skin. Even better than that was the fact that he needed her touch as well.

Before they'd been rudely interrupted, every kiss had held a promise that their pasts could fade away as long as they were together. They needed this.

She wiggled in her seat again. Her panties were so wet they were uncomfortable. She wished she knew for certain if he took them off that she wouldn't end up where he'd been a few hours before.

"You okay, baby?" He squeezed her hand as open fields full of cornstalks flew past the windows.

"Not really."

"What's wrong? Need me to stop?"

"Don't stop. Get there faster."

His right eyebrow ticked upwards. He glanced at her. "You wet for me, baby?"

"Yes." Her vow was a half-whispered plea.

Another one of those hungry groans filled the truck. He slowed down. She huffed out her frustration. "I'm gonna take good care of you, sweetheart. I swear to you. I'm gonna make everything feel better. Do you know who owns this land?"

Furrowing her brow she studied the surrounding cornfields. They were almost to the railroad tracks that ran behind the one road that made up Pleasant Glen. "This is Kilroy land."

"Any of the Kilroy boys go wandering around in their fields at night?"

"Are you asking if they'd care if we park out here for a little while?"

He nodded.

"Tucker has been Luke's best friend since they were in kindergarten. He wouldn't care if I was out here no matter what I was doing."

There was a slip of land between two fields. The corn was almost ready to be harvested. It was taller than the truck. Aaron expertly hid them away. She launched herself into his lap.

"Nat, baby, you are driving me wild." He had her shirt unbuttoned in three seconds flat. A confidence she only felt when she was on top of a horse surged through her. Her brain and her body aligned for once in her life. The fear slipped further away. She couldn't even access it.

Rising up on her knees she pressed her crotch to his and slid down against the fierce rigidity of his cock. Pleasure sizzled from her clit outward. Another surge of wet heat coated the lips of her pussy. "Oh God," whimpered from her much too loudly.

"Feels good doesn't it, baby?" He popped the snap of her jeans and lowered the zipper. "My God, you are soaking wet. So needy. It hurts doesn't it? Can I touch you, Nat? Can I make it feel better?"

"Yes, now." Pride and need welled in her soul. She wasn't afraid.

His fingertips tenderly traced along the top of her panties. A shiver worked through her.

"Let me feel how wet you are for me."

Her breath stalled in her lungs. She writhed against him. Longing clawed under her skin. The air around her took on her frantic pulse. He teased at the curls covering her mound. She rose up on her knees again. His tender touches zinging through her until she was dizzy with need. Finally, mercifully, his fingers circled her clit giving her sweet relief.

His cock throbbed against her. She needed more. The emptiness physically hurt. It burned. She needed to be filled.

"Aaron, please."

He growled out his pleasure. "Tell me what you need."

"Please, please." She wasn't certain what to ask for. "More."

She rose up on her knees again. His fingertips traced lower, exploring her lips. They felt swollen against his touch. Pressing against her clit with the palm of his hand, he gently slicked two fingers at her opening. "So fucking wet. My God, honey. You are ready aren't you?"

"Please." She gripped his shirt and scratched at his chest seeking anything to cling to. He dipped one finger deep within her. Her body cinched around him as she bucked.

"Look at me," he demanded. The commanding thrum of his voice pushed her closer to the edge.

Her eyes fluttered open. Primal urgency blazed in his gaze. It burned away her ability to think at all. "You want more, honey? Tell me. You're so fucking tight. I don't want to hurt you."

Her mind scrambled. Whatever he'd offered she wanted. "Yes," flew from her lips. He opened her wider. Her body rejoiced. The pressure increased, coiling constantly behind her mound. He pressed deeper, taking more.

His lips latched around her right nipple under the lace of her bra. She whimpered as he sucked. The ministrations of his mouth made her raw. She understood. The pain registered instantly as pleasure.

Some sound she didn't understand shattered through his masculine moans.

"What...?" she tried to determine what was ringing.

"Right here, baby. Keep your eyes on me. Let me give you what you need."

Another grind. She walked a cliff of arousal. Afraid to fall. Afraid not to. She shook. The pressure mounted until she was certain she could feel it all the way up to her eyeballs. "That's it. Let it feel so good for me."

The ringing increased in volume. It was ceaseless. She stopped moving. "What if...?"

"Come on, Nat. Ignore it," he demanded.

She couldn't. The texts alerts on his phone came between every ring. "What if someone needs you?"

"You're the only one I give a damn about, baby." Frustration ground in his voice.

"Check that." She stopped altogether, shuddering as he eased his fingers away.

"Whoever the fuck this is I'm going to kill them." He jerked his phone off of the console. "What?" he seethed.

But a moment later the frustration melted from his face. Concern replaced it. His jaw tensed with every "Uh-huh," he spoke. "I'll be right there."

"Who was that?"

Still unable to process much beyond the fact that he'd had Natalie ten seconds away from an orgasm, Aaron cranked the truck. The musk of her arousal clung to his fingers. God, when he got Griff and T out of whatever fucking trouble they were in, he was going to kill them.

"Aaron?" she was frantic with worry now.

Trying to come up with something to tell her that wasn't a complete lie, he drew a deep breath only serving to bring more of her flavors to his nostrils. "Uh, it was T. Remember they had a thing they were doing tonight?"

"Oh my God. They're hurt aren't they? They got caught or something. I had a bad feeling as soon as T said that."

"They're not caught, but T is hurting. Things didn't go quite the way they'd planned though. I need to go pick them up."

"I'm going with you."

Given the fact that T was currently hiding in Moorer's woods behind the library in Pleasant Glen and couldn't find Griff there was no way that was happening. "No, you're not. I'm taking you home." *The long way since Sheriff Wilheim is apparently camped out in the library parking lot with his lights on.* He couldn't let her see that.

"What if you get hurt? I can't... You have to take me with you."

"Baby, I can't take you with me. I'm sorry."

"But I won't know if you're okay."

Once again the remnants of his heart swelled in his chest. For a second, they almost felt whole. Sweet angel. No one had ever worried over him like this except maybe his foster parents. "I'll be fine, sweetheart. I'll call you when I find them and get them out."

"You don't even know where they are?" Her voice rose several octaves.

"I'll find them."

"You better call me and come to my house when you're done so I know you're okay. I want to see you so you don't just say you're okay if you aren't."

"I promise, and Nat, I'm sorry this night sucked."

"It didn't. I loved most of it, just not this part. Are you sure you're okay to go help them? Maybe Voodoo or Echo should go. Won't that remind you of...?"

"I'll be fine."

CHAPTER TWENTY-THREE

"Why are you going this way?"

Damn, he'd hoped she wouldn't notice. "Just did it out of habit I guess." The number of times he'd lied to her in the last five minutes made him sick.

T had said they had the name of the man who'd hurt her. That kept Aaron from losing it. He'd get them out of whatever trouble they were in and then demand they tell him everything they'd found. After that, he'd go to her house and if she'd let him, he'd make her come all night long. On his fingers, on his tongue, on his cock, however she'd allow him to make this up to her.

He circled Rural Route 11 and sped toward Camden Ranch, making it to the North gates, instead of the main entrance, in record time.

"Aaron, promise me you'll be okay."

"I swear, Nat. I'll be fine. Don't worry about me. Go on to sleep."

"No. Not until I see you." Her stubborn cowgirl pride was out in full-force. "I could help you, you know? I've been out to Cottonwood Springs loads of times. I know my way around."

"Nat, come on. You know I can't take you with me." Aaron recalled T-Byrd telling her they were working in Cottonwood that night. Between his own lies and his teams this was going to get tricky.

"Why?"

"I don't know what I might find when I get there."

"All the more reason I should go."

"No."

She turned away from him glaring out the passenger side window. Shit. As furious as he was with T, he was angrier with himself. He'd set this whole thing up. He reminded himself that he had to know who'd hurt her. He had to end them.

"Just let me off here. I'll walk," she demanded. They were passing her parents' house and almost a mile from her own.

"No. I have to know you're home safe."

"Exactly. You get to know I'm safe but I don't know if you are."

Fuck it. "Nat, I was a Green Beret. I've done stuff far more dangerous than this will be half asleep. I will be fine. I'll come here as soon as I get them back to wherever T's truck is."

"You better." She flung herself out of the truck when they came into sight of her house. Aaron slammed on the brakes before her feet hit the ground. She gave him one more vicious glare when she turned.

"Hey, Nat." He went with it. He had to. Nothing about it made sense but she had to know. In that moment he desperately needed to offer her the single truth he prayed would make all of the lies he'd told that evening worth it.

"What?"

"I'm pretty sure I'm in love with you. I'll be back later."

Her mouth fell open. "You're just going to tell me that before you go off and do whatever it is you're going to do?"

"Yeah, because you deserve to know. I love you. There, I said it, but I have to go, babe. Please don't be so mad at me. I can't stand for you to hate me." *I'm doing this for you.*

"I don't hate you." The wind captured her whispered words. He read her lips instead.

"Good." Reaching across the truck cab, he pulled the door shut and backed up. He had to go rescue his friends. It was what he did. It was who he was.

There was only one road through the Glen. Aaron parked his truck at Old Man Rasmussen's. Racing into his home, he cleared his mind, refusing to fully focus on what he knew he needed to do. Going on with it, he pulled a baseball cap low over his eyes, emptied the change from his pockets, and put on a black hoodie. He silenced his phone and removed his belt. No noise. T thought someone was looking for them.

Easing out the door after a quick pat to both of his dogs, he walked into town following the tree line, staying off the road.

He texted T. *Passing the bar. Sheriff's car is still in front of the library but the lights are off.*

A response came almost immediately. *Griff's here. We've moved further into the woods. A klick due south from library.*

Sit tight.

Cutting behind the dumpsters at Saddlebacks Aaron mentally calculated how far the library was from the bar. T's truck was in the parking lot. Praying everyone assumed he'd gotten lucky and had gone home with some cowgirl, Aaron focused on his current mission. He needed to head southeast to avoid being seen by the Sheriff or anyone else out at this hour. He had to bisect the prairie land between the back of the buildings that ran behind Main Street and Moorer's Woods.

The cold Nebraskan dirt would offer him no coverage. He had to get to the woods quickly. They'd have to wait until the sheriff left to make their escape. It was a clear night with a three-quarter moon. He could do this without a flashlight. His gut was a better guide anyway.

Pulling out his phone again, he flipped to the picture he'd taken of Natalie just before he'd lost his fucking mind. That smile. Those eyes. Jesus Christ, those lips. The way she looked at him. If he just kept her in the forefront of his mind, hiking a klick through the woods to find members of his team wouldn't rush the past back into the chasm he'd carefully crafted between him and what had been. The space had to remain empty. He couldn't traverse it, couldn't attempt to recall any part of it, couldn't resurrect anything from its barren landscape. Keeping it at arm's length was the only way he remained sane. Its intrusion that very night proved he wasn't strong enough to allow it to have any part of his life now.

Natalie. She was the only thing that mattered. This was all for her.

He'd find the man who'd effectively draped a dark cloak over her light, taking something that never belonged to him. He'd end him. He would keep her from ever having to be afraid again. He loved her too much to ever let her fear hurt her again.

Softening his footfalls, he listened intently. Something was moving. The rhythmic crunch of leaves sounded human. Slipping into the shadow of a Birch, he barely breathed. He wasn't even half a klick away from the bar. There was no way this was T or Griff.

The low beam of a flashlight bounced in the distance. Aaron's training took over. Pulling the hoodie over his hat, he crotched low keeping himself in the darkest sliver of shade. He pressed his body against the massive tree trunk. A cluster of dead leaves remained low on the Birch. The autumn winds hadn't gotten to them yet. He accepted their offered coverage.

Running his fingers through the dirt at his feet he dusted it over his face to keep the moonlight from outing his location. Bile swam in his throat. The last time he'd done that... No. He wasn't going there. He couldn't.

The hardwood at his back absorbed his pulse. He kept his breaths shallow and steady. He had no weapon, save a jack knife in his pocket. Silently, he reached into his pocket and eased it out.

How fucked up was it that they were in this mess because he'd asked for their help? If it weren't for himself, he'd be tucked up in bed with Natalie holding her in his arms, safe and warm. And yet, the only way to know she would always be safe was to go on with his mission.

That was always the way. The give and the take of every assignment. He'd played the game. He'd known the risks. He'd made it work until the amount that was taken was simply more than he had to give. The scales had tipped so far out of balance he could never restore them and yet here he was.

The footsteps grew closer. Who the fuck was out in these woods in the middle of the night? More importantly, *why* were they out here? What exactly had T and Griff done on his behalf?

"Dang blastit, you kids! We've got you dead to rights! I heard you walking," rang through the air in a decidedly Southern accent.

Aaron fought not to even grin though he wanted to laugh. Deputy

Clarke Newsome had to be one of the biggest idiots Aaron had ever met. He had a hearty case of Barney Fife syndrome and didn't seem willing to seek treatment. Bring it on, Deputy. You want to play with Berets let's see how well that works for you.

Jerking his hood back, Aaron stood and stalked toward the Deputy.

"Now, you just stop right there. I hear you," the Deputy screamed to the trees behind him, the opposite direction from where Aaron was walking. Dear God, this was almost comical.

"Deputy? That you?" Aaron called.

"Who's there?" Newsome spun.

"It's me, Aaron Weber. Saw some guys running behind my place and followed them out here. They went that way." He pointed the opposite direction from where Griff and T were hiding out.

"It's the ones who busted into the library. I knew we'd find them out here. I've been telling the town council for a coon's age that we need to cut back Moorer's Woods. It's a hotbed for thugs and criminal types. I hate to say I was right but here we are."

"You want to cut down the woods because of a nonexistent crime problem in town?" Aaron spoke quickly.

"Absolutely. You give 'em an inch they take a mile. I'll just bet it was them Culver boys. Nothing but trouble."

Aaron knew Ted Culver. Poor guy had four sons all of whom had enough energy to run a nuclear sub station. They weren't bad kids just ran a little wild from time to time.

"Don't go too hard on 'em." He edged closer. "Bet they didn't really mean to do any harm." Having the deputy convinced it was someone else worked well for Aaron, but he hoped the Culver boys all had alibis.

"I told the Sheriff that Brock's wife must not of locked the library up the right way and they popped the lock. Doesn't look like they took nothing, but still, that's a B&E."

"Breaking and entering?" Aaron sighed. Why the library? And he'd bet Hope Camden had locked up the library perfectly well. Griff could pick any lock anywhere. He refocused. "Want me to help you look for them?" Solidifying his own innocence in one quick offer. Intelligence 101. Would never have worked on anyone with any experience whatsoever but Aaron played the hand he'd been dealt. He also knew Deputy

Newsome would want full credit for finding his imaginary perpetrators. He'd never accept help.

"Nah, now I know you've got some military experience what with them tattoos and muscles and all, but this is police business. It's way out of your league. You head back on to Rasmussen Farm and stay inside. This could get ugly."

"Yeah, this is definitely not something I've done before." Aaron rolled his eyes. "Hey, did you say the Sheriff is staked out at the library?" He hadn't, but working this particular target was just too easy.

"Yeah, he keeps thinking whoever broke in will return to the scene of the crime. It's hogwash but he says he's gonna stay up there for a while. I'm out doing the real police work. I just hope you citizens remember this when I make my run for sheriff."

"Oh, I have no doubt we'll remember all you've done for the community. Like I said, they headed that way."

"I heard ya the first time." Newsome bathed the quiet woodland with yellow light from his flashlight before he headed the direction Aaron needed him to go.

Natalie paced from her living room to her kitchen and back again. She was going to wear holes in the parquet if she kept this up. The way he'd thrown his body over hers when his mind told him they were under attack replayed over and over in her head.

Maybe if he hadn't had such a rough night she wouldn't worry this way. Shaking her head, she knew she would, but he had no business throwing himself back in any kind of situation that might bring on another flashback. God, why were men so stubborn?

"You cannot just tell someone you're in love with them and then leave and go do something stupid," she shouted at the emptiness in her home. "Ugh." Had he said that because she was mad? Did he really love her? They'd only really just begun dating. And if they did love each other what did that mean? Did things change? Is this how it worked? All of her brothers and even Holly swore they'd fallen head over boots for their spouses the moment they saw them. It was supposed to be the Camden way of falling in love.

Well, that was stupid. That couldn't possibly be how love worked. Could it? The first time she'd seen Aaron he'd been shaking Ed Olsen's hand. He'd just accepted the open bartender position at Saddleback's.

That same kind of strange flutter she'd experienced the night before had begun in her belly and moved outward until it had taken over her brain. She'd tried to introduce herself and couldn't seem to recall her own name. No other man had ever had that effect on her. He was gorgeous but that wasn't what had tangled her vocal cords that afternoon. It had been the pain in his eyes, the lost hollowness she wanted to erase from existence. It had been the easy tenor of his voice and his hands. She would readily admit to falling in love with his hands the first time she'd seen them. But him? Is that what this was? She was furious with him for leaving, and yet, she couldn't wait for him to return. She wanted to hit him and be wrapped up safely in his arms and never leave.

A soft knock sounded on her door and she propelled herself to it. Her feet barely touched the ground. Jerking it open, she gasped when she saw her mother standing on her front porch, dressed in her favorite flannel pajamas and worn terrycloth robe. She was carrying a plate of oatmeal raisin cookies, Natalie's favorite.

"Mama, what are you doing here?"

"I know I'm not who you were wanting to be standing here, but I went out to check that late calf we had yesterday. I saw your light on and thought I'd come check on you, too, since Aaron's truck raced by my house about an hour ago."

"It's two o'clock in the morning."

"I'm not sure if you noticed darlin' but mothers don't really get time off. It's pretty much a twenty-four seven commitment. I petitioned for Sundays off but I was denied, twice."

"Well, come on in."

Natalie led her mother to the kitchen, hating that she'd worried her enough to get her out of bed.

Jessie pulled the plastic wrap off of the plate while Natalie made two mugs of tea. They settled at the kitchen table. "Now, Aaron isn't here and you're madder than a freshly baptized cat. You wanna tell me what happened?"

"While we were at the fair in North Platte, he had a flashback to some time when he was under attack in the Middle East. The fireworks got to him. He was so embarrassed and he doesn't need to be. Then his friends from when he was back in the army called him and needed him to come rescue them or something. He could be in danger or he could have another flashback and I..."

"And you are in love with him and more scared than my fearless girl has ever been in her life."

"I'm not fearless."

"Interesting that's the only thing you denied."

Natalie huffed. "I can't be in love with him. I've only been dating him a few days."

"Doesn't even take that long and you've been in love with him for years, sweet girl. But you come by your stubbornness honest so go on with it."

"I'm mad at him." There, she'd said it. "He's supposed to be here with me. Then I would be with him if he has another flashback and I could—"

"Take care of him?"

"Yes."

"You ever think that whatever he's out doing is to take care of you?"

"What? No. He's out helping his friends. It doesn't have anything to do with me."

"Funny thing about love. Turns out once you fall in it everything you do is about the other person. Even the most inconsequential things."

Natalie took a cookie off the plate and picked one of the plump raisins out of the top. They were her favorite part. Her mother chuckled. "Before your daddy and I married I was living here on the ranch but didn't know nothing about how to run it. He told me he was going burnin' one day. I didn't know what on earth he was setting fire to but I remember thinking I wished it was your uncle."

Natalie huffed. "Too bad it wasn't."

"Anyway, he set out and all I could think was he was messing around with fire and how that didn't sound too safe to me. I realized in that moment that it didn't matter if I'd only been with him for a week or two I couldn't make it without him. My entire life had changed in a split second. Scared the pure piss outta me. I was hell-bent on helping him do whatever it was he was gonna do because you see, me not knowing a dang thing about ranching *clearly* meant I was gonna be able to save him from something he'd been doing all his life." The lift of her mother's eyebrows accentuated her point.

Natalie rolled her eyes. "Daddy didn't have PTSD and he hasn't lived through what Aaron's lived through."

"But you have?"

"Well, no, but—"

"But you're certain if you were with him everything would be all right. And that right there is how I know you finally found the man who's worthy of my little girl. He's got some scars, had a few days I'm sure he'd much rather he didn't have, but so do you. You may not be able to help him do whatever it is he's out there doing, but you want to help him. You'd do most anything to protect him, just like I wanted to do with your daddy on that fire truck. The fact that you're fighting mad tells me all I need to know. That's the thing about love and fear. They couldn't be more different and yet most of the time they go hand in hand. Difficult thing to love something so much you're terrified to ever let it go."

"Why do you always have to be right?"

Her mother laughed. "I'm not always right, Nat, but I can tell you this, he loves you, too. And you're not the only one who's scared, sugar. Long row to hoe between here and where you're headin' and you gotta walk every blasted mile of it. I know this, too, no matter what happens between here and there, no matter how hard you have to fight, it will be worth it.

"There were weeks of your life that I wasn't sure I'd ever see my baby girl smile again. Past few days, it's all you do. Even when your brothers and your daddy are beating their proverbial chests trying to protect you, all you do is grin. You keep this faraway look in your eyes, like you've just discovered a secret that makes life worth living. And, sweetheart, I s'pose you have.

"You've come so far from those dark days. I'm so proud of you. I know how hard you've fought. Just look at my girl now. You're so strong and brave, Natalie. Never forget that. Never forget your own strength. I'll tell you this, too, he needs you, baby girl. He's been strong for so long. He stopped fighting an endless battle in that desert over there but he never stopped fighting the battle in his mind. Difficult thing teaching a man how to be in love when he doesn't believe he deserves to be loved."

"How do you know he thinks like that?"

"A mama knows, and when I get done beating your daddy and your brothers back out of their caves we're all gonna love up on him. Not gonna be easy, but it's gonna be worth it. Love always is. I 'spect he knows what he's doing with his friends tonight. He'll be all right, but making him believe he's worth lovin', well, that might take more strength that you ever knew you had. I know you have it. I've always known."

"He told me he loved me just before he left. Do you think he said that 'cause he knew he was pissing me off?"

Her mother's laughter filled her kitchen. The cold evening air that had settled in her old house took on the warmth of the laughter, like her mama had wrapped a soft quilt around her shoulders and brushed a kiss on her cheek. "No, I 'spect he said it 'cause he means it."

Natalie considered that, weighing her next question terrified if she allowed it to escape the tight seal of her lips her words might somehow bring it into existence. She bit her lip, frantic to keep the words locked away where they couldn't cause any harm.

Her mother reached across the worn wood table and squeezed her hand. "Ask me."

"Do you think he said it tonight, just before he left, because he's gone off to do something dangerous and maybe he won't...be able to say it later?"

Her mother shook her head. Tears sprung to her eyes.

"Why are you crying?" Panic jolted through Natalie.

"Not because I think anything's gonna happen to Aaron, sugar. You really think if I believed for a moment that my future son-in-law was gonna go out risking his neck and not be just fine that I woulda let him off of my ranch? I thought you had more faith in me." She winked at

Natalie. "I'm cryin' because I'm gonna have to put up with your daddy losing another one of his baby girls and Lord help me he don't handle that well." She laughed again.

"Mama."

"I'm teasing you. I'm crying because it's hard to watch your young'uns grow up and fall in love. I'm crying because one minute I look at you and all I can see in my mind's eye is the braids I put in your hair flying out behind you when you rode your horse faster and harder than any of your brothers. The next moment I see my beautiful baby girl all grown up ready to take on this world with a man who's deserved someone like you in his life for so long. And the Good Lord's finally seen fit to get you two together, but that don't make it easy to let you go.

"He's already telling you things he won't even tell himself. Bet that'll drive him up one hay bale and over another when he realizes it. Let out a little rope, baby girl, and settle on down in that saddle. Getting Aaron Weber where he needs to be is gonna be one hell of a ride. You remember all them times Sundance hurled you to the ground when you were trying to break her?"

"Yeah, my ass still hurts just thinking about it."

"Things worth having in this life don't often go down without a fight."

CHAPTER TWENTY-FOUR

Aaron gave another two-toned deliberate whistle followed by a higher pitched one. Scanning the trees and brush surrounding him, he got no response so he hiked deeper into the woods. His next signal was met with a matching whistle. He followed the sound another hundred paces.

"T?" he called.

"Right here."

Aaron almost tripped over him. He was burrowed down in the leaves. "You are aware this is the Pleasant Glen Sheriff's Department after you not M.P.'s right?"

"Hey, I wasn't taking any chances. I'm not going to jail tonight, and I can't run."

Griff stepped out from behind a tree, buckling his belt. "Sorry. Had to piss."

"What the hell did you two do?"

"Well, we found your guy for one."

Aaron sank down beside his friends. "Talk."

"It's more like show but I'd rather do this in my truck than in the woods. Can we get back?"

"Not sure. According to the deputy, the sheriff is staked out at the library convinced you'll return to the scene of the crime. We can head that way but I'm not sure we can get to your truck without him noticing. Assuming he's still out there."

"You talked to the deputy?" Griff asked.

"Yeah, he was heading this way. I saved your asses, once again."

"Hey, man, you may be out but you'll always be Triple A," Griff vowed.

"Amen," T agreed.

"Just tell me what you found."

"I've got something you need to read, but apparently it was her uncle." T turned his phone on. "I'm almost out of battery so look quick." He revealed a picture of what looked like a rewritten will.

"Who's Micheal Camden?" Aaron enlarged the photo.

"All I know is he has a son named Brock."

"Holy fuck. It never even occurred to me that Brock wasn't Ev and Jessie's." Somewhere in the recesses of his mind Aaron had known that. He was a cousin not a sibling. He'd just never put two and two together. Some intelligence officer. He'd clearly lost his edge. "So, where is he? He's not in the Glen. I know that."

"Looks like he was banished from Nebraska itself. I have no idea where he is but I'll figure that out once I get back to the office. I can't promise you he's still living."

"He is. I can tell when she thinks about him. I can see it in her eyes."

Moon-washed sorrow formed on T and Griff's features. Natalie would hate their pity. He hated it on her behalf. "By the way I'm gonna kill you for what you interrupted."

Griff chuckled. "Sorry, A. We thought we were had. We both dove out of back windows. My phone shattered when I fell and this is not exactly territory we know a lot about."

"We did find your guy. That should count for something," T argued.

"Doubt it replaces him getting down and dirty tonight," Griff goaded.

"Thanks for figuring it out. I appreciate your help," Aaron offered.

"That's our job."

"Can I ask why the hell you went to the library?"

"Because that courthouse file room is less organized than a circus sideshow," Griff huffed.

"That explains nothing."

"I wanted to see what was in the papers the weeks surrounding the incident," T elaborated. "I don't know who the hell figured out we were in the library, but that's where I found the letter."

"What letter?"

"Not out here. I want you to be able to really see it. It's gonna piss you the fuck off. I'd rather not be there when you read it, actually. We were looking at old newspaper clippings when two people stumbled in. Pretty sure they were drunk. I didn't stick around long enough to figure out why the hell they were in the library, however."

"This has to be the most action this town has seen in a decade. Nothing ever happens in the Glen. That's why I like it here."

"You know when we come to town shit gets interesting." T laughed.

"Why's the letter gonna piss me off?"

"Telling you is the same as you reading it. I don't want to be around when you start putting your fists through trees. Plus, you have to figure out how to get the damned thing back in Hope Camden's desk before she realizes it's gone."

"Fuck. All right, let's head back and see if the sheriff's still on his stakeout," Aaron commanded. "I need to get back to Nat. She was all kinds of pissed I left her."

"She's got it bad for you, brother. Hope you're ready to settle down."

Aaron offered no response.

"Question remains, now that you know who hurt her what are you gonna do about it?" Griff demanded as they began their slow trek back toward town, offering T hands when he needed them.

"I'm still working on that. First person I want to talk to is Brock. I plan on sending this uncle of hers straight to hell but how I go about it remains to be seen."

"You sure that's a good idea?" Concern riffed in Griff's tone.

"I will not let someone that scares her like he does continue to walk the face of this planet." Aaron tried not to be offended but truthfully he was.

"You ever think she might not want you risking a life in prison for killing this douche?"

"I won't get caught."

"A, man, this isn't Iraq. You don't have license to do this no matter what he's done."

"I'm still gathering. I'll let you know when I plan to move."

T shook his head. "I need you to tell me that you know getting her isn't the prize for choking whatever little life is left in this bastard. Don't get this fucked up in your head, A. Don't trade in everything you've got sitting in the palm of your hand because you think you haven't done enough to earn it first."

"Fuck off, T. Thank you for your help. I'll get you out of here, but I don't need you telling me what needs to happen in my life after here. You got that?"

Griff huffed. "That ain't the way this works and you know it. We're a team, A. Always will be. Whether you want to work for the agency or not, we're not gonna let you fuck this up with Natalie. Go back and talk to your shrink or do whatever you need to do to get your head straight. This isn't some random shitstack that no one knows and no one will miss if we let you off him. This is her uncle. I know you never believe us when we say this but, no matter what he did, killing him isn't gonna absolve you of whatever shit it is you feel like you've got to make up for. You don't owe anybody anything, not even her."

Rage snarled in Aaron's head. Never before had he wanted to beat the shit out of one of his remaining team members. His jaw tightened until his molars ached. Griff had no fucking clue what he was talking about. It wasn't his fault half their team was murdered in cold blood.

"Let's just get out of here."

It was just after three when Aaron's truck spit gravel from his back tires in an effort to get down the long gravel road that would ultimately lead him to Natalie's home. He prayed she'd gone on to sleep but knew she wouldn't.

He silenced his truck engine near her carport but hadn't made it out when she propelled out the side door and flew to him.

Catching her in her leap, he chuckled. "Hey, baby." Her legs wrapped around his waist and she squeezed him for all she was worth. The letter was tucked inside his T-shirt and the waistband of his jeans. He had to read it and then figure out how to get it back inside Hope's desk.

For the moment, he told himself to enjoy the feeling of her wrapped around him. "When I saw you running out here I didn't know if you were coming to hug me or whip my ass. Figured I'd let you do either."

"Would you shut up for a minute," she huffed.

"Yes, ma'am. Shall I carry you back in the house before you freeze your gorgeous little ass off?"

"I told you to shut up. Do it." Her index finger landed on his lips. He kept her balanced against him with ease.

Trapping his laughter behind his lips, he kissed her fingertip and then followed orders.

"Good. Now, I love you, too, you big stupid army man, and you better not ever scare me like that again."

That did it. All of the terror and insanity the night had held burst out of his mouth in delirious laughter. "Big, stupid army man? What am I like some kind of life-sized G.I. Joe figure or something?"

"You are still talking. Stop it. I'm not finished. I know we're both scared and I know you hate what happened tonight with the fireworks but I don't want you to hate that. I understand what it's like. Just please don't be ashamed of anything. We have to figure out how to be in love, because I love you, too."

"You keep saying that."

"Again with the talking."

"Sorry. Go on." He tried to contain the mountain of questions behind his smirk. She couldn't possibly love him. Even if she did she wouldn't if she ever found out how badly he could fuck up life if given half a chance.

"I do love you. I'm pretty sure I always have. I used to have a Cowgirl Barbie doll. She was the only one I ever played with but she annoyed me because I couldn't get her boots on and her outfit was stupid. I also cut that ridiculous rainbow braid off of her horse's mane but that's beside the point. I left her nekkid most of the time and I used to put her in bed in our dollhouse with one of Grant's G.I. Joe dolls because he was way hotter than Ken."

"Am I allowed to talk now?"

"Yes."

"Only thing I really hated about tonight was leaving you needy. I'll figure the rest of the shit out. Right now, I need to take care of my girl."

"Did you get the point of my story?"

"About the Barbie?"

"Yes."

Aaron racked his brain. It seemed like she was just recalling a humorous moment from her childhood. He'd hoped she clung to more of those than the awful ones. He also hoped Grant didn't mind her calling his G.I. Joes dolls. That was all he'd come away with. "Maybe I didn't get the point, baby. I'm sorry."

She gave him her customary eye roll. His cock twitched anxiously and that damned letter burned on between them. The corner of it dug into one of his scars with every minute adjustment of her body against him.

"The point is I'm ready. I'm not scared, just a little nervous maybe."

Ready to do what? The late hour, the flashback, the fight with Griff it racked in his gut. He was exhausted and living on nothing more than the memories of her on the brink of orgasm in his truck. Realization erupted in his foggy brain. Holy fuck. She was ready.

"Baby, even if you do love me, that doesn't mean we have to push this or go faster than you're ready. It's only been a few days since we decided we were doing this."

That earned him another eye roll. "Get me nekkid, take me to bed, and let's pretend we're Barbie and G.I. Joe."

He couldn't. If for no other reason than he had to get rid of the letter before he could strip. She could never know what they'd done that night and what they'd figured out.

"Let me get a shower first." There was dirt ground into his face. He was covered in leaves and a shower would buy him some time. "Then if you're sure, we'll see."

She leaned her head into his sweatshirt, inhaling deeply. The letter crinkled against his jeans. "Will you just tell me where you were exactly? You smell like Moorer's Woods."

Using every ounce of Special Forces training he'd ever been given, he kept his panic at bay. "Moorer's Woods has a smell?" He knew it did but tried to sound surprised.

"Yeah, it's because all of the Cedar trees. I love it out there."

"There are Cedar trees in Cottonwood, too, babe. I was out there looking for Griff and T who were being dumbasses and almost got caught. Nothing more to it. I got them out." Half-truths were still lies. He doubled down on his own self-loathing. She wanted to sleep with him. She trusted him enough to do that and all he'd done all fucking night was lie to her.

Ripping him out of the abyss he'd hurled himself into, her fingers tunneled through his dirty hair. A heartbeat later, her lips were on his.

She tasted like warm cookies and cinnamon tea. Sweet and spicy innocence. The flavors of her. God, he needed more. The combination was intoxicating. He wanted to steep himself in her juices. Wanted to make her come on his tongue and drown himself in her cream. Let it flow down his throat while he feasted on her. The wants listed quickly in his mind and turned instantaneously to life sustaining requirements.

The rest of the world, what her uncle had done to her, Griff, and T they could all just take a fucking number and wait outside. He owed her this. He owed *them* this. She lifted her head. His lips slid to her throat. Her sweet little whimpers and moans filled the cool air around them. He wanted to drown in them.

She licked her lips. Every nerve ending in his body honed in on her tongue. Then her mouth crashed down on his again. He parted her lips and explored. She opened willingly, just like he'd make certain her pussy did that night all for him.

"Nat," he jerked away before he got in way over his head. "Baby, are you sure you're ready?"

"I'm sure." Confidence played at the fringes of her vow. She wanted to be sure. That wasn't good enough.

"Let me get a shower. I'll take care of that and we'll go to sleep."

He gestured to his raging hard-on he was certain she felt pressing against her.

"No. Well, I mean, if you want to do that in the shower I want to watch, but then I want to have sex."

He grunted at the thought of her watching him get off. "Killing me, baby. Fucking killing me." There was so much he didn't yet know. Was that touch of curiosity a bit of voyeur in the making? She didn't even know her own preferences. She didn't know his. But she would. He'd make certain of it. Every single fantasy she longed to explore, he would fulfill.

"Please, Aaron."

"Jesus, I love the sound of my name on your lips."

"Want me to say it again?"

"Yeah, I want you to scream it while you come over and over again all night."

"I can do that."

His entire body went rigid with hunger. His veins throbbed with adamant need. "Fuck. Shower first." That damned letter. Why hadn't he shoved it in the glovebox?

The glovebox. "Hang on one sec, babe." Keeping her in his arms, he carried her back to passenger side of his truck.

"Are we gonna do it in your truck?"

"Eventually." He brushed a kiss on her forehead. "But not tonight. Your first time is gonna be in your bed where I know you're comfortable and we're taking it nice and slow. Just needed to get these." He grasped one of the boxes of condoms and the lube he'd purchased that morning.

"Oh. Yeah. Kind of forgot about those."

"I'll always take care of you, Nat, in every possible way."

"Do we have to use them? I like the way your skin feels."

"I'm gonna blow before I get you in the house."

"Sorry."

"No. It's fine. I want you to ask me anything you want to know. I'm clean, baby, but I'm doubting you're looking to get pregnant tonight, and unless you're begging me to unload all over you I plan on coming inside you over and over again."

The thought of coming all over her perfect ass was followed instantly by thoughts of him soaking down the tight walls of her pussy. He burned. His cock begged for relief. Every muscle in his body was ragged with desire.

"How many come in a box?" Curious little thing tonight wasn't she. His vocal cords were just as ragged as the rest of his body.

"Uh," he tried to blink the haze of lust from his eyes as he headed inside. "I don't know. Something like twenty-four, I think. Why?"

"How many are we using tonight?" This question revealed a quiver of nerves. So that was it.

"Let's try out one and see how you're feeling."

"I have a vibrator," spilled from her lips as he set her down on the linoleum in her kitchen.

Yet another image chiseled itself into his brain. Natalie Camden, his baby, sprawled out on her bed, naked, writhing with a vibrator in her hand. Army training in the event of capture made its way through the need swamping his every thought. *Aaron Alexander Weber First Sergeant, United States Army, 321-72...* She was torturing him and she had no idea. *Get it together, Weber. You're better than this.* "You want to play with that, baby, I'm all over it."

A quick swallow preceded her shaking her head. "No. I meant it probably won't hurt so much because I've used that before."

Every ounce of practiced patience drained from his body. All restraint disintegrated. All composure depleted. The hunger and need liquefied in his veins. It ran hot and hungry through his body. The man he'd been before surfaced after three long years.

Gripping her upper body, he hoisted her up onto the counter. Her quick gasp was followed by a throaty sound that threatened to drive him wild. He jerked her forward until her pussy collided with his cock. The thin nightgown and panties she was wearing did nothing to keep her from understanding his need. "Stay with me, honey. Eyes right here on mine. I fucking need you to understand something."

Her breaths fragmented but she locked her eyes on his.

"Your innocence, the things your body knows you need, and most definitely your sweet little cherry, I'm about to take them all. It all belongs to me. All for me not some fucking toy. You got that?"

"Oh, yeah. I got it."

You're gonna terrify her, asshole. The voice in his head was choked out by his own need. It was fighting a losing battle anyway. His cock was running the show. She kept licking her lips. Any chance he had of regaining control was erased with the quick darts of her tongue. Her eyes were dark and hungry. Every golden fleck was on fire. Her nipples were rigid pebbles tenting the loose fabric of her gown. Her body rocked against him. She wasn't scared. She was turned on. Oh fuck, yeah.

"You like it when I talk like that, honey?"

"So much. Please, Aaron. Do it. Take them."

"I'm gonna show you, honey. I'm gonna fucking teach you how good it can be when you let me show you what you need when I want you to have it."

"Yes. Now." She didn't yet understand how this would work, but she'd learn.

She bucked against him. The corner of the letter stabbed into him. He winced as a jagged edge tore at one of his scars. He had to get rid of the damned thing.

Backing up, he tried to clear his mind and his lungs with a deep breath but he only succeeded in bringing the intoxicating scents of her to his nostrils. His body shook with greed. "Let me get a shower. Go get in bed. I'll be quick."

"You have to let the water run for a while before it gets warm." She hopped off the counter. Her eyes never left his form.

"A cold shower would do me some good. I'll be right back."

Sealing himself behind her bathroom door, Aaron switched on the shower water not particularly caring if it ever heated. Ripping off his sweatshirt, he watched the letter fall to the tile floor. Incensed rage ate at the desire swimming through his veins. The two things he most wanted were on either side of the door. Being with her and protecting her from the man who'd hurt her went to war for dominance in his mind.

His glance flipped back and forth from the letter to the door. He'd left her high and dry a few hours before. He wasn't doing it again and he had no idea how infuriated he would be when he read whatever the douchebag had written. T had assured him it would piss him off. Tonight he wanted no part of it. His desire won out over his vengeance. Tonight, his only requirement was her satisfaction, her climaxes on his tongue, her sweet sticky juices all over his fingers, his cock so deep inside her she forgot everything but his name. Tomorrow, he would deal with her uncle.

Grabbing the letter, he rolled it in his sweatshirt, stripped, and folded the rest of his clothes around it.

CHAPTER TWENTY-FIVE

Natalie stared at her own bathroom door like it might've contained a live lion. Her mind was divided in battle between summoning all available courage she had, stripping, and joining him in the shower or putting on several extra sets of clothing and hiding under the covers of her bed.

"You're a fucking cowgirl. Get it together," she commanded herself. She'd finally told him she loved him. She'd suspected that she'd fallen in love a while ago, just like her mother had said. She just had no way of fully understanding what that meant or what to do about it.

"People have to call it making love for a reason." She spoke through her teeth as she wriggled out of the old nightgown and flung it on the bed. He thought she'd somehow missed him saying that she *thought* she was in love with him.

People said she was stubborn. Clearly, they'd never tried to convince Aaron Weber that they were in love with him. Shaking her head, she slipped her panties down her legs and kicked them away. Remembering her mother's words that he didn't believe he was worthy, determination sluiced through her, stiffening her spine and enlivening her body. This wasn't a one way deal. He needed her to teach him something as well.

She paused for one more moment, remembering the rough gravel of his voice when he'd informed her that her innocence belonged only to him and the feel of his stubble on her neck and his fingers on her hips.

A shiver quaked her. More than anything else in that moment she wanted her body to belong to him, wanted him to fill the emptiness, wanted to hear the sounds he made and the commanding tenor his voice took on when he forgot how little experience she had.

That was all it took. Her wants and needs tangled in her mind. She understood only small parts of each. She needed him to unfold them, to suss out the puzzle pieces she'd been missing for far too long. She needed him to show her what it could be like between them.

And she would show him what love really was. Despite the hell her uncle had put her through, the rest of her family had always stood by her side and loved her through it all. She knew how to love even if she wasn't certain exactly how to make it.

A wall of steam greeted her when she opened the bathroom door. His clothes were rolled in a ball on the countertop. The shower curtain swayed. She could just make out the shadow of his masculine form behind the cloth barrier. Longing clogged her throat. She continued to watch him for far longer than was probably normal. His body dominated most of the space in her shower. She couldn't look away.

Her heart beat out a frantic SOS. She needed to be back in his arms but her feet refused to move. Her chest rose and fell in rapid pants. The humid air made it difficult to breathe. His hands skated down his chest until his right hand wrapped around his cock.

A small squeak of approval escaped her lips. Suddenly, the curtain was jerked aside, revealing the ropes of chiseled muscle that comprised his body and the intricate tattoo work that made her weak with desire.

His eyes devoured her with need that bordered on possession. "You like watching don't you, baby?"

With that question her mind flatlined. Words seemed a foreign concept. A hive of responses buzzed in her head. They made no sense. Yes. Maybe. Was it wrong if she did? Was it weird if she didn't? Who wouldn't want to look at him? He was so gorgeous it was almost painful.

"Come here to me." It wasn't a request. Nothing about his tone said she had any other options than to comply with his summoning. It was a command she willingly obeyed. The cold tile registered on the soles of her feet. It juxtaposed with the fiery heat roaring in her belly and singeing her cheeks. Once she stepped into the shower, there was no going back.

Inventorying her mind, she located no regret. For as long as she'd been able to remember she'd wanted to shatter her past into diminutive pieces so tiny they could never be restored. He offered his hand to help her make the final step. She was certain it was an invitation to sin if ever there was one. She grasped it firmly and threw herself into his arms under the rapid fall of water.

"So damned beautiful," he grunted in her ear. He cradled her against his chest using his body to keep the water from her eyes. "I wanted to be the one to strip you, baby. I wanted to take my time. I want to study every square inch of your body. But you coming to me like this... it's better than anything I've ever fantasized about and I've been dreaming about you naked under me for so fucking long."

His cock was an iron brand against her. His scars were pressed to her abdomen. She longed to touch both. She could bring relief to the fierce strain and tender skin. She knew how now.

Having never showered with a man before, she had nothing else to draw on but what she'd learned the evening before. Easing back a half centimeter she scaled her right hand between them and ran her fingers over his cock. Rivulets of water and pre-cum flowed down him. She followed their trail. A ragged growl echoed around her. His girth and length registered in her mind prodding at the hive of nerves that had robbed her of words. The pain everyone seemed concerned about finally worked through the hunger that had deadened the words of warning she'd heard since she was a teenager.

Seeking reassurance from him, she blinked back the water that rushed into her eyes when she sought his gaze.

His arms wrapped back around her, crushing her to him and keeping the water at bay. She clung to the only anchor she'd ever really wanted. "Are you scared, baby?"

"No." The single word was lost in the drumming beat of the water. She lifted her head. "Just nervous."

He nodded his understanding. Beads of water rolled down his shoulders. She wondered what they tasted like mixed with his sweat. She longed to know what would happen if she bent and tasted the pearly mixture weeping at the head of his cock. She wanted to know his flavors, wanted to breathe him in, to absorb him with every single one of her senses, wanted to know everything there was to know about him.

"We're gonna take it nice and slow. I'd never do anything you didn't want, Nat. I got a little crazy thinking about you with a vibrator. I know I scared you."

"You didn't." She spoke with more authority now.

He eased her away from the water. "It's okay to be nervous."

"You're so... big," she finally confessed.

His body shook with one of those intoxicating chuckles she'd fallen hard for two seconds after she'd met him. "Damn but you're good for my ego. I'm gonna get you nice and ready for me, baby. Open you up for me. Fit you to me. I'm gonna make it feel so good. I promise."

Her nipples throbbed against him, urging him onward. Her body was awash with nerves and raw with need. Her confidence was fleeting, making its way down the drain with the rest of the water.

"Hey, look at me," he soothed. She lifted her head. Once again he blocked the water from her face with the expanse of his back. "First time you learn to HALO jump, you jump tandem with an instructor. Not gonna lie to you, I was more than nervous. I was pretty much scared shitless."

A grin returned to Natalie's face. A sense of why she was standing in the shower with him washed over her. His voice steadied her. She was right where she needed to be.

"Instructor told me there were only two things I had to remember for my first jump. Breathe and hold on. Can you do that for me? Just do those two things and I'll take good care of you. I'll do everything else. I just need you to breathe for me and to hold on to me. I'll never let you go. You're not free-falling alone in this, okay? I'm right here."

Pressing her body to his, she held on for dear life. He was right there with her. He'd never let her fall. She knew that. Even that night she'd run from, him she'd known he'd be there waiting on her return.

"I want you." The only words she'd really wanted to say that night finally took flight from the buzz in her brain. "Now."

She was so soft. God, she felt so damn good. Aaron kept her cradled to him. His hands explored her back and then he mercifully granted himself access to the finest ass he'd ever seen. Cupping her backside, he gauged her, plying and squeezing then softening his touch. Her moans increased in volume as he neared her pussy. She spread her legs without his prompting. So damn needy. So fucking hungry for him.

"Let me see you, honey. Let me look at you."

"I thought I was supposed to hold on," she chided.

Thrilled she wasn't too nervous to joke, he shook his head sending water shooting out from his hair. "Careful, baby. It's taking everything I've got to keep my baser nature locked up tonight."

She did step back. Intrigue danced in her eyes as she raked her teeth across her bottom lip. "Meaning what?"

"Meaning if you want that lip bitten I'll be the one doing the biting and if I tell you to let me see you, you do as you're told. After tonight, and when I know you're ready, whenever we're in bed I call the shots. Believe one of your requests was that I show you the less vanilla side of sex."

Her eyes narrowed and those perfect pink lips of hers twisted in consideration. "I don't normally like being told what to do." Her eyebrow lifted. She was testing him, wanted to see what he'd make of that.

"Trust me, honey, you'll like doing as you're told when you're with me."

"Yeah, I'm pretty sure you're right about that, just don't let it go to your head."

"Too fucking late." He crashed his mouth down on hers, unleashing unrelenting devastation on her mouth. His tongue dove past her lips, hungry and demanding, all the things he was. All the things he'd always been for her.

He swallowed her moans. He swore they slipped down his throat and wrapped themselves forcefully around his cock. Nipping at her lips, he cupped her breasts, drawing them together.

Stepping back, he made certain she was with him, staring into his eyes, still every bit as hungry as he was. "I fucking love your tits. Small and perfect. Makes me want to sit you down in front of me and let you watch while I come all over them."

"Oh God, yes," she whimpered. Perfection. He needed her drunk on him, intoxicated with all of the things he wanted from her, and desperate to comply.

"Mm-hmm, I knew you'd like that. They hurt though don't they, baby. They swollen for me?" He traced his index fingers around her nipples, dark with her arousal, sweet little peaches too long on the vine. He refused the thing he knew she most wanted. His muscles pulsed to the hammering of his heart. His cock throbbed anxiously.

A low throaty hum was her only response. Another circular trace of his fingers elicited a gasp of pure need. Her body rolled against the tile wall as she tried to press her nipples into his palms. He rolled them between his fingertips instead.

Convulsive waves jolted through her body like she'd pressed her hands to an electric fence. "Oh God, yes, please," she panted. Fucking hell, she was going to kill him.

He closed her his hands over the swells, giving her what she couldn't seem to ask him for yet. "You could come like that couldn't you, baby? So sensitive for me." His mind instantly conjured up an image of her in clamps. He damn near lost it all from the thought alone.

He swallowed down a possessive growl that threatened to tear from his lungs. *First time. It's her first fucking time* became his mantra. Tonight wasn't about what he wanted. It was about what she required. He'd get his later and he'd wait a lifetime to see her come full circle, giving her pleasure over to him entirely.

He followed the fall of water as it moved over her svelte abdomen and gathered in the curls that covered her sweet little pussy. This was where things could get dicey. "Look at me, Nat." He kept his voice calm and in control, leashing the demanding edge successfully for the moment.

Her eyes flew open. They were jewel drenched pools of confusion and need. "Stay with me, baby. Here's where you hold on." He gathered her hands in one of his own, leaving his other free to explore.

Other than his good girl slip, he had no idea what that piece of human waste had said to her before he'd touched her. Revulsion drove away a little of his own frantic desire.

"Can I touch you, sweetheart? Can you spread your legs for me?" She'd been all about this in his truck but this was different and they both knew it.

He prayed nothing that came from his mouth would summon any of the demons that had been so cruelly forced on his baby. The demons he would damn back with everything he was, the ghosts of her past that he would smother and cage, the fears he would starve for so long they no longer held any power over her.

"Please," sang from her lips as she revealed herself to him. She kept a tight hold on his hand. His eyes drank her in. Her long hair fell in soaked curls over her shoulders. Her soft belly was pulled taught. Her eyes closed once again. She writhed.

With precise gentleness, he circled her mound with his free hand. Her breaths stuttered from her chest. "Still with me, honey?" He ran his middle finger up her slit, back and forth watching as she bloomed for him.

"Yes. Just please. I need…" Her plea dissolved.

"I know what you need, baby." He slowly dipped his finger between her lips, so ripe and full of heat she shook for him. "I know what you want. I know you're so fucking hungry for it right now it hurts, and I'm gonna give it to you. Someday soon I'll have you just like this. I'll spin you around against a wall and give you exactly what you're wanting hard and fast, make you scream for me. But tonight, we're going nice and slow." He punctuated the last three words with teasing strokes over her clit.

Her fingernails dug into his hand. A harsh cry whimpered from her.

"Feels so good right there. I know, baby. I know it does." He continued his ministrations until her body opened and her clit sought out his touch. "That's it, honey." He increased his pace. Her pussy clenched against his fingers, hungry to be filled.

"Please, please."

"Feels empty doesn't it? So needy for me."

"Yes, God, yes, please."

"You beg so sweet my stubborn little cowgirl." He chuckled. Giving her what she craved he dipped his middle finger back. Rotating his thumb around her clit now, he pressed inside her. "Jesus Christ you're so damn tight." Every cell in his body vibrated with greed. "All for me."

She rode his hand in earnest now. Back and forth, her body pulled at his finger. "That's it. Take what you need. Can you feel that, Nat? Can you feel your body pulling me in? You need it. Give it to me."

Moving their joined hands over her head and pinning them to the shower wall, he leaned and latched his mouth onto her right nipple sucking hard. Her entire body tensed, the tight walls of her pussy cinched against his fingers, and then she shattered on his hand, calling out his name. Her honey flowed over his knuckles. His every fantasy in living form.

Easing his finger away for the moment, he wrapped her up in his arms offering her a sanctuary from any fears that might've brought back. "I'm right here. I've got you. You come so sweet, baby. God, I can't wait to feel you on my cock." He planted a kiss against her wet scalp. "You okay?"

He got a single nod in response. For tonight, he'd take that. "I'm not finished, not near finished," he warned.

"Good," panted from her.

"I'm gonna taste everything you just gave up for me. Plan on half-drowning myself in your sweet snatch."

She jerked back but before he could panic her hands landed on his shoulders. She attempted to push him downward. "Do it. Taste me."

He fell to his knees. The unforgiving tile sent a tremor of pain up his thighs. He didn't give a damn. "Just hold on to me and breathe. Okay?"

"I will."

Water flowed freely down his face. Squeezing his eyes shut, he let the perfume of her arousal fill his nostrils. Sweet and spicy nectar, ripe with abandon. He ran his tongue over her lips, bathing her before he opened her with his thumbs.

Her legs spread farther. Her grip on his shoulders increased. Starved for her flavors, he pressed his tongue over her clit. He'd imagined this hundreds of times. Not one single wet dream or stroke session held anything over the heavenly reality of tasting her.

Burying his face against her, he worked his tongue inside her, letting her ride his face this time.

"Oh my God," she screamed against the pounding water as his whiskers chaffed at her lips.

Still driving constantly toward his ultimate goal, he slipped his tongue out of her opening and spun it around her clit. Dipping two fingers through her swollen tissues, he used more force this time. She ground harder, clawing at his neck and hair now. As soon as he got her through this, his sweet baby was going to like it rough. Perfection.

With each pass of his fingers she slowly stretched open. He worked quickly, pounding his fingers into her faster, sucking harder. Leaning back in, he bathed that warm bundle of nerves with his tongue and let his teeth scrape against her folds. The next moment, she spiraled over the cliff once again.

His own accomplishment and satisfaction rode on her juices as they flowed over his tongue. His muscles throbbed with accomplishment but his own hunger pulsed under his skin as well.

Standing, he returned to his previous position, wrapping her up in his arms, making certain she was still with him in the present, proving to both of them that he'd be both her lover and her protector.

Her hands slicked down his back. She grabbed his ass, seeming to need the moment to explore his strength pressed against her softness.

"That was incredible." She spoke into his chest.

"I agree. Sweetest candy I've ever tasted. Let me take you to bed, baby. We're not finished yet."

He shut down the shower as it lost its warmth and wrapped her up in the towel he'd hung on a nearby hook. The flavors of her saturated his every sense. He was insane with need. His cock was strung so tight he hurt. Every muscle in his body was poised to take. The last thing he wanted to do was rush her, but he was walking a fraying tightrope of greed.

Grabbing another towel from the cabinet, he ran it over his back. She squeezed the water in her hair into her towel and then wrapped it around her body. When her hand hesitantly reached out and touched the scars marring his abdomen, he forced himself to let her explore. His eyes closed, sealing away the memories.

"I want to know what happened." Her voice was a half-haunted breath laced with the desire he'd worked so hard to achieve.

"Not tonight, baby. Come here to me." Lifting her into his arms, he carried her to bed.

CHAPTER TWENTY-SIX

A rush of excitement spiraled down Natalie's spine as Aaron carried her. Other than feeling as if her bones had been robbed from her body, it was the only discernible feeling she understood.

Every time he'd forced an orgasm from her, she'd flown so high she was certain she'd never reach the ground and now, he was laying her out tenderly in her bed. There was so much more to come.

The worn sheets enveloped her overly heated body. Familiarity calmed her fraying nerves. Glancing down at her own chest, which Aaron couldn't seem to stop looking at, she checked to make certain he couldn't actually see her heart beating its way out of her ribcage.

He stood at the foot of her bed over her. His greedy gaze ate her up. Resisting the urge to cover herself, she focused on his cock instead. He could work magic with his tongue and his fingers. What must he be able to do with that?

"Aaron, please," she finally begged. Drawing it out was unfair. She needed him in every possible way she could have him.

He licked his lips. "Let me enjoy this, honey. You are so fucking beautiful and all for me."

"Then take me."

"Plan to." He lifted her leg and painted tender kisses up her calf.

She tensed when he reached her knee. That wasn't where she wanted his mouth. Why did it feel so good? Impatience made her writhe. He spread her legs and continued kissing a trail of fire up her thighs. Each touchpoint of his lips brought another rush of wet heat to her pussy. The breath swept from her lungs. Her legs trembled. Her body ached.

Put on the condom. Stop making me wait. Let me touch you. Let me feel you. Open me. Fill me. Do something. He stared at her like he could hear the silent frantic pleadings of her mind. He answered only with a dark, sinful chuckle. "When I say, remember, sweetheart?"

"Now," she demanded.

"So impatient for me." He made no effort to speed his ascent up her body.

"Please, Aaron."

"Mm, honey, you have any idea how much I like hearing my name on your lips? Next time I bring you I want to hear my name over and over, but right now, hush." He leveled her body with his and brought his mouth to hers.

This kiss was somehow different than all the others. His lips demanded more. Pressing her into the mattress, his tongue dove between her lips and tangled with hers. She could taste the greed and necessity. This kiss demanded everything.

He took. She gave as good as she got.

Bracing her foot against the bed, she bucked against him, desperate to feel more of his skin on hers. The rough abrasion of hair coupled with smooth plains of muscle and tender lines of scars. The combination had every nerve ending in her body on high alert.

A low, greedy growl sounded in her ear. He eased down her body and licked the remaining bath water from the underswells of her breasts. Each kiss worked closer and closer to her right nipple but he refused what she so desperately needed.

"Tell me, baby. Tell me you need me to suck you," he ordered. His index finger circled the raised bumps surrounding her nipple, throbbing out their need for his mouth.

"Please." She writhed again.

"Please what?"

"Suck me," she finally managed in a breathless pant. Her back arched pushing her nipple closer to his mouth.

"That's it."

A heady sense of power pulsed through her when he complied. Drawing her nipple, so raw it was painful, into the soothing velvet heat of his mouth she groaned out her relief.

There it was again. That knot of need that tightened behind her mound when his mouth was on her breasts. She still had no idea how he accomplished that. All she knew was she never wanted him to stop.

His fingers stroked along her pussy managing to add ecstasy into her bliss. "Yes," she cried out for him.

"Relax for me, Nat. Just relax. I need you to take a little more from me." He spoke as his lips travelled from one breast to the other. She couldn't fully understand his request through the haze of pleasure in her mind until he slipped two fingers back inside her and then slowly, and ever so gently added a third. "Breathe, baby. Let me open you. Just relax for me."

Relaxation wasn't an emotion she was capable of reaching just then. The pressure separated into two distinctive camps, pleasure and pain. His mouth latched onto her other nipple and the bands of pleasure working throughout her body vanquished the pain. She gave herself over to the pleasure.

"That's it." He continued to stretch her with delicate precision. A half-second later he shifted and she heard what sounded like the pop of a plastic cap. Her eyes flew open when he eased his hand out of her, poured the lube on his fingertips, and then returned them to her pussy. "You still breathing for me?"

She nodded. Her wet hair drenched her pillow. She didn't care. He pressed deeper and stroked that spot so deep inside her she could never quite reach it. The delectable pain and pleasure went to war once again. Her body sought both.

"So fucking tight. You're gonna feel so fucking good." Intensity weighted every word. Once again he leaned across her body and drew her left breast back into his mouth and once again the pleasure spiraled out from her core, dancing along her limbs and making her feel like she was flying off the highest mountain with no worry of ever falling down.

"Aaron, I think I'm gonna, mmm..." Her teeth sank into her lower lip. Every stroke of his fingers orchestrated the impending climax.

"I know you need to, baby. It's right there isn't it, but not yet. Let it build for me. Let me make this feel good." He pressed deeper, faster. Tearing the breath from her lungs. How was she supposed to stop this? He had to know what he was doing. "Not yet, honey. Not 'til I say. It's all mine. All for me. You'll go when I say."

She whimpered out her need. Surely, he would let her have what he offered her so expertly. Her body rocked against his hand. *Please. Please.*

The crinkle of the condom wrapper distracted her slightly. She watched him slip it over his cock with one hand and refused to think about where he'd learned that particular skill.

His body loomed over hers, braced on his forearm yet he managed to keep his fingers stroking to the rhythm of her body with ease. Once again she was swept back into the heavenly sensations he provided her.

Her legs tensed against his forearm. She needed more. This fullness wasn't enough. "Please," she begged again.

"You ready for me, Nat?"

"Oh God, yes." She was more than ready.

"You come when I say, understand."

"As long as you say now," she whimpered. He pounded. She surged higher. He stroked. She reached the apex. Her body began its spiral toward pure bliss.

Another chuckle sounded in her ear. "All right, honey. Let me hear my name when you lose it. Come for me." She flew. He catapulted her from the sky and yet she flew higher, singing his name like a prayer on from her lips. The only hymn she'd ever understood.

His fingers vanished from her body replaced by the head of his cock. She gasped as he slowly dipped inside her, inch by inch.

Still in throws of the orgasm he'd made her wait to have, her body guided him deeper, begging for more.

This time he readily gave. She desperately took.

A ravenous moan thundered from his lungs. No part of her was unaffected. All of the missing pieces were found. She was unable to move, too busy trying to understand how every hollow had found fulfillment, every need satisfied. The pain was there. The pleasure was more. The pressure eased as he tenderly withdrew but grew with every thrust.

Her body seemed unable to contain him and yet needed him to make sense of life itself. Her hands sought his back, clinging to the only thing she fully understood, they needed to be together.

"That's it. Just hold onto me and breathe, remember?" he choked.

She did just that.

Excruciating pleasure consumed Aaron with every tender thrust he made. Stripping away every mask he'd ever worn, every identity he'd taken on under orders that weren't his own, every person he'd tried to become to keep from being who he was.

He tried so hard to be gentle, but the only thing his body understood was that deep within her lay his redemption. A tidal pool of atonement she freely offered him. Every single thing he refused to forget slipped through his hands like hot grains of the sand that had robbed him of everything. Every baptism of his cock deep inside her made it as if they'd never existed at all. No need to remember. No need to forget. Nothing existed but her and him.

She was so tight there was no room for him to be anything but the man he was put on earth to be, the man who lived to protect and worship her.

"Natalie. Mmm. So tight. Ah, Jesus, so good," sang from his lips, a feeble supplication to the sins she absolved. His unworthiness washed away as well.

His mind spun, wringing out the memories he'd clung to for too damn long. His body pressed deeper, so needy for her to replace them with her love.

Her love. Holy fuck. The knowledge aligned with the all-consuming ecstasy she flooded through him.

Rapture thundered in his veins. Every carnal need he'd ever had was satisfied. Her swollen folds drew him in, drowning him in her healing nectar.

Another groan ripped from his lungs. He gave her everything he had. Her eyes closed in ecstasy. His name whispered from her lips as she started to meet his thrusts with tiny lifts of her hips.

On her next lift he wrapped his arms around her, clinging tightly to his saving grace.

He rocked his body back and forth. He knew the pain he'd brought had robbed her of another climax and yet she wanted him to continue. Her eyes were seeking. Her body riding the waves of his own. She gave with no requirement that she also receive. Next time, he would make certain she received over and over again.

This time was for them together, not them apart. It existed only between them. He pressed in again. His body on the precipice of explosion. The pressure built.

His sac drew tight. His cock throbbed constantly. He wished he could strip off the condom and soak down the walls of her pussy. He longed to bathe her in him the way her juices washed him clean. He wanted nothing between them.

Another pump. He tensed. A ragged groan shook from him, ridding him of more of the pieces of himself that had never belonged.

"Oh yes." She urged him onward.

Her pussy flexed against him. That was it. He was done for. All will to fight on was leached from his body. On his next pump, he collapsed against her. Spurts of hot cum filled the condom and hot tears filled her eyes.

CHAPTER TWENTY-SEVEN

"Hey, shh, it's okay." A slight shudder he couldn't halt, worked through her body as he withdrew. Working quickly, he shed the condom and disposed of it. He wrapped her up in his arms, rocking her gently. "I've got you. I'm right here, Nat."

She jammed her fists in her eyes and tried to forcefully rid herself of the tears. Aaron had been expecting this. She apparently had not. "Why am I crying? That was amazing."

Trying to conceal his grin, he brushed a kiss on her head. "It was incredible."

"I'm not crying because I'm sad. I am not sad," she finally determined.

"Did I do anything you didn't like, baby?"

"No. It's just... I don't know. I don't have anything to compare it to."

"I'm sure this makes me a possessive asshole but I happen to love that fact."

She managed a half grin before she buried her face in his chest again. Leaning with her in his lap, he turned off the lamp, shrouding them in a cocoon of darkness. The sun would be up soon. He needed to get her to sleep if she could.

When she lifted her head and stared him down he knew neither of them was going to be sleeping anytime soon. "But you do. You slept with other people, people you didn't really care about, right?"

Every intelligence officer reached the points of no return in negotiations. The place where no amount of lying was going to achieve the goal. The place where you either walked away or told the truth. The moonlight danced in her tear-soaked hazel eyes as she studied him, seeing beyond what anyone else saw, what anyone else had ever looked for. He knew this was the point where only the truth would set him free.

"Yeah, more times than I care to remember. But, Nat, I swear they meant nothing, and you... my God, you mean everything."

"I know. That's my point. You've had that before with other people and I need to know if this was different. It felt like it was different than I thought it was supposed to be. It...sort of...felt like...more." She stumbled through her own confusion.

He reclined in her bed and guided her onto his chest. "It was more. More than anything I have ever experienced, more than anything I could ever have fathomed, and you gave me more than I will ever have to give to you but I swear, I'll be more somehow." There, the truth, both barren and bold, hollow and hallowed, all he was, and all he ever hoped to be for her.

"But you did. You gave me everything. Thank you for that. You don't need to be more for me."

"Trust me, I'm the one who should be thanking you. Are you sore, honey? I can give you a bath. It'll ease a little of the strain."

"We just took a shower. I'm okay. I just want you to hold me."

He strengthened his arms around her. "I don't ever want to let go."

"Good."

He watched her sleep as the sun pierced the darkness bringing a hesitant glow to the deep purple night. Aaron shifted his body to keep it from awakening her. He needed to go read that damned letter but he couldn't let her go. She needed him and he would never let her down.

Tucking her hair behind her shoulders, he let himself drift on the edge of sleep as her scent and her warmth contented him. A relaxation he had no recollection of ever experiencing before kept him at ease.

The memories he both hated and refused to forget were too far away to be reached that night. She kept them at bay. An angel to pull him from the depths of hell where he'd resided for so long he no longer knew which way was up. She took his hands and guided him home.

The nightmare always started the same way. Natalie tried to shake free from it. The skirt of the dress that matched Holly's, the ones their grandmother had given them, flew out to the sides as she jumped from hay bale to hay bale. The wind lifted the dress higher.

Uncle Mick leaned against the barn. Three broken beer bottles were at his feet. Another was in his hand.

No.

Her fists collided with something. Skin and muscle. Someone.

"Nat!" His voice tried to reach through the terror. "Baby, wake up." She couldn't reach it. Her uncle's hands gripped her arms. They held her captive. She couldn't run.

Someone sat her up and shook her. "Natalie, baby, it's okay. Wake up for me."

She clung to something. His arms. A lifeline.

"Natalie!"

His voice shattered the icy hands that held her captive. Her eyes flew open. Air rushed into her lungs in a frantic gasp. Aaron's gentle hands cupped her face. "Look at me, Nat. Right here. You're right here with me. You're safe. I've got you. It's over, sweetheart. Never again. Okay, I will never let someone hurt you again."

She collapsed into him and washed his chest with another round of tears her uncle didn't deserve and she hated herself for crying in the first place.

"Deep breaths for me, okay. I've got you," he kept speaking the words that steadied her breaths and her heartbeat. "I'm right here. I will always keep you safe."

She tucked herself closer to him. He wrapped his arms and legs around her, a shield against her past. His right hand cradled her head, keeping her from having to see anything at all.

His left hand pulled the sheets up over them. He covered her completely. "I've got you, baby." His kisses wiped away every escaping tear. His hands kept her in the here and now. She just needed him to stay forever. If he was there, nothing could get to her. She was safe. "I'm right here."

CHAPTER TWENTY-EIGHT

The sun was far too high in the sky the next time Natalie woke up. She groaned. The cattle had to be fed. Sundance was probably anxious to get going. Her family surely had already eaten breakfast without her.

But Aaron's arms were still around her and the perfection of it all was simply too good to end just yet. Her family would get over it. Her horse would understand. And the cows, well, God knew her brothers owed her years' worth of chores for all the times she'd done theirs for them.

Sighing, she buried her face back in Aaron's chest determined to go back to sleep. His breathy chuckle kept her from her mission. "I'm perfectly happy to hold you all day long, baby. I do need to go feed Buster and Lulu eventually but they can wait."

"Can I go with you?" She sounded like a dying frog. How hard had she been sleeping? The nightmare. It rushed back into her consciousness. Bile lodged in her throat.

She chanced a peek at Aaron. Understanding settled in his eyes. "Still right here," he reassured. "And of course you can go with me."

"No, it's okay. I promised I wouldn't be clingy and I have to go feed Sundance."

"Hey, you're not being clingy. I love when you want to be with me. Kind of goes with the loving you thing."

A few of the better memories of the night before swept the nightmare away. She focused on those. "You still love me?"

"Did you think I was going to change my mind, sweetheart?" Concern erased the understanding from his gaze.

"Just making sure."

"You still think you love me?" He didn't seem to even try to hide his incredulity.

"Did you think I was gonna change my mind, G.I. Joe?"

He laughed. "More like I think you should."

"Well, I'm not."

"Stubborn cowgirl."

"And proud of it."

"Thanks for not asking me about last night. Thanks for knowing I don't want to talk about it." There, that's what she'd been trying to say for the last five minutes.

"Not a stranger to nightmares, sweetheart. I know how awful they are. Just know if you ever do want to talk I want to listen."

Forcing her body to rise, she pulled her knees to her chest. Okay, that was a little tender. She tried unsuccessfully to hide her wince.

"You're sore aren't you?"

"Just a little."

"Not sure there's any way around that but I hate I made you hurt."

"I'll be fine. It'll go away."

"How about that bath?"

"I have to go do chores." Rubbing the fog from her eyes, she finally noticed the red rims of his. "You didn't sleep. Oh my gosh, you stayed up with me and never went back to sleep."

"I told you I will always take care of you, Nat. I'm fine. You can take a nap with me at my place when we go feed the dogs."

"I'm sorry."

He shook his head, sat up, and planted a kiss on her forehead. "You have absolutely nothing to apologize for."

"Are you working the late shift tonight?"

"Yeah, and it's Saturday so we'll be slammed. I still want you there though."

Natalie refused to admit to him how much she disliked the bar. Drunk men were frightening. She hated the terror that always resided just under her skin while she was there. Why couldn't they just stay on the ranch? Not that nothing bad had ever happened there. She reasoned her way through their evening plans. If Aaron was there, she'd go. "Okay."

"Bar's closed tomorrow. You want to go up to the lake or something? Or you could finally show me your favorite place in the Glen."

The entire day and night with him the next day definitely made up for having to hang out at Saddleback's. "Yeah, that would be fun."

Tempted to rip the top sheet from her bed to wrap herself in it, she debated the best way to get to the bathroom without him seeing how much her ass jiggled when she walked.

Her bladder told her to get over herself. She slipped out of the bed and attempted to walk backward toward the toilet.

"What are you doing, Nat?" He laughed at her outright as he climbed out of bed in all of his Greek statue perfection.

"Going to the bathroom."

"Mm-hmm, I figured that but why the hell are you going backwards?"

"No real reason."

He studied her with that look that said he was combing through her mind and was highly likely to land on the very thing she was trying to hide. His long legs ate up the distance between them. "Few things I might've failed to mention last night. One, I am an unapologetic ass man. Two, your ass is so fucking beautiful I can barely keep my hands off of it. Three, attempting to hide it or any other part of your drop-dead gorgeous body from me will result in my hands paddling your fine ass until I turn it as pink as your cheeks get when you get embarrassed. That all good or shall I review it again?"

She narrowed her eyes in an effort to look annoyed. Truthfully, the fact that she'd had one of those stupid nightmares with him here and he was still willing to go on with everything he'd promised, everything she so wanted to explore, delighted her.

"Yeah, you can get pissy about it if it makes you feel better, but I know you like what I just said. Turn around and shake it for me, honey."

She edged closer to the bathroom, keeping up her glare for appearances sake alone. At that last moment, she spun and shook her ass back and forth. His growl echoed around the room. She loved it. She loved flirting with him. She loved the intensity of his hungry gaze. She loved him.

He reached for her. She slipped into the bathroom, slammed the door in his face, turned the lock, and laughed triumphantly.

Rushing to the toilet she sat down. Okay, that definitely burned. She didn't have time for a bath but maybe a quick shower would help.

Aaron glared at the door between them but knew she needed some time. Before he could settle back in the bed, the door opened. He stepped toward her, but she shoved the ball of his clothes out with just her hand. "My daddy's not gonna like it if we leave here while you're buck nekkid."

He grabbed the clothes and far more importantly the letter concealed in the pile. Holy fuck, that was close. Far too close. He'd forgotten the letter. He had to focus. Letting her nightmare drive him, he concocted a plan.

The shower water turned on. He counted to sixty and listened. He could just make out the shuffle of her feet on the tile. The tub creaked when she stepped in and he flew into action.

Pulling on his clothes like a man on his way to put out a fire, he stalked quickly to her kitchen memorizing the pops in the parquet hallway so he'd know the sounds of her approach. Moving to the back corner of her kitchen where there was a built-in desk, he leaned up against the wall granting himself an ideal vantage point of the rest of her home.

Vile repulsion shot vomit to his throat as he opened the damned thing. He didn't want his hands to have contact with the man who made her have dreams like that. He considered locating a pair of oven mitts to read the damn thing with but he was burning precious time.

The letter was worn. He checked the postmark date. Two months ago. Fuck, how many times had Hope read this letter? Summoning control of his own fury, he made certain the shower water was still on and unfolded the foul thing.

His eyes scanned the jagged handwriting. His biceps flexed of their own accord. *I'm gonna end the motherfucker.* He promised himself he wouldn't let her have any reason to have nightmares like that again.

His lip curled when he read Brock's father's plea that he get to see his grandkids. Brock and Hope had two sons. He wondered what Hope had made of him wanting to visit. Most mothers were protective as hell over their kids. Not his mother so much but she wasn't the industry standard by a long shot.

He read on.

His eyes fell to the line, *I plan to make a trip to Pleasant Glen. I deserve to see my son and I deserve the right to make an apology.*

"Like hell you do, you pathetic piece of garbage," Aaron spat. "You're not coming anywhere near her."

Gall roiled in his gut. He had to know if Hope had responded to this. He had to know if Brock knew his father was planning a trip. All of his training said Brock had no knowledge of the letter. Hope had kept it at the library and out of their home. Once people brought things into their intimate spaces there was some degree of acceptance and communal sharing. She hadn't wanted the letter near Brock. Had she pretended it away without a response? Or had she accepted his request and chosen to let it be a surprise to her husband?

He had to figure all of this out before Natalie was forced to see the rat bastard again. He also needed to get the letter back in the library before Hope discovered it was missing. Nothing like being backed into an impossible situation. How did you interrogate someone about something you weren't supposed to know existed? Maybe an impossible task for most men, but Aaron had thrived on this very thing. He had the skills. He'd handle it.

He restored the letter to its envelope. The need for actionable intel locked in his musculature. The shower was still on. He settled at her laptop. One quick search. He'd figure out her uncle's address, erase the history, and have something to go on.

Running his finger over the touchpad his leg shook while he waited on the laptop to come back to life. As soon as the screen lit, shame lodged in his gut. Natalie had eleven tabs open in her internet browser. Every single one of them was either about PTSD or the precious little information the army released about Green Berets. His flashback the night before, the shame he'd felt, the life he'd lived, the diagnosis he hated, it all stared back at him, a one-dimensional definition of the weakness he would never accept.

"You could've asked," he breathed. *She tried.* His brain came to Natalie's defense. So he wasn't the only one doing some research. They were both fucked up. For what had to be the thousandth time since he'd been diagnosed he tried to be okay with it. Only problem was, her issues she'd had no control over. She was brave and had worked through most of it. Everything that had happened was his fault. There was no working through it. He couldn't even make it through a fireworks show without flipping the fuck out. She deserved better. She deserved a whole man.

The absence of the shower water finally registered. He rushed the letter out to his truck. Throwing it in the glovebox, he slipped back in the house and returned to his corner willing the computer to go back to sleep.

When it didn't, he flew to the bedroom needing to keep her there for a few minutes more.

She was fully clothed, much to his chagrin. He willed his pulse back to a normal tenor.

"Where'd you go?" she demanded.

"Uh, was gonna try to make you coffee. Couldn't figure out your maker." He loathed the lies. He just had no other available options.

Her sweet grin only rubbed vinegar in his wounds. "Yeah, Mama and Daddy gave it to me for Christmas. I don't have any idea how to use the grinder thing or the hot tea deal. I just know how to make regular coffee. It has too many buttons."

"Guess I'm better at beer taps."

"Hey, Aaron." She cleared her throat.

"Yeah, baby?"

"Can I say something weird?"

The way she reached through all of the shit his life held astonished him. "I always like your kind of weird."

"This wouldn't make any sense to anyone that hadn't been through the things we've been through."

Interesting. "What have we been through, Nat?"

"You know all the things we don't talk about." She gestured to his gut. The scars. There was so much more to it than the scars. He only offered her a nod.

"You trying to say that I get you?" He drew her closer telling himself he was offering her a place to hide. In reality he used her to cover the scars. She wrapped her arms around his waist and another remnant of his shattered heart seemed to find its way back to life.

"Yeah, I'm saying that. And I wanted to say thank you for teasing me about my butt and about spanking me, even after that nightmare. Most people would've freaked out and..."

"And?"

"And not remembered that I can be strong and brave, too. That I'm not always weak. And how nightmares and flashbacks aren't your real life. They're from a time that doesn't have to exist anymore. You can move on from them."

Can you? He wasn't certain he could. "Baby, you are never weak. And this is the part where I thank you for not freaking out about the fireworks thing. I hate myself for doing that. I probably scared the fuck out of you."

She stepped back. Her hands landed on his face. She gave him no option but to stare into her eyes. "Never ever hate yourself for that. Never. Do you hear me? If you hate yourself for that, I'll hate myself for my nightmares and I'll think I'm weak again. I know you don't want me to believe those lies. And I will not let you tell yourself you're weak either. You, well, you're the strongest person I know and you did not scare me. You never scare me! Stop saying that. A lot of people have assumed a lot of things about me but I will never allow anyone to underestimate me."

Well, damn.

"You promise me right now you won't feel any kind of shame or hate or anything like that for a flashback. I won't let you. I know what they're like. I know what it's like not to be able to breathe for hours after they're over. I know what it's like when you throw up everything for days afterwards. I know what it's like to feel so weak and have no other options except to be strong. I will never let you hate yourself for anything. You got that?"

"Yeah." He managed a slight nod. "Okay."

"Good."

"I never underestimated you, Nat. Never. Okay?"

"Yeah, I know. You underestimate yourself and think that doesn't affect me. You want to blame yourself for everything without thinking about how that makes me feel. I told you I love you. I meant that. At least I'm aware that the things I don't want to tell you affect both of us."

Willing away the irritation ticking in his blood, he shook his head. "Doesn't seem to matter. You still won't tell me."

She edged closer, determination set in those fierce eyes of hers. "Tell me how you got all of those scars. Tell me why you aren't in the army anymore."

"No." God, he couldn't. He wished he could tell her everything. But the inevitable shame she would feel and the pity...he couldn't take the pity. "I wish I could, but I can't. I can't go back there. Not today."

"Yeah, see, I get that. I don't want to go back either. So, can we please just go forward?"

"Baby, I'll go anywhere in this world or any other with you." *Please, just don't walk away.* He reached for her hands. She accepted.

"Good. I'm going to the kitchen to make coffee and eggs and then I'm going to the barn. After that I'm going to go get Lulu and Buster and bring them over here where they can run and play to their hearts' content. I feel bad they haven't seen you much since you started staying here and I don't like Old Man Rasmussen. I don't like Lulu and Buster being there without you."

She still wanted to spend the day together. Relief swept over him, making him dizzy for a moment. He sank down on the bed. "You really think we can do this, Nat? You really want to have this with me, still?"

To his shock, she crawled into his lap and curled herself up into a ball. "More than I have ever wanted anything else." He wrapped her up in his arms certain his next breath depended on having her beside him.

"I'll try to get my shit together."

"I don't need you to get anything together. I just need you to stop blaming yourself for everything. Come on."

CHAPTER TWENTY-NINE

Caught somewhere between hating herself for letting her temper get the better of her yet again and being proud of herself because she fully believed that Aaron needed a little tough love, Natalie scooted the spatula around the skillet keeping the eggs moving.

"I can do that, baby. I should at least be making you breakfast." He kept pacing behind her. She knew he needed something to do. His restlessness was getting to her and he seemed to grow more frantic with each passing moment.

"Why don't you make us toast?" She pointed to the toaster.

"I'm pouring you coffee first."

"Because I'm being bitchy?" She sighed. So she had come off too harshly. She just couldn't stand it when he insisted that he was weak or that he scared her.

"No." He swept her hair away and a kiss landed on the back of her neck. A shiver she couldn't stop coursed through her. "I'm making you coffee because you love coffee. You are never bitchy." Before she could argue, his hand landed on her ass with a pop.

She spun around nearly knocking the skillet off of her stove.

"Say it again and see what I do." His eyebrow lifted in challenge.

She narrowed her eyes. "That a dare?"

A cocky chuckle preceded his smirk. He poured two mugs of coffee with that goading grin on his face. She wanted to kiss it off. "Try me, sweetness."

"I would but I'm pretty sure we'd both enjoy it and I still haven't forgiven you for not forgiving yourself for the thing last night at the fair."

"Stubborn through and through. Pretty sure that's one of the first things I fell for."

"That works well for me. You know how you can't always turn off the lie detector thing?"

"Yeah."

"Well, I can't turn off the stubborn thing. It's gotten me through too much."

"Strongest, bravest person I know."

"Right back atcha, G.I. Joe. Sit down and eat. This is one of the only things I can cook."

"I haven't made the toast yet."

"Then get your ass in gear."

A half hour later, they walked hand in hand to the horse barn. The tender rubbed sensation between Natalie's legs grew more and more apparent with each step she took. By the time they arrived she was quite certain mounting Sundance and riding was going to hurt like hell. She needed to ask Holly when this went away or maybe take him up on that bath.

Sundance was the only horse in the paddock. Everyone else was either out in the fields or being ridden.

"You okay, baby?" Aaron asked yet again.

"I'm fine."

"I don't think so." He grabbed two folded horse blankets from a nearby shelf and set them on a low stack of hay bales. "Sit."

Natalie reluctantly obeyed. Maybe sitting for a few minutes would ease the slight stinging sensation. Sundance immediately walked in from the paddock, leaned her head down, and nuzzled Natalie's neck. Natalie kissed her muzzle. Aaron beamed at them. "See, even she knows you need to take it easy. She's checking up on you."

Chuckling at that, she hugged her horse. "She's the only thing on this ranch more stubborn than I am. She's always gotten me, but what she wants right now is to eat the hay I'm sitting on."

"You hungry, girl?" Aaron patted her side. He pulled another bale of hay out of the stack along the wall, popped the twine holding it together, and spread it in Sundance's stall. The horse gave Natalie another nuzzle before she went after her breakfast.

"We should go riding together someday. You think your brothers would let me borrow one of their horses?"

"Of course. That would be so much fun. I didn't know you could ride."

"It's been years, but we used to have two horses at my foster parents' farm."

Ridiculously pleased that there was something else life giving she could do with him, she debated the best time for their ride. "We could go today after I check to make sure my brothers fed my stock and we go get the dogs."

"I'm doubting you're up to riding today, baby." He leaned down and kissed the top of her head. "Isn't there some other way to check your cows?"

"Yeah, I'll go out in my truck in a little while. Maybe we could ride tomorrow."

"We'll see."

Aaron tried to discreetly check the clock on his phone. The library was opening in five minutes. Surely Hope was already there. He had to get that letter back before she realized it was gone. Natalie needing to take it easy after all they'd done the night before helped his mission, not that he didn't hate that she was hurting. "Honey, why don't I take you back home? I'll go get the dogs and come right back."

"No, I'll be fine. Maybe we could take that bath before we go get Lulu and Buster. The shower didn't help."

Shit. Of course she wanted to take a bath now. Certain he was being rent in two, the head on his shoulders and the one in his jeans were once again at odds. He had to get the letter back and find out how Hope had responded. Holding Natalie naked against him in the bath, soothing her, making up for the inevitable pain he'd caused held far more appeal, however.

Before he could tell one of his heads to get over itself, Brock and Holly came into the barn. No one else would ever have noticed. Aaron's constant awareness of Natalie and his particular skill set honed in on the way she leaned away from Brock, moved her arms in front of her chest, and kept her gaze on the ground. Three minute movements she accomplished instinctively.

Instantly hating the man in the barn for carrying Micheal Camden's DNA, Aaron turned, keeping himself between Brock and Natalie. His arms crossed over his chest and he widened his stance, making himself her physical shield in every possible way. *Never again, baby. I'll never let anything scare you again.*

Confusion furrowed Brock's brow as he dug in a bucket full of deer-skin gloves. "It's nice to see you around here so much lately. How are you?" he offered politely.

Fuck, Brock wasn't his father. Aaron eased his positioning. "I'm with her so I'm good."

Brock gave him a genuine grin. "Yeah, I get that. Hope's at the library today. Damn, if I don't already miss her."

Okay, that was as honest an answer as Aaron had ever been given. Brock was trying to build some kind of friendship. Aaron had to figure out what he knew.

"You okay, Nat?" Brock asked next. "Sundance didn't throw you again did she?"

"I'm fine."

Holly however looked like she'd just been named queen of cowgirls. She leapt from the barn door to the hay bales where Natalie was seated. Certainty radiated from her. She threw her arms around Natalie's neck and squealed like only girls can do.

"Women," Brock shook his head. "Been married for six years. Still can't figure why they do that."

"Holly, remember when we talked about you switching to decaf? I really think you should," Natalie chided. She winced as her sister's excitement rocked her back and forth on the blanket.

Dec stalked into the barn next. It took him a few seconds longer than it had taken his wife to figure out why Natalie was seated and why Holly was so excited. He laughed outright.

"Holl, darling, let her breathe."

"We're going to talk," Holly announced. She jerked Natalie up and tugged her out of the barn.

"Uh?" Aaron took two steps toward them when Natalie spun back around.

She wrinkled her nose. "Do you mind going and getting the dogs? Let me just talk to her for a few minutes."

She played right into his hands and he hated everything about it. "Sure, baby. I'll be back in a little while."

She blew him another kiss. He repeated the motion of catching it and bringing it to his heart. Dec and Brock both laughed. He didn't care.

"You are aware it's all over with, right, my friend? She's it. You're here. I'm going to need to see if I can keep seeing you even though we're going to be related by marriage," Dec goaded.

"Yeah, I'm in love. Doesn't mean we're getting married."

He noted the concerned gaze Brock and Dec shared. He needed Dec to leave. He might never get another opportunity like this. Brock wanted to bond on some level and they were almost alone.

"You keeping your Monday appointment?" Dec quizzed.

"I'd planned to."

"Good." Dec slapped him on the back and then left the barn carrying two bales of hay. He slung them in Holly's truck and drove away.

Aaron turned on Brock calculating the best place to start. "Yeah, I'm not sure what that was all about." He gestured to the hay the Camden sisters had just evacuated.

Brock smirked. "Oh, I kinda think you might." He pulled on his gloves. "Nat's a sweet girl. For some reason she hates me, but that doesn't mean I won't have plenty to say about it if you break her heart. Fair warning."

Ah, another threat, something Aaron could work with. "Never got the impression she hated you. Why do you think that?"

"I was kind of hoping *you* could tell me why. Way you acted when I walked into my own barn..." He shrugged. "Like I was gonna attack her or something. I figured she must've told you what I did that upset her so much. I wish I knew. I'd apologize. I just have no clue what I'm apologizing for. I kept thinking maybe she'd up and tell me eventually. Been here a long time now though. She's never said a word."

Holy fuck. He had no idea. The information worked through his mind. Natalie's father knew. Luke knew. Austin seemed to know. Brock hadn't a clue. How in the hell had that worked out?

"I'm just extremely protective of her. Got nothing to do with you." Another lie. This one rolled through his conscience leaving no guilt behind.

"We got along all right when we were kids. She's competitive as hell, but that never bothered me. If me or her brothers did something, she wanted to do it better. Most of the time she did it, too. I don't know what I did exactly but I figure she must not like it that Uncle Ev gave me half of the ranch a few years back. She wasn't all that kind when Hope and I moved up here."

"That doesn't sound like her."

"Yeah, I know. She's nice to most everybody else unless they tell her she can't do something. Like I said, it's me she don't like."

"So, why did Ev give you half the ranch? I thought Luke was the oldest kid." Aaron kept a great deal of nonchalance in his voice as he pressed harder waiting on Brock to correct him.

"He is. Well, I mean he's their oldest. I'm not their kid."

Aaron feigned surprise. "Don't guess I ever realized that."

"Yeah, I'm just a cousin."

Aaron honed in on the word *just*. Brock didn't think he was worthy. "So, you'd moved away or something? You said when you moved back."

"Yeah, I went to high school in North Carolina. That's where I met Hope, actually." His cell phone buzzed in his pocket. He answered it immediately. Aaron mentally cursed the caller. "What? Broken into?"

Shit. Aaron was out of time.

"Nah, now just hang on, I'll come out there." Brock listened again. "Hope, I know you're fine, but I still want to come out there. I'm on my way just let me see if Aunt Jessie minds watching the boys a little longer. I don't want you there by yourself. I'm on my way." Dispensing with the gloves, Brock headed out of the barn.

"What happened?" Aaron followed him.

"Apparently, someone broke into the library. Can't fathom why the police didn't let her know this last night when it happened other than the fact that our deputy couldn't find his ass with two hands and a mirror. I need to go make sure she's okay."

"I'll go with you."

Brock halted. "Thanks, but you don't have to do that. It's like you said about Natalie, I'm awfully protective of Hope. You understand?"

"Sure. But I used to work in military criminal investigation command for the army. Like you said, the deputy's dumber than his boots. If you want whoever did this caught, let me see what I can find. I'd hate for something like that to happen while Hope was there." Fear was often the most accessible bait at an Intelligence Op's disposal. The suggestion of something happening outside of the source's control generally worked, especially if the source couldn't identify any harm in the operative's suggestion.

"Yeah, I guess, but it was probably just some kids messing around. This is Pleasant Glen not Omaha."

"Can't hurt to check though."

"I s'pose."

Timing was going to be everything. Brock had to go talk to his aunt. Aaron arriving at the library ahead of her husband would confuse Hope. In the realm of confusion, he could access information. Assuming she hadn't realized the letter was missing, it would also give him a chance to get it back in her desk without having another set of suspicious eyes on him.

Brock headed toward the farmhouse. Aaron hightailed it to his truck.

CHAPTER THIRTY

"Just don't ride today. By tonight you'll be fine. But I want details, woman."

Natalie listened to her sister's advice while giving her an eye roll. "I'm not giving you details."

"You have to give me something."

"No, I do not." Yanking her jeans off, Natalie pulled on a pair of her favorite jogging pants. The discomfort disappeared. She had no desire to share anything that had happened the evening before with anyone but Aaron. The connection they'd made wasn't something she had the capacity to verbalize. It was indescribable.

"Come on, Nat. Did you like it?"

With the force of a jackhammer, her sister kept pushing.

"I more than liked it."

Holly sank down on the sofa. Delight broadcast from her, filling the room with her own special brand of sunshine. Just like always, Natalie succumbed to her sister's loving warmth. "It was amazing," she finally confessed. "More than I could ever have imagined."

"Oh my gosh, Nat, I'm so happy for you."

"Me too. I just kind of keep thinking we'll eventually have to work through all of our stuff but I don't want to worry about that right now."

"Are you gonna tell him what happened?"

"He keeps asking me to but you already know a bunch of stuff happened to him when he was in the army and he won't tell me about that. We're at some kind of pleasant impasse."

Holly's brow furrowed. "Pleasant impasse?"

"Yeah, we'll talk about it when it feels right. It doesn't feel right, right now. I mean, unless you could tell me more about what happened to him. What exactly caused the Post Traumatic Stress?" Natalie called herself a rat for going behind Aaron's back but she needed some idea of how to help him deal with everything.

"I honestly don't know. He's Dec's patient. I only know his diagnosis. Just don't let this pleasant impasse go on too long, okay?"

"We'll figure it out. We're good just like we are." Natalie debated but went on with her confessions. "He told me he loved me last night."

Holly's jaw unhinged. "Wow. Nat, that has to be huge for him."

"Yeah, that's what Mama said, too."

"Do you love him back?"

Natalie scooted closer to her sister. "How did you know for certain you loved Dec?"

A watercolor depiction of memories painted themselves in Holly's eyes. "Honestly, the moment I realized I loved him was one of the most terrifying, awful moments of my entire life."

"What?"

"It was when he walked in the lecture hall and I realized he was my professor. If we kept dating and got caught I would get thrown out of school and even worse he would lose his job and lose his green card. I sat there dying inside and then I realized I didn't care. I didn't care if I didn't get my degree. I didn't care about anything but being with him. If he'd gotten sent back to London, I would've given up everything here to go with him. That was when I knew it had to be love."

Natalie considered that. No one was asking her to give up anything for Aaron, but she knew there was no cost too high. There wasn't one thing she wouldn't do to be with him. She loved being a cowgirl but that no longer felt like her purpose on this earth. Her purpose was to show him that he was worth being loved. "When I'm with him it just feels like everything is more."

Holly beamed at her. "Yeah, I get that. Kind of like it's *more* than love."

"Yeah, like maybe it's... magic. I know I sound completely ridiculous."

"Hey, Nat..." Tears pricked her sister's eyes. "You don't sound ridiculous. You deserve all of the magic in the whole world. Please don't let what happened with Uncle Mick come between you two. He stole your magic a long time ago. I can't stand to think he might still have that power over you. If Aaron asks about it again, maybe tell him, even if he can't quite talk about what happened to him yet."

"Yeah, maybe I will."

Charging up the stairs to the library, Aaron methodically assumed yet another identity. Recalling everything he could about the temperament, verbiage, and demeanor of a criminal command officer, he slipped into character.

He hadn't had to deal with them often, but on occasion their paths would cross. Since taking on other identities was the name of the Special Forces game, he let his training take over. Hoisting the door open, he took quick inventory of the main room in the library. Sheriff Wilheim and Hope were standing at her desk. Not ideal but he'd figure it out.

"Aaron?" Hope offered him a forced smile. "I haven't officially opened just yet. Was there something in particular you were looking for?"

"No, ma'am. I was out at the ranch when you phoned Brock. Thought I'd come by and see if I could offer any assistance. He'll be here in just a few minutes."

"Well, thank you but neither of you really had to come. Other than the busted lock and shattered windows nothing seems to be out of sorts."

"You're certain nothing is missing, Hope?" Sheriff Wilheim was making notes on a clipboard. Aaron pretended to check around the shelves nearby all while waiting to hear Hope's response. She'd burned her three to five seconds with silence. Never a good sign. Whatever was about to come out of her mouth was going to be a lie.

"Uh, well, nothing of any importance." Her fingers swept over her mouth and then landed on the top drawer handle of her desk.

Shit.

"I need to know if anything at all is missing, even if it doesn't seem significant," the Sheriff sounded irritated. Aaron wondered how long this interrogation had been going on.

"Well, I haven't had a chance to inventory all of the books but nothing seems to be missing. The microfiche machine was moved but it's still on the shelf where I keep it. Have you talked with Mrs. Lee yet? You said the door between the library and the newspaper office had been opened. Maybe she knows something."

She wanted the Sheriff to leave. Aaron knew it but so did Sheriff Wilhelm. Almost without thought, she ran her fingertips over a framed photograph of her and Brock.

"My deputy is over there now. Nothing missing from there either and they had an unlocked drawer full of cash that had been taken out of the paper's vending machine in front of Saddleback's. All the money is still there. Odd case."

"Yes, it really is." Her eyes flew from the front door back to her desk. She popped open one of the side drawers, searching through it frantically. "See, nothing seems to have been taken or even moved."

Aaron wondered if the Sheriff had picked up on the disappointment in her declaration. Something was definitely missing. Something she didn't want anyone to know about. Something that was most likely the very thing shoved in the waistband of Aaron's jeans. If she already knew the letter was gone, he sure as hell couldn't return it.

He needed a reason to stay at the library a little longer. He needed to know what she was going to tell Brock. Guilt played cruelly in her eyes. She was going to confess, not to the Sheriff but to her husband. Aaron would bet everything he had on it.

Shaking out of his criminal investigative command identity, he slid back into friendly neighbor. "Hey, Hope, Rasmussen has a scrap wood pile he's not doing anything thing with. I'm sure he wouldn't mind me grabbing some plywood from there and fixing the windows for you. Looks like rain's coming in." It didn't but that was beside the point.

That got him a genuine smile. "Oh, Aaron, you're so sweet but you don't need to do that. Brock used to build houses. I'm sure he'll take care of it for me."

"Hope, baby, you okay?" And there was her superhero. Instead of a cape he was wearing a tool belt and carrying two pieces of wood the approximate size of the back windows of the library. Every curse word Aaron knew and a few he made up on the fly gathered on his tongue.

"I'm fine. Just kind of shocked. Nothing ever happens here and why would anyone break into a library? I only charge ten cents a week for overdue books and we've only collected twenty-two dollars from the book drive. Twenty of it Uncle Ev gave me. It's not like I have any cash here. Are the boys okay?"

"They're fine. Playing with J.J. and Hank. Aunt Jessie said for me to stay as long as you need me."

"I'm not sure cash is what they were looking for. Ms. Lee says a few rolls of microfiche were out of place. You said the machine had been moved. Seems like whoever broke in was looking for something that was on one of those rolls of film. My illustrious deputy still hasn't figured out that the windows were shattered from the inside out. They didn't break them to get in. They broke them to get away. Lock was already popped on the door. Why not go out the way they got in? Odd case indeed," the Sheriff urged.

"Other than breaking in, it's not illegal to look at microfilm," Hope offered.

"No, it's not, but why not do it during regular business hours?" the Sheriff countered.

"Maybe it was just a bunch of kids who wanted to see if they could get in, mess around, and get out the windows." Brock sighed. "I had friends who did crap like that back in school. Tell you God's honest truth, every year at the beginning of school we used to dare the new freshman on the football team to do stuff that could've gotten them in a lot of trouble. We thought of it as a rite of passage, but we were also idiots, for what it's worth now."

It was a decent theory. Aaron had to give him that.

"School year did just get started. Dates on the moved film were about this time of year. Could've been some kind football glory prank I suppose." The sheriff made another few notes on his board.

"Just doesn't seem malicious to me," Brock vowed.

"Me either," Hope agreed.

"Committing a crime for any reason is still against the law. Let me know if you see anything suspicious. If anyone comes in the library in the next few days who's never been in before I want to know that as well," Sheriff Wilheim ordered.

"I'll let you know," Hope assured him. Aaron wondered if it would occur to her that he had never been in the Pleasant Glen library before that moment.

"Mr. Camden, Mr. Weber." The Sheriff nodded to them as he made his way out.

"If you're sure you don't need any help with those windows, I'll head on over to my place. Need to feed my pups." Aaron pressed humility into his tone. Come off as a friendly everyday hero people would believe you were.

"Thanks for stopping by." Brock offered him his hand. "You probably don't have to work this hard to get Uncle Ev to like you, but I'm much obliged anyway."

The assumptions people made often became the very excuse you needed. Aaron smiled. "Didn't figure it could hurt. He's not my biggest fan."

Hope laughed. "He's just awfully protective of Natalie and Holly. We all think you're great. He'll come around, just give him some time."

Summoning a concerned but hopeful expression, Aaron pretended to check a few things on a nearby shelf then walked to the restroom. "I'll be around until Natalie orders me away. These the windows they broke?" He opened the door wide.

"Yeah, but just one here and one in the newspaper office." Hope and Brock followed after him.

"Offer still stands, if you want some help boarding them up, I can give you a hand." This time Aaron made the offer to Brock. He knew he wouldn't take him up on the help, but he needed the bathroom door to remain open.

"I've got it. God knows I've installed windows more than a time or two. I'll get 'em boarded up."

Hope went back to fidgeting with things on her desk. Brock noted her nervousness. Perfect.

"I'll be on my way then." Aaron saw himself out. As soon as the front door slammed shut, he slipped to the side of the library and silently eased to the back near the shattered windows. Hope was going to make her confession soon. He knew.

Cautiously avoiding the crunch of decaying leaves on the ground, he slid along the brick building, getting as close as he could to the broken window and leaving himself an escape into Moorer's Woods if Brock should decide to come do the window work before Hope made her admission.

"Baby, what are you looking for? You said nothing was gone." Brock's question grew louder and then softened as he passed by the opened bathroom door. He must've walked to the desk. Aaron chanced edging closer to the window.

"I wouldn't have even noticed that it was gone if I hadn't checked to make sure the book drive money was still here. I'd almost forgotten about it," Hope's explanation was riddled with guilt. Aaron regulated his heartbeats.

"What are you talking about? Forgotten about what?"

"It was a... I wasn't even going to mention it. Why would someone take that?"

The rustle of papers muffled her voice. Aaron's jaw clenched. He chanced one more step toward the window.

"Hope." Brock's tone took on an edge of worry with a shot of irritation. "What are you talking about?"

The rustling papers silenced. Aaron halted his breaths.

"It was a letter."

"A letter from who?"

"From, uh, well... it was from your father."

The wind itself took up Aaron's cause and ceased its restless whips.

"What the hell did he want? And why the hell was he writing to you?"

Seemed Brock disliked his own father almost as much as Aaron did.

"I have no idea. He's never written me before. I wasn't even sure he knew we'd gotten married. He basically demanded to see you and the boys. Said something about deserving forgiveness. I wasn't going to tell you. I know you never want to see him again and neither of us would ever let him near the boys, not after the things he did to you. It makes you so angry to even think about him. I don't know why I even kept it except something about it was strange."

"Strange how?" Brock's two-word question held more than a note of hurt and accusation.

"Weird like he almost alluded to being sick. Kind of seemed like he wanted to see the boys before he... isn't here anymore, I guess. I know I should have told you about it. He mailed it here to the library which is weird in and of itself. But even more strange is why on earth would anyone take that?"

"How does he know you work here?"

"That's my point. Does he have some kind of spy in the Glen? He's never contacted me before. I promise. I'm sorry I didn't tell you."

"I don't like you keeping things from me, Hope, even if they are things you know I don't want to hear."

"I know. I'm so sorry. I honestly forgot about it until I went to look for the money and remembered I'd shoved it in my drawer."

"Did you answer the letter?" Brock sounded like someone had punctured his lungs.

"No."

There was the answer Aaron needed. Unfortunately, just like any mission he'd ever worked before, the answer only brought on more questions.

"Do you want me to?"

"Fuck no. I don't want you, or my kids, or anyone I love having anything to do with the likes of him. It'll be over my dead body that he gets anywhere near Camden Ranch."

So, Aaron did have an ally in that respect. He counted that as a blessing.

"That's probably why he sent me the letter instead of you. Maybe he thought I'd invite him up. Maybe he actually thinks I've forgiven him for the horrible things he did to you."

What had he done to Brock? Yet another question.

"Dad's never been afraid to use people to get what he wants. I don't know if he was planning on taking advantage of how sweet you are or if he figured I couldn't read the letter if he had sent it to me."

Aaron's brow furrowed. What the hell did that mean?

"You read perfectly well now." Tender pride welled in Hope's affirmation.

"Yeah, but he doesn't know that."

"It doesn't matter why he sent it to me. I want to know why someone took it. Maybe they were after the money in my drawer and got interrupted or something. Maybe that's why they broke out the window to get away. Maybe there's actually two culprits."

"You playing Nancy Drew, baby?"

"I was a big fan of the *Babysitter's Club Mysteries*."

Brock's easy chuckle said Hope was forgiven. Silently, Aaron slipped away. He waited on the train whistle that always sounded at 9:57 to crank his truck and drive away.

CHAPTER THIRTY-ONE

"You get the letter back in the drawer?" T answered on the second ring.

"Nope," Aaron sighed. A cocktail of nerves stirred in his gut. He couldn't quite put his finger on what was wrong but something was amiss.

"How come?"

"Got there too late. Hope already knew it was gone. It's still on me."

"Fuck."

"Yeah."

"You think she'll say anything to Natalie about the letter?"

"No. She didn't even want to tell Brock about it. His father is apparently hated by most everyone. I doubt she'll mention it ever again. She never responded to it."

"I'm sorry, man. I should've just snapped a pic of it. We got sloppy because there's no security in that town. I never dreamed anyone would figure anything out. I do have a peace offering for you though."

"I was an ass last night. You don't need to give me a peace offering." Aaron hoped that would be enough of an apology.

"You are always in a much better mood after you get laid. How was she?"

"Don't make me murder you, too."

T laughed. "You're not gonna tell me anything? Come on."

"She was perfect. Now shut the fuck up."

"I knew it. You never sound this happy after a misstep in a mission. She's good for you."

"Fairly certain I told you to shut it."

"Fine."

Aaron heard T's fingers on a keyboard again.

"I am currently looking inside Micheal Camden's house."

"You're kidding."

"Nope. There's a tire swing hanging in the backyard which makes me want to murder him twice. It seems anyone who's had the great misfortune of interacting with him calls him Mick."

Vomit swirled in Aaron's mouth. "He's listed as a sexual predator though, right?"

"Nope. He has a fairly lengthy record but they're all public drunkenness or drinking and driving. Nothing like what happened to Natalie. That is what happens when families don't report things. On the other hand, what parent wants to put their kid through having to testify to shit like that? Keeping in mind that this was someone she probably trusted at one time, she may not have even been capable of testifying about it at eleven. Fucked up all the way around."

"I'm gonna make sure he burns. Don't worry."

"Yeah, well, you know we're going with you if you go."

"I need to know where I'm going first."

"He lives in a tiny beach town near Wilmington, North Carolina, called Gypsy Beach."

"Fuck. That has to be more than a thousand miles from here. I was kind of hoping the postage on the letter was because he sent it on vacation or something."

"Gypsy Beach is fifteen hundred eighty-seven miles to be exact. He's lived there since he was thrown off of Camden Ranch. That's a two-day trip minimum even if you flew."

"I can't afford to fly."

"You want some money?"

"No. Even if I flew down there, beat the shit out of him, did him in, and dumped him in the Atlantic, where the hell am I gonna tell Natalie I'm going?"

"Personally, I'm far more concerned about your new mailing address being in the North Carolina state penitentiary."

"He doesn't deserve to live."

"I'm not disagreeing, but you do."

Clearly having spent a good deal of time on a cattle ranch lately, Aaron only grunted his response. He didn't necessarily agree with T's assessment.

"Tell you what, you stay in Pleasant Glen with your cowgirl and keep doing things that make her smile. I'll keep eyes on Uncle Mick."

"What's that mean exactly?"

"Means he won't so much as sneeze without me knowing about it."

"I still plan on choking him with his own sac."

"Good thoughts. For now, go see if Natalie might be up for another round. You're getting pissy again."

Natalie laughed as Buster and Lulu shook the old towel she'd given them to play with back and forth with utter delight. "You'd think it was covered in bacon." She scratched behind Buster's ears.

Aaron grinned. "They love you, too."

All of the discomfort the evening before had provided was gone by noon. In fact, the emptiness she hadn't missed was returning.

She chanced another glance at Aaron as he downed the last of the Dr. Pepper she'd given him. There was an ease to him now. He was seated on her couch, where they'd taken a nap earlier. His eyes were clear. His beard a little longer than he normally kept it. The muscles that had cradled her so gently all afternoon were still relaxed. Like the picture her mother had taken of her and Sundance on the table nearby, he seemed to belong. The room wouldn't have felt complete without him.

"When do we have to leave for Saddleback's?"

"Just a few minutes. I have to clock in at five."

"That sucks."

"Believe me I'd much rather stay here, but having a paycheck, small as it is, does come in handy."

"I know. I was just wishing we had time for you to carry me back to the bedroom." She tried for a flirtatious smile.

The low hum she'd needed to hear sounded from him. "I kind of pride myself on how long I can go, sweetheart, but that's awfully damned tempting. Not sure you're quite ready for us to get down and dirty that fast, anyway."

"You're going to stay with me again tonight, right?"

"Unless you're tired of looking at me."

"I'm definitely not."

He lumbered upward and made his way to her. Hungry intention locked in his gaze as he tipped her chin upward. "Don't worry. As soon as I get you back here, I'm gonna rock you to sleep. Back and forth. In and out. Listen to those sweet little gasps and moans you make when I take what belongs to me." His lips swallowed down the approving squeak she made. There was a hint of the syrup from the fizzy drink she'd given him on his tongue, she pressed hers deeper needing the flavors of him.

He turned his head and kissed along her jawline. When he nipped her earlobe she gasped. God, who knew ears were an erogenous zone? She ran her hands over his shoulders and down the ropes of muscles that comprised his massive arms.

"You have any fucking clue how much I love the fact that I'm the only man who knows you, baby?" Another kiss on her lips. Another moan. "The only man who knows how sweet you come." And another, this one slower and deeper. "How sweet you beg." His hands gripped her ass rocking his erection against her. "The only man who knows how wet and needy you get for me. Knows how good you taste." Another greedy kiss. "Knows how to make you come. And tonight I'm gonna feel you come on my cock, honey, over and over again." His raspy tone carried the current of desire directly to her core.

"Oh God."

His hands slipped to her breasts. He caught her lace trapped nipples between his thumb and index finger. "Yes." She couldn't help herself. Every time he touched her there, the entire world tilted off its axis. He pressed harder and she bucked against him, unable to keep herself from him.

"Can't you be late?" Her nipples puckered and throbbed, begging for more of his touch.

His throaty chuckle tangled her in knots only he could untie. "Anticipation is a good thing, baby." He took one more kiss before his hands returned to her back and he cradled her to him. "I have a question for you."

"Should you ask me while we drive?"

"Probably. You sure you're okay with the dogs staying here?"

"Of course."

CHAPTER THIRTY-TWO

"What were you going to ask me?"

If she hadn't asked Aaron was going to let it go. He was pushing too hard yet again. "Don't worry about it."

"Tell me."

"If this wigs you out, just say so."

"Okay."

He chanced a quick look her way. The sinking sunlight melted into the cornstalks outside his windshield and played in the strands of her dirty-blonde hair. It highlighted the strands of gold. Innocence and devotion to him had her seated right beside him, clinging to his arm. For a half second he swore there was an actual halo around her head. "I'm a bastard. You should dump me now."

"Would you stop it? What the hell? You're pretty much the greatest guy ever."

"You don't know what I was about to ask."

"It can't be that bad."

"It pretty much was."

"Just ask me."

"Nope."

"If you don't ask, I'll pinch you and I rope better than Austin. I'll make it hurt."

"Ironic," he sighed.

"What?"

"Fine, I'll ask. Your answer will be no which will only cement me as the world's biggest jerk. Least that way I'll get the idea out of my system. Maybe."

Her fingers dug into his thigh. It didn't hurt but the girl was strong as hell. "Hey, I said I'd ask you. I thought I only got pinched if I didn't."

"That was for you calling yourself a jerk."

Aaron laughed at his own ridiculous idea in hopes she'd let this go.

"So, ask me."

"Fine. Do you know what nipple clamps are?"

"Well, not exactly but I'm going to go with clamps you put on your nipples." Her hand flew back to the charm on her necklace. He lambasted himself for ever bringing them up.

"Good guess."

"They sound interesting." Her right eyebrow arched.

"They can be."

"I take it you think I might like them."

"Most of them are way too much for you. I don't mess with that shit. Never have. Don't do torture. There are others, just for pleasure play, I think you might enjoy."

"I don't like the word torture in any scenario ever."

"Me either."

"And do you own a set of the other kind or something?"

"No, baby. Haven't been with anyone but you in a long time, remember? Just thought I could get you some if you want to experiment."

"You cannot order those and have them sent to your house. The mailman opens everything. You know this."

"I wasn't going to order them. I may be a rat bastard but I'm not an idiot."

"I mostly just like when your hands are on them." Heat bloomed across her cheeks.

Unable to help himself, he leaned and brushed a kiss over her fevered skin. "Trust me, I love that, too. I'm more than happy to improvise some clamps with my fingers. Just trying to figure out your kink level, I guess."

"I'm not sure how kinky I am. I'll probably bore you soon."

"Natalie Jessica Camden, if I wasn't driving I swear to you I *would* turn you over my knee. What the hell? I'm in love with you. That's not gonna change. I don't give a damn if you never want to get kinkier than we already have. Never say that again."

His vehemence eased the tension slowly knotting itself in Natalie's stomach. Talk of nipple clamps had her on edge. She found herself giggling at his irritation. "Only my mama yells at me with all three names. When did I even tell you my middle name?"

"Uh, you mentioned it one night when we were talking a few months ago."

If it hadn't been such a trivial thing, she would've sworn he was lying. His knuckles whitened against the steering wheel. Before she could contemplate further, they were parking behind the bar.

Readying herself for a night of loud music, louder cowboys, and general annoyance, she hopped out of the truck when he opened the door for her. "Mama would tell me to thank you for always being a gentleman and opening the door for me and stuff."

"Babe, I just asked you about nipple clamps. Definitely not a gentleman but don't tell your mom that."

"I like your gentlemanly and your not so gentlemanly sides."

"Oh yeah?" He wrapped his arm around her and guided her in the back door.

"Definitely."

"Hang on let me grab an apron."

"Look at you two lovebirds. Sweeter than a pig in poop." Eliza slapped her own thigh and then dragged Natalie in for a full force hug. "Does he kiss as good as he looks like he would? You know I always say Little Red Riding Hood shoulda up and gone after the big bad wolf. The bad boys always do very good things with their mouths."

Aaron coughed to cover his gag. Natalie bit her lips to keep from guffawing. "Um, he does everything well, Eliza. I'm a lucky girl," she finally managed.

"You sure are. Mm, mmm, mmm what I wouldn't give to be twenty-five years younger." She released Natalie and ran a long red fingernail down Aaron's bicep as she passed by.

"You look completely horrified," Natalie informed him as she followed him behind the bar.

"I am beyond horrified. In fact, I'm pretty sure I have a sexual harassment suit in the works."

"That might be why Ed hates you so much."

"I can't win for losing."

"She was right about all of the very bad, good things you do with your mouth." Natalie waggled her eyebrows at him, loving the flicker of heat that lit in his eyes.

"Just wait, baby, I'll show you all of the very good, bad things I can do with my mouth as soon as I get you home."

"I'm hoping."

Aaron tested a few of the taps and then lined up shot glasses and beer mugs. As much as she hated being in the bar, she loved watching him work. That was the reason she usually agreed to come along when her brothers and sisters wanted to spend the evening at Saddlebacks.

He popped a crick out of his neck and swung his arms back and forth, loosening up for the hours he'd be working. He winked at her as patrons made their way toward him. "What can I get you, Duke?" he offered Duke Kilroy Jr. a kind smile.

"Give me a shot of Crown. No, make it a double." Duke slunk down on the stool beside Natalie.

"Rough day, man?" Aaron didn't quite give him a double shot, Natalie noted.

"Mother-in-law's in town."

"Ah."

Another round of giggles threatened to take Natalie over as Aaron added a little to Duke's glass.

"She got into it with Cassie about starching my boxers and feeding the kids them dinosaur chicken nuggets. I swear sometimes that's all they'll eat and I don't want my drawers starched. I came to my wife's defense and then I got myself thrown out of my own house." Duke downed what was left in his glass. "Give me another."

"One more but then you're eating something and I'm switching you to beer. Cassie's gonna want to make up when you get home and you don't want to disappoint."

"You think?"

"Didn't some kind of argument lead to all four of your kids, man?"

The tension bled from Duke's face. He laughed. "Yeah, s'pose you're right. Just switch me to beer now."

As if he could read the man's mind, Aaron handed him the beer he'd already poured. He'd never even picked the Crown bottle back up. Duke lifted his glass to Aaron and headed toward one of the checkers games going on.

"How did you know that about their kids?" Natalie leapt as soon as he was out of earshot.

"I'm the local bartender, sweetheart. People tell me stuff. Part of my job."

"Do they ever tell you anything you wished they wouldn't?"

"Sure, but I figure everyone needs someone to talk to. If I can be that for them, I'm okay with it."

"Is that what Dec is for you? Is he who you talk to?"

Aaron studied her for a long moment before he answered. "I guess so."

"Do you think I could ever be the person you could talk to?" She needed to know if there would ever be a time when she would be enough to help him deal with all of the things that had fragmented his soul. "It's okay if I can't be that. I just kind of wondered."

She watched his long black eyelashes blink in consideration. "Kind of feel like that question is a two-way street, Nat. You ever think I'll be someone you could talk to about what happened?"

"Should have guessed that's what you'd say." Disappointment crashed through her.

"That's not really an answer."

"You didn't answer me either."

"Fine. Yes, someday I'll try to explain all of the complicated shit

that's in my past. It's just not something I want to pollute our relationship with right now, okay?"

Well, that was something. Maybe they were getting somewhere.

"Give my girl something pink with an umbrella." Wyatt Jenson
slumped against the bar. "Hey, Nat, what's up with you?"

"Hey, Wyatt. Not much. How's the corn?"

"Taller than me but that ain't saying much." Wyatt laughed at his
own expense. "How's the cattle?"

"Fat and happy just how we like 'em. Who's your new girl?"

"Wyatt finally talked Amy Scofield into going out with him a few
weeks ago." Aaron supplied Wyatt with Amy's drink. "I take it things
are still hot and heavy with the two of you."

"Not near as hot and heavy as I hear you two are gettin' on." Wyatt
elbowed Natalie.

She rolled her eyes. "Don't believe everything you hear."

"Nah, now Amy says he up and overpaid for a few things at the
drugstore the other day. She got to digging and figured there was a
pregnancy test missing from stock. That must be why he overpaid,
right? When's the happy day, Nat?"

Natalie's mouth hung open. Her body vibrated like she'd been
struck by lightning. Aaron was vehemently shaking his head but he
knew something. She could tell. Flinging herself off the barstool, hot
tears stung her eyes. Who the hell was he buying a pregnancy test for?
Bile singed her tongue.

"Nat." Until Aaron's hand landed on her arm she wasn't aware she'd
been racing out the door. "Stop."

"No. Who is she? I thought you said..."

"I love you. I said that and I meant it. Just come here." Fury and
rejection made her woozy. As she swayed, he was able to pull her
behind the bar. He didn't stop until they were back in the kitchens. "I
didn't buy that for me."

"Obviously," she snarled.

"Shit. Natalie come on. I bought it for Austin."

"What? Do you actually expect me to believe that?"

"Yes, I do. I've never given you a reason not to trust me and Austin didn't want people bugging Summer about the pregnancy yet. Did you know she had a miscarriage a few months ago?"

That settled her on her boots. Trying to force the images of her torching his truck from her mind, she had to admit he wasn't lying to her. No one outside the family knew Summer had lost a baby back in May. Austin must have told him.

"I was in the drugstore getting the condoms. I ran into Austin and I helped him sneak out with the test. He gave me a twenty to leave on the counter. Call him and ask him. I am not lying to you."

"Summer hasn't ridden in two weeks."

Aaron raised his eyebrows in expectation. Natalie squeezed her eyes shut wishing she could erase the last five minutes of her life. "Sorry. I shouldn't have jumped to conclusions."

"I forgive you. That had to be a shock to hear."

"Why didn't you tell me about Summer?"

"Babe, I kind of figured that was Austin and Summer's story to tell."

"Maybe, but all the stuff we aren't telling each other is starting to get to me."

"You want to talk, I'm right here."

"Yeah, I know. But it's just like you said, that street goes both ways."

"I need to get back to the bar. You gonna be okay?"

"I'm fine."

"You sure about that or are you just saying that?"

"I'm really fine."

He offered her his hand. She took it and let him lead her back to the bar. "Hey, how about this, I could tell you something I've never told anyone, not even Dec? That sound good?"

"Very good."

Leaning on his elbows so they were face to face, he glanced right and left to make certain everyone else was busy. "I'd never tended a bar when I took this job. Not even once."

"Are you serious? I can't believe Ed hired you with no experience." Natalie kept her voice to a whisper.

"Oh, I told him I had a ton of experience. I spent ten years in the army learning to blend in to any situation they put me in so I figured it out as I went. Spent the first three months Googling any drink that wasn't a whiskey shot or a beer. I made do."

"So, you just went all over the world pretending to be different people?"

"Kind of. It's a little more complicated than that."

A spike of nerves twisted in her stomach. "That must've been hard."

"Not nearly as hard as I am standing here looking at you." This time his flirting didn't settle her. He'd spent so much time being other people. Who was he now?

CHAPTER THIRTY-THREE

"At what exact point do you throw them out?" Natalie's fascination with his work made it infinitely more fun to tend bar that night.

Aaron refilled Ty Lorner's beer while keeping an eye on the couple all but humping on the dance floor.

"Ed'll let 'em stay as long as they're paying to drink. Eliza usually cheers them on. I tend to tell them to find a room if any skin that should be under clothing is revealed to the bar at large." The couple was rapidly approaching Aaron's line.

Natalie was laughing and gazing up at him like he was a fucking superhero.

"What did I do to earn a look like that? Whatever it was I sure as hell want to do it again."

"I was just thinking about you helping Austin and about how even if you did have to pretend you were all those different people that it was such a brave thing to do. Kind of made me worry at first but I'm over it."

"Why'd it make you worry, baby?"

She shrugged and shook that necklace back and forth yet again. He caught her hand. "Tell me."

"I guess I kind of worried about who you were being with me."

"Nat." He swore she killed him with her honesty. Honesty was never a good idea in foster care and never allowed in Army Intelligence. There was a time when he'd wondered if he would even be able to recognize the truth when it stared him in the face. Then he'd met her. "You want to know what just one of the most incredible things about making love with you last night was?" Unable to keep his hands from her, he traced the soft angles of her face. She nodded. "It was the first time in a lifetime when I felt like me. The first time I understood who I used to be and who I wanted to be for you. I wish I could explain it better. It was incredible."

"You keep making me fall more and more in love with you." Her tender vow mended another portion of his tattered heart.

"I plan to keep doing that if it's okay with you."

"It's definitely okay with me."

Ripping them from the moment of precious intimacy two of Amy Scofield's girlfriends burst through the door, hooting with laughter. Aaron cringed. Natalie rolled her eyes.

"Great. The entire Pleasant Glen gossip column just arrived," she said through her teeth.

"Maybe they'll order wine. At least that'll settle them down."

Amy beelined over to them. "Did you all hear about the library getting broken into?"

Aaron grabbed a bar cloth and edged closer.

Natalie's brow furrowed. "The library was broken into?" She joined their conversation. The ladies didn't look any too thrilled with her interjection.

"That's what she just said," Tilda Herker huffed.

"Does Hope know?"

"Well, I'm sure she does since the sheriff was up there talking to her all morning."

"She didn't say anything to me about it."

"Do all of you Camdens walk around your big-ass ranch telling each other every little thing, Natalie?"

"Do all of you Herkers have the corncobs shoved up your ass

professionally installed or is it a do-it-yourself project like your boob job, Tilda?" Natalie thrust her finger at the wad of tissue emerging from the top of Tilda's blouse.

Aaron choked back hysterical laughter as they shared a conspiratorial grin. Shoving her homemade padding back in its proper location, Tilda followed after Amy and Heidi Conlin like hens heading to the house.

"She is such a bitch," Natalie fumed.

"I love you."

"You keep saying that."

"Well, that's because I do." He wondered how much of the library incident she would focus on.

"Did you hear that about the library?"

Weighing his options very carefully, Aaron knew if his conscience had any chance of survival he had to tell as much of the truth as he was able. "Yeah, I went up there this morning when I went to get my dogs. I was with Brock in the barn when Hope called him. It was right after you left with Holly."

"Why didn't you say anything?"

"Once I'm with you I can't think of anything but you." That was the truth with a twist, he decided.

"Was anything taken?"

"Didn't look like it. Brock thinks it was probably some kids, some kind of football prank or something."

"That's strange though. Nothing ever happens here."

"I got the impression Sheriff Wilheim is sick of people reminding him of that."

"It's true though. Why would anyone break into the library? Do people actually steal books?"

"People steal e-books all the time. I doubt they steal books from libraries too often though. Didn't sound like they have any idea who did it." A fact Aaron was supremely thankful for. "You want something to drink?"

"Sure. Whatever you want to kiss off of me." That little mischievous grin she sported whenever she flirted with him shot another jolt of lust through him.

"Whatever I want to kiss off of you, huh?" Grabbing a glass, he made her a soda water. "I just want to taste you, baby. In every possible way I could mean that."

He stared unabashedly at her tongue as it teased her bottom lip and then disappeared. "I want to do that too, you know."

His cock leapt to attention. His crown swelled out a salute. Images of her on her knees before him, of him fucking her mouth filled his mind. "Oh yeah?"

"Yeah." She leaned closer so no one could hear their dirty banter. "I want to know what you taste like."

A low grunt clawed up from his lungs freeing the question he longed to ask. "And if I ask you to swallow everything I give you what happens, honey?"

"I do it."

"You drive me fucking wild, Nat. I swear you were a sub in a former life or something."

"Maybe I just like you directing things. Maybe that really turns me on."

"Maybe so." He breathed the word across her lips as he leaned over the bar and devoured her mouth. To illustrate his point, she coaxed his tongue into her mouth and began sucking. She was timid and unsure. That only made it better. She wanted to learn to blow him. He sure as hell would teach her.

A rumbled growl of approval spilled into her mouth. Later, he'd spill himself between her lips, tell her to let him see it before she swallowed. Then he'd kiss his flavors from her mouth.

"Weber, you think you can get your tongue outta her mouth long enough to serve drinks?" Ed fumed.

Jerking away, Aaron counted backward from five. "Sorry, sir."

"I don't recall it being bring your girlfriend to work night. You're this close, son. You ain't the only idiot who knows how to pour shots in the town."

Devastation cast Natalie's beautiful face. Her lips were kiss-swollen and so ready for more. Aaron hated his job more and more with each passing moment.

"Hey, lay off him, Ed. Two kids in love. Nothing wrong with that," bellowed from Mayor Kilroy who'd come in to check on Duke. "Whole damn town's sick of your loud mouth anyway."

A chorus of yeahs chanted from the crowd. Aaron caught the damp towel Ed hurled at his gut before he stalked back into the kitchen. Eliza's scolding shrieks spilled out into the bar almost instantly.

"Sorry." Natalie cringed.

"I feel like I should get a fucking medal for not ringing the last call bell after what you just offered me. He threatens to fire me at least once a week. As you can see, I have a bar full of job security. Don't worry about it."

If she traced her finger along the woodgrain in the bar once more, Natalie was going to lose her mind. Her fingertip was raw. It was five minutes until last call and she was counting the seconds. Flirting with Aaron made the time fly by but she would not lose him his job.

Constantly reviewing everything she'd admitted to him in the last two hours simultaneously served to embarrass her and enliven her. A heady sense of power was birthed deep inside her when she'd admitted that she liked when he directed their lovemaking. Tonight, she wanted more than she'd had the day before.

Eventually she wanted to know what he was like in full form. The same set of adjacent emotions taunted her again. She both appreciated the women who'd come before her and hated them.

"What's the frown for?" Once again his voice reached through the mire of confusion in her head and pulled her out of the tidal waters.

"Nothing." She refocused on those deep blue eyes.

"Not nothing. Tell me."

"Eventually I'll figure out how not to feel ashamed about the things I want to ask for and I'll stop being afraid that if you do something I'll have a panic attack, right? Time is supposed to heal all wounds or whatever."

Compassion, worry, and love paraded through his gaze right after a flash of vengeance. Her heart pounded out a warning. "I'm not sure time does heal all wounds, sweetheart." He came around the bar and wrapped his arms around her.

"You're going to get in trouble again."

"I don't give a shit. You need me. That is all that will ever matter to me." His pecs flexed against her cheek as he reached over her head and rang the bell just a little early. Tremendously thankful, she squeezed him tighter.

"What does heal wounds if it isn't time?" she asked almost an hour later when he'd finally been able to leave the empty bar. The crunch of gravel under her boots disturbed the quiet night. Pleasant Glen was tucked in safe and secure just like always.

"I kind of figure it depends on the wound." Exhaust assaulted the cool air as he cranked his truck. "Do you remember when you told me that your therapist explained to you that sometimes your dreams are your brain's way of healing?"

"Yeah. Of all the times I talked with her that was the one thing that helped the most I think. It made me not hate myself for having them."

"It kills me that you hated yourself for anything but I think fantasies can be the same way. That was the way Dec explained it to me anyway. Trusting me with some of them can help you keep what happened in the past from being in the present."

"You talked to Dec about your sexual fantasies?" Natalie tried to process that. The thought of it scalded her cheeks.

"Not much. He knows a little bit about my past."

"Oh." So, Dec can know but I can't. *It's a two-way street, Nat.* Her mind readily came to Aaron's defense, even taking up his verbiage as its banner. Sometimes she hated her brain. "What's one of your fantasies then?"

She felt the hot lick of his gaze as he turned toward her. "I plan on showing you as soon as I get you home, baby."

"But I want you to tell me now."

"How about I tell you one we're not going to do for a while?"

"Okay."

"You on your knees, your hands behind your back, me feeding you my cock slowly and then faster. Seeing my pre-cum cover your sweet little mouth. My hands wrapped up in your hair. Feeling you moan instead of just hearing you. Then pulling out and coming all over your tits, watching it drip down your nipples. But I told you I like it dirty."

Wet heat rushed to fill the lips of her pussy, readying her for him. It seeped into her panties. She needed him to free her from their constraint. "I like your kind of dirty."

"Let me guess, I don't get to hear one of yours."

The direct challenge stirred the very marrow of her bones. She was a cowgirl and this time she wasn't going to shy away. "You naked, tied to my bed with one of my lariats. I get to touch, and lick, and feel all of you. I don't even know exactly what I want to do once I have you like that, but I know I want to taste you and to climb on top of you and ride you. I want to see the way you look when I do that. I want to be in control just for a little while. It morphs from there."

An anguished sound of pure need filled the truck cab. "Morphs into what?" Carnality dominated his question.

"Into you taking control, taking what you want, making me beg just like you like."

"How wet are you right this moment, sweetheart? How wet does me taking control make you?"

Riding the arc of electricity between them, she popped the snap on her jeans. "Why don't you find out?"

Instead of his hand diving inside her panties like she'd envisioned, he stroked his fingers outside the cotton crotch. Her jeans trapped his hand there. Each touch made her eager for more. "Touch me," she whimpered.

"No, baby. Tell me how bad you want my fingers against your clit. Tell me how empty you feel. Beg me."

"So bad. Please." Her body rolled. She spread her legs farther. "Please, please."

Three fingers pressed wet cotton to her clit. The fabric amplified every stroke. "So wet, baby. You get so nice and wet for me."

"Please touch me."

"Not yet. Not until I'm good and ready." He circled his fingers. The elastic bands taunted her lips. She wriggled in the seat and clawed at his forearm.

He growled out his adamant approval. "When I get you home, baby, my God, we are gonna make your fantasies come true. Every fucking one of them and a few of my own. Be ready for me. I'm gonna keep you so wet we have to change to sheets. I'm gonna make you drip for me. Down my throat, all over my cock, all over me."

CHAPTER THIRTY-FOUR

The rear tires on the truck skidded as Aaron slammed on the brakes outside the largest barn on Camden Ranch.

"Why did you stop?" Her breathy inquisition did nothing to stem the tide of his wanton desires.

"Get a rope."

Realization slowly softened the furrow of her brow. "Are you serious?"

"Now."

Without further prompting she hopped out and returned with a well-worn round of rope. Every fiber of his being hated what he was about to do but loved her enough to do it.

Carrying the rope in her trembling hands, she managed to flip on a light switch as they entered her home and a few more on the way to her bedroom.

"Nat, look at me."

She obeyed readily. "A few things you need to understand. There's a give and a take between the Dom and the sub. It's in constant flux. Back and forth. The yin and yang of it. They must always remain in balance. The desires for power and control are in all of us. It's a universal thing. Everyone has them. Never believe for one second that wanting to tie me up and having me at your mercy is something you should be ashamed of wanting to experience. But far more importantly I need you to understand that wanting to be dominated by me, you wanting me to be in control, is a normal healthy desire. That also exists in every human being."

"I know."

"You're the one holding the rope, Nat. If you know, why do you look more terrified than I've ever seen you?"

"I don't know what I'm doing."

Cradling her face in his capable hands he willed her to understand. "You're going to allow yourself to take what you want, to explore. You're going to leave all of the rules and other shit society tells you not to want outside your bedroom door. You're going to fight through the fear and find the pleasure, baby. You're going to take away the power it's held over you for so long. You're going to give it back to yourself and ultimately I want you to trust me enough to give it to me. Can you do that?"

A timid nod stroked his thumbs against her cheeks. "I already trust you that much."

"Good. There's one more thing I need you to know." He waited on the heat of her gaze to return to his. "I do not give up my control, ever. I have never done this with anyone and I would never do this for anyone but you. Do you understand what I'm saying to you?"

"You don't have..." She offered him the rope as her lips sealed shut.

"I love you. I will always give you anything you need. Tonight, you need to be in control. All I'm asking is that you recognize that this isn't easy for me. Also understand there are very few physical situations I can't get out of. I spent months in Special Forces training learning to get out of most anywhere. I sure as hell can get out of a fucking lasso. I'll do my best but I make you no promises that I will remain bound."

"Okay."

"Then let's do this."

Refusing the haunting memories, damming every recollection of bindings on his young body, denying the knowledge of the scars her hands would touch once he was tied to her bed, Aaron took the rope from her. He tossed it on the bed. This wouldn't be the first time he'd been held. It sure as hell would be the last. "I undress you," he informed her.

"Yes. Now."

"Not feeling particularly gentle tonight, baby, you sure you want to do this?"

"I don't want gentle, Aaron. I want you."

"If you want me to stop, I will. Just speak up."

"If you need me to untie you..."

Laughing at the very idea, he shook his head. "I won't."

Jerking her forward, he thrust as her mound collided with his cock. "You feel how hard you make me?" She nodded. "Good. You want a ride, honey, I'm gonna let you ride. But after that I'm gonna turn you over and take you exactly the way I want. And what I want tonight is every bit as hard as I feel right now. Say you understand."

"I more than understand. It's exactly what I want, too." Another one of those delectable little trembles shuddered through her.

"Good. Take your boots off." Once again she complied.

His fingers made quick work of the pearl buttons on her blouse. Her jeans were already unsnapped so he continued his downward trek, stripping her of the denim blocking the wet heat he'd already explored.

Determination glimmered in her eyes from the lamplight. She stood before him in nothing but a lace bra, a pair of socks, and a pair of wet panties. Her shirt hung open, framing the tender swells of her breasts. Innocence personified. Everything he was about to give at odds with everything he would take away.

Tracing his fingertips along her collarbone he eased the shirt from her shoulders. Her eyes closed and she swayed with the motion. "The things I want to do to you, honey. The things I want to teach you..."

"Do them. I want them." Her breathy vow was fervent. Her fingertips brushed over his zipper line. Her palm centering on his head and crown. His cock throbbed out its demand to be released from his jeans. A low murmured moan escaped her lips. "I want it to do that in my mouth. I want to feel it." Certainty seemed to be erasing the hesitant doubt locked in her limbs.

"Fucking hell." He seized giving himself one moment to rock against her hand. "Trust me, baby, my cock's gonna love being in your mouth." Shoving the sleeves of her shirt down her arms, he dropped it in a pile of cotton at her feet.

He heard Lulu pawing at her bedroom door. "Should we let them in?" Natalie sounded horrified by the idea of a canine audience. Aaron happened to agree.

"No. I'm not putting on a show tonight. They can come in when we're finished." Refocusing her on her mission, he swept his palms up her belly and wrapped his hands around her breasts. He pressed the lace of her bra to her and groped.

Her nipples obediently tightened beneath his touch. Tearing off his shirt, desperate to feel her skin on his, he stalked behind her and returned his hands to her breasts. "Feels so good doesn't it, honey?"

"Oh God," she hummed. Using one hand to pop the clasp of the slight bra, he exposed her all for himself. She let it slip to the floor with her blouse.

"There. That's what you wanted isn't it?" With practiced patience, he lifted her breasts letting her nipples spill between his fingers. He squeezed. She cried out for more. Her ass rocked back against his erection, decimating any hope he had of drawing this out.

"Someday, sweetheart..." his right hand skated down her abdomen and pressed her back against him, "...someday I'm gonna take that gorgeous ass, too. There won't be one thing on your body that doesn't belong to me."

"Yes." She rocked harder. Every contact point of her back to his chest sizzled with a hunger he wasn't certain would ever be satisfied. He'd never get enough of her, enough of this. Nothing else made sense but to take more, to take every single thing she offered him.

Making another turn, he fell to his knees before her. Impatience surged through his bloodstream. "Before you tie me up, I need another taste, Nat. I want more of that sweet cream you make so good for me."

"Please. Now." She hooked her thumbs in the elastic band of her panties but he caught her hands.

"Look at me."

She obeyed.

"Who undresses you?"

"Oh God, you do."

"That's right."

"Do it faster," she whimpered.

"I love that you're not afraid to tell me how bad you're needing it, baby. How fucking much you want me to take you. But you need to remember who's in charge for the moment." Rotating the wet cotton against her clit, he listened to her moans turn to pleading. Slipping the panties slowly down her legs, his mouth watered, his eyes centered on the glistening pearl of her clit with laser-sight precision. Dragging his fingers up and down her wet curls, she begged in earnest now.

"Open yourself for me, baby. Show me where you want my mouth."

Apprehension flashed in her eyes, but again she complied. Her hands trembled as she gently spread the lips of her pussy with her fingertips.

Blowing a quick cool breath over her, he reveled in her anguished choke of his name. Leaning in, he caressed that tiny bundle of nerve endings back and forth with his tongue. She rose up on her toes, making him chuckle.

Ever resourceful, she spread herself with one hand now, and tunneled her fingers through his hair granting herself leverage. She tried to push his face back to her pussy. "Please, please," sang from her constantly.

"Fucking wish I'd recorded you swearing to me you'd never beg," he taunted. Clamping his hands on her ass, he gave her two more languid laps with his tongue. Standing, he lifted her into his arms and laid her out on the bed. He spread her legs with a ragged warning. "I need more."

Taking her hands in his own, he relocated them both back to her pussy. Remembering the two words he would never utter again, he skipped his typical statement of encouragement. "Hold yourself open just like that. Do it until I tell you to stop."

She writhed and bucked so anxious for his mouth only amping the edgy spike of hunger consuming him. Zeroing in on her slippery clit he coaxed it into his mouth. She rocked against his mouth, pressing her thighs against his beard.

"No, baby. Open for me." He pinned her thighs back to the bed and returned to his work. A ragged growl tore from his lungs as her juices filled his mouth. Dipping low, he drank at her inner folds then pressed his tongue deep inside her and spun it back to where she most wanted his attention.

"Oh God, I'm gonna..." she cried out in warning.

He backed off. "Say please, honey." Slowing the strokes of his tongue, he licked at her fingers still dutifully trying to hold herself open.

"Please," cried from her in a shudder of pure need.

Widening his tongue, he lapped at her pearl back and forth then circled until she was unable to do anything more than moan. Drawing it back into his mouth he suckled and teased at her opening with his index finger. He gently raked his teeth across her sensitive tissues.

She broke on a wail of his name. Her hands flew to her face. Her thighs clamped around his jaw. This time he allowed it. At the peak of her climax, her cream coated his chin. He wanted to drown in her flavors. Delving deeper, he feasted on everything he'd forced from her body. The sweetest confection with a liquid chaser of sin.

Standing, he ran the back of his hand over his mouth and stared at her limp with satisfaction in her bed.

He'd promised her something. As much as he would hate being bound, she needed this. She needed to own her desires, needed understand what she did to him, needed to be willing to explore.

Natalie forced herself to sit up as the last quake of her orgasm shook through her. What happened next? She was just as unable to believe that he was going to let her tie him to her bed as she was that she'd actually told him that's what she wanted.

Her eyes flew to his package as he slowly unbuckled his belt and popped the snap on his jeans. He refused to meet her gaze as he lowered the zipper.

Wet heat had gathered in a circle in his boxers at the head of his cock. He kicked off his boots and stepped out of his jeans. His boxers were next. "Do you know how gorgeous you are?" She'd wanted to ask him a thousand times. How could he not know?

"I'm glad you think so, baby. You ready for this?" He gestured to his rope on the other side of the bed.

Commanding her legs to support her, she stood. "If you're sure this is okay. You don't seem too thrilled about it."

He reclined in the bed and propped his hands behind his head. His calm, cool position in direct opposition to the dark fire in his eyes and the tense grip of his jaw. "There are parts of it I'm going to enjoy the hell out of."

"But the other parts?"

"Not the first time I've been tied up, Nat, but this is the first time for pleasure."

Oh my God. Had he been captured? Is that what had happened to the Sevens? "You mean when you were in the army?"

"No. Leave it, baby. Just get on with this."

"No. I'm not doing this to you."

"You are. I'm not taking no for an answer."

"Are you sure?"

"Sure as I'm ever going to be."

"You always ask me that. If I said I was as sure as I was going to be about whatever you were asking to do you'd refuse to do it."

"I'm sure."

With the rope in her hands she somehow managed to forget every single thing she'd ever known about what to do with one. She'd been roping and riding since she was five. What the hell was wrong with her?

Ordering herself to get it together, she hesitantly took one of his hands in her own. Nothing about this made any sense. "I don't know how to do this." Judging from T's teasing quip at Saddleback's the other day, Aaron had tied up lovers before. She could use a little guidance.

"Here." He took the rope. "Do you want them tied together or do you want one on each bedpost?"

"Which way would you prefer?"

His soft laughter grounded her and somehow eased the tight wire of tension that ran from his shoulders all the way to his ass. "You are quite the Domme, sweetheart. Maybe I'll get you a whip for your birthday."

Rolling her eyes, Natalie tapped back into her own stubbornness. Jerking the rope out of his hands she flung one end behind three spindles in the middle of her headboard and pulled it back through the other side. She brought his hands together. Laying them on a pillow, she worked a quick, effective farmer's loop and bound them over his head. "There."

"Very nice." He angled his head, eyed the knot, and quirked a smile. A half-second later he settled back. All concern was erased from his features. He licked his lips and gestured to his cock slowly softening without any attention. "Believe you wanted a ride, cowgirl."

"There's other stuff I want to do first."

"Take what you need, baby. I'm all yours."

Considering for a moment, she let her eyes feast on him splayed out naked all for her enjoyment. Power surged through her. Every inch of him was perfection. There was so much she wanted to do and it was all entirely up to her.

She climbed onto the bed beside him, longing for the warmth of his skin near hers. Caressing her hands over his pecs, she traced the disks of his nipples, loving the way they tightened with need. The chiseled valley in the center of his chest beckoned her. Feathering light kisses over the smattering of hair, a close-mouthed hum of approval sounded from him.

"Do you like that?"

"Your hands and mouth are on me, Nat. Doesn't really matter where they are, I'm in heaven."

"I'm kind of overwhelmed at all of the stuff I want to do and to taste."

"I'm liking this being tied up thing more and more. You can taste to your heart's content."

Continuing on her explorative journey, she spun her tongue over his right nipple, reveling in the way every hill of muscle in his chest and abs tensed in pleasure. Blazing a hot trail, she whispered kisses up to the cord of muscles that comprised his neck. She splayed her hands wide to cover more ground on his chest.

Summoning what she hoped was a sex cat pout, she leaned low over him and stared him down.

"You keep looking at me like that I'll break the damned bed to get out of this tie-up and show you precisely what you're doing to me."

Pride welled from her soul and flowed out to her limbs. A broad grin replaced her pout making him chuckle. She didn't care. She was doing this. She was taking what she wanted and more importantly what she needed.

Spinning her tongue at the hollow between his chest and stomach, she let the salty tang of him saturate her senses.

Slinking down his body, she hesitantly traced along the deepest scar that ran from his navel to the enticing valley between his right leg and his cock. Unwilling to keep herself from anything, she teased at the thatch of hair surrounding the base of his erection.

He growled. She giggled.

"Are you laughing at me, cowgirl?"

"Yes. I like making you growl."

"Oh honey, I'm gonna growl for you. If you don't move a little faster I might cry."

"I doubt that."

"Beginning to think you're a cock tease."

Going on with one of the things she most wanted, she brushed a kiss along one of his scars. "Still won't tell me what happened will you?"

His Adam's apple bobbed. Her gaze flew back to his neck and then slowly back to his eyes.

"There's not all that much to tell you, babe. I got shot."

"I know. Please tell me this happened when you were serving."

"Does that make it better?"

"No. Not at all. I'm just trying to figure out your life before me piece by piece."

"Yeah, well my life before you existed in nothing but pieces."

Natalie lingered over his scars hoping that every kiss she painted over them would bring him healing. She'd never been the kind of girl who believed in fairy godmothers or shooting star wishes. Until she'd met Aaron, she'd refused to even believe in any kind of magic. As her lips encountered another deep puckered groove in his abdomen she would have given anything to get back all of the wishes she'd never made during her childhood. She would wish that her kisses and her love really could make things all better.

CHAPTER THIRTY-FIVE

Aaron tensed as her silky hair brushed over his cock again. Caught somewhere between absolute heaven and pure hell, part of him loved every minute of her ministrations over his scars. Another part wished she'd forget they were there altogether.

Another one of those gazes from her preceded her spinning her tongue over the head of his cock. He came up off the bed. "Fuck. Do more of that."

"I will in a minute," she promised. Instead of obeying, she moved her lips to the scars on the other side of his body. Agony seared through him. Concentrating on her to keep from losing his mind, he watched head bob and forced himself to feel her lips press to his skin.

He owed her this. Her eyes flitted back to his and some bizarre form of comfort worked through the haze of confusion and denial that choked out every other emotion in his mind.

"I love you," whispered from her lips. And she did. He knew. He had no idea how the hell that could be possible. He'd never deserve that but as she returned to her healing work he began to understand.

She didn't seem to see his scars as brands of his ultimate failing. They weren't red flags of warning that he was nothing more than a disappointment.

Another kiss grazed over the bullet hole near his hip bone. "I love you so much," she assured him yet again.

"You shouldn't," he choked. No one should love him. No one should look at him like that. No one should see his scars as openings where they can pour in their love. That couldn't possibly be what they were. He'd failed. And yet she continued to kiss them and to heal the invisible wounds hidden much deeper in his body.

"Yes, I should. And even if what you said was true, I'm way too stubborn to stop loving you. Fastest way to get me to do anything is to tell me not to." That truth was followed by her tongue dancing from the base of his cock to his crown.

"Jesus Christ, that's so good, baby."

"I've never done this before," she stated unnecessarily.

"I'm good with anything but teeth."

"But I've imagined doing this to you so many times."

"Nat." He couldn't catch his breath. Every nerve ending in his body sizzled with greed. He thrust into the air, so needy he was almost ashamed. "Suck me."

"Mmm, yes, sir."

"Holy fuck," he grunted as she drew him in. What she lacked in experience she made up for with exuberance. Her tongue lapped at his head, dragging him rapidly from want to fervor.

She experimented with sweet kisses and soft suckles and just when he was certain he would die from the torture she would draw him deep and suck hard. "I don't fucking believe you've never done this." He thrashed in the bed. Creaking loudly, her headboard banged against her wall from his force.

Another moan vibrated down his shaft before she lifted her head with an audible pop. "Show me, baby. Show me my cum on your lips." So much for letting her run the show. One of those sweet little hums sounded from her as she licked his pre-cum from her lips. Those need-you noises were almost better than her screaming his name when she came. Every single thing about her only served to make him love her more.

"I love the way you taste. Like man and you and... sex." She returned to her work with vigor.

He fought the cloud of lust threatening to take over his senses. Not yet. Not fucking yet. "Nat, baby, listen to me. Relax your throat muscles and take me deep. I want to feel you swallow with me at your throat."

She did as she was told. Her teeth scraped at his shaft as she slowly took him deeper and deeper. The slight pain registered only as unadulterated pleasure.

Her cheeks hollowed. The warm wet haven of her silky mouth suctioned to him. He dug his heels into the mattress. The bed gave audible warnings of him testing its construction.

She sucked harder. The muscles of her throat flexed against him.

"Swallow me," flew from his lips as a command.

Brilliant, beautiful woman had already figured out one of his many kinks however. The first milky spurt of his cum she swallowed. The next, she lifted her head and let him see it on her lips and tongue before she closed her eyes and swallowed again. The final landed on his abs.

"Finish it." All sense of restraint gone, he gave another order. Her tongue lapped him clean. His entire body shuddered as she brushed one more kiss on his now flaccid cock.

Full of a heady sense of power over the fact that she'd given him that slack-jawed, dazed expression, Natalie debated what to do next. "How long does it take it to get hard again?" She wrinkled her nose wondering if that was something she should have asked.

He shook his head at her, that half-smirk firmly in place on his lips. "Come kiss me. Let me taste myself in your mouth and give me about five minutes."

"Should already have known it would be something impressive."

"I was a Green Beret, baby. We penetrate deeper, last longer, recover faster, and carry a heavier payload."

Laughing at that, Natalie straddled herself over his hipbones. That was the first time she'd heard him joke about his time in the service since they'd been friends. Perhaps underneath all of the scars both visible and invisible he carried, there were moments he'd enjoyed. Maybe she could help him reach more of those moments.

Laying out over his chest, she taunted him keeping their lips just far enough apart that he couldn't reach her. Her nipples pricked at his chest. Her own wetness coated his cock already stiffening against her. Tingles of awareness overtook her body.

Unable to tease any longer, she pressed her lips to his. He didn't require his hands or even his arms to take control of her. Every connection of their lips made her long to be devoured entirely by him. His saliva was spiked with possession. His lips full of sinful seduction. She wanted it all.

Once again the bed protested him pulling at his restraints. He turned, angling his head the other way. "You taste like mine, baby. Say it for me. Tell me who you belong to."

"You." Her vow was a breathy moan. She rocked against him with more force.

"That's right." He bucked for her bringing his cock to the wet folds of her pussy.

Still so hungry, she dove in for another kiss. Drawing her tongue between his lips he began to suck. She canted her hips faster. He was hard again. Jerking back, driven only by her own desires, she gripped his cock and held it to her clit.

"I fucking love when you take what you want," he groaned.

She rocked back and forth. The pressure so good it was almost unbearable. He thrust against her, giving her more, knowing she needed it.

Sliding against him, every pass over his crown shot a flash fire of heat throughout her. *More. Take more.* The friction was a drug. She'd never get enough. That knot of pressure deep within her tightened with every pass. His moans were equally intoxicating. She wanted more. The need was oppressive. Her next breath depended on him setting her free.

Rising up on her knees, she positioned his head at her opening starved his fullness.

"Jesus, I deserve a fucking crown for stopping you, but don't forget the condom, baby." His body continued to rock against her. He flexed his ass constantly, pressing himself between her lips. It wasn't fair. Stopping even long enough to put on a condom felt like she was being tied and quartered.

Whimpering out her frustration, she jerked one out of the box on the bedside table. He squeezed his eyes shut for two breaths. "Pinch a little at the top so it doesn't break when I come and then roll it on."

Tearing the package, she followed his instructions. Every roll of her fingers down his shaft made him tense. Bringing his head back to her opening she made another swipe with it back and forth, soaking him down with her cream.

A string of expletives flew from his mouth. "Nat, baby, I haven't opened you. Untie me and let me get you ready. I don't want you to hurt."

"This is precisely the kind of hurt I want. I'm not some kind of delicate flower, Aaron. I'm a cowgirl." With that she sank down his cock. The first two inches robbed her of breath, but the driving force was all-consuming. He groaned in agony. She pressed further but struggled. "Help me."

"Just remember you said that in the morning." He thrust hard up into her penetrating her fully.

"Oh, yes." She gave an inquisitive rock. That thatch of hair at his base teased at her clit. She pressed harder.

"It's good isn't it, baby? It hurts so good."

"Yes," she sang. "More. Please more."

Every thrust became a dedicated assault on her senses. He pounded into her. "Look at us, Nat," he commanded. "I know I'm not the only one who loves a show. Watch your greedy little pussy swallow me up."

Clawing at his chest, she lowered her head to see. Her body was a live wire electrified by the sight. Faster and harder she road with everything this was.

"Jesus, so fucking tight, so fucking good."

"Oh God, more."

Suddenly, a loud crack drowned out her moans. His hands flew forward and the splintered pops of the wood made her gasp.

"I'll fix it for you tomorrow. Keep fucking riding me."

CHAPTER THIRTY-SIX

Lightning fast, just like he'd been trained, Aaron extended his arms fully, flattened his palms together, and jerked his right hand free. Tossing the rope aside, he never missed a thrust.

She threw her head back. Her tits bounced with every roll of her body. One thing was for certain, his cowgirl knew how to ride.

Pressing his thumbs to her hip bones and digging his fingertips into her ass, he held her to him pumping hard and fast.

Anticipation thundered in his blood. She milked every twitch of his cock. The fluid flexes of her pussy threatened to destroy his resolve.

She trembled. She was right there. Dragging his right hand to the precise spot where they were joined, he rotated his thumb against her clit.

"Oh...yes...mmm...Aaron...mmm," she panted. He continued his relentless pounding.

"That's it isn't it? You're right there, baby. Let me have it."

She collapsed on his chest breaking on a haggard moan of his name. Gripping her ass, he held her to him while he filled the condom in a series of tensed muscles and wild groans.

Drunk on the aftershocks of their climaxes, he moved his hands to her back and cradled her far more gently than he'd held her captive a moment before.

Still quaking, she turned her head and buried her face in his neck.

Smiling at that, he brushed the damp hair out of her face. "You okay?"

That wispy sigh of satisfaction quickly ranked as yet another of his favorite sounds.

Her pussy gave another tender flex against his cock. His breath stalled momentarily as he reveled in the sensation. "Baby, you're gonna have to ease off of me for me to get out."

"I don't want you to get out. I like you there."

After all he'd done, after all he'd survived when others hadn't, after all he'd tried so hard to pay back, could he possibly deserve her? It had to be some kind of fevered dream. "Believe me, being deep inside you is pretty much heaven, but let me clean you up." Cradling her head in one of his hands and wrapping his other around her back, he rolled them to the side and withdrew as tenderly as he was able.

She poked her lip out in an adorable pout. Chuckling, he brushed a kiss on her forehead. "You just keep making me fall more and more in love with you." He quoted her line back to her.

"Good." Slowly, she sat up and rubbed her hands over her eyes. "Oh my gosh, you broke my bed!"

A sly grin he made no effort to conceal stretched the width of his face. "Yeah, I did."

She punched him in the shoulder. "Don't look so smug. I will never live this down. My brothers will talk about this for the next fifty years."

Rubbing his shoulder more to make her think she'd actually hurt him than anything else, he chuckled. "I wasn't going to tell them, sweetheart."

Studying the headboard, he doubted it could be fixed. The three center spindles snapped in jagged lines. Two of them were lying with their splintered remains on the floor below. The other he tore away from the bed to keep either of them from impaling themselves on it. "Now that I look at this I'm thinking particle board might not have been the best thing to tie me to."

"Now you tell me."

Brushing a few remnant crumbs of wood in the floor, he winked at her. "If you don't lay back down on my chest I'm probably going to beat it Tarzan style."

Laughing hysterically, she settled back on top of him. "I can't believe you broke my bed."

"I do what I can, baby."

"Aaron, do you know what my family is going to say when I have to have a new bed delivered here? Can we fix it?"

"I can put new spindles on it but they'll never match. What if I bought you a king? That would only make them think I'm going to be staying over often and I would actually be able to stretch out."

"But my horseshoe sheets won't fit on a king." She dissolved in another fit of giggles.

In that moment, something akin to wholeness filled his chest. Her warmth penetrated his skin once again and banished the dark chill from him completely. "I'll see if I can find you some more horseshoe sheets, baby."

Beaming at him she eased up on her elbow. "I like the way you look in my bed better anyway."

"You still have stuffed animals in your closet don't you?"

"I'm not answering that." Tucking her head back on his chest she burrowed until her face was no longer visible. He laughed at her outright.

"And are you not answering on the grounds that it might incriminate you?"

"Yes," sounded from somewhere in the vicinity of his arm pit.

"Hey, Nat..."

"Do not go in my closet."

"I was gonna say I love you."

"I love you, too." She surfaced. Her hair was a halo of dirty-blonde waves. Her cheeks were flushed with her embarrassment. Satisfaction was still etched on her lips and eyes.

"Let's see here, if I were a betting man I'd say there's more than one Beanie Baby in there."

"Only the horses and one cow because he was too cute to give away."

"And a teddy bear, maybe? No. Not you. That's too clichéd. I know one of those stuffed animal kitties."

Her hands flew to her face and another round of hysterical laughter broke over her. Pinning her to the bed, he tickled her sides. "I'm right aren't I?"

"How do you do that?" She wiggled trying to escape and clamped her arms down to block his fingers from her sides.

"I'm just that good, sweetness."

"You just leave Mr. Sniffles out of this. He's missing an eye."

"I knew it."

"Seriously, how do you do that? Did you go through my closet?"

"I would never go through your closet. I just happen to be an expert on your kitty." He waggled his eyebrows.

"Well, my broken bed and Mr. Sniffles better never come up at your monthly sessions with the Sevens, you got that."

"Nat, come on, you know I'd never tell anyone about anything that goes on between us. I don't share. Did Mr. Sniffles lose his eye in a tragic accident? Cat fight maybe?"

Her attempt at annoyance lost all of its believability when she continued laughing. "I may or may not have smacked Luke in the face with her when I was six. He and Brock said they'd play hide-and-seek with me. I went to hide and they just never came to find me. I was out in the hayloft for an hour. They were just mad because I dared them to a horse race and I kicked their butts."

"That's my girl."

A frustrated whine accompanied a set of paws scratching at her bedroom door. "Oh, I almost forgot them." Standing, Natalie attempted to walk to the door. Her legs wobbled and she gripped the footboard to steady herself.

"Seriously, I'm not going to be able to get my ego out of your house in the morning." He laughed again.

Rolling her eyes at him, she let the dogs in the room. They promptly leapt up on her bed. "I don't think so," Aaron started to scold.

But Natalie crawled in between them, giggling. "They get to sleep here too because they did not break my bed." Lulu licked her face and then settled protectively beside her. Buster took post at the end.

"And where exactly do I sleep?"

"Here." Natalie scooted to the side moving Lulu behind her. Aaron curled himself up tighter so he could put her on his chest. "I've never felt so safe."

"Good." Contorting himself so he could turn out the light he brushed a kiss on her head and settled in.

Surrounded by people and animals who really did seem to love her, Natalie knew she had to tell him. There was so much that needed to be said. She wasn't certain how to verbalize most of it but he deserved to know.

"Hey Aaron?" she whispered in the darkness, thankful for its cover.

"Yeah, baby? You okay?"

"I'm perfect."

He shifted to his side and stared down at her. A sliver of moonlight betrayed the darkness she clung to. His hand caressed her cheek. "What's wrong, Nat?"

"Nothing's wrong, honest. I uh... I wanted to say... thank you."

"For what?"

"For everything we did tonight. You have no idea how much that meant to me, what that did for me."

"Will you tell me?"

"I'll try."

The tender touch of his lips to her forehead bolstered her courage. "Take your time, sweetheart. I'm right here. I'm not going anywhere. I know you don't really believe this, but nothing you say is going to shock me."

"You can't possibly know if that's true so just let me say this."

A single nod was his only response.

"It was like everything was my choice. And it was incredible. It's always incredible to be with you but this time I didn't feel..."

"You didn't feel what, Nat?"

"Guilty."

"Baby." His arms wrapped around her. He shielded her completely with his body. "I know. Okay, I know."

"You do not. You can't possibly. It was all so confusing."

The hint of light in her bedroom displayed the raw pain in his eyes. "Of course it was."

"And I didn't understand any of it. I wasn't even completely sure..."

"I know, baby."

"But tonight... tonight everything was my choice. It was all up to me and that means I'm..." She sank her teeth into her bottom lip to trap the confession.

He tightened his hold on her. Lulu edged closer and nuzzled her nose against Natalie's back. Buster stood at the end of the bed. His hunter green eyes alight in the darkness keeping constant watch.

"That means you're allowed to enjoy it." He gave voice to the words she couldn't speak. "That means there is no shame in it feeling good. You knew it was wrong when it happened but you had no idea why something wrong still felt good. You did nothing wrong. Nothing about being confused was wrong. You hear me? Nothing. Absolutely nothing about any of the emotions you went through or are still going through is wrong. What he did was wrong. All him. Not you. And absolutely nothing you want to experience with me is wrong. And if we do something you want to do and then you feel guilty about it let's talk about that because that's a very real thing. Okay? I never want you to feel anything but how much I love you, but I know it's not quite that easy. I swear to you I will be right here to deal with anything either of our pasts might throw in our path. I don't know about you but I'm tired of all of the shit that happened before right this moment fucking everything up. Somehow we're going to heal together. I won't allow there to be any other options."

"Thank you." She managed to push the two words past the boulder in her throat. He really did understand. For a girl who'd convinced herself that no one would ever understand it was unfathomable. Blinking rapidly, she focused on the navy blue, star-strewn sky outside her bedroom windows. Maybe all of those shooting star wishes she'd never made had culminated into the man laying in bed beside her. Maybe all of the hell they'd been through had a finish line. And maybe they were closing in on it.

CHAPTER THIRTY-SEVEN

Nuzzling his face against her neck, damp with sweat, Aaron kissed and licked indulging himself in the flavors of her. She was sound asleep beside him. His sweet baby had slept peacefully through the night. Her evening confession had cost her so much. He had to do something to prove to her that nothing she'd said had shocked him.

She grunted and wiggled deeper below the covers.

Lulu took up Aaron's cause and licked her face. He laughed.

"I'm asleep," she declared though she wrapped her arm over Lulu to cuddle with her.

"What happened to all of that nonsense I used to hear about how early you get up to go out and cowgirl?"

"That was before I realized how well I sleep when my bed is full of you and dogs."

"I changed my mind. If the dogs get to sleep with us I'm getting you a California King."

Her eyes blinked open hesitantly. "We'd have to put it out in a pasture because my room is not that big."

"Few more rounds of rough sex and I'll see if I can knock the back wall out for you. Consider it creative demo before an addition."

"You probably would if I'd let you but my granddaddy built this house and I happen to like the walls where they are."

"The granddaddy that lives down in the cottage at the entrance gates?"

"Yep."

"Is that where Brock got his contractor skills?"

"How did you know Brock used to be a contractor?"

Shit. Mentally lambasting himself for forgetting that not everything had been revealed the night before, he shrugged. "He said something about it at the bar one night."

"I honestly have no idea where he learned to do all the building stuff. I don't really remember him working with Pops all that much. Where did you learn how to do stuff like that?"

Aaron waited on the inevitable dread that he associated with discussing his time in the Army. For some reason, it remained absent, perhaps hidden somewhere with the chill he knew would return as soon as she was no longer in his arms. "Army SF isn't always about going in and fucking people's lives up if they disagree with our mission. A lot of times we went in to help. Of course our help was usually a means to an end, but that's not necessarily a bad thing. Voodoo is practically a walking hospital. I've seen him deliver babies, give vaccinations, and operate on animals all in the same day. We spent a good bit of time working with the CoE to build dams and even restructure community centers and shelters, stuff like that."

"I'm going to need to know what S, F, C, O, and E stand for."

"Sorry. SF is Special Forces. CoE is Corp of Engineers."

"So, you're even better than G.I. Joe. You're basically Superman."

"I prefer Batman since there's definitely a dark side. You can be Catwoman. I'll get you a black leather leotard to go with your whip."

"Very funny."

"No, now come on this could work, Mr. Sniffles can be one of Catwoman's cats."

"I'm pretty sure Catwoman's cats are girls. Mr. Sniffles is a boy."

"Yeah, the mister part of his name clued me in." Running his fingers through her hair, he let her contented sigh wash through him. If he could just keep her making sounds like that, he'd figure the rest out.

Her uncle. His past. Her fears. His needs. He'd make it all work somehow.

"Is it ridiculously girly that I love it when you play with my hair?" Her eyes fluttered closed.

"What's wrong with being ridiculously girly?"

"So it is."

"I never said that, just wondered why it should matter."

"I guess I've always prided myself on being tougher than all of my brothers."

"Being tough as hell doesn't mean you can't like me loving on you. Or does it go something like you were afraid to show off your softer side because you'd already been forced to do something you didn't want to do? There's nothing wrong with protecting yourself, Nat."

"Yeah. Maybe it went something like that. I was so awful to Brock and Hope when they moved back here. I feel so bad about that."

Holy fuck. Did she realize what she'd just said? Summoning nonchalance, he brushed a kiss on her cheek as if nothing out of the ordinary had happened. "How come?"

Panic throbbed in Natalie's head. *Oh no. No. No. NO. Me and my stupid mouth.* She'd already confessed more than she'd ever intended to. She refused to talk about Uncle Mick and the vile things he'd done anymore.

Lifting her head, she brought her lips to Aaron's. There was one surefire way to distract him. She ran her right hand over his pecs, satin covered steel. Refusing to ignore his abdomen anymore, she softly tended the scars and then wrapped her hand over his cock.

"Nat, baby, I'm loving that, but last night was pretty intense for your second time. You have to be sore this morning." The way he came back in for another kiss assured her that it wouldn't take much to convince him to go on with this.

Adding her confession about Brock and Hope to the locked safe of things she refused to talk about ever again, she brought his hand to her breast.

"Mmm," he grunted.

"I'm not sore. I just want you." She was a cowgirl. Being sore was part of her job and the slight rubbed sensation between her legs this morning was nothing.

"You're sure?"

"So sure."

"Then give me just a second." He crawled out of bed and clicked his mouth to summon the dogs. "Out ladies and gents. What I'm about to do is for my eyes only."

Natalie gave both of the dogs a pat as they followed their daddy's orders. Aaron came back to bed and arranged himself against the portion of her headboard that wasn't broken. "Lean back against me."

She scooted until she was seated between his legs with her back to his chest. His hands cupped her breasts, squeezing and massaging until she wriggled against him desperate for relief.

An embarrassingly loud moan spilled from her lungs as he rolled her nipples between his thumb and forefinger. "God, why do I like that so much?"

A wicked chuckle sounded in her ear. "I fucking love making you moan, making you so needy for me. Drives me wild."

Pressing her breasts together with one hand, the other trekked down her stomach. She spread her legs praying he'd give her what she so desperately needed.

"I also fucking love how small you are, love that I can touch all of you, and fucking love your tits."

Her back arched as she began to rock. His fingertips teased at the wet curls covering her pussy. "Watch, baby. Watch me get your body ready for me."

"Oh yes," she gasped. He ran his middle finger between her folds. She shivered at the sight.

"So beautiful." When he added another finger and circled her clit she gasped. Her fingernails dug into his muscular thighs. His hungry growl said he didn't mind.

"You see that, Nat? See how juicy I can get you?"

Her breaths came in quick staccato pants.

His lips found her throat. He dragged his knuckles through her wetness now. His other hand taunted her nipples constantly, one and then the other. He shamelessly used everything he'd expertly learned about her preferences to drive her insane.

"More."

"Mmm, my sweet baby gets so impatient for me."

"Please."

"Not yet. I'm enjoying the view."

Wiggling again, she positioned his cock between her asscheeks, fairly certain that would speed things along.

"Playing with fire, sweetheart."

"Good," she challenged.

"Oh, I'll make it good for you when you're ready for that, but it isn't this morning. Let me enjoy you." His cock throbbed against her, just as anxious as she was. The chains that had held her own sexuality hostage had been shattered the night before. Channeling brazen femininity she'd had no hopes of accessing before, she recalled a few of the most intriguing things she'd seen on Tumblr.

His rough-skinned hands slid along her sides and her ass as she crawled forward. Leaning her head down she kept her ass in the air on all fours. "Bet I could make you hurry it up." She turned back to stare him down.

"Holy mother of God."

She giggled triumphantly before resuming her sex cat act. "Take me."

The wiry hair on his legs scraped at the back of her thighs as he positioned himself behind her. His hands gripped her hips with fervor. Oh, this was going to be good. She knew.

"Dying to tell you how naughty you're being but terrified to say something I shouldn't," he admitted.

"I think I like being naughty."

"Oh yeah, baby? You want to be fucked dirty like this? I'll give what you're begging for but I'm pulling out and coming all over your ass. Fair warning."

"Yes." The thought alone made her tremble. She'd spent years listening to her sister and her sisters-in-law go on and on about dirty sex. Now she knew why they couldn't shut up about it.

His fingers parted the lips of her pussy, and pressed inside her.

Her body drew them deeper, begging for more even if she wasn't capable of finding words to make her requests. Pressing back against his force, the tight ball of tension in her core kept time with her pulse. Her nipples ached. Every nerve ending from the top of her scalp to the bottom of her feet throbbed to the slow pump of his fingers.

"I was gonna take you nice and gentle. Slow and steady. But that's not what you want is it?" His low intonation turned the consistency of gravel.

"No." The low hum in her head kept her from elaborating. She gripped her sheets in her fists as the pressure threatened to overwhelm her. She flexed against his talented fingers.

Starved and yet so satisfied, he rendered her mindless. Using one of his thighs he spread her legs farther giving her the friction she hadn't thought to ask for.

The climax ricocheted through her body before she fully understood that she was going to come. A fiery detonation of pure pleasure. She felt herself weep for more as he jerked his fingers away. *More. Please more.*

She shook, riding the waves of her climax.

"The next one you have to beg for," he ordered. "Nice and slow. Feel me." True to his word he fed his cock into her agonizingly slowly, only allowing her his head at her opening. She tried to press back, so hungry for his girth to stretch her. His firm grip on her hips kept her right where he wanted her, reminding her who was in control this time.

She gave willingly. She had no doubts. She trusted him above all others.

There was nothing between them this time. She felt his crown breach her. "Please, please." She thrashed.

"So greedy, baby." He allowed her another inch. She was certain she'd never needed anything the way she needed him to bury himself to his hilt. He'd sworn he couldn't read her mind. She wasn't sure that was true. Instead of giving her more, he pulled away and then came back only pressing slightly farther on his next thrust.

She climbed with every pass. Higher and higher. The air stretched so thin around her she couldn't breathe. She could only feel. The constant tension tied her knots. "Please," choked from her in a breathless pant. He ratcheted her higher still, keeping himself from her fully.

Finally, mercifully, he sank himself to his hilt in a dedicated thrust. "Like that, sweetheart? That what you needed? My sweet dirty girl likes to be full of me, don't you?"

"Yes," sang from her.

He pulled away and came back faster now. Warmth licked up her spine. Reckless abandon rode the fluid flexes of his thighs with every connection of their skin. He pounded harder.

Her back arched. "OhGodYes," blended into an indecipherable exultation from her lips.

"You like when I play with your hair, Nat? Bet you'll like this more." His hand fisted in her hair, yanking her head upwards. Her body rejoiced. He pulled gently with every retreat and pressed harder with every thrust.

She felt herself milk him. He growled his adamant approval. "Not yet, baby." His warning, his dominance, only rocketed her higher.

But she couldn't wait. She flew. Jolts of pleasure quivered through her. She came in a rush of heat and hunger.

"Aw, fuck," he rasped. Suddenly, hot splashes of cum landed on her back and her ass. This only served to rev her more.

She turned back to see him grip himself as he came all over her. His head was thrown back. His body tensed with every spurt. Gruff words, some sexy, some sweet, some nonsensical, flew from his mouth.

Collapsing to the mattress simply unable to hold herself up any longer, she chased her breath. He reclined beside her.

"At some point I'm going to have fucked you enough to not be so weak when it comes to you."

"What about that was weak?" A rogue aftershock of her orgasm had her tensing yet again.

He grinned at that. "If you weren't sore after last night, which I know you were lying to me about, you sure as hell are now."

"I was only a little sore. No big deal. And that was amazing."

"Yeah, well I happen to agree. Someday I'll figure out how to keep your orgasms just out of reach longer than that, too."

"Well, we have lots and lots of time for you to practice."

"Oh yeah? You're not tired of me hanging around so much already?" He winked at her.

"Pretty sure I'll never be tired of you."

"Good to know. Now, you are keeping your sexy ass in bed today. I am going to make you some breakfast and we are not doing that again for a long time."

"Does a long time mean in a few hours?"

"No, cowgirl. It means... fuck, I don't honestly know how long I'll be able to hold off. You're just too good."

"You know I like to be the best at most everything," she laughed.

"Trust me, you're the best. Now let me grab a towel and clean you up."

CHAPTER THIRTY-EIGHT

"Are you aware that you've been smiling for the past four days straight?" Holly inquired as she and Natalie heaved bags of cattle feed onto the platform cart in the Feed and Seed.

"There something wrong with that?" Natalie's grin expanded. Thinking about Aaron when she wasn't with him was addictive. A byproduct of her addiction was smiling about it.

"Hell no. I'm happy for you. Still curious why you tackled me in your hallway today so I couldn't get to your room, but happy none the less."

"You... just didn't need to go in there."

"Nat, not that I really care but last week you showed up in my bathroom while I was showering. We tell each other everything. What is up?"

Glancing around to see which other residents of Pleasant Glen might be in listening range, her eyes landed on Old Man Rasmussen. A wave of cold dread steamrolled her. He was thirty feet away but she swore the hateful glare he always gave her lowered the ambient temperature to somewhere near arctic tundra levels.

Her smile disappeared altogether. Utter hatred filled her. With a bag of feed hoisted on her shoulder, Holly turned to see the old man's disdain. Narrowing her eyes, she flung the bag on top of the others. "We know we're beautiful but staring is rude."

"Fucker," snarled from Luke's mouth as he returned with bags of calf milk replacer and cattle meds. "Walk away, Rasmussen. You mess with my little sisters I'll make it so you can't see anything ever again. You got that old man?"

Hating that her big brother had defended her yet again, Natalie was secretly relieved. Wishing for the hundredth time that day alone that Aaron was there she wondered what would have happened if he had been. Rasmussen was his landlord. Aaron hated him but didn't have a lot of other rentals available to him in the Glen.

Rasmussen walked away mumbling under his breath.

"You didn't have to do that," Holly huffed. "We can take care of ourselves."

"Yeah, well, I was here and I didn't much care for the way he was lookin' at you. 'Sides he made a snide remark to dad about my wife a couple of weeks ago. He's lucky to still be alive. Dad chewed him up and spit him out. Beating the piss out of an old guy ain't exactly the honorable way of a cattle rancher but that don't mean I won't do it."

"What did he say?" Natalie demanded.

"I ain't repeating it. You two ready?"

"Since you're here and wanting to flex your ego why don't you haul feed bags? I want to look at the boots," Holly taunted.

"Yeah, fine, just hurry up. I want to watch the Huskers game."

Following after her sister, Natalie ran her hands along the cool metal shelving in the store. "Do you know why he hates me so much?"

"He hates all of us, not just you." Holly plucked a box of snip-toe Corral boots off of a low shelf.

"It feels like it's just me."

"He's an ornery old coot. Mama says he doesn't have sense God gave fleas. He was a friend of Uncle Mick's so that should tell you something."

So that's why. The cold dread plunged through her like a blade once again. Trying to take solace in the fact that no one in town knew the real reason her uncle had been banished from the ranch, she forced herself to draw slow, steady breaths.

Her phone buzzed in her pocket. *I miss my girl* flashed on the screen. Her broad grin returned. His warmth chased away the chill that had overtaken her. She missed him, too. He was working the afternoon and evening shifts that day and wouldn't be over until late.

"You would look sexy in these, Nat, try them on." Holly thrust the pair of boots she'd just tried on at her. They were pretty. Pointy toed with a teal lace design, much fancier than anything she ever purchased for ranch work.

"I thought you were getting them."

"The heel is too high for me and I have fancy boots. You don't. I bet Aaron would trip over his own tongue if you wore those with say a g-string and nothing else." Holly waggled her eyebrows.

"I don't own any g-strings, Holl." Sitting on a nearby bench, Natalie tried on the boots.

"Then I know what we're shopping for next. You said Aaron was working both shifts today. We're going to Ogallala for some sisterly shopping."

Turning her foot to see the design, Natalie had to admit the boots did look good. She stood and tried to see herself in the plastic stick-on mirror.

"Damn, damn, damn." She gasped as Aaron stalked to her side. His appreciative whistle delighted her almost as much as his appearance.

"What are you doing here?"

"I told you I missed you."

"I miss you, too, but aren't you supposed to be at work?"

"Threatened to report Ed if he didn't start letting me take real breaks. He's bitching about it but knows it's illegal not to. Figured I'd come down here and see if you were still buying feed."

Natalie threw her arms around his neck. "I'm so glad you decided that."

"Babe, your ass in those jeans and those boots, my God. I'm gonna be hard up for days," he whispered in her ear.

"Bet I could help you out with that tonight."

That shuddered growl she loved came next. The perfect antidote to Rasmussen and life in general kept tight hold of her. She was pretty sure heaven couldn't be any better.

"Get the box. I'm buying those for you." He patted her backside. Holly giggled.

"You are not buying these for me."

"Watch me."

"Let him spoil you. It's fun," Holly assured her.

After the boots were purchased, Aaron took her hand and guided her out of the store. "Guess I need to get back to the bar."

"I need a kiss first."

"Oh honey, trust me, that was my plan." He leaned in. His breath whispered across her lips.

"Natalie Camden," rang from the most annoying voice she'd ever heard. She jerked her head away from Aaron intent on telling Cheryl Crawford to take a long walk off a short pier. "Just what are your intentions with Thomas?"

"Who is Thomas?" Natalie demanded.

"T-Byrd." Cheryl preened like a rooster with a rock up its ass.

Aaron's brow furrowed but he said nothing. Rolling her eyes, Natalie spat, "I have no intentions with T other than to be his friend. Now, we were busy so, bye, bye."

"Well, it certainly didn't seem that way to me when I confronted him last week right in front of the courthouse about not returning my phone calls. He said he was here to see you. Acted like there was quite a bit going on between you two and here I see you making out on the sidewalk with someone else. Thomas has feelings you know. You Camdens seem to think you can just have your cake and eat it, too."

"What?" Utterly confused, Natalie turned to Aaron for a little help. She swore she saw a flash of panic in his eyes before he composed himself. What the hell?

"T was probably messing around. He came to see me and to bring Nat her jacket. Why do you care so much, Cheryl?"

"What T and I shared was special," she whined.

"Really?" Aaron huffed. "He took you home one time and then failed to return your calls and texts for a year and you thought it was special?"

If Natalie hadn't been so annoyed, she would've felt bad for Cheryl. If Cheryl wasn't more agitating than an ass boil, she might've even been irritated with T for doing her that way. As it stood, she wanted Cheryl to evaporate so she could get back to kissing Aaron.

"Well, now that he's lost all of that money in Alaska I thought maybe he could use some comfort. If he started one successful company surely he could start another. He just needs some encouragement."

Aaron rubbed his temples and Natalie bit her lips together. "I'm doubting he has time for *comfort* since he's so busy in Alaska working..."

"On the pipeline," Cheryl supplied.

"Right. The pipeline. That's difficult work." Aaron played her like a fool. "I hadn't even seen him in ages. Poor guy."

Natalie choked back laughter.

"Wait just a second." Cheryl leaned in. Aaron stepped between her and Natalie. "If you aren't seeing T then how did he have your jacket?"

Tongue-tied, Natalie tried to formulate a believable lie.

"He and Nat have been friends for ages. He actually introduced us. He'd had the jacket for a couple of years just keep forgetting to get it back to her. Wanted to return it before he headed back to Alaska." Aaron, however, lied like it was his job. She reminded herself that at one time it had been.

"Oh. Well, when I saw him at the courthouse and heard him talking about you I got to wondering if maybe there was something serious between you. I don't share."

I'm gonna kill him. Aaron seethed. If he'd still been his C.O. he would've give T months of hard labor for being so reckless. What the hell was he thinking chatting up Cheryl outside the very building where they were breaking in? Praying Natalie didn't think too hard about the courthouse comment, he cleared his throat.

"Next time I talk to T I'll let him know you were thinking of him." *I'll let him know by shoving my fist down his throat for being a dumbass.*

Before Aaron could come up with some way to get Cheryl to walk away, Holly and Luke were at their sides. "You ready, Nat? Katy wants us to pick her up so she can go to Ogallala with us."

"You're going to Ogallala?" Aaron prayed he could distract her.

"Yeah, but we won't be back too late."

"Have fun, baby. I got to get back to work." Despite Cheryl, Holly, and her most overly-protective big brother standing nearby, Aaron plastered his lips to Natalie's. If she found the kiss mind-blowing all the better. His right hand raced down her side hinting at the tender swell of her breast. His left grasped her ass. He called himself a fucker for using the things that drove her the craziest against her.

Cheryl's angry huff assured him this was working. The click of her boot heels echoed against his skull as she marched away.

Natalie swayed against him as he eased back. Her eyes were at half-mast. Her lips puffy from his force. He knew she was wet. Trying to remember why he kept his job in the first place, he clenched his jaw until his molars protested. "I'll see you tonight, babe."

She nodded as Holly took her hand and half-dragged her to Luke's truck.

"I'm gonna fucking rip your arm off and beat your ass with it," he informed T as he stomped back to the bar.

"What did I do now?"

"Cheryl." Aaron spoke through his teeth making certain no one on the street was paying him any attention.

"Dude, that was over a year ago. What is it with you and Griff hanging her over my head?"

"Not that."

"Then what?"

"I can't tell you right now. I'll text it to you on my next break."

"Well, now I'm curious."

"Why don't you tell me about your other mission."

"If it will get you to chill, fine. The dude basically sits on his ass all day. Must've been a smoker. He's on oxygen. Only leaves his house to go to the gas station to buy milk and off-brand cookies. His ex-wife went by there yesterday."

"Wonder if she knows what he did."

"No idea, but she was carrying casserole dishes and an envelope I'm betting had pics of those grandkids he's wanting to see."

"She has to know." There was no way the Camdens threw the entire family off the ranch without her knowing.

"You said Brock doesn't know. Maybe she doesn't either. On the other hand, if she does, she struck me as the type who would consider it her duty to feed the lowlife piece of garbage even though they're divorced."

"When did they divorce?" Aaron held the phone between his shoulder and ear while he tied on his apron.

"Yeah, I wondered exactly what you're wondering. It was approximately ten seconds after their beloved son graduated from high school. She was protecting Brock from his father."

"Interesting."

"Agreed."

CHAPTER THIRTY-NINE

"You're sure you want me to show you this place?" Natalie asked Aaron yet again. He watched her teeth sank into her bottom lip as she piled a quilt and a picnic basket into his arms.

"If I bite your lip for you, would you finally believe me?"

She rolled her eyes. "It's just not the most exciting place in the world."

"It's your favorite place in this tiny town. To me that's all kinds of exciting. Plus, I get to spend the afternoon with you. Nothing better than that."

She followed him out to her truck. He set the picnic and blanket in the bed. "I've never shown this to anyone else. I'm not even sure my brothers and sisters go out there."

"Then I'm honored, baby. You want me to drive?"

"Nope." She hoisted herself into the driver's seat and slammed her door. When he'd climbed in beside her she gave him that grin that he swore could light a thousand distant suns. "But hang on tight. It's a rough ride."

"My favorite kind." He winked at her and fastened his seat belt.

Instead of heading to the gravel road that would lead them off of the ranch, she turned the other direction and drove over grass. "I take it your favorite place is somewhere on this ranch."

"Yep." Her spine was straight as a board and she kept gnawing that lip.

"Are you scared to show me, sweetheart? You don't have to." He reached for her hand.

"No, I want to show you. It's just... well it would kind of be like showing you Mr. Sniffles."

Smiling at her creative descriptions, he brushed a kiss across her knuckles. "Sharing a pretty important part of your life with someone is scary. I get that. Offer still stands. We can do something else tonight."

"Just don't ever tell anyone about this place. I don't ever want it to change."

"Classified information is definitely something I can deal with."

They drove over cattle guards and enough pasture land he was shocked they were still on the same ranch. When they reached rocky terrain, she slowed the truck. "It's not far." The truck bounced and creaked as they traversed a ditch Aaron was concerned it couldn't handle.

The grass turned to clumps of dead weeds and dirt. She kept going. A slight elevation was ahead. She parked the truck just before they reached it and hopped out. Aaron followed her up the hill.

"So, this is it." She spread her arms and he took in an endless expanse of nothingness. Mounds of dirt ran all the way to the sinking orange sun set against the blue sky. "I know the grass is more picturesque or whatever but just look at it. No telephone or electric poles. No fences. No worn places from where we drive the feed trucks over and over again. If you just look at it and pretend, you can't even tell what decade it is. It's like time doesn't exist here. Nothing exists here but us."

"Hey." He wrapped his arms around her. "You don't have to explain it, baby. I get it. Believe me, I get it."

"You do?"

"Oh yeah." He sank down on the ground and pulled her into his lap. "You already know I grew up in foster care. The year before I started high school my social worker got wind of just how bad the place I'd been in was. She shut that home down and pulled a few strings on my behalf. I got sent to this farm in Gentry, Missouri. Whole entire town only had like fifty people living there. My new foster parents owned a farm. I got out of my social worker's car prepared for the worst and walked out on the most beautiful bit of pastureland I'd ever seen. I stayed there until I joined the Army. There used to be a dirt field just like this where I'd go when I wanted to think. I was finally in the middle of a place where people cared about my well-being and that field in the middle of that farm felt like all of the shit I'd been through belonged to someone else's life. It couldn't reach me there."

"You do get it." She wrapped her arms around him with enough force that he swore her love was going to be enough to hold him together forever. "Thank you for telling me that."

"Thank you for showing me this."

"Do you ever go back to Gentry? Do you ever go visit your foster parents or your field?"

"No." Aaron drew a hard line there. He'd already shared as much as he could. Going back to Gentry wasn't an option. He couldn't look Ms. Campbell in the eye. Not after all she'd done for him and how badly he'd let her down.

Natalie stared at him. He swore she was searching for his soul. She hadn't quite figured out that his heart and his soul resided in her. "You can come to my field any time you want."

"I plan on bringing you out here as often as you'd like."

"Come on there's something else I want to show you." Crawling out of his lap, she took off.

"I'd follow you to the ends of the earth, Nat." She was too far away to hear him but that was a truth he'd never hesitate to tell her.

Clutching the stitch in her side, Natalie panted as they came into view of her old barn. She tried not to be annoyed that Aaron wasn't even breathing hard. Stopping a few yards from the door, she grinned. "So, this is the oldest building on the ranch. I have no idea when it was built but as far as we know it wasn't built by a Camden."

His hands traversed the crumbling dirt and stone structure. "Pretty rudimentary construction. Could be hundreds of years old."

"Isn't that cool." She rushed inside, coughing from the dirt soaked air.

"Careful, baby. This roof could go at any moment."

"I know but you have to see this." Determined to go on with this even if it was lame, she scooted into one of the ancient horse stalls. "Look" She pointed to a pile of old metal horseshoes, mostly broken.

He grinned. "Kind of cool to think about people back then ranching the same way you all do, isn't it?"

"See, I knew you'd get how cool this is. I love it up here."

He knelt down to touch the horseshoes and his brow furrowed. "What's that?" He pointed to a mound of dirt in the corner of the stall.

"I'm going to go with dirt."

"No. Underneath it." Prying a clod of earth out of his way, he shook off a stack of papers.

"Oh my gosh." Thrilled with a new discovery in her barn, she snatched them out of his hand. "These don't look very old." Shuffling through a bunch of yellowed slips she tried to determine what she was looking at.

"If you'll hand them back I might be able to help you figure out what they are," he goaded.

"Sorry." She handed over the find.

Stepping to the doorway he held one up to the fading sunlight. "They're old horse race betting slips."

"Can you see a date on them? This is so neat. I wonder if there used to be a track around here somewhere a long time ago?"

"Babe, you were right. These aren't that old."

"Then how did they get here?"

"No idea but these are from the nineties. Look they're carbon copies."

Her parents never gambled. They wouldn't even allow the boys to play poker until they were grown and living on their own. No one she knew gambled. Her father wouldn't even hire hands who occasionally bet on a Huskers game.

A sudden memory ripped the breath from her lungs. He'd been

there. He'd been in her barn. How dare he? This was hers. And just like everything else he'd taken from her he had no business there. "Oh."

Time came rushing back to her. She couldn't push it away.

"There's something else in here."

She could barely make out his voice. The screech in her ears drowned out his curiosity. He flipped through the massive stack of yellow slips until something else came into her view.

His eyes goggled and all of the color bled from his features. He jerked his head away from whatever he'd seen like he'd been slapped. She didn't want to know but she had to ask.

"What is it?"

Not even the hatred and fear that had etched his face the night he'd had the flashback could compare to the raw fury in his eyes.

"Tell me." She told herself to let it go but couldn't.

"No. Let's just go," he choked.

"I already know whose gambling slips they are so just tell me." She gagged, certain she was going to be sick.

"I don't want to tell you, Nat. Please let's just burn them or something."

"So, they're pictures right? Pictures of me I'm assuming."

A single nod. Driven only by her own gall, she jerked the stack of slips out of his hand once again. Flipping to the thicker pieces of paper hidden in the stack, she found two photographs.

Both were of her and Holly standing on their parents' front porch when they were in late elementary school. Mud was caked in their hair and covered the steps and porch railings. Her mother was doing her best to rid them of the mud they'd been playing in all morning. She'd stripped them and was toweling them off.

The picture had been snapped from so far away only their backsides were truly discernible. "Guess it could've been worse." The papers fluttered to the ground as she turned and flew out of the old barn.

She didn't stop until she reached her truck. Leaning against the door, she refused to feel anything at all. She would just pretend she'd never shown Aaron the barn. They'd just stopped right there in her field. The dirt she'd kicked up burned her throat and stung her eyes. She blinked rapidly trying to erase the things she refused to feel.

Fifteen minutes later, Aaron returned to her.

"What took you so long?"

"I had the lighter in my pocket for the candles you packed for the picnic. I burned them. Had to make sure it didn't burn down your barn because I will not let whoever took those pictures take that place from you. I won't. And if he were here right now, it would be him I'd be setting on fire right after I beat him senseless."

"Thank you," she managed in a haggard choke.

"Come on, baby, talk to me. Tell me how to help you handle this."

"I don't know."

"Then I'm taking you home and I'm gonna hold you until you're ready to talk."

"I'm never going to be ready to talk."

"Then I guess I'll be holding you forever because I'm not going anywhere."

CHAPTER FORTY

Spreading the quilt out on her living room floor instead of in her favorite field, Aaron set up the picnic as best as he could. The dogs were stretched out nearby, eyeing the picnic basket hopefully. He already had a fire roaring in her fireplace. If it weren't for her sicko uncle, this would've been nice.

Using the same lighter he'd used to incinerate the photos, he lit the candles he'd set on her coffee table. "Come here," he held out his hand.

"You didn't have to do this." She started to sit beside him on the floor, but he guided her into his lap instead.

"I told you I will not let him take anything else from you. Not your barn. Not this picnic. Not your dignity. Not your field. Not anything else on this ranch that you love. And sure as hell not me."

If he hadn't been hell-bent on never leaving her side, he would already have driven back to his house and beaten the fuck out of Rasmussen. Her uncle's name wasn't the only one on those slips. He'd recognized the old man's handwriting before he'd even found one with his name on it.

There were only two possible reasons Rasmussen hated her so much. He was afraid someday she might find physical evidence against him and press charges, or he blamed her for keeping him from his sick hobby. He was too stupid to know the old betting slips weren't enough to convict him in a state courtroom. Aaron didn't give a damn what a judge might rule. He'd execute the man himself. He stopped short of listing ways to murder his landlord while making it look like an accident.

"I don't want to remember that part of tonight. I want to remember all of the other things that I liked about it."

"Okay." He rocked her back and forth. "Then that's what we'll do. Your field is beautiful, baby."

"I still love it."

"Good. I want you to still love it. Never stop going there. Don't give it up."

"The barn is still really cool but I..."

"Don't want to go visit that for a while."

She nodded.

"You tell me when you think you're ready. I'll take you back up there and I'll be right beside you the entire time. Okay? Bet I could even get all of your big brothers to go with us. I know they make you feel safe."

"They do, but I don't need them so much anymore. I have you."

"Always."

Cosseted safely in Aaron's embrace, Natalie quirked one eye open the next morning. *Make it stop.* She whimpered. The buzzing continued.

Sitting up, she grabbed her cell phone from her bedside table. "Hey, Mama," she yawned.

"If you'da told me a month ago that my girl was gonna fall in love with a man who'd make her sleep in late, I woulda called you a liar."

"Sorry. Rough night."

"Something happen with you and Aaron?"

"Not exactly. We're fine. What did you need?"

"Well, your brothers are fit to be tied over doing your chores for you so after you go check your cattle bring Aaron down for breakfast. I'm making strawberry pancakes."

"Yum."

"Hurry up and you can lick the beaters on the mixer," her mother bribed.

"Are you making strawberry whipped cream, too?"

"Does your mama ever do anything halfway?"

"Definitely not."

"Then I'm making strawberry whipped cream. Get your behind over here."

"Okay. We'll hurry."

"We'll hurry to do what?" Aaron's entire face contorted with his yawn.

"Mama's making strawberry pancakes. She makes them with the preserves she puts up. They're amazing. But I have to check my cattle first, so get up."

"If I go down there with you, is your daddy gonna take pot shots at me?"

"Possibly, so just stay behind me." Natalie giggled.

"Not a fan of the idea of using you as body armor but your daddy definitely won't shoot you so I may take you up on that." Aaron crawled out of bed, grinning at her. "Feeling a little better this morning?"

"Much. And no nightmares so that's good. Plus, strawberry pancakes improve all situations."

"Let me find clothes and feed the dogs."

"I'll make us coffee," Natalie called as she headed down the hallway.

An hour later, the horses were fed and her cattle were all accounted for. They were just pulling into view of her parents' house when a loose steer darted in front of Aarons' truck. He slammed on the brakes missing the steer but causing Natalie to dump hot coffee all over her lap.

"Oh God, baby, I'm sorry."

Natalie held up her hand willing the hot sting to cool. "I'm fine and I'll dry. Spilled coffee is way better than a dead steer."

"Let's get you inside so I can get that coffee off of you."

"I'm fine." Natalie popped open his glove box searching for napkins.

"Nat, don't." He grabbed her hand but it was too late. Instead of the napkins she'd been expecting to find, her hand landed on a letter address to Hope.

Jerking away from him she stared from the letter to him. "Why do you have a letter for Hope?"

"I, uh... it was in the..."

"How did you get this?" Her body flushed hot and then ran ice cold. The acid in her stomach swirled into a maelstrom. She recognized the scratchy handwriting from the betting slips she'd seen the night before. Tearing open the envelope, she jerked open the letter. "Tell me how you got this. Tell me right now."

"T took it." His voice was a half-haunted whisper. T. The library. Cheryl seeing T at the court house. All of the pieces fit far too neatly. "You broke into the library didn't you. You took this from her desk or something. You were the one who broke the lock and the windows. You and T, right?"

"No."

"Stop lying to me!"

"It was T and Griff. It wasn't me."

"Oh my God. The night at the fair. When you said you were going to Cottonwood. You *were* in Moorer's Woods. You went to get them because they'd found this."

"They almost got caught at the library. I had to rescue them. You wouldn't tell me who'd hurt you. I just... Nat please. Please, I'm so sorry."

"So, what, I wouldn't tell you so you hired your friends to find out everything about me. Is that it?"

He had the audacity to nod. Bastard.

"The courthouse. Oh my God. Cheryl saw T outside the courthouse. Did he break in there, too?"

"They were looking for the wills."

"I trusted you." She raged in his face. "I trusted you with everything!" Flinging the door open she bolted toward her parents' house. "I hate you. I never want to see you again," she screeched as she reached the porch.

Her parents and brothers all raced outside. Dec, Holly, Brock, and

Hope followed after them.

"Nat please," Aaron continued to beg as he raced after her.

Shoving past Luke, Natalie took the stairs two at a time. "Tell him to leave," she shrieked before slamming her door.

"What the hell?" Luke and Austin made it to Aaron first. If they wanted to beat the shit out him or kill him in cold blood at that moment, he would have let them. "What did you do?"

He'd made a career out of always having the right thing to say at the right moment. Lies. Truth. Half of both. It never mattered. But he'd reached the end of the rope. There was nothing but the truth. It was the only thing he'd ever owed her and it was the singular thing he'd withheld. "I tried to find your uncle."

Every single member of the Camden family froze where they were. Dec's eyes closed for the better part of a minute. Ev's mouth was still hanging open.

"Why would you want to find my father?" Brock finally asked.

"We'll talk about that later," Jessie decreed. "Aaron, sweetie, let me talk to her. Let's just let her cool off a little."

Shaking off his shock, Ev approached Aaron. "Take a walk with me, son."

"Sir, I have to beg her forgiveness. I... have to... do something."

"We'll get to all that. Right now, we need to chat." Unsteady on his own feet for the first time in his life, Aaron found himself being led out toward the pasture nearby. They were five hundred paces from the Camdens' front porch before Ev started talking.

"So, what were you planning to do to him when you found him?"

"Uh, pretty much to kill him, sir." Any ability to lie seemed to have been drained from his consciousness.

"If I'd a known that, I woulda told you where he is. Wish you'd just asked me."

"I have to talk to her."

"Oh, she ain't gonna talk for a while. Got more temper than her mama and that's saying something. Just so I know how deep a ditch you've gotten yourself into and so I can figure how exactly to get you out of it, how did you go 'bout finding him?"

"In a former life, I was a Special Forces intelligence officer for the Green Berets."

"Impressive. Thank you for your service, son. So, you called the Pentagon askin' 'bout my brother or something like that?"

"No, sir." The need to do more than chat with her father seared through his brain preventing him from coming up with any actionable plan. "Uh, some friends of mine from back in the army run a security firm that specializes in finding people who don't necessarily want to be found. They helped me."

"Heard her say something 'bout the library. I'm guessing you and your friends are why it got broken into but nothing was taken."

"Yes, sir."

"Wouldn't have thought that kind of thing would be in the library."

"It wasn't. They broke into the courthouse as well. They, uh, they found your wills."

"Thorough ain't they?"

"Yes, sir."

"You know, I could be pissed about you upsetting my baby girl, but honest to the Good Lord up above you impressed the hell out of me. I thought about driving down to that stupid beach town in North Carolina and putting a bullet in his head more times that I can count. But you see, son, I finally realized that me festering in it wasn't gonna help her go on. I tried to do everything a daddy can do when one of his babies has been hurt like that. I would've given anything to have killed him before he ever got to her. Sick bastard." Ev spat on the ground.

"You moved his son back up here. She hates that." Being angry at someone else just felt too damn good. It brought breath back to his lungs. It made him able to fight again.

"She did. She don't so much anymore. I never dreamed Mick wouldn't leave Brock with us when I told him I'd kill him if he ever so much as crossed the Mississippi again and bury him so deep no one would ever find him. Brock is nothin' like my brother. This whole damn town wants to hold him accountable for his father's sins, the ones they know about, anyway. I wasn't going to do that. Boy deserved another chance. And my daughter deserved to know how strong she is. She never has to forgive Mick but carrying around all of that hatred was hurting her, too."

"Guess we'll agree to disagree on that. She deserves to hate whoever she wants, including me."

"She don't hate you. If she hated you, she wouldn't be up in her old bedroom crying over you. She'd be out on her horse thinking up creative ways to set your truck on fire."

"I'll hand her the matches. I deserve worse."

"You know, Natalie has always needed one thing me, and her mama, and her brothers, and her little sister just didn't have it in us to give her. But I think you might just have it in you."

"What? Anything."

"She needs somebody more stubborn than she is. Somebody who ain't gonna roll over and play dead just 'cause she told 'em she don't never want to see 'em again. You know anybody willing to fight *with* her *for* her?"

"Yes, sir." Fragments of an idea began to take shape in his mind.

"Kinda thought you might. I knew I liked you."

"You did?" The man had hated the very earth Aaron walked on a week ago.

"Just 'cause I threatened to kill ya don't mean I don't like you. I just love my girl."

"I love her too, sir."

"Then batten down the hatches, son. She's real likely to come out of my house guns blazing."

"I need to get a few things."

"You go on. I'll see if Jess and Holly have had any luck getting through to her. They won't but they'll try. It'll be a good long while for she even comes outta that room. She'll go from there straight to her house."

"I'm sorry I hurt her. I never meant to do that. I..." he choked.

Natalie's father put his hand on Aaron's shoulder. "I know you never meant to. Let her simmer down. Lying to her was a bad plan. Protecting her wasn't. I should've done a better job of that when she was a little girl. I'll never forgive myself for what he did to her. I shoulda taken a page from you. Course I didn't know then what I know now. But I like the idea of her being with a man willing to go to prison to keep her safe."

"I would."

"Oh, I know, son. I ain't so much worried about a prison cell though. I'm more worried about getting you out of the doghouse."

Aaron had his phone to his ear as soon as he cranked his truck. "Get him on a child pornography charge. I want him to burn," he snarled.

"What?"

"Mick. If I can't kill him, let some inmates do it on my behalf."

"Dude, what the hell is wrong with you?"

"Natalie found the letter. She pretty much hates me for lying to her."

"Fuck."

"She took me out to this barn on her ranch that she loves. We found some old betting slips and there were pictures of her and her sister when they were young."

"Jesus. I hope he does burn but it won't be in the state pen. He doesn't even own a computer."

"How the hell do you know that?"

"I am looking inside his house, A. I'm telling you. He's got nothing there that's illegal. Guy doesn't even drink anymore. How are you going to get Natalie back?"

"I'm not sure I can." The idea Aaron had come up with seemed more and more ridiculous the farther he drove away from the ranch. He didn't deserve to get her back. Why would this mission go any better than his last?

"Fuck that. You're getting her back. You two were meant to be. Why the hell do you think you stopped your truck in that tiny ass town years ago? You were supposed to meet her. I know it. I can feel it."

"I stopped here because it reminded me of Gentry not because of her."

"Uh huh. You ever think all the shit that you went through as a kid, Gentry, what happened in Najaf, all of it has been leading you right to her. I'm not letting you give up without a fight just because you're damned and determined to be punished for something that wasn't your fault. You get your shit together. We're going wheels up at 1100 hours."

"What?" The call had been ended.

Fight with her for her. It ricocheted around in his head making him dizzy. How exactly did he do that when she refused to come out of her parents' house? Nothing else came to him so he went on with his original plan.

Tearing open the boxes under his bed, he found his old combat tent. Flinging away meritorious promotion paperwork, combat medals, and his purple heart, he dug until he located his old rucksack and sleeping bag.

With each memory that surfaced, he tried to disassociate himself from them in preparation for the battle ahead. If she wouldn't take him back, he had no interest in going on. This was the fight for his life.

Needing some piece of Josh with him, he slipped his tags around his neck and dropped them behind his shirt. Another shattered fragment of his heart found the whole Natalie had been reconstructing.

Standing, he flung away his Wranglers. If he was going in, he was going in in fatigues.

He was shoving protein bars in his ruck sack when his front door was kicked open.

"Good, we were all on the same page." Griff assessed the disaster in the floor. Every remaining member of the Sevens was dressed in black T-shirts and camo pants. "Packs are in the trucks. I went by Supply and got enough M.R.E's for a month. Wheels up."

"I take it the drop zone is approaching." Smith chuckled as T drove them through pastureland toward Natalie's house.

"You don't have to do this with me. I'm the one who fucked everything up."

"We are the United States Army Special Forces Operational Detachment Alpha 1167. Where you go we go," T vowed. "High time you got over yourself and figured out what to do with your life. Natalie is what you do with your life in case you had any doubt."

Honored, humbled, and humiliated, Aaron had never been more

thankful for his team in his entire life. He followed them out of the truck and started setting up camp in her front yard.

T stabbed a metal pole in the ground with a paper guidon flag attached to it. Aaron shook his head. The Special Forces arrows were in the center just like their old guidons. However, unlike their old flags, the team number was now a 69 and the company name was no longer a single letter it was an A and an N.

Griff unfurled a full sized army surplus tent. When it was erected, he hung a sheet of poster board on the side facing Natalie's house declaring that this was Camp Take Him Back.

"Where the hell did you get a tent like that?" Uncertain how to feel about all his team had done, it was the only question that came to mind.

"I refuse to answer that on the grounds that the army might want it back and decide to incriminate me." Griff smirked.

"All right we need some mission parameters and specs. Basically, I'm asking what the hell happened and how are we going to fix it."

The look on her face when she pulled that stupid letter from his glovebox sucker punched him yet again. "I shoved the letter in my glovebox. I wanted it on me in case I stumbled up on an opportunity to get it somewhere back in Brock and Hope's house or her pocket-book or something. I've been on the ranch so much I figured I had a fair chance to stick it somewhere and make Hope believe she hadn't left it where she knew she did. A cow ran in front of my truck this morning. I slammed on the brakes. Her coffee went all over her. She was looking for napkins I guess. Found the letter. Put all of the shit I'd been shoveling in a pile, told me she hated me, and that she never wanted to see me again."

The weight of every lie he'd told crashed down on him. He sank to the ground under the strain of his shame.

"All right so obviously you can never lie to her ever again. Not even for a Christmas present or about a burned dinner or anything else triv-ial." T, in ready form, began planning.

"Yeah, I figured that out all on my own."

"As for you going behind her back to find shit out, you weren't the only one on your own intel gathering mission."

"What the hell does that mean?"

"She asked us about what happened to you," Griff supplied. "The scars, all of it."

"When?"

"That night we were in the bar."

"Yeah, I got a phone call from your girl a couple of nights ago. She pretended to want to know what your favorite meal was. She said she wanted to surprise you. Can't lie to save her own life. She finally got to asking me if we'd all gotten deactivated at the same time," Smith supplied with a life of his eyebrows. "Made me wonder where she got the correct army term. I figured it was from you."

"What'd you tell her?" Inventorying his mind Aaron could find no irritation that Natalie had asked his friends about him. Only hope and regret. He clung to both. Clearly, they both needed to stop talking to his team and start talking to each other.

"Nothing. But that's not the point."

"She didn't get the term from me. She's been Googling."

"So, I'd say you've got a better than a fair chance of showing her you weren't the only one who went around your ass to get to your elbow as far as finding shit out about each other goes."

"Yeah, well I'm sure as hell not gonna go in pointing that out. I have to apologize on my knees. Swear I'll never lie to her again."

"All in due time, brother. All in due time." T sank down to the ground beside him. "You'll get your chance. First course of action is to get her out of her house."

"We can't bomb her out, T." Smith rolled his eyes.

"I'll come up with something slightly less destructive," T assured them.

The sound of approaching footsteps had all of the team standing. Dec offered them a kind grin. "Gentlemen."

Aaron cleared his throat. "Dec this is T-Byrd, Griff, Voodoo, and Echo, my old team. Guys this is Dr. Declan St. James, my shrink."

Dec got several appreciative nods.

"Currently, I'm here as your friend. Although I would be remiss not to remind you that I told you not to do this. That being said, my wife is holed up in there with her sister and I thought I might see if I could lend a hand to your mission. I'd like Holly to come home at some point. I know my wife. She won't leave Natalie's side until this is all resolved and you weren't the only one asking the wrong people for answers."

"What's that mean?" Aaron demanded.

Dec shook his head. "If we manage to suture the cavernous wounds both of you tore in your relationship, promise me you will come see me together."

"Not really in a position to promise anything on her behalf," Aaron huffed.

"Good answer. Let me talk to her."

"Just what the hell does he think he's doing?" Fury radiated from Natalie as she peeked out of her blinds to spy on the army camp set up in her front lawn.

"You fell in love with a Green Beret, sis. Looks like he's not going down without a fight." Holly wrinkled her nose.

"Yeah, well maybe he should've thought of that before he decided to have his friends spy on my life and then lie to me about it." Pleased his dogs were in her house, Natalie continued to play with Lulu's ears. Eventually she'd have to return them to Aaron but for now she needed their comfort.

"I know you're hurt, Nat. I just..."

"Do not make excuses for him."

Holly's sigh was interrupted by a knock on the front door. "Holl, love, it's me. Let me in." Dec's soothing intonation quelled a little of Natalie's rage, but only a little.

Holly swung open the door. "I'm not getting anywhere with her."

"Let me try," Dec assured her.

"Do you people think I'm deaf?" Natalie snapped.

"Hard of listening, maybe, but not deaf," Dec challenged. "About two weeks ago, a woman who bears a striking resemblance to you waltzed in my home early one morning demanding answers on the man camped outside in some bizarre combination of army meets cattle ranchers. When I refused you, you got them out of your sister. Now, how exactly is that different from the things he did?"

Incensed ire rode on the bile that shot to her throat. "Well, for one I did not break into businesses to find out about his PTSD."

"So, you're mad he's better at it than you are?"

"Get out of my house," Natalie menaced.

"Nat, come on. He's right. You both did the same things. He just went above and beyond, which is kind of his motto, isn't it?" Holly pointed out.

"On that note and since it is painfully obvious that there needs to be absolutely no secrets between the two of you, I'm going to once again do something I shouldn't. Aaron decided to take himself off of all of his anti-depressants when you two started dating. They can have sexual side effects. To my knowledge he'd never experienced any but he wasn't taking any chances when it came to you. Understand that in doing so he was willing to return to the nightmares and the flashbacks coming far more often than he could really deal with."

The night at the fair whipped through Natalie's mind. Guilt taunted the fringes of her anger. She tried to refuse it but failed.

"When a soldier with Post Traumatic Stress who blames himself for the trauma comes off of the meds there is an extremely common occurrence."

"Superhero syndrome," Holly gasped.

Dec nodded. "Yes. Exactly."

"What is that?" Natalie sank down on her sofa under the weight of all that had happened. Her steady foundation was shaken and cracked, but maybe it wasn't quite broken.

Holly sat down beside her. "It's a different scenario for each individual experiencing it. In this case it means his brain sort of went into overdrive. He convinced himself that he needed to be better than human for you. He didn't feel like he deserved you. He had to earn you so to speak."

"Something like that," Dec agreed. "His mind concocted the idea that he had to end anything that had ever frightened you. Your uncle being right at the top of his list. It was the only way he believed he'd ever be good enough for you. His psychological trauma is significant, Natalie. He's still not well."

"I know that."

"Does that mean you'll give him a chance to at least apologize?"

"No."

"Nat..." Holly pleaded.

"No. I don't know what I'm going to do but I shared everything with him and he lied to me over and over again."

"But you didn't share everything with him. If you had, he wouldn't have gone on some bizarre mission to figure out who'd hurt you." Holly crossed her arms over her chest.

"I don't have to share that with anyone."

"No, you don't," Dec agreed. "But don't sit there playing judge, jury, and executioner based on false evidence. You did not share everything with him. You shared a few fragmented pieces of your soul, and that took tremendous courage. No one is saying that it didn't. But as you can plainly see the parts you left hiding in the dark are the ones that have gotten us here."

"This is not my fault," Natalie snarled.

"Of course it's not," Holly huffed. "But you two are the only two people who can fix this."

"I don't think I can ever trust him again."

"Coming from us..." Dec put his arm around Holly, "...two people whose entire relationship existed because of complicated lies we told everyone around us, I can tell you that the trust you had before can never be rebuilt, but you can build a new kind of trust, a better kind of trust, one that can't be broken," Dec concluded.

CHAPTER FORTY-ONE

The ache of his feet in his boots was all too familiar yet Aaron continued to pace. He tried to believe that somehow some way this would all work out. There had to be something he could do or say to convince her to give him a chance. He marched on. It was all he really knew how to do. He needed her. Every breath, every heartbeat hinged on the belief that he could hold her in his arms again. Somehow.

Dec closed the door behind him. He offered Aaron a consolatory half-smile. "Give her a little more time. The Camden women like to get everything sorted out in their minds before they take action. She's still processing."

"She told you to leave didn't she?" Aaron knew.

"I didn't listen but yes."

"Got any other ideas, Doc? I'm losing it."

"I can go to the office and get you enough samples to get you through the next few weeks."

"I will not be drugged into believing that I haven't just ended my own life."

"You've gotten through so much, Aaron. This isn't over with. You're just going to have to give her a little more time."

"My life depends on her opening that door."

"I know it does. I promise you I will not let you lose her, too. You have room for one more in this camp?" He asked the team.

"You got food?" Voodoo grinned.

"I'm a decent cook and I can let you men make use of both my pantry and my plumbing facilities instead of digging a latrine."

"The more the merrier, Doc."

"Did you boys really think I was gonna let you camp out on my ranch and not feed you?" Jessie and Austin approached carrying platters of food. Grant pulled up in his truck.

"Ms. Camden you don't have to feed us." Torn between wanting his friends to have plenty to eat and not wanting the Camdens going to any more trouble on his behalf, Aaron shook his head.

"She's gonna feed you and she's almost as stubborn as her daughters are, so eat," Austin directed.

Grant hopped out of his truck and pulled a folding table and a stack of chairs from the back. "You want these in the big tent?"

"You really don't have to..." Aaron started but T glared at him.

"Shut it, man. They want to help and Jesus Christ himself knows you need to learn to let people help you."

"Put it in the tent, Grant. Is Katy coming down?" Jessie commanded.

"I ain't letting her sleep on the ground with us, but she's bringing coffee, and fixins, and her cherry pies."

"Dude, where were they when we were in the sandbox?" Smith chuckled.

Austin unfurled a Coleman sleeping bag before Aaron could stop him. "You don't have to..." he tried again.

Austin held up his hands. "One, I want to see somebody out-stubborn my sister. Two, I owe you one. Three, Summer's mighty ornery right about now in her pregnancies. I ain't making much of a sacrifice being out here 'stead of in there. And four, my young'uns love to camp out, so they think this is great fun and it'll get 'em out of Summer's hair."

"I'll agree on the first point," Grant explained as he arranged a sleeping bag beside his brother's. "On the other hand, Katy gets sweet and cuddly right about now so this is a little more of a sacrifice for me. But it's worth it to see my sister finally have to admit she mighta been wrong and that she might have to give a little latitude every now and again."

Aaron was quick to correct him. "She isn't wrong. I've been lying to her the whole time. I was wrong."

Grant shrugged. "I ain't one of those people dumb enough to believe that lying for a good reason is as bad as lying for the wrong reason or for no reason at all. Way I see it you had the cajones to actually do what we all been wishin' we could do for years now. If I get the chance, I'll tell my little sister that, too. And don't tell my old man but me, Austin, and Luke got a pool going on how long she'll make you wait out here 'fore she caves. I got a hundred dollars on tomorrow afternoon if you want to keep that in mind."

"She ain't goin' down that fast," Austin huffed. "This is Nat we're talking about."

Mr. Camden's dirty boots hit the dirt next. He chuckled as he entered the camp area. "Nice job, if I do say so myself. You know I think I got an extension cord long enough to run from Dec and Holly's out here if you want me to bring a TV. I got a buncha old army movies we can watch while we wait."

Aaron stared skyward not certain what he was praying for. Half of him believed he was back on those painkillers they'd given him after his surgeries that made him hallucinate.

"Ev, no one wants to see *The Thin Red Line* with you, honey. I'm sure these boys have seen all kinds of real red lines and they don't want to see any more. Now, have you talked to our daughter?" Jessie rolled her eyes.

A foreign sensation overtook Aaron. It took him a minute realize that he was chuckling. Nothing made sense without Natalie beside him. He longed to tell her how kind her family was and how funny. *She knows that, moron.*

"I ain't talked to her yet 'cause all of you who've already tried are wasting your breath. You gotta let her stew on it."

"Well, when do you plan on talking to her? 'Cause this is plain ol' ridiculous. So, he wanted to kill Mick. Ain't like every single one of us out here ain't had thoughts like that most of the time we've known him."

"It's not that. It's that I lied to her, ma'am. She has every right to hate me."

"She don't hate you," Jessie assured him. "If she hated you your truck would already be in flames."

That was the second time that oddly specific warning had been given. "Did she actually set someone's car on fire at some point?"

Ev and Jessie nodded and then both doubled over with laughter.

"When she was about nine, calf thieving around here was pretty common. They'd take 'em before we could get 'em branded. Then they'd try to sell 'em back to the ranchers they'd taken them from," Grant explained. "One day, this old truck with a trailer pulls up to Mama and Daddy's and our calves are in the back. We knew what was up but before Dad could get the cops out here, Nat snuck outside and stuck a pack of fireworks in the hood of the truck while they were in our kitchen horse trading on our own cows. They realized we were on to them, took off, firecrackers went off, truck went up in flames. She single-handedly caught the thieves. She's never lived it down though."

"That's my girl," Aaron vowed without thought. She wasn't his anymore.

"She don't take well to anybody trying to take advantage of anybody else," Grant explained.

"Yeah, but life's not always fair," Jessie commented. "She knows that. She just don't like it. I'm going in and Everett Camden you are coming with me."

"All right, fine." Ev set down a fried chicken leg he'd taken from one of the baskets Jessie had provided. "If we ain't back out here in a half hour start thinking up a rescue mission boys," Ev commanded T-Byrd.

"We call them tactical evacuation missions, sir, but we won't let you down. If you want to do a little recon for us while you're in there, we'd appreciate it."

"You got it, son." Ev saluted and every member of Team Seven bit back hysterical laughter.

"Seriously, what the hell happened to your bed?" Holly dissolved in another fit of giggles.

Natalie kept her glare trained on the camp right outside her front door. "I cannot believe Grant and Austin are taking their side."

"Oh, I'm on their side, too. I'm just in here with you because you're my sister and I don't like to camp."

Whirling around to glare at her sister instead, Natalie didn't get a single word out before there was another knock on her front door. "So help me if they think they're getting in here to use my bathroom."

Holly joined her at the bedroom window. "It's Mama and Daddy. Come on. We cannot let Dad see your bed." She jerked Natalie down the hallway and let their parents in. Before she closed the front door, her mouth fell open. "Oh my gosh, did Katy make pies?"

"Yep and Indie's on her way with her potato soup," Jessie informed them.

"It's a good thing I love you, Nat," Holly huffed.

"I don't think he's going anywhere, baby girl. Why don'tcha just hear him out?" Her father tried.

"Because he lied to me about basically everything."

"He did not lie to you about everything. He lied about trying to figure out who'd hurt you and about his friends breaking into half of Main Street," Holly explained yet again.

"I can't believe you all are on his side."

"I am not taking sides," her mother assured her. She went to the kitchen and poured a mug of cold coffee. "I'm just here because it don't matter how many holes are in the waffle it does always have two sides and I want to hear both of 'em. So, start talking my stubborn little cowgirl."

"Let's see here. I trusted him with everything and he lied."

"Once again, you did not trust him with everything, Nat." Her sister was officially on her nerves.

"Did he ask you who'd hurt you, Natalie?" Her mother stared her down.

"Yes."

"And did you tell him?"

"No."

"And why was that?"

"I didn't want Uncle Mick to have anything to do with me and Aaron." Just saying her uncle's name swirled bile in her stomach.

"Fair enough. Did you explain to Aaron why you wouldn't tell him?"

"Yeah."

"Seems to me he was trying to respect your mission while conducting one of his own. You didn't want to think about Mick. He wanted to kill him. The way a man's mind works the two never had to cross paths."

"That's ridiculous. He cannot kill Uncle Mick."

"Why not? I almost did several times. Most of the time I wish I'd succeeded. If it weren't for your granddaddy, I would've, too," her father vowed. "And every single time you had one of them nightmares after it happened, I swore to myself I was gonna drive to North Carolina and shoot him, beat him, and drown him one after another."

"Please try to remember that Aaron is also not thinking entirely clearly," Holly leapt in again.

"How could I forget? You bring it up every five minutes."

"All right you two. Now, the night I was out here and we had tea you told me you were worried sick about him because of his PTSD. Did he tell you about that?" Her mother already knew he hadn't. Natalie could tell.

"No."

"So, how did you go 'bout figuring that out?"

"She asked Dec, and then she asked me, and then she researched it. Oh, and she also asked several of his friends about it behind his back."

"Ain't that interesting. Tell me, cowgirl, did you tell Aaron you were researching his diagnosis?"

"No, I didn't." Natalie ground her teeth.

"And why not?"

"I didn't want to upset him."

"My, my, my. Pot meet kettle. And why did you do so much research, sweetheart?"

Natalie refused to answer.

"Mm-hmm, I'd say it has something to do with the fact that you love him and you want to protect him. I'd bet every head of cattle on this ranch and a few on another that those are the very reasons he didn't tell you what he was doing."

"That doesn't make it okay to lie."

"No, it don't, but love and protection are two pretty good places to build a relationship. I saw the look on the boy's face when you went running up to your old room. If you don't want to trust him right now, trust your mama. He ain't ever gonna lie to you about anything ever again. People do make mistakes, sweetheart."

"Nat, baby, you know trust doesn't have to be all in or all out." Her father winked at her. "You can build it back slowly over time. Take a little faith, turn that into trust, and go from there."

"You never lied to Mama about anything," she reminded him.

Her mother choked on a sip of coffee. "Dear Lord," she cleared her throat. "Your daddy likes to forget the part of our getting-together story where he'd been seeing someone else on occasion when he picked me up on the side of the road. What was her name, Ev?"

"I don't remember."

"Uh-huh, well she shows up on the ranch demanding to know who I was. I started demanding to know who she was. Your daddy kept assuring me she was a very distant cousin."

"Well, that was kinda true if you think about us all being related 'cause we all came from the people on the Ark and all."

Her mother rolled her eyes so hard Natalie was momentarily concerned they were going to lodge in her skull.

"Another time, I went back to Denver to help my mama move into assisted living. You all were little but your daddy kept assuring me he could handle everything. When I got back, Luke had a cast on his left arm and his right hand. Grant hadn't bathed in a week. Austin had tied four saddles onto three heifers. You had a calf up in your bedroom you'd dressed as a cowgirl princess that your daddy didn't know was there, and Holly had learned to curse and had finger-painted all over my walls with the manure she found in your bedroom. Whole time I was gone he kept telling me how everything was totally under control."

"So that's a good example of your mother's forgiving nature and learning to trust me again." Ev sighed.

"She also never left all of us with you again," Natalie pointed out.

"That ain't the point."

"Holly said shit more than she said mama for an entire year, Everett."

Natalie hated the loneliness she'd felt as soon as she'd banished Aaron from her life almost as much as she hated that he'd lied to her. The desire to hear the entire story straight from him continued to shimmer in her mind. "So, all men lie. That's what you're saying."

"There you go, Jess. Turnabout's fair play ain't it? You want to correct her or shall I? What was it you told me when I asked you 'bout a dozen times if you were sure you'd ridden a horse before?"

"I told him I'd ridden my whole life. I'd never ridden. Got my ass thrown in the dirt. There I lied, too. I was trying to impress him."

"Then she got mad at the horse and hit me when I went running out to make sure she was okay."

"As long as we're on the subject I might also have lied to your daddy more than a time or two about how much a pocketbook cost. And... I might've let him think that I got to keep my employee discount at Dillard's for a year or ten after I quit my job there."

"Mm-hmm." Ev shook his head.

"Fine. I will think about maybe, possibly talking to him but not right now," Natalie conceded.

"No time like the present, darlin'," her father reminded her.

"Not. Right. Now."

CHAPTER FORTY-TWO

"What are the chances she'll hate me more if I just kick down her door?" Aaron fumed as night fell. Despondency had set in. He could no longer make out the green grass or the hazy orange sunset. Colors leached rapidly from the world around him. How had he lost the one and only thing he'd ever really wanted to live for?

The tags against his chest agitated his skin. It was the only feeling he could decipher beyond the pain that made him unable to breathe. How could he have been so stupid? How had he really believed he could orchestrate a mission that wouldn't end in disaster? He had precious little evidence to prove him otherwise.

"I wouldn't do that." Luke cringed. "Better than decent chance she'd come up with some way to hate you more."

"Yeah, well, it'd have to be better than sitting our here worrying about her."

"A, deep breaths. She'll come around eventually. Deal him in," Griff ordered Austin who was shuffling a pack of cards.

"Don't you fucking get it? I don't need to play cards, or to drink, or to do anything other than beg her forgiveness. I need her. I don't want to walk, talk, breathe, do anything unless she's mine again. None of it even fucking matters."

"Could someone please tell me what the hell this is all about?" Brock appeared out of the enveloping darkness. "My dad is a grade A asshole. We all know that. But what does he have to do with Natalie? I've been walking around this ranch trying to put the pieces together because I can't stand that he's divided this family again. Why were you looking for him? Why did you want to kill him? I'm not even necessarily opposed to the idea I just... I think I deserve to know why."

Every eye in their makeshift camp turned to Aaron.

"Son, well..." Ev started but Aaron was tired of the lies.

"Your father sexually abused Natalie when she was a little girl."

"What?" Brock jerked back like he'd been physically struck. "No way. He... God please tell me... Are you...? Oh my God. That's why she hates me. That's why you made us leave."

Ev stood. "It wasn't because of some fight Mick and I had. I never dreamed he'd actually take you with him, but I had to help my daughter deal with what had been done."

"I have to apologize to her, offer to move, do something." Brock swayed but then directed his boots toward Natalie's door.

An audible gasp worked through the crowd when the door swung open. Instinctively Aaron moved toward her.

"You don't have to apologize for what your father did, Brock," she choked.

"Yes, I do. Nat, I had no idea. I would've asked you before we moved back. I would've done... something." Brock held his hands up. "Jesus, do I scare you? I know I favor him. I never meant to."

"You used to but not so much anymore. Just maybe don't ever grab my hands."

"Never. I swear. If you want Hope and me to move, we will. I just never..."

"I don't want that and Daddy did ask me if it was okay if he offered you your land back. I told him yes."

With magnetizing force, Aaron marched forward. Desperate but driven. "Nat, baby, I..."

"You, on the other hand..." she narrowed her eyes hatefully, "...have a lot of apologizing to do."

"I'm so sorry. I swear I never meant to lie to you."

"Dammit, did anyone have tonight in the pool?" Austin inquired.

"She ain't forgiven him yet," Grant reminded everyone.

"You never have to forgive me. I don't deserve that. I just need to apologize. I just need... you." Aaron would beg for as long as she'd let him.

Holly whipped around her sister and bolted out the door. "You two go talk."

Praying to any deity willing to listen, Aaron crossed the threshold of her home, thankful she'd allowed him that much. She shut the door behind him.

"I want answers to every single question I ask and so help me if you lie even once, I'll never speak to you again, you got that?"

"I swear. I will never ever lie to you again."

"When were you shot?"

"July 11, 2013."

"Who shot you?"

"The first two shots were by a man named Samer. I never knew how to pronounce his last name and I don't want to lie to you. I don't know the name of the man who shot me the third time. I woke up on the helicopter. Remember, I told you that. Voodoo managed to get enough of the fragments out of me that he could get a few stitches in so I didn't bleed to death before he stitched himself up."

"I thought you were going to say the bad guys shot you. You actually knew the man who shot you?" Her lip quivered but he didn't need her pity he needed her forgiveness.

"Yes. We'd been working with his men trying to train up the Iraqi police force. They turned on us."

"Oh my God."

Frantic to answer every single thing she wanted to know, he swallowed down bile and vomit from the memories. "It was my fault."

"How? Why? You keep thinking everything was your fault. How on earth were you supposed to know they were going to do that?"

"I was the intel officer. It was my job to know. I knew... I just had this feeling something bad was going to happen, but I kept telling myself I felt that way because of something else. CIA intelligence was coming down the line to me. That would have been the proof I needed. It just didn't get there in time."

"That isn't your fault."

"Seven men who were brothers to me, Nat, all lost their lives because I didn't fucking figure it out. I was trained. I knew what I was doing. I was the best and I blew it."

"I'm so sorry."

Aaron shook his head. "I'm here to say that. You have nothing to be sorry for."

"So, that's what the stars on your arm are for?"

"Yeah." Blinking back the sting of liquid memories from his eyes, he turned his arm over. "See, these are their numbers under each star."

"How did? I mean, why didn't we hear about that over here? We should have known that."

"One of the reasons we do what we do, the reason we fight, is so that your lives are never interrupted. It's the sacrifice we make and it being all over the news doesn't bring them back. They're still just as gone."

"Is the guy in that picture one of the men who was killed?"

The picture? Aaron racked his brain. His brow furrowed.

"The one I saw on your counter. The one from when you were younger."

"Oh. No. He didn't go into Special Forces. But, uh, he did take his own life about a month before we were shot. It took my foster mom that long to get word to me. I'd just found out the day before. That's part of why I wasn't... at my best, maybe."

"Oh my God, Aaron. Why did he?"

"Found out his wife was cheating on him."

Her hand flew to her mouth. She shook her head.

"Nat, I should've respected the fact that you didn't want to tell me about your uncle. I had no business getting them to find him. I just... it killed me that a man who'd hurt you, one who still scares you, went on wasting oxygen. I'm so sorry I lied so many times. And I know, okay, I know the truth out of a liar's mouth is worthless but I swear I wasn't lying when I said I loved you. I wasn't lying when I told you about the field or how beautiful and strong you are. I love you so much, Nat. I just..."

Suddenly, she was in his arms again. Breath rushed back to his lungs. His heart finally found a steady beat. The constant pain eased its icy clutches. He clung to her terrified to let her go.

"Wait." She wiped tears out of her eyes. "You said your foster mom. Did he live in Gentry with you?"

"I'll tell you everything but can I maybe just keep holding you while I do it?"

A heartbroken smile tipped the corners of her mouth. She took his hand and led him to the couch. Once he was seated, she curled up in his lap. "Thank you."

"Talk."

"Remember when I told you my social worker pulled a few strings to get me to the farm in Gentry? Well, Josh Campbell was my foster parents' only biological child. He was my age. He was the first friend I ever really had but it was more than that. I lived there five years. He was my brother. We joined up together. The one thing my foster mom said to me with tears in her eyes the day we got on that bus was to please take care of Josh. They'd saved my life and I failed to do the only thing they'd ever asked of me."

"Aaron, surely she knows it wasn't your fault. Oh my gosh, is that why you haven't been back to visit?"

He managed a haggard nod. "I get a paycheck every month from the government for being a Beret and being airborne and all that, even though I'm doing nothing to earn it. I send it to her. My foster dad can't farm anymore so..." he shrugged, "...that's why I don't have a lot of money like T and Griff and all of them. And there's this other thing I need to tell you. I've never said this out loud to anyone. I've never even told Dec this. Whenever I have a flashback, and I go back to when I was shot, I don't get it right. My brain always puts Josh there with me. I keep trying to save him and I just... can't."

"I'm so sorry I got so mad at you," she whispered.

"No, baby, no. You have every right to be mad at me. I lied to you and I went against your wishes. I'm the one who's sorry."

"It's just that it takes more than it should for me to trust someone.

I don't have a lot of experience with it, I guess. So, the story goes that my uncle kept touching me. He'd try to find me when I was alone. It happened a lot. One day he grabbed me in the barn, but he was drunk and didn't realize Holly was there. She screamed and my parents figured out what was going on. After that, I never really left the ranch. I trust my family and never anyone else. So, when I trusted you..."

"You were trying to trust me with a few other things so you could see if you could trust me with more. I know. I fucked it up. I failed the test. And knowing the story doesn't make me want to murder him any less."

"You didn't fail anything, Aaron. So, we have to start out with a lot of faith and build the trust from there. I want to do that. Just please tell me everything, okay? Even if you think it isn't important."

"Okay. Uh, let's see here. Where do you want me to start?"

"I kind of meant from here on out but I'd like to know if you knew your biological parents."

Digging deeper into reserves than he had in three long years, determination locked in his musculature. "Yes, I knew them. My dad was in the army actually. He left when I was five. I have no idea why. I just remember telling all of the kids in my class that he was coming back. He never did. He was my hero and then he was gone. My mom found chemical ways to avoid the pain. I was put in foster care when she held up a drug store at gunpoint looking for pain meds."

"Oh my God."

"As far as I know she's still in prison. Don't really have any desire to see her."

"Well, I don't want you in prison for killing my uncle. I swore to myself a long time ago that I wouldn't let him steal anything from me ever again. Today, I almost let him. I was so embarrassed that your friends had figured everything out and that I believed you when you were lying to me."

"You didn't," he vowed.

"Yes, I did."

"No, you didn't. Not really. Every single time I covered something up this flash of questioning would go off in your eyes. You chose to ignore it but your radar was trying to warn you. I could see it. Part of me wished you'd call me on it. I hated lying to you, but the other part of me just wanted to bury the bastard in the ground and piss on the dirt."

"Can't we just let him die in North Carolina and never think about him again?"

"I'm more than happy to let him die, but baby, every part of both of our pasts affects our present and our future. Dec said if I ever got you to talk to me again, we should see him together."

"That's probably a really good idea. Therapy refresher would be good for me, even if he is my stupid brother-in-law."

"He's helped me a lot. He even told me not to go after your uncle. I just didn't listen."

"He told me you went off your medication for me. You didn't have to do that."

"I wanted to. I'm still glad I did. I hate I had a flashback with you but that's part of my truth I guess."

"Yeah, and I love every single part of you."

A tremor of disbelief jolted through Aaron. He strengthened his hold on her. "You do? I mean, you don't have to. I lied to you."

"I know you did and you better never do that again. But even when I was furious with you I still loved you. That's how love works. You don't have to earn it."

Someone knocked on her front door with enough force to shake the foundation of her house. Natalie started to get up but Aaron held her tight. "Little busy right now," he shouted.

"A, it's me. Let me in. We have a situation." T sounded frantic.

Aaron beat her to the door by two paces. He jerked it open. "What?"

"This." T held up his phone.

"What? It's a blinking red dot in the middle of Missouri." Aaron sounded as frustrated as Natalie felt.

"Yeah, that blinking red dot is her uncle's car."

"What?" Instinctively, Natalie gripped Aaron bicep. "Why is he in Missouri? He's not allowed."

"Yeah, well, I hadn't had time to check on him this morning before you called me. He must've left after my last check yesterday. He's seems to have stopped for the night."

"How did you make there be a dot on his car?" Natalie knew she sounded like an idiot but none of this made any sense.

"There's a Beret training facility in North Carolina. T called a friend of ours who's stationed there. He bugged your uncle's house, set up surveillance cameras, the whole deal. He also attached a tracker device to his car," Aaron supplied though his words were laced with fury.

"I see we've already taken a vow to tell her everything now." T sighed.

"I'll never lie to her again."

His promise was barely audible over the sirens blaring in Natalie's ears and the panic clawing under her skin. She couldn't see him. She didn't know what to say to him. He couldn't come to Camden Ranch. Her carefully orchestrated world had begun to unravel that morning when she'd found out about Aaron's lies. Now, the seams were splitting, audible rips and pops in her mind so loud she didn't understand how no one else heard them.

"Look, give me some kind of directions or coordinates or however you guys work and I'll go meet him. I'll tell him to turn around and go home," Brock vowed as soon as he got back to the door.

"We're too far out. Coordinating you two would be next to impossible. Ever try to work one of those word problems about the trains heading towards each other on parallel tracks at different speeds? That's basically what we'd be dealing with," T explained. "We'll have to wait until he's closer."

"Are you sure he's coming here?" Natalie finally located words that made sense.

"No. Just seems that way. If he stays on his direct course, he'll end up right here."

"Could we just call him and ask him what the hell he's doing?" Brock sighed.

"No cell phone." T and Aaron answered simultaneously.

"Go get packed, Nat. We're leaving. I'll take you anywhere you want to go, but you're not facing him." Aaron had located his voice as well.

"I'll get you a plane. Fly her anywhere you want," T readily volunteered.

"No." A still, small voice erupted from the vicinity of Natalie's chest. It took her two breaths to recognize it as her own. Her hands on Aaron steadied her. Her heart lurched back to life. The steel blade she'd longed for so many times in her life finally made its severing cut.

The malignant fear and anger she'd clung to for so long dissolved in the sea of all she'd lost and all she'd gained. "No. I will not run from him or from this. I am not a little girl anymore. He has no power over me. I won't let him. I refuse to be afraid of him. I refuse to let him run me off my ranch. This is my land. This is my family's land, a family he isn't a part of. If he's coming, let him come. God knows I have plenty I'd like to say to him." There. For the first time in years, she knew she was the one that held all of the power.

Aaron turned and cradled her face in his hands. "Look at me and tell me you're absolutely sure you want to see this man."

"I am just as sure of this as I am that we are going to figure out some way to move past all of the lies and sneaking around both of us did. He isn't going to hurt me. I can take care of myself now. I'm a cowgirl and he can bring it on."

"You're not facing him alone," Aaron informed her.

"Oh we'll be there, too," T vowed. "You want to take on one of ours you take on all of us."

"She's right." Brock smiled at her. "Nat's never taken any shit off of anyone. She's not gonna take any off of him and I have a few questions I'd like answers to as well. My shitlickin' sperm donor can look me in the eye and tell me what he did. I make no promises he'll still be standin' when I'm finished with him but I'm not a kid anymore either."

"Baby, you have every right to stand up to him. But hear me say this, he so much as looks at you wrong I'll kill him." Aaron's vow held no notes of indecision or even consideration.

"Yeah, well, you can get in line, son," Ev spat. "I told him a long time ago if he ever came up here again it'd be the last thing he ever did."

"No one is going to kill him." Natalie shook her head at her would-be defenders. "He is nothing but a lazy coward with a sick mind. Let him burn when it's his time."

CHAPTER FORTY-THREE

Natalie's resolute decision gnawed at Aaron's desperate need to protect her above all others. Her eyes followed him in his relentless pacing.

The Sevens were all sitting in her living room. Holly and Dec were among them along with her parents. Camp was still set up outside but her brothers had returned to their homes. At least that's what they'd said they were doing. Aaron had a feeling they were out somewhere on the ranch conducting target practice.

"He's stopped at a hotel somewhere. Car hasn't moved in three hours," T gave another report.

The clocks in her home chewed through the time too quickly. Aaron wasn't convinced she was prepared to face him again no matter how certain she seemed.

"I don't care. He'll be here when he gets here. Don't you get it? A lot of victims have to live with their abusers for years. I didn't. And... I kind of think we each have to handle it our own way. There is no wrong way to deal with it. It sucks but there's really no way out of your only life. In fact, I don't want a way out. I happen to like my life. So, he's coming here. I want to deal with this by facing him, telling him exactly what I think of him, wishing him well on his one-way trip to hell, and then I want to get back to living my life."

"My big sister is kind of a badass." Holly winked at her.

"Yeah, she sure as hell is," Aaron agreed. "*My* beautiful badass."

"Oooh maybe I'll get a tattoo that says that." Natalie laughed. Unable to believe she was actually laughing in the face of this, he just fell more in love with her.

"Baby girl, your daddy's heart has been through a lot this evening. Could you not get a tattoo until I've had time to process this day?" her father begged.

"All right, Daddy, but why don't you all go on home? I am fine. He's not going to show up tonight and if he does I have a horsewhip."

"She is handling this remarkably well," Dec quietly informed Aaron as he passed by his chair.

"Yeah, but I'm not."

"I'd say it's high time you let her be strong beside you. She doesn't need you to be strong for her."

"I'm trying."

Members of the Camden family begrudgingly left after making both Aaron and Natalie promise to alert them when her uncle returned to the road.

After seeing her parents out, Natalie spun to face the Sevens. "I am not an egg or some kind of china doll. I'm not going to break. But since it doesn't seem like you're leaving I want to know exactly what happened with the courthouse, and the library, and Cheryl."

Griff cleared his throat. "Basically, we all love you for loving Triple A and once we discovered that someone had hurt you we were like rabid dogs. A might've asked for our help but it wasn't all him. I went as far as to lift your jacket that night at the Hi-Way to have an excuse to come out here and find the fucker who'd hurt you."

T nodded. "Yeah, and Griff and I got greedy because I've seen Cracker Jack boxes with higher security than this entire town. We shouldn't have done it in the first place but we had what we were looking for at the court house. The library was us being dumbasses."

"What were you looking for in the library and how does that letter play into all of this?"

"They went in the library to look at old newspaper reels from the week when your family threw your uncle off of the ranch. T found the letter in Hope's desk. Mick had written to her asking if he could visit his grandkids. When I read that, I went insane. I had to find out if Hope had told him he could come.

"The morning I left you here to go get my dogs I stopped by the library, snooped around, and eavesdropped on a conversation between Brock and Hope about the letter. Guess I owe them an apology, too." The weight of all he'd done, all the lies he'd told her hung like a noose around Aaron's neck.

Her willingness to forgive him gave him steady footing. He was no longer swinging but that damned rope was still wrapped tight.

She shook her head at him. "When you all set out to do something you go all out."

"Kind of what we were trained to do," Smith tried to explain. "Since the doc walked, I'll offer up a little of my own psychobabble the dudes at the VA keep telling me. You gotta remember the missions we went on, the things we did, we were never allowed to tell anyone about. Hell, my own sisters had no idea where on the globe I was for years. Triple A was running a mission in his mind. He couldn't tell you even if he should've. We all have a little trouble converting back to life outside our army boots. There's this significant separation between life then and life now and it's not always so easy to traverse back and forth."

"I already forgave all of you, just don't ever do anything like this again."

"Despite everything that came out of it, thank you for doing all of this for me. I... can't thank you enough for being there today." Aaron searched for more words to offer his old team but none came to him. The full range of emotions he'd experienced that day had him bound.

"You tell her what happened in Najaf?" Griff asked.

"Yeah."

"K, now I'm gonna tell her what really happened."

"Did you lie to me about Iraq?" Natalie huffed.

"He didn't lie to you. He just doesn't quite remember it the way it actually went down."

"Yes, I do."

"No, you don't. Triple A kept telling our detachment commander that one or more of the men we were working with was sour. He didn't have proof but he knew. Commander didn't believe him. Kept telling him to let it go, so he took it to our operations sergeant. Got turned down there, too.

"It was just supposed to be a gas refill in the vehicles. No big deal. When all hell broke loose, Triple A threw himself on top of a nut job who felt his sole purpose in life was to blow himself up to kill all of us. He was five feet away from three dozen ten-thousand gallon tanks of gasoline. If he'd detonated himself, none of us would be here to be telling this story. Guy shot A twice at point blank range in the gut. Triple A shot him the head and then threw himself between me and a guy with an M-16 we'd given him. He saved my life, too. So, all of his bullshit about it being his fault, that's the one and only lie he can't seem to figure out isn't the truth."

"Aaron," Natalie couldn't believe what they were telling her. How had he survived? How could he possibly believe he wasn't worthy, even if he had lied to try and protect her? Flinging herself into his arms, she tried to hug him hard enough to make him believe their truth if he didn't believe his own. "You are never ever allowed to do anything dangerous ever again."

She heard his team chuckle but he just held her tighter. That was all that mattered.

"Hey, doll baby, you know you got a massive splinter in your finger?" Voodoo asked her as he passed by her on his way to the kitchen.

Aaron set Natalie down and grabbed her hand.

"I knew I had it. I just had a few other things going on and asking mama to take it out for me would've meant leaving my house this afternoon, and I am stupidly stubborn enough to have not wanted to give you all that satisfaction. You work on the lying thing and I'll work on the stubborn thing."

"You got it, baby, but let me take it out for you. Where'd you get it anyway?" Aaron's gentle touch on her hand erased the slight pain from existence.

"From my bed." She spoke through her teeth.

Voodoo laughed. "Oh, there's definitely a story I want to hear, but I am the team medic so step back Triple A. Let Voodoo do what he do."

"Little bit worried about exposing my girl to the things you do," Aaron teased. Relief flooded through Natalie. It was so good to hear him joking around again. With everything else this day had held, she needed that.

Voodoo waggled his eyebrows and Natalie giggled. "I only want to get freaky with him..." she pointed to Aaron, "...but I'll let you take this splinter out for me."

"Hello." T leapt to attention. "Just how freaky does Triple A get? We need something to harass him about."

"I get just as freaky as my girl likes, not that either of us will be telling you about it, perv," Aaron harassed.

While Natalie was laughing, Voodoo expertly pulled tweezers from a pack strapped on his thigh and removed the splinter. She didn't feel a thing. "You're really good at that." She stared at her finger to make certain he'd really performed the task that quickly and painlessly.

"I'm really good at a lot of things, baby doll."

"If I didn't owe you all so fucking much, I'd throw you out just for that comment," Aaron informed his friends.

"No. I don't want you to have to go all the way back to Lincoln tonight. I have two spare bedrooms and the couch folds out." The bravery she'd clung to all night long was still with her. She had every intention of confronting her uncle, but having a team of Green Berets nearby wasn't something she planned on turning down.

"We did pack for a week," Smith shrugged.

"You were going to stay out there an entire week?"

"I would've stayed out there a lifetime, Nat. I don't want to do life without you," Aaron readily informed her.

"I'm not the only stubborn one I see."

"Hey, your daddy told me the one and only chance I had was to out stubborn you. I followed orders."

"That sounds like my daddy."

"Kinda think he likes me now."

"Yeah, well, you're good for me."

"I try to be, Nat. I swear I'll never stop trying to be good for you and to you."

"All right, let's let him get sappy with her in private. Direct me to sleeping quarters," Smith ordered.

"Take your pick and thank you for staying."

"It's like Griff told you, we love you 'cause you love Triple A. You two end up getting married you'll basically be taking us all to raise. Fair warning."

"I might've had a decent chance of her saying yes 'til you told her that." Aaron feigned irritation.

"I'm going to need more information on what exactly taking you to raise means."

"Can you cook as good as your mama?"

"No. But my mama will feed anyone who sits at her table anytime they're sitting there."

"Sold. I'm moving out here." Smith laughed.

CHAPTER FORTY-FOUR

Thankful for every step she allowed him, Aaron watched Natalie slip off her shirt. A hungry moan he'd tried to dam back vaulted from his lungs. "Sorry."

"Why are you apologizing?"

"I spent a good portion of today certain I'd never get to see you like this again, Nat." Unable to resist, he folded her into his arms. The lace of her bra taunted his pecs. He longed to pop the clasp, to have her naked in his arms once again. It was the only way this fucked up life made any sense at all.

"Yeah, I was terrified of that, too. I should've heard you out to start with. I was just so shocked. And then I was embarrassed and I do incredibly stupid things when I get embarrassed."

He placed his index finger on her lips. "You did nothing wrong. I'm just thankful I get the chance to prove to you that I'll do better. I'll never lie to you again."

She kissed his finger and then pulled her head away. "Can I tell you something that's the truth?"

"I kind of think that should be our gold standard from here on out."

"Me, too. And I'm not so much scared to see my uncle, but maybe I am a little nervous." She buried her head against his chest.

"Bravest woman I've ever met. Most people would be a helluva lot more than nervous, sweet heart. I will be right there, right beside you, the entire time. And if you change your mind and want to take off anytime, you say the word and we'll fly. Okay?"

"How long do you think it'll take him to get here?"

Wishing for the thousandth time she'd ask him to take her away and keep her safe, he refused to beg her. He would never do anything that would make her think for one moment that he doubted her strength. "It's about seven hundred miles between Pleasant Glen and Gentry. He made good time from North Carolina. Depending on what time he leaves, he could be here tomorrow evening."

"You know I didn't so much lie to your face but I lied to you, too, by omission. You'd ask me stuff and I'd use sex to distract you, and I asked Dec about you, and your friends. I'm sorry."

"I already knew all of that."

"I'm still sorry."

"Oh, and my favorite meal is you, but my second favorite is probably Spaghetti O's. I like the kind with meatballs. Somebody might've mentioned that you'd asked them about it." He chuckled, still unable to believe he was standing in her bedroom teasing her.

"Can't believe he ratted me out like that." Her sheepish grin was worth more than every brick in Fort Knox.

"Oh, and I'm pretty sure after that flashback I had you led me to believe that you hated fireworks, too. Come to find out, you made good use of them incinerating a truck when you were a kid."

She laughed. He kissed her open mouth. "Can't believe I get to do that again either."

"Don't guess we can have make up sex with all of your friends here."

Unable to hide his smirk, he shook his head. "You just get too loud for me."

"Would you shut up and take me to bed?"

"Yes, ma'am."

When she shimmied into her Buck Off T-shirt, he sank his teeth into his tongue to keep from protesting. If she needed coverage that night, he would provide. He would always put himself between her and anything that wanted to do her harm. It was who he was. But if she needed the familiarity and the perceived security of her favorite T-shirt so be it.

"I can totally make you Spaghetti O's, but meatballs happen to be the one and only thing I make better than Mama. I can also boil noodles like a pro."

"Oh yeah? It's like we were meant to be."

"I think so, too. Are you going to be able to sleep tonight?"

"Probably not." He readily admitted. "I might doze if you do."

"I like this truth thing."

"Yeah, me, too."

"I don't want you to stay up all night."

"I don't want you to be scared."

"Guess we don't always get what we want."

"Trust me, baby, I've lived enough life to assure you we don't, but sometimes life does give you exactly what you need." He guided her onto his chest and wrapped his arms around her.

"Life's kind of cool like that."

"For a long time I didn't think so, but right now it seems pretty fucking awesome."

Try though she might, she couldn't sleep. Natalie kept her eyes closed hoping Aaron would doze like he'd said. She tried to recall her uncle in better detail. Her mind had fragmented his features. She remembered his hands and the old pair of black boots he used to wear but she couldn't recall much else. She remembered the revolting way he always smelled like moonshine and rotting meat. He'd turned into a faceless nightmare. Never a man, only a divided entity that had altered the course of her life in ways she would never fully understand.

What would it be like to see him again? What would she say? All of the times she'd envisioned what she would do if she ever had to see him outside the oppressive cloak of her darkest memories she'd just imagined vomiting on him. It seemed the only fitting response to a monster.

She wondered why he'd come back to Nebraska and why he'd chosen to do this now. Did he honestly believe that she would allow him to live on the ranch again with her nieces and nephews? She would personally freeze hell first.

The only thing the next evening would bring to her uncle would be a trip back to North Carolina. Was he even coming there to see her? Did he somehow believe he could come on the ranch and only see Brock? Was he that stupid? Did he think she would forgive him? Would it be better for her if she tried?

Turning on her other side she tried to push the thoughts away again without success.

"I know you're not sleeping, Nat. Wanna talk?" Aaron nuzzled her hair until he located her cheek and peppered it with kisses.

"Yeah. Talking sounds good. I have all of these questions no one but him has answers to. It's frustrating."

"Like what, baby?"

"Why is he coming back now? I mean why all of these years later?"

"In the letter he indicated that he wasn't doing well. Maybe he's convinced himself if he can get you to forgive him he'll have a bastard's chance in heaven."

"Tell me more about this letter."

"It's still in my truck. Do you want to read it?"

"Kind of but I don't want you to leave to get it. Just tell me what it said."

"One of the reasons I was chosen for intelligence when I was in Q training was because I'm pretty good at figuring out what's written between the lines. Want me to speculate?"

"Okay, so I do kind of like your superpowers when you're working for me instead of against me."

"I will always be working for us, Nat. I swear to you."

CHAPTER FORTY-FIVE

"He's an hour out," T announced to the crowd gathered in Natalie's mother's kitchen.

"If he keeps that up we're gonna have a real deal shootout at Saddleback's on our hands," Jessie whispered in Natalie's ear. "Your brothers are way too twitchy for my liking."

Giving her mother a nervous grin, she nodded. "I know but I can't exactly ask him to stop."

"You know I can outshoot all of ya, so why don't I just go sit in my truck at the entrance gates, blow his ass to hell when he arrives, and the rest of you can go on about your lives," Jessie asked the crowd at large. "I can't take much more of this. Lord have mercy on my indigestion."

"It's true," Ev agreed. "She can shoot a gnat off a bull's ass but you ain't gonna blow anybody to hell tonight, darlin'. Less he gets ornery, which I've never known him not to be, so maybe I oughta go on and put a down payment on your bail."

"No one is going to kill him," Natalie ordered yet again. "You all are making me crazy. I'm going riding."

Rushing out of Aaron's arms, she raced down the steps and headed to the barn. He was on her heels a half second later. "I'm going with you."

The air in her parents' home was so thick you could've cut it with a dull ax. At least outside she could breathe. Corn-sweetened, manure-laced air rushed into her lungs. She closed her eyes and soaked it in. This was her home. She worked for it, played in it, kicked her boots up on it, dug her heels into it, and sweated and bled on it. She would bet her very life on it. This was who she was. Nothing was going to keep her from it.

"Fine, but I'm going fast."

"Works for me."

With every thundered gallop of Sundance's hooves, her mind settled. Aaron had saddled Grant's horse and he had no trouble keeping up. They flew together. The wind whipped in her face and cleared her mind. He was coming. She was standing firm. He was going straight to hell. As soon as she'd had her say she was going to bed with Aaron and they were going to heaven.

Her heart timed itself to every rhythmic gallop. It was the music of her soul. She was a cowgirl. He was nothing. Taking off up another trail, Natalie let her instincts guide her. A few minutes later, her field was in view. Her ass bounced against her favorite saddle. Leaning in, she held on tight as Sundance flew over the deep ditch that kept the rest of her family away.

Laughing, Aaron managed the same jump without quite as much grace. Pulling up on the reins, Natalie gasped for breath when she came to a stop. "You're not half bad for a farmer's kid," she goaded.

"I feel certain my cowgirl can teach me a few tricks of the trade."

"Speaking of that, you ever think about becoming a cattle rancher?"

"I'm definitely not opposed to the idea. It'd beat having to put up with Ed and Eliza. Getting to work with you every day sounds like perfection to me. Don't know much about how it all works though."

"I could teach you. There was one other thing I wasn't completely honest about."

"What's that?"

"I hate going to Saddleback's. I don't like drunk men. I'm pretty sure they'll always make me nervous."

"Nat, I wish you'd said something."

"I know, but I wanted to be with you so I didn't."

"Want to maybe figure out what to do with the rest of our lives after tonight?"

"Probably a good idea." Clicking her mouth, she canted farther out in the field so she could see the sun set over the ranch.

When she'd run out of places to ride and the air was dark and cold enough she could see Sundance's breaths, she headed back to the barn. Surely her uncle was there now. They took their time brushing the horses and giving them treats.

"Nat, we don't have to go back over to your parents," Aaron offered again.

"I know, but I want to get this over with. Constantly waiting on whatever is going to happen to actually happen is making me crazy. I want to yell at him and then tell him to get his ass off of my ranch and never to come back. Then you're taking me to bed."

She recognized his single nod as the one he gave when he'd been given orders he didn't like. He managed to keep his arm wrapped around her shoulders and her slightly behind his body as they walked back to her parents' home.

There were no strange cars parked anywhere. Relief and confusion fought for dominance in her mind.

"He isn't here, baby girl," her father immediately assured her.

"So where is he then?"

"He's in town. Out on Holly Hill near Main." T stared at his phone.

"That's my place." Aaron sounded as surprised as she felt.

"Why is he there?"

"He's with Rasmussen." Her mother rolled her eyes. "Kind of like rats, you see one you got more."

Brock was seated at the table with his head in his hands. "The only human being on the planet that doesn't hate him. I'm going out there. This is insane. He's not getting anywhere near Natalie, or my kids, or my wife."

"I'm going with you," Natalie informed everyone.

"If she's going I'm going," Luke huffed. "Shoulda whipped his ass a long time ago." A chorus of me toos flew around the kitchen.

Jessie sighed. "Fine, we're all going. If you married one of my children you all know I love you more than the ones I birthed, but if you'll stay here with the young'uns? I think my children have something they'd like to say to their uncle."

Her mother's determined dignity gave Natalie another round of strength.

"Of course," Indie agreed. "You all go. Luke honey, if you need me to bail you out, call me. I'll be right there. And I might've put a few extra tire irons in the back of your truck last night should you need one."

"Oh, that reminds me. Grant, do you remember when you bought that Louisville Slugger for Keith and I told you he was way too young for it and stuck it in the garage?" Katy asked.

"Yeah." Grant smiled.

"It's not in the garage anymore. It's in your truck."

"I have always liked the way you think, Katy Belle."

Dec lifted Holly's chin. "You're sure you want to go?"

"Definitely."

Certain he was going to crush the steering wheel with his own fists, Aaron followed Luke's truck. Natalie was seated right beside him with her arms crossed over her chest. Determination rolled off of her in waves.

"You're awfully quiet." She finally spoke.

"Taking everything in me not to just keep driving until we're somewhere in the vicinity of Oregon, taking a boat from there to anywhere he isn't. I don't want you to do this. There. That's the absolute truth."

"I know but *I* want to do this."

"That's the only reason I'm going along with it. Grant handed me a pistol when we left. I'm taking it in with me, although Indie's tire iron idea has merit."

"If anyone gets to beat him with a tire iron it should be me, or maybe Brock."

"Fine. I'll hold him for you."

A line of Camden trucks filled Rasmussen's yard. Aaron had gone into battle with a lot of different kinds of men. This was the first time he'd fought alongside cattle ranchers. He was beyond certain they were America's finest.

The Sevens took the front line as they headed up to the front porch. If Rasmussen and company hadn't seen them coming, they were in for one hell of a surprise.

The front door swung open before Griff could kick it in. "What the hell do you think you're doing?" Rasmussen demanded. His dentures were out making his attempt to sound tough oddly humorous.

"We're here to talk, old man. Move or be moved," Aaron snarled.

"Let 'em in." A voice from inside the house had Natalie gripping his arm tighter. A shiver worked through her.

"Baby, we don't have..."

The fierce clinch of her jaw said she was doing this. Aaron kept her behind his body as they entered the house.

CHAPTER FORTY-SIX

Natalie could barely see Mick between the men standing in front of her. The odd rasp of his oxygen chaffed at her nerves. Most of his hair was gone and the liver spots on his hands looked nothing like Brock's now.

She pushed between Holly and Austin, edging closer.

"Mick, I swore to you I'd kill you if you ever came back up here. Only thing that makes any sense at all is that you're looking to die tonight." Natalie had only heard her father so furious one other time in her life.

"How'd you even know I was here?" He asked in odd fragments of speech punctuated by the puffs of air. Her heart pounded frantically. She wanted to run and she wanted to fight. Neither option offered her an acceptable outcome.

"Word gets around when dirty snakes slither, fucker," Luke spat at Mick. "Answer his question. Why the hell are you here?"

"I needed to see my son."

"I saw enough of you for four lifetimes in the eighteen years I endured living with you, Dad. I've still got the scars to prove it. You can go straight to hell. I know what you did to her." Brock pointed to Natalie. "I honestly never thought you could get worse and yet somehow you managed that, too. So, now you've seen me. I hate you more than I did the day I moved out. Leave and never come back. You're dangerously close to Camden land and you will never be a Camden."

"That what you drove all this way to hear, Mick? You need to hear him say he hates you again?" Ev demanded.

"I deserve forgiveness from all of you."

Pure, unadulterated rage rocketed up Natalie's spine. "Move," she shouted to Griff and Voodoo. They edged to the side ever so slightly. Aaron was right beside her. "You deserve our forgiveness, old man? Did you actually just say that to me?" She lunged toward him. It took the strength of three former Green Berets to hold her back. "The only thing you deserve is to spend an eternity in hell which is right where you're going."

"I've asked God for forgiveness for what I did to you, Natalie. I suppose I'm sorry."

"Are you? Are you sorry for every single time I sobbed, for every hour I spent listening to therapists tell me it wasn't my fault, and the years and years I told myself it was? Are you sorry for the nightmares and the panic attacks? Are you sorry for the other little girls in my class who I asked if their uncles touched them the way you touched me? Are you sorry for every single twisted lie you told? Are you sorry for all of the hell you put me through? Are you? Tell me."

"Yes."

"Good. I hope you are. I hope you fall on your weak ass knees every fucking night and beg for forgiveness from God himself because trust me you'll never have it from me. Never. You aren't worth it. You are not even worth the gunpowder it would take for us to blow your sorry ass to hell.

"Eventually, I learned to fight for myself. I learned to stand up to bullies who pick on little girls who trusted them. I learned how to fall in love. I learned how to have all of the experiences you took from me. So, I hope you spend the rest of your life praying, Uncle Mick. I really do because I'm done. I'm done being afraid of you. I'm done letting the memory of you ruin my life. You are nothing but a waste of the oxygen some doctor gave you. After everything you did to me, there is only one thing I should thank you for and that's how fucking strong I am. So, you get back in your car and you drive yourself back home, because if you ever darken the Nebraskan state lines again, I'll know. And it won't be Daddy or Luke or anyone else you need to worry about shooting you. It'll be me. And I won't miss."

"And I see you still can't keep your children under control, Everett."

Natalie gasped as Aaron's fist collided with her uncle's jaw. His head whipped to the side. A loud pop exploded in the air. Blood flew out of his mouth and teeth clinked against the hardwood flooring. "Say one more word, motherfucker. I fucking dare you."

"Damn," Luke admired.

"Knew I liked him," her father agreed.

"Figured you'd come back eventually and get your forgiveness before you died, didn't you, old man? But you had to wait on the statute of limitations to run out. Even stayed in Missouri instead of driving on yesterday. I know why you're here. Her birthday is next week. Timed it out perfectly didn't you. You never crossed the state lines until today. No one can press charges now. Sick bastard all the way to the grave," Aaron snarled.

"I really wanted to be the one to hit him," Brock huffed.

"Be my guest." Ev directed Brock to the front of the line.

Aaron remained two inches from her uncle's face. "Leave. Now. Because if I ever see you again, after she shoots you, I'll bury you so deep God himself won't be able to find you to give you all that forgiveness you think you deserve."

Suddenly, Sheriff Wilheim walked through the door. "What on earth is going on here?"

"Couldn't have planned this better if I'd tried." Aaron spat. Natalie had no idea who'd called the sheriff but the neighbors must've hear her shouting. Aaron didn't seem surprised to see him there though. "That computer right there," he pointed to an ancient computer in Rasmussen's living room. "Turn it on."

"Now you just wait right there, Sheriff." Rasmussen was panicked.

Sheriff Wilheim held up a folded piece of paper. "Got a tip you might have something in this house that'll send you up to the penitentiary for a long, long time, Rasmussen. I have a warrant. State police are pulling up now."

"Once we all escort this shithole outside, open any available file on that desktop. That should be all the evidence you need." Aaron stood. "You okay, baby?" He blocked her uncle from view with the expanse of his body.

"Better than I've been in a long, long time."

"Good. We're done here."

It was almost one in the morning when Natalie finally fell asleep in his arms. Aaron continued to run his fingers though her hair. Smith and Voodoo had volunteered to follow her uncle to the state lines to make sure he never decided to turn back.

He prayed she'd sleep. He prayed his foster parents would've been proud of him that night, both for his aggression and his restraint. He prayed the families left behind from both war and abuse eventually found peace. He prayed he'd always be enough for her. He prayed he could learn to be a cowboy because nothing else would ever suit her. He prayed for forgiveness he knew he'd already been given. He prayed for them.

CHAPTER FORTY-SEVEN

"I tried to talk myself out of this for a solid week and I couldn't," Aaron admitted as he drove them across the ranch a week later.

"I have no idea what is in that huge box but I'm so freaking excited." Natalie laughed as the truck bounced over the cattle guards. "Why are you so nervous?"

"It's your birthday. What if you hate this gift?"

"I won't. It's from you."

"Yeah, but my girl's kinda picky." He winked at her.

"Well, I picked you so I think I have good taste. Are we going to my field?" Bliss, once again, danced in her belly. This was exactly how life was supposed to be.

"Yep, we are. You know, I considered taking you skydiving for your birthday."

"Oh, my gosh, please tell me there is not a parachute in that box."

"I was a little worried all of my memories of the last jump I made might make me have another flashback. That would not bode well for our safety, so I went a different way. This was actually what I wanted to do. The sky diving was me trying to talk myself out of this, like I said."

"You definitely made the right choice. I like my boots being on the ground more and more lately."

"Oh yeah? I thought you loved to fly."

"I prefer the kind of flying you make me do in bed with you."

"Mmm, baby, we'll get to all of that after our picnic redo."

"It's sweet you wanted us to do this tonight."

"I want you to have better birthday memories. I'm going to do my damnedest to give you those."

"Is it that you're finally going to agree to move in with me since the city is seizing Rasmussen's house and property because he's going to rot in jail?"

"We've only been dating a few weeks, babe."

"I don't care. We Camdens know who we're gonna spend the rest of our life with, right off."

"That so?"

"Yes, it is. Ask Daddy to tell you about it sometime. He loves to tell that story."

"I'll have to do that."

"So, you'll move in with me then?"

"How about this? I will only move in with you if you end up liking this birthday present. And remember our deal, no lying even if you hate it."

Natalie's brow furrowed. What on earth was in that box?

Aaron slowed the truck as the terrain got rougher. A few minutes later, they'd bounced their way into her field.

Natalie bailed out of the truck before he had it in park. "Anxious, sweetheart?" He asked as he pulled a blanket and picnic basket from the back.

"Yes. I love presents."

He took his time perfectly arranging the blanket and basket. Pouring them glasses of wine and opening the containers of Spaghetti O's she'd prepared for them.

"We should eat first don't you think?"

"I think you just like making me wait for the things I want the most."

"You comparing your birthday present to all of the orgasms I give you?" He waggled his eyebrows.

"Yes. I should get to open my presents first."

"But Katy baked us a cake."

"And we'll eat that after."

"All right, I guess I'll let you but only because you're adorable bouncing up and down like that."

"Yay!"

"You're going to need to sit down for this."

"Okay." She sank to the ground and he placed the box in her lap.

"Go for it, sweetheart."

Ripping open the paper, she paused to wad it into a ball so it wouldn't fly away in the wind. Getting up on her knees, she pulled open the flaps on the plain brown shipping box. Reaching inside, she removed a bottle of beer.

"Uh, thanks…"

"There's more in there, Nat. That's just my way of telling you I turned in my notice at Saddleback's."

"Oh my gosh, thank you." She threw her arms around him. "That is a fantastic birthday present and I love it so you can move in with me."

"No, that's not how it works. You have to love everything in the box that much."

"That's really all you had to get me."

"I like spoiling you. Keep going."

She pulled out a plastic grocery sack next. Untying the handles, she discovered Red Vines, Flamin' Hot Cheetos, Airheads, Nerds, jelly beans, and a six pack of Dr. Pepper. Laughing, she kissed his cheek. "You got me all my favorite junk food. I love it."

"But you have to wait to eat it."

"Okay, wait until when?"

"Get the next thing out of the box."

"It's a map." She unfolded it and grinned. "It's of Gentry. Show me where the farm is."

She spread it out on the blanket beside her.

"I'd like to show you the real thing. I called my foster parents a few nights ago and apologized for not coming to see them. I needed to ask if it would be okay if I didn't send them my whole paycheck this month. They insisted that I not send any more money and told me all the wanted was to see me and to meet you. I was hoping you'd go on a road trip with me next weekend. Ed's making me work every shift for the next two weeks but I talked him into giving me next weekend off. We can leave Friday."

"I would love to go with you. I'm so happy you called them. Seriously, best birthday gift ever."

"There are a bunch of one more thing in there. Keep going."

"I cannot believe you did all of this." She reached inside one more time to pull out another box. Opening it she revealed dozens upon dozens of lottery scratch-offs. "Aaron, this is amazing," she gasped.

"There's always a chance, right?" His voice quivered.

When she lifted her head from the tickets, he was down on one knee holding an open ring box. The lottery tickets spilled all over the blanket when the box slipped out of her hand. "Oh, my gosh."

"I know it's fast and that we still have a lot of stuff to work on, but I just wanted you to know that I'm in this, Nat. I'm in this forever. And for the forever after that and for as many forevers as God will give us. I don't want one second of one forever that doesn't have you in it. I spent most of my life pretending to be people I was never meant to be. Until the first time I took you to bed, I wouldn't have even recognized myself. And you... you loved me enough to show me exactly who I was meant to be, the man who loves you and adores you and protects you forever. I love you so much and you may have to keep teaching me exactly how to love you the right ways, but I'll learn. I want to be there for every single thing you do. So, will you marry me?"

"Yes. Yes. Yes. A thousand, million, quadrillion times, yes!"

Every time she looked at the rather large diamond he'd procured with an entire month's paycheck on her left land, he grinned.

After they'd practiced feeding each other cake, they'd lain out on the blanket to watch the sunset.

"You know, for the longest time I didn't think I would ever get a happy ending," she admitted.

"Baby." He was at a loss for any other words beyond that.

"I didn't. Then I saw you shaking Ed Olsen's hand in Saddleback's that day you accepted the job and something deep inside of me thought if I was ever going to have a happy ending I wanted it to be with you. It just took me a little while to work up the courage to ask you for it."

"You deserve every happy ending in the world, Nat."

"So do you." Her vow was fervent. She turned to stare him in the eye.

"You said yes so whether or not I deserved it I got it."

"I want you to believe you deserved it."

"I'm working on that. Need a little more time. Kind of hoping seeing the Campbells next weekend will help me get there."

"I'll take that for now. I can't wait to meet them."

"I can't wait for them to meet you."

An ocean full of memories threatened to pull him under as Aaron drove them down the tiny two-lane road that made up most of Gentry, Missouri.

"I'm nervous," Natalie admitted. She threw another Cheeto in her mouth.

"They'll love you."

"I hope so."

"Is it awful that I hope they've changed Josh's room?" He'd been wanting to ask for the last two hours.

"No. That isn't awful at all. It's a real thing, just like you tell me when I feel guilty."

"Okay, then I hope they have."

"I've never been to a town smaller than Pleasant Glen."

"It's barely even a town. It's more like a few streets off of this street. And..." he turned down his foster parents' long gravel driveway, "...this farm."

"You okay?" She squeezed his hand.

"Not sure."

"Deep breaths."

"Yeah. Doing that."

His foster mother opened the driver's side door before he'd even shut down this truck. "Aaron," she hugged and laughed and cried all at the same time. He didn't know which thing to respond to so he hugged her back as best as he was able. "I'm so glad you're finally back."

After he'd extracted himself from the truck, he opened Natalie's door. She received an equally voracious hug. "You must be Natalie."

"Yes, ma'am. It's so nice to meet you. Uh, my mama sent you jam and my sister-in-law sent pies." She held up the basket she'd barely managed to save from the onslaught of the hug.

"Well, come on in. Gary can't wait to see you."

Measuring his breaths and timing his own heartbeats, Aaron wondered if this had been a terrible idea. The first breath of the kitchen that had at one time been the only home he'd ever thought of as his, brought back every memory he'd tried to forget.

There were pictures of him and Josh all over the farm from their youth. "Aaron, I can't get out of this chair to hug you the way I want to but come here, son." Mr. Campbell held up his hands.

The hug cemented him in the world once again. They didn't hate him. They didn't blame him for Josh's death. They still loved him.

"I was beginning to wonder if we were ever going to get to see you again. The day before you called us I'd decided we were going to drive to that town in Nebraska and find you. Don't you ever stay away this long again."

"Yes, sir."

"I promise. I'll bring him back." Natalie's grin expanded the width of her face.

"Uh, Mr. Campbell, sir, this is my fiancée, Natalie Camden."

"It's so lovely to meet you, sweetheart. You let me know if he ever gives you any trouble."

She giggled. "He won't, but I will."

"Sit down, sit down," Mrs. Campbell directed. "Natalie brought pie and I want to hear how you two met."

Aaron sincerely doubted his foster mother wanted to hear about Natalie asking him to sleep with her so he decided to tell their original truth. "Honest to God, it was love at first sight, just took me a little while to convince myself I was good enough of a guy for her to date."

"Then it took me a little while after that to work up the courage to ask him to go out with me again," she concluded.

"Well, sometimes the best things in life take time and the time you spend building the life you want is always worth it." Mrs. Campbell squeezed Aaron's hand. "I'm just so glad you have you here. I swore I wouldn't cry, but I am."

"I'm sorry I stayed away so long. I never meant to hurt you."

"Honey, I knew you blamed yourself for Josh. We all needed time to work through that. But now I want to celebrate life with my living children. I'll see him again someday and then I'll spend every moment I can with him."

"Mrs. Campbell we'd really love for you to come out to the Glen and come to the wedding. I'd like to do it before the first snowfall. We've put off happiness for so long I don't want to wait anymore." Natalie seemed to know the perfect things to say. Aaron wasn't even surprised. She was perfection.

"We'd love to come. Were you thinking of having a big service, Natalie? Aaron says your family has quite the ranch."

"We do have a big ranch but I don't want a big wedding. Just family and of course the Sevens."

"Of course," Mrs. Campbell chuckled. "I know it's silly but I used to imagine that Josh and Aaron would both have their weddings here. Your parents are probably beside themselves with excitement."

"Actually, all but one of my brothers and my sister got married in the Glen. Mama and Daddy are probably sick of having them by now. Why don't we do it here?"

"Are you serious?" Aaron loved the idea but wanted their wedding to be whatever she wanted.

"I'm completely serious."

Tears sprang back to his foster mother's eyes. "Oh, honey, I never meant to make you think you should do that for me. I was just dreaming out loud."

"Mrs. Campbell, ma'am, you loved Aaron and took care of him when no one else had ever done that for him before. I want him to get married here. It's the way it should be. It's perfect actually."

"When would you like to have the ceremony? I can take care of anything you want." The ladies sprang into action. Mr. Campbell and Aaron just smiled.

"What if we did it Sunday?"

"Like in the day after tomorrow, Sunday?" Aaron wondered if all of the sugar she had in the car was making her a little nuts.

"Why not? You both just said you'd put off happiness for too long. You think you can get your family out here tomorrow?" Mrs. Campbell asked.

"Of course, and I'll get my sister to bring her gown."

"Nat, we've only been engaged one week. I don't have you a ring yet." The thought of being married to her in two days' time was just too good. He couldn't possibly have it. "I haven't even had time to save up for our rings yet."

"I have plenty of money for rings, Aaron. Surely there's some kind of jewelry store we can get to from here."

"Kansas City is only an hour and a half away."

"There you go. Please." She turned the full power of those gorgeous hazel eyes on him.

"Like I would say no. I just want you to be sure."

"Just like every other time you've asked me if I was sure of something, I am very sure."

"Speaking of you needing to save up for things, Judy, hand me that paperwork." Mr. Campbell pointed to a stack of papers on the kitchen counter. "Even though I told you not to, you kept sending us all of that money. I got tired of trying to get you to stop so I had my financial advisor invest it for you. Should be a nice little nest egg for you and your lovely Natalie. We don't need your money, son. We just need to see the two of you a little more often."

"You saved all of this." Aaron stared down at the rather large amount of money in the balance column of a high interest savings account.

Ms. Campbell nodded. "Every penny. It was never your job to take care of us, Aaron. It was our job to take care of you. I worry we didn't do all we should've. We should've figured out how to come see you when you got back to the States. I just didn't know if I could handle seeing you wounded after everything with Josh. Then Gary had his fall and that took some adjustment, but never, not for one moment, were we not thinking of you and wishing we were with you. I kept telling myself you'd come see us and we could give you the money. I hope you've had enough to live on. I worried myself sick over that."

"I was fine, Mrs. Campbell. Thank you for this. I just wanted to do something for you. You did so much for me."

"That's the thing about family, son, you don't have to repay people for loving you. You are a fine man who has done things far and above the call of duty. We could never be more proud of you and for you," Mr. Campbell vowed.

"Thank you, sir."

"See, I told you we both deserve a happy ending," Natalie reminded him.

"You were right. We do."

CHAPTER FORTY-EIGHT

That evening in his old bedroom, Aaron wrapped his arms around Natalie's waist. He'd made it all the way through dinner barely touching her. He was starved for the feel of her warmth against him. He was an addict and there was no going back.

"You know, there used to be a rule about having girls in my bedroom when I lived here before." He nuzzled his beard against her cheek until she leaned to expose the tender skin of her neck. He helped himself to a taste.

"Well, since we're getting married in two days maybe they won't mind."

"Can't believe you're really going to be my wife on Sunday. I want you to be sure. It's really quick. I don't want you to have any regrets."

She spun in his arms and laid her head against his chest. "I have a lot of regrets, Aaron. I've done and said some awful things in my life. But I will never regret this. I told you I'm tired of waiting on us to get to be together. The farm is so beautiful and it means so much to them. I can't wait."

"Our wedding isn't for them, baby. It's for us. It means the world to me that you want to do this for them, but..."

She kissed him. Their tongues tangled, each one anxious for the other. Another remnant of doubt erased from his mind.

"I'm just going to kiss you every time you think I don't want to do this."

"You are really, really bad at punishments, my sweet little Domme."

"I'm serious. I was never one of those girls who dreamed about a big fancy wedding with a dress that looks like a cupcake swallowed her whole and dozens of people I barely know watching me walk down the aisle. That entire scenario makes me want to gag, honestly. This is perfect."

"As long as this is what you want, I couldn't be happier. Is there anything you want to talk about before you vow to put up with me for the rest of your life?" He needed to make certain she knew what that might mean. "I'm still not quite the way I'm supposed to be."

"For me, you're completely perfect." She rose up on her tiptoes to plaster her mouth to his again.

Until the moment he'd slipped the engagement ring on her finger, every kiss had been seeking, asking questions, a test of sorts. She'd shattered the invisible bounds her uncle kept her in, even after his banishment. She'd forgiven Aaron for his transgressions. Now, their kisses were full of answers and promises of what was to come.

She stepped back, her eyes full of wanton heat. Her tongue darted out over her lips. She whipped her shirt over her head. Her breasts were full of heat. Those perfect peach nipples pressed to the lace of her bra.

A moan tangled in his throat. "Keep going."

"Yes, sir."

"Jesus. The things you do to me, Nat."

Keeping her gaze locked on him, she toed out of her boots and slipped the button on her jeans from its enclosure. His eyes widened as she shimmied them down her short legs.

"Holy fuck," he panted as she revealed a light pink g-string that covered nothing at all.

"Holly made me get it. Now I see why." She giggled. "Don't drool, honey."

One step forward and he crushed her body to his. His hands dove down the slight elastic straps of those panties that should've been illegal, and unabashedly groped her ass.

She pressed her pussy to his cock still bound behind far too many layers of cloth. Gripping her ass, he thrust against her until she whimpered. "Shh, we have to be quiet, baby."

"Oh God, I want you," she panted.

"I'm gonna give you all of me, over and over again."

"Now."

"There's my impatient girl." Lifting her up, he half-tossed her on his old bed.

"Now who's being impatient?" That impish grin did him in.

Tearing off his clothes, he lifted her feet and dispensed with her socks. He trailed long, languorous kisses from her calves up her thighs. When she spread her legs for him, he paused reminding himself never to let that feeling of being offered heaven from an angel become insignificant.

His cock throbbed out its need. Reaching her hand up she stroked him. He choked back a growl. Suddenly, she sat up. A desperate shudder quaked through him as her lips circled his head and her tongue cleansed him. "Hungry, baby?"

"Yes." Slowly, deliberately she slid her mouth down his cock, tasting him.

"It's all for you. Take it."

She sucked with more vigor. His hands dove to her hair, tangling in the long strands. He allowed himself one lengthy moment of ecstasy before he pulled back. "Tonight, I want to come deep inside of you."

She reclined, offering herself to him like a delectable feminine feast.

Working quickly, he popped the clasp of her bra and dispensed with it. Her nipples visibly throbbed out a needy call for his attention.

For the moment, he ignored them. Moving his hands to her panties, he gently slipped them down her legs. "Naughty little panties make me want to do all kinds of naughty things with you."

"Good."

He brought the scrap of satin to his face and inhaled the soft spicy nectar of her.

A breathy moan escaped her throat.

"Shh," he reminded.

She shifted so he could pull down the soft worn sheets and blankets. He wanted her comfortable and safe. Needed her warm and hungry all for him.

His fingers trailed up her inner thigh. Her heat invited him to her core. "All for me," he whispered as he gently opened her.

Her eyes fluttered closed. Her mouth parted on another slight moan.

"You're so hot and wet for me, baby. How long have you been thinking about this? How long have you needed me to take care of my girl?"

"I never stop thinking about it. I always need you."

He took her mouth with his own and pressed his fingers fully inside her, conducting an assault on her body.

Instinctively, he moved his fingers right where she needed them. He knew precisely where to go. She jerked her head away gasping for breath, and rocked against his hand. Back and forth to the rhythm she needed.

"Feels so good right there doesn't it. I know. I know right where my baby needs me to touch, needs me to suck." He spun his tongue over her right nipple as she arched her back. Her fevered pulse was alive in her clit and her nipples. Her entire body honed in on his touch. Perfection.

Her jaw tensed. Heat streaked from her breasts to her pussy. Her body begged for release. Giving her the friction he knew she required, he captured her gasped groan of his name in his mouth.

Unable to draw this out any longer, he left her only long enough to grab the condoms from his bag. The next moment, he was on top of her, penetrating her fully in one long fluid thrust.

She bucked against him, anxious for his fullness. His mind spun. Every heartbeat timed itself to hers. He pressed further, taking every centimeter all for himself, in the bed of his youth.

His worlds collided and then as her eyes opened and her body accepted him so fully he could no longer tell where he stopped and she began, his worlds aligned. Every regret, every mistake, the penitence he owed, it all dissolved in the heat of her gaze. "I love you so much, Nat."

"I love you, too." She wrapped her arms over his back drawing his scars to her body, the only antidote to his pain.

And there in that room, in that home, in her body, he found the sanctification he'd so desperately been seeking. In her devotion he baptized himself. Every tainted memory of his life before was washed away.

She trembled. He clung to her as they came together two halves of a whole.

They'd been all over each other every available moment for the last week. Something about that night was different. Natalie sighed as she lay naked in his arms with soft flannel sheets scattered around them.

"That was amazing," she whispered in the darkness.

"It's always amazing with you, but that was something else, something beyond amazing."

"Yeah. That's what I was thinking, too." She traced the loops and lines of the wings tattooed on his chest. The man who protected her, loved her, and worshipped her was also the man who made her fly. They were getting married in two days. She had no doubts.

"Can I ask you something I've been wanting to talk about?" His voice trembled.

"Of course."

"Do you want to have kids?"

Natalie considered that. "I love my nieces and nephews. I just never thought about it. That seemed like part of that happy ending I was never going to have."

"It kills me when you say that. Like physically hurts me."

"I'm sorry."

"No, baby. I'm sorry for everything you endured that made you think even for one second that you didn't deserve a happy ending."

"Do *you* want to have kids?" she asked him.

"Yeah. Some of our own and maybe some that aren't ours."

Realization formed in her mind and crystallized in her heart. "You want us to be foster parents?"

"Only if you want to. It might be tough. Kids like me, we aren't always so easy to love."

"Yes. I want that. Oh my gosh, that's perfect. I never even thought of it but that would mean so much to me."

"You know, a lot of times when kids get removed from their homes it's because of..."

"Things like I went through or things much worse. I know. That's part of why I want to do this so badly. Believe me, I get making yourself unloveable to protect yourself. I can relate to that. How do we do it? How do we foster?"

"I have to ask Dec if I'd even be a candidate. We might have to wait until the PTSD is no longer such a factor in my life, but someday, I'd really like to do for kids what the Campbells did for me."

"Me, too. I want to use what we both went through for good. It will never be worth it but that isn't the point. There are kids that need the kind of help we can give them."

"Hey, Nat?"

"Yeah?"

"Thanks for being you, and for loving me, and for giving me a happy ending."

CHAPTER FORTY-NINE

Natalie's family caravanned all the way to Gentry with the Sevens. They tripled the population of the town when they arrived.

"Oh my gosh, you're getting married," Holly squealed as soon as she got out of the truck. They hugged in the front field of the Campbells' farm for five minutes straight.

"Guess this was one thing she wasn't gonna let simmer." Ev helped Jessie out of the car.

Aaron couldn't help but laugh. "We let things simmer for years, sir. We're ready for a new life."

"Well, welcome to the family, son. Same things still apply. I like ya. Heck, I'll even learn to love ya like one of my own. You hurt her or you ever lie to her again I'll kill ya. Just that simple."

"You have my word, sir. I'll never hurt her or lie to her again. I was raised better than that." Aaron nodded to his foster parents. "Ev, Jessie, this is Gary and Judy Campbell. My parents."

They hugged and started talking like they'd known each other their entire lives.

"Dude, when she puts you on a leash, she pulls it tight," Voodoo goaded. He handed Aaron his dress uniform. "Had it pressed for you and I brought you Josh's tags. Kinda thought you might want them."

"No leash required and thanks, man. I owe you one."

"You owe me so many more than one, which is why I did not get you a wedding present."

The next morning, Aaron stood in front of a new mirror in his old bedroom. He held the green beret in his hands seeing a thousand memories staring back at him instead of his own image. Josh's tags were laying on the bed.

"Want some help with that?" Mrs. Campbell peeked her head in.

"Uniform still fits." He was strung tighter than a racked pistol. The past two days had gone by in a blur and by the end of the night he was going to be married to Natalie Camden. How had he ever gotten so lucky?

"You look very handsome." His foster mother smiled at him and dabbed the tears in her eyes.

"Been a long time since I wore it."

"Maybe you should put it on more often. I bet Natalie will love you in it."

"I can't believe she loves me out of it."

Mrs. Campbell laughed.

"Didn't quite mean it like that."

"I wasn't offended. I'm not sure I've ever seen you so nervous and that includes the day you first arrived here."

"I wasn't all that nervous that day. I just remember being so damn tired."

"You did nothing but sleep and eat for a week straight. Then we finally got to know you."

"I remember."

"Don't you sometimes wish life was kind of like a pencil? That one end had an eraser so we could erase all the parts we wish weren't a part of it?" She took the beret from his hands.

"I used to wish that but Nat told me one time that there's no way out of your only life and that even with all of the bad stuff she went through she didn't want out of hers. I decided if she's in it I don't want out of any part of mine either."

"Sounds like she's a very smart girl."

"She is."

"Aaron, you do know Josh would have been so proud of you."

"I just wish I'd been here for him when he needed me."

"We *were* here. We thought things were getting better. I refuse to believe any of us could have stopped him. You know what depression can do. Please, don't blame yourself for what happened."

The last words Aaron needed to hear to have total forgiveness reached his ears. "I miss him so fucking much."

"Me too. Every single day."

"I kind of like thinking that he can see us. Maybe he'll get to watch me marry her. Maybe he'll see that I'm okay now."

Ms. Campbell scooped Josh's tags off of the bed. "He's right here whenever we need him watching over us all. And he is most certainly out there now. I kind of like to think he has the best seat in the field." She pressed the cool metal into his hands. "Lean down just a little."

Aaron did as he was told. She placed the beret on his head. He stood back and looked at himself in the mirror. For the first time in his entire life he knew where he was going and he knew it was a place he wanted to be.

"It's too long," Natalie fussed as the hem of her sister's wedding gown dragged the flooring.

"That's why I brought you my highest heeled boots," Holly handed over the shoes.

"You look beautiful." Her mother wiped away a few remnant tears.

"Thanks, Mama. I wish I wasn't nervous."

"I'd say it's normal to feel nervous, cowgirl. I couldn't even eat for two days before I married your daddy. I got down the aisle and almost fainted from hunger."

Natalie had been avoiding the mirror in Josh's old room, that had indeed been partially redone, all morning. She hated that she didn't recognize herself in the dress. This was her life. Why couldn't she quite understand that she got to live it?

Her mother tucked a stray strand of hair back into the low bun at the nape of her neck.

"Did I ever tell you the first thing I thought when they handed you to me after you were born?" Her daddy's smile couldn't quite rid the liquid emotion from his eyes.

"No, I don't think so." Natalie shook her head.

"The doc wrapped you up in this tiny pink blanket and put you in my arms and I just couldn't take my eyes off of ya. Never tell your brothers this, but I'd had more than a few talks with the man upstairs about wanting your mama to have a little girl. But they handed you to me and I knew it wasn't your mama who needed a baby girl. It was me. I swore right then and there, I'd never let anything hurt my baby. I'll never forgive myself for not keeping that promise."

"Daddy, you did..." She shook her head.

Her father kept talking. "I spoiled you rotten but I couldn't help myself. You were just this perfect little angel with a crooked little smile that brought me to my knees no matter what you'd done. Soon as I saw ya, I knew I'd never deserve the life God had seen fit to give me. I finally figured out those times when you can't quite believe you got what you have, that's when you know what you're doing is the right thing to do. Sometimes this world don't make a dang bit of sense, but every now and then it all lines up just right and you can't believe you get to be the one to live it." Her father shrugged. "You made my whole life make sense, baby girl. Seems to me maybe your Green Beret makes your life make sense, too."

"Daddy." Natalie threw her arms around his neck. "He does."

"Then we better get." He took her hand and helped her walk out to Aaron's field.

"You're sure this is how you want to do this?" he asked her as they came to the back of the aisle she was to walk down.

She took one long look at the line of men in uniforms standing beside Aaron and the man in the wheelchair who was standing in for his son as the best man. Her destiny awaited her. This was so much more than a happy ending. He was her happy beginning.

"Yes, this is perfect. This is exactly how I want to walk down the aisle. I wish it was Sundance but this will do."

"All right then cowgirl, saddle up."

Natalie held out the skirts and slips of Holly's gown and positioned herself in the saddle. Her father led the horse down the makeshift aisle the Campbells had created. The entire town of Gentry had shown up. It ended up being much larger than she'd originally imagined and even more perfect.

When she reached Aaron, she hopped off the horse and took his hand.

"There's my girl," he whispered.

EPILOGUE

"Seven minutes," Aaron informed his wife as he scrubbed down the bar top at Saddleback's one last time.

She'd asked to come with him that afternoon since it was his last shift. Eliza had insisted she stay behind the bar with him.

"I'm enjoying your countdown to our honeymoon." She giggled again.

"You laughing is the best damn sound in the whole world."

"Really? And I thought you liked the way I moaned."

"Okay, you laughing is the second best sound."

Shaking her head at him, she slid a few clean glasses into their racks. "So, what exactly are we going to do for the next week in a chalet in Vail?"

"Well, first, Mrs. Weber, I'm going to get all up in your business. You thought I was invasive before you haven't seen anything yet."

"Oh yeah?"

"Oh yeah, baby."

The clatter of a thrown skillet sounded from the kitchen. Aaron rolled his eyes and started back there. Holding up his hands, he stopped himself. "You know what, it's no longer my problem."

A man Aaron had never seen before sank down on a barstool with his cowboy hat pulled low over his eyes. "Get you something to drink, sir?"

"Uh, sure. Can I ask you something?"

The man looked up and something in his eyes struck Aaron. "Do I know you?"

"Not unless you've ever spent any time in Holder County, Oklahoma."

"Never been down there. You just look familiar I guess. What can I get you?"

"I'll take a whiskey neat. This is Pleasant Glen, right?"

"The one and only. If you blink, you'll miss it so we get asked that pretty often."

"Can I ask you something else, man?"

"For the next three minutes, I'm the bartender here so you can ask me anything you want."

"You get fired?"

"I quit. Learning to be a cattle rancher instead."

The man laughed. "I wish you the best. Cattle ranching's a crap shoot on a good day."

"You sound like all of my brothers-in-law."

"Then they're probably straight shooters."

"They are but you were gonna ask me something else."

"Yeah, you ever heard of the Camdens? They own some land up here or something."

Natalie whirled around. "I'm Natalie Camden. Well, actually I'm Natalie Weber but I'm still a Camden. My family owns the largest ranch in Lincoln County. Did you need something, sir?"

The man looked like she'd backhanded him.

"What did you say your name was?" Aaron asked.

"Uh... my name's uh... Colton. Colton Holder."

He'd spent the first three seconds of his response making up a lie about his name. Aaron eased Natalie away from the stranger. "Holder, huh? Got a good friend from Oklahoma named Maddox Holder. I think he's even from Holder County. He used to be a Screaming Eagle from the 101st. He any relation to you?"

"Mad-do... No. Never heard of him."

"Interesting." Aaron nodded. To have never heard of him he knew his nickname. "Well, my time's up. We're heading out of town. It was nice to meet you."

Aaron removed his apron, took Natalie's hand, and got her the hell away from whoever that guy was.

"We're going home to tell Daddy about him before we go to Vail aren't we?"

"Yeah and I'm all kinds of pissed about our delay but that isn't his name and I want to know what the hell he wants with your family."

WAYWARD SON

Colton Holder isn't his name but he is on a mission. Find out who he is, what he wants, and why he's looking for the Camdens in my upcoming novel, *Wayward Son*. Join my mailing list to get clues, excerpts, and gossip about what happens when he finally confesses the reason he's in Pleasant Glen. You'll also get all of the insider info on my upcoming series, Holder County.

Wait there's even more you can learn about if you join my mailing list. I'm also launching a Western Military Romance series. Read all of the stories of Team Seven as they each find their Happily Ever After! Griff's book, *Dirty HALO,* will be out in the Spring of 2018.

Join my mailing list now!

ABOUT THE AUTHOR

Bestselling author Jillian Neal likes her coffee strong and sweet with a shot of sinful spice, the same way she likes her cowboys. In fact, her caffeine addiction is quite possibly considered illicit in several states as are a few of the things her characters do. When she's not writing or reading, you'll find her in the kitchen trying out new recipes or coming up with ~~excuses~~ reasons to purchase yet another handbag or make an additional trip to Sephora. Though she'll always be a Bama girl at heart, Jillian hangs up her hat and kicks up her boots outside of Atlanta with her hunk-of-a-husband and her teenage sons.

For more information...
jillianneal.com
jillian@jillianneal.com

ALSO BY JILLIAN NEAL

THE GIFTED REALM SAGA

GYPSY BEACH

GYPSY BEACH TO CAMDEN RANCH

CAMDEN RANCH

THE GIFTED REALM: ACADEMY

Free, web serial